Praise for *New York Times* bestseller *Lady Sophie's Christmas Wish*

"An extraordinary, precious, unforgettable holiday story… An unconventional storyteller who knows exactly how to touch a reader's heart and reach deeply into the soul."

—*RT Book Reviews* Top Pick of the Month, 4.5 Stars

"My Christmas wish for you is that Santa brings you this book… a joyful, sensual read."

—*USA Today Happy Ever After*

"Shines with love, sparkles with humor… Breathtaking."

—*The Long and Short of It Reviews*

"Supremely sexy, emotionally involving, and graced with well-written dialogue… a fascinating, enjoyable read."

—*Library Journal*

"Yet another outstanding Regency romance featuring the Windham family… each book is a treat that shouldn't be missed."

—*Night Owl Reviews* Reviewer Top Pick, 5 Stars

"A Gem of a Read! A rapturously entertaining story that warms the heart just in time to bring in the holiday season with yuletide cheer."

—*Romantic Crush Junkies*

"Grace Burrowes has given us the most romantic story of Christmas miracles… a touching story that takes time to peel back all its layers and reveal the hidden delights of true humanity."

—*Yankee Romance Reviews*

"The characters are lovable, the dialogue entertaining, and the story heartwarming."

—*Drey's Library*

"Poignant and tender. No one does emotional and magical romance like Grace Burrowes!"

—*Bookaholics Romance Book Club*

"Another Grace Burrowes masterpiece that hits all the heartstrings."

—*Bookloons*

"Grace Burrowes gives readers a novel that will pull at their heartstrings and renew their faith in miracles."

—*Debbie's Book Bag*

"A delightful holiday story of longing, hope, and love… Sweet, but ever so tantalizing."

—*Anna's Book Blog*

"Grace Burrowes gives us yet again a magical delight that I, for one, will carry in my heart for years to come."

—*Dark Diva Reviews*

Praise for *Lady Louisa's Christmas Knight*
A *Library Journal* Best Romance of 2012

"Lavish and seductive... Delightfully charming and lovable characters... Burrowes crafts yet another winning romance."

—*RT Book Reviews*, 4 Stars

"Excellent dialogue and terrific characters rest on a bedrock of realistic relationships and deep family love. Exceptional writing and deft timing will keep readers smiling and the pages turning."

—*Publishers Weekly*

"Humor, strong female characters, and fresh situations are hallmarks of this award-winning author... Fans of Amanda Quick and Loretta Chase will enjoy Burrowes."

—*Booklist*

"A warm and enchanting romance with its share of humor and emotional moments. I was thrilled by this beautiful love story."

—*Night Owl Reviews* Reviewer Top Pick

"I absolutely love this family and their stories... thank you, Grace Burrowes! A luscious romance that is rich in everything we could possibly ask from Santa."

—*Yankee Romance Reviewers*

Also by Grace Burrowes

The Heir

The Soldier

The Virtuoso

Lady Sophie's Christmas Wish

Lady Maggie's Secret Scandal

Lady Louisa's Christmas Knight

Lady Eve's Indiscretion

The Courtship (novella)

The Duke and His Duchess (novella)

Mary Fran and Matthew (novella)

The Bridegroom Wore Plaid

Once Upon a Tartan

Darius

Nicholas

Ethan

Beckman

Gabriel

Grace Burrowes

Cover design by Anna Kmet
Photography by Jon Zychowski
Cover model: Leah Lehr/G&J Models

Published by Sourcebooks Casablanca, an imprint of Sourcebooks, Inc.
P.O. Box 4410, Naperville, Illinois 60567-4410
(630) 961-3900
FAX: (630) 961-2168
www.sourcebooks.com

Printed and bound in the United States of America
VG 10 9 8 7 6 5 4 3 2 1

To my brother Dick, my first and most enduring hero

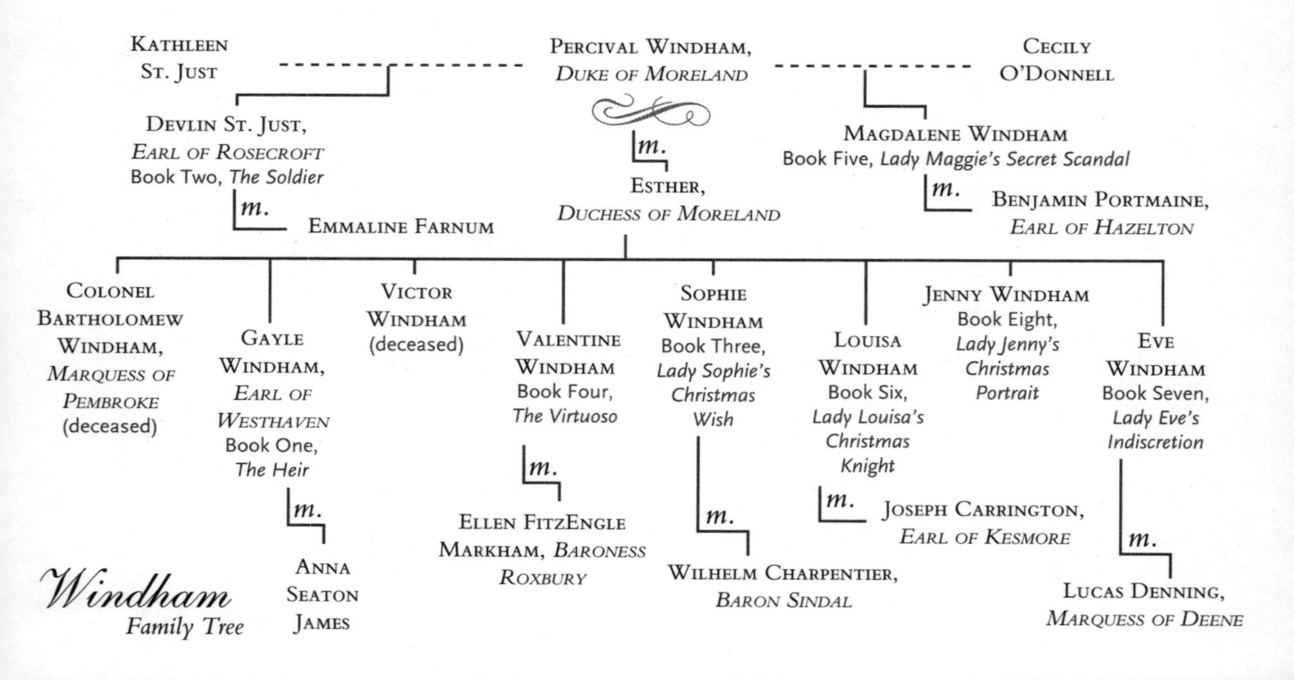

Kathleen St. Just
Percival Windham, Duke of Moreland
Cecily O'Donnell
Devlin St. Just, Earl of Rosecroft
Book Two, The Soldier
m.
Emmaline Farnum
m.
Esther, Duchess of Moreland
Magdalene Windham
Book Five, Lady Maggie's Secret Scandal
m.
Benjamin Portmaine, Earl of Hazelton
Colonel Bartholomew Windham, Marquess of Pembroke (deceased)
Gayle Windham, Earl of Westhaven
Book One, The Heir
m.
Anna Seaton James
Victor Windham (deceased)
Valentine Windham
Book Four, The Virtuoso
m.
Ellen FitzEngle Markham, Baroness Roxbury
Sophie Windham
Book Three, Lady Sophie's Christmas Wish
m.
Wilhelm Charpentier, Baron Sindal
Louisa Windham
Book Six, Lady Louisa's Christmas Knight
m.
Joseph Carrington, Earl of Kesmore
Jenny Windham
Book Eight, Lady Jenny's Christmas Portrait
Eve Windham
Book Seven, Lady Eve's Indiscretion
m.
Lucas Denning, Marquess of Deene
Windham Family Tree

One

Either Lady Genevieve Windham didn't recognize Elijah Harrison with his clothes on, or she had reserves of self-possession he could only envy.

"Sir, may I be of assistance?" She hovered in the door, a blond angel on a miserable winter night, not welcoming him inside and not refusing him entry—a succinct metaphor for Elijah's dealings with Polite Society.

"I must beg your hospitality, my lady, for my horse has gone lame, and the weather is worsening. Elijah Harrison, at your service. I left the last posting inn some miles back and have seen no other hostelries along the way."

He shivered in the wind and sleet and tried not to let his teeth chatter. He was ready for her to refuse him or tell him to go 'round back and seek entry of the cook. The very fingers by which he made his living—and a number of other parts—were long since numb, or he would not have knocked on even this door.

The lady stepped back and gestured him inside.

"Gracious heavens, Mr. Harrison, come in this instant. I hope the grooms are seeing to your horse?"

Her green eyes were lit with concern, and not—bless her—for his horse.

"My thanks." He passed into the warmth and quiet of the Earl of Kesmore's country house as she closed the door behind him. "When last I saw him, the beast was being led into a cozy stall, his limp improving apace at the prospect of straw bedding and a ration of oats."

"I'm Jenny Windham," she said, and that she would eschew her title—as he had eschewed his—caught his curiosity. "The servants are quite done in, today being Stirring-Up Sunday. Let me take your coat."

She hefted the sodden wool from his shoulders and hung it on a hook, spreading the capes and sleeves just so, the better for the garment to dry. This attention to Elijah's outerwear gave him a moment to study her the way a portrait artist was doomed to study all others of his own species.

Her hands had a competence about them he would not have expected from a duke's daughter. She dealt with wet fabric as any yeoman's wife might, then held out a hand for Elijah's scarf.

"I've never seen it rain ice," she said. "An occasional sleety afternoon, yes, but not this… this"—she grimaced at his scarf—"unending mess. Nobody will be going anywhere if they have any sense. I hope you hadn't far to go?"

Again the concern in her eyes, and for an uninvited guest who had no business inconveniencing her.

Elijah focused on peeling off damp wool and sopping gloves. "A few more miles yet, but I'm not familiar with the neighborhood, and nothing good ever comes of forcing a lame horse to soldier on."

"Nothing good at all. You must accept our hospitality tonight, Mr. Harrison. You'll come with me to the library."

She did not explain to him that the earl and his countess would be down shortly to welcome him properly, though Elijah well knew this was Joseph Carrington's house. He would not have presumed to knock otherwise.

And yet he followed Lady Genevieve down a dimly lit corridor without protest, watching the way her carrying candle and the mirrored sconces moved light and shadow across her feminine form. By the time they reached the library, Elijah's feet were starting the diabolical itching that accompanied a thawing of limbs too long exposed to winter's wrath.

"You can warm up in here, and we'll have a room prepared for you," Lady Genevieve said as she set her candle on a delicately scrolled chestnut sideboard. When his gaze fell upon an embroidery hoop left on the sofa, Elijah realized the lady herself had occupied the library earlier.

"You're burning wood." The sweet tang of wood smoke blended with other scents—beeswax, cinnamon, and something floral, an altogether lovely olfactory bouquet.

"Lord Kesmore prefers to burn wood, and his home wood is extensive. If you'll give up those boots, Mr. Harrison, I'll have somebody take them down to the kitchen for a polishing. Leave it any later, and the boot boy will have gone to bed."

Stirring-Up Sunday saw the plum pudding tucked into its brandy bath. The kitchen had no doubt been a merry place for much of the day, and the help would need to sleep off the results of their exertions.

How he loathed Christmas in its every detail.

"I'll wrestle my boots off, but please don't put anybody to any trouble. I would not want to impose on his lordship's staff unnecessarily."

He did not elaborate, leaving her another opportunity to explain that his lordship wouldn't find it any imposition, and would be told immediately of his visitor.

"I'll see to some sustenance for you, Mr. Harrison. Please make yourself comfortable."

She bobbed a curtsy; he bowed. The moment she left the room, Elijah picked up the embroidery hoop to study the gossamer-fine chemise it held. The itching was climbing from his feet to his calves, and would soon overtake his thighs, but he'd seen such needlework only on his mother's very own hoop, and the artist in him had long grown used to ignoring all manner of bodily inconveniences and urges.

Jenny returned from the kitchen to find her guest standing before the fire in his stocking feet and shirt-sleeves, her embroidery hoop in his hands.

Which would not do. It would not do *at all.*

"Come eat, Mr. Harrison. I gather the making of the plum pudding occasions something of a celebration among the staff, and so the larder boasted impressive offerings. They'll be decorating the house tomorrow in anticipation of the Yule season."

His dark brows lowered and, more importantly, he set her embroidery hoop on the mantel. "I apologize for my state of undress, but my coat was damp."

Said coat—more sopping than damp—was now draped over the back of a chair set close to the fire, steam rising from the fabric.

Which accounted for the wet-wool scent accompanying the cozier fragrances wafting through the library. Jenny set the tray on the low table before the hearth just as the eight-day clock in the hallway chimed the hour.

"Don't stand on ceremony, Mr. Harrison. You must be famished."

And as for his state of undress… Jenny knew firsthand that for all his height, he was lean and hard, every muscle and sinew in evidence when he was naked. Every rib, every pale blue vein, every dark, curling hair on his chest… and elsewhere.

"May I pour for you, sir?"

"Please."

She took a place on the sofa while he remained standing, which reminded her that whatever else was true about Mr. Elijah Harrison, he had the manners of a gentleman. "You must sit, or you will get crumbs all over the countess's carpet, and she will not be pleased."

He came down on the sofa, making the cushions bounce and shift with his weight. "I gather mine host and his countess have already retired?"

A maiden-aunt-in-training ought to expect such questions.

"I would not know. They are from home, and I am

keeping my nieces company in their absence. How do you take your tea?"

He was given to silences, which Jenny should have expected from a man who painted for a living. Some artists were so mentally busy trafficking in images that words came to them only reluctantly—a sorry, second-rate form of communication.

"Lady Genevieve, if I know we are without chaperonage, then I will mount my lame horse and find other accommodations. I account Kesmore among my few friends and would not want to give him offense."

To go with his beautiful body and his beautiful hands, he had a beautiful, masculine voice. She could have listened to that voice recite Scripture and still pictured him without his clothes.

"My aunt is abed on the next floor up." She paused midreach for the teapot. "You used my title."

His mouth didn't shift, but something in his eyes suggested humor. "I make a habit out of attending many of the London social functions. Because I must work in all available daylight hours, I spend most of my evenings dozing in the card room. Even so, I have observed you often from a polite distance."

Something about the way he used the word *observed* had Jenny fussing with the tea things. She was rattled by his disclosure, so rattled she fixed her own cup of tea first, with both sugar and cream.

Did he know she'd *observed* him as well, for hours, when he'd worn nothing but indolence and an offhand sensuality?

"You are prescient," he said, lifting the full cup. "You know how I like my tea."

The humor had found its way to his voice, which made Jenny curious to see what a smile would look like on that full, solemn mouth. For all the parts of him she *had* seen, she had never seen him smile.

"A lucky guess," she said. "Just as finding your way to Kesmore's doorstep tonight must have been good luck for you."

"And for my horse." He saluted with his teacup, his fingers red with returning circulation.

"Eat something." Jenny passed him an empty plate. "Chasing the chill from your room will take some time, and you have to be hungry."

As he filled a plate with as much buttered bread, ham, and cheddar as any one of Jenny's brothers might have consumed at a sitting, Jenny indulged in closer study of her guest. His dark hair was damp, and around his eyes, fine lines gave him a world-weary air. He was not a boy, hadn't been a boy for years.

She'd had particular occasion to admire his nose. The nose on Elijah Harrison's face announced that no compromises would be made easily by its owner, no goal casually cast aside for costing too much effort. Had she not seen the entire rest of him, she would have chosen that nose as his best feature.

He paused between assembling his meal and consuming it. "You're not eating with me, Lady Genevieve?"

He'd said her name with a little glide on the initial *G*—"Zhenevieve"—the way a Frenchman might have said it. He had studied in France. Somehow, despite the Corsican's protracted nonsense, Elijah Harrison had managed to study in France. She envied him this to a point approaching bitterness. "I'll nibble some cheese."

"Like a starving mouse?"

"Like a woman who had a decent meal not that long ago." Like a woman who knew it was time to have done with visually devouring her guest. "What brings you to our neighborhood, Mr. Harrison?"

"Work, of course. Some sentimental old fellow has taken it into his head—or perhaps his lady wife has taken it into her head—to have portraits done of his youngest progeny. If I'm to present myself to the world as a well-rounded portraitist, then I must add children to the subjects in my portfolio."

He said this as if painting children was an occupational hazard, like napping in card rooms.

"Is it difficult to paint children?" Between one heartbeat and the next, Jenny realized Elijah Harrison knew a great deal that she wished she could learn from him. He'd travel on in the morning, but for as much as the next hour, she could interrogate him to her heart's content.

He didn't answer immediately. Instead, he put bread, cheese, and some apple slices on a plate and held it out to her. His gaze held a challenge.

Over a simple meal? Abruptly, Jenny wondered if he'd recognized her.

She took the plate and tossed her list of questions aside.

Genevieve Windham was not pretty, she was *exquisite*.

Pretty in present English parlance meant blond hair and blue eyes, regular features, and a willingness to spend significant sums at the modiste of the hour.

Unless a woman was emaciated or obese, her figure mattered little, there being corsets, padding, and other devices available to augment the Creator's handiwork. Failing those artifices, one resorted to the good offices of the portraitist, who could at least render a lady's likeness pretty even if the lady herself were not.

Lady Jenny left pretty sitting on its arse in the mud several leagues back. Her eyes were a luminous, emerald green, not blue. Her hair was gold, not blond. Her figure surpassed the willowy lines preferred by Polite Society and veered off into the realms of sirens, houris, and dreams a grown man didn't admit aloud lest he imperil his dignity.

The itching over Elijah's body faded in the face of the itch he felt to sketch her.

She had certainly sketched him, after all.

"Have some sustenance, my lady. For me to eat alone would be rude, and I intend to consume a deal of food."

Lady Jenny took the plate, and though he was ravenous, he wanted to watch her eat more than he wanted to fill his belly. "My thanks, sir."

So… small talk. His livelihood depended as much on his ability to make small talk as it did on his talent for slapping paint onto canvas. "How fare my lord and lady Kesmore?"

"When did you first know you wanted to paint portraits?"

They'd spoken at the same time, though he'd put his question to her, and she'd directed hers to the plate of gingerbread on the tray. Elijah added a slice to her meal and waited.

"Lord and Lady Kesmore are in good health and wonderful spirits. They look forward to the holidays, as do their children."

Not an answer, but rather, a recitation.

He offered reciprocal superficiality. "I was born with an interest in the arts."

She glanced over at him, her expression suggesting he was a plate of holiday treats she must not be caught snitching from. "An interest in the arts? A general interest only?"

His answer was the one he gave whenever members of the Royal Academy asked the question Lady Jenny had. The Academy boasted sculptors as well as painters, and one was elevated to membership by vote of the Royal Academicians. A general interest had struck him as the more politic reply.

Lady Jenny was not considering him for membership in the Royal Academy, and would never be in a position to do so.

"Painting has been my preoccupation for as long as I can remember," he said. "When the other lads were clamoring for a pony or playing Robinson Crusoe or longing to explore darkest Africa, all I wanted to do was paint."

In some regards, he would have been better off in darkest Africa. Rather than ponder that unhappy truth, he popped a bite of gingerbread in his mouth.

"And where did you study, Mr. Harrison?"

This mattered to her, or mattered more than ham, cheese, gingerbread, apples, and hot tea. "Might I prevail upon you to pour again, my lady?" Because he'd downed his tea in one hot, indecorous gulp.

"Of course."

"I studied here and there. I have French cousins on my mother's side, and while Paris was no fit destination for an Englishman for quite some time, my cousins sought refuge in Italy, Denmark, and Switzerland. I made a royal progress of visiting them and their drawing masters. My mother spoke French to me from the cradle, so France was not as risky for me as it would have been for others."

Her Exquisite Ladyship fixed his second cup of tea, while he forgot his meal and instead focused on how firelight reflected off the tea service and off her hair. Lady Jenny was not a woman of angles; she was a woman of curves—an elegant curve to her spine in particular suggesting she'd eschewed stays due to the lateness of the hour, or perhaps—being in the country—she had settled for stays without boning.

The teapot was not the tall, silver, decorative variety, but rather, a round, porcelain confection with pink roses and green vines twining about the glaze. The curve of the pottery spout mirrored the curve of Lady Jenny's neck and shoulder. The green of the leaves was only a shade lighter than her eyes, and the gold tracing on the teacups a near match for her hair. If he were painting her, he'd find ways to echo the lines and colors, in the pattern of the curtains, the curl of a cat's tail, the foliage of some lush, flowering houseplant or—

"Your tea, and I can find you a book to take upstairs with you tonight."

She passed him the cup and saucer and decamped for the rows of shelves at the other end of the room.

Being a gentleman, he couldn't very well remain on the sofa if she wanted to wander the room, despite the fact that he was damp, hungry, and exhausted. He followed her between two rows of shelves, bringing a candle with him.

"You'll need some light, unless you have Kesmore's library memorized?"

She didn't take the candle, so he held it higher, the better to illuminate books, titles, and one lovely, if shy, woman. "One could not memorize the contents of Joseph and Louisa's library. They're always acquiring more books, lending this volume, trading that. Louisa is mad for books, and Joseph is mad for his lady."

"Their collection is to be envied," he said, studying the titles at eye level. Elijah's estimation of Kesmore rose—or perhaps widened—as he regarded the spine of an illustrated volume of erotic Oriental woodcuts. Beside that was some French erotic poetry, and beside that—

Lady Jenny was not as tall as he'd first thought her. The titles he regarded would not have been visible to her.

Mentally, he shook his imagination by the scruff of its shaggy neck and wagged a finger in its panting, eager face: *small talk*. "I enjoy Wordsworth." As a soporific, anyway.

"His poetry is lovely. I'm partial to—"

She fell silent as the library door clicked open, followed by the rapid patter of what sounded like small feet.

"Let's be quick, Manda. Papa always keeps it in his desk for when we rescue him from the ledgers."

"Hush, Fleur." The little feet crossed the library. "If Aunt Jen finds us, she'll be disappointed in us."

"I *hate* when she's disappointed in us."

Lady Jenny started forward, clearly ready to rain down disappointment in torrents, but Elijah caught her with an arm around her waist.

"Wait." Whispering in the lady's ear meant he had to bend close, close enough to catch the light, lovely scent of jasmine.

She turned her head to whisper back. "They should have been in bed hours ago. Let me go."

The sound of a drawer opening carried across the room. Through the stacks of books, Elijah saw two small girls, both dark-haired like Kesmore, both swathed in thick flannel dressing gowns. They plundered their father's desk, intent on some mischief.

"Aunt Jen won't be mad when we draw the pictures. She'll help us with them and make them ever so much prettier." This came from the smaller of the two, Fleur. "And Papa won't be mad when he opens our present."

"Mama can help us make it into a book, just like her books."

Against Elijah's body, Lady Jenny felt as if she were quivering with a need to herd these juvenile felons back to the nursery, while Elijah quivered with something else entirely.

Her scent was marvelous; her curves were marvelous; her focus on the children and complete lack of awareness of him was not marvelous at all, though it was exactly what he deserved.

"Which is your favorite?" Amanda asked as they closed the drawer.

"I like them all. I wonder which is Papa's favorite?"

Elijah's favorite was the manner in which Jenny Windham's backside fit exactly against the tops of his thighs, though the way she'd gone still and relaxed against him made a close second.

"Probably the one about the crow who fills the pitcher of water with stones. Papa likes cleverness and not giving up. Per... Per-something."

They trundled out, discussing the moral merits of various of Aesop's fables, while Elijah realized he'd been trapping his hostess against his damp self for far longer than was wise.

He let her go and retrieved the candle from the shelf where he'd perched it.

"Those are your nieces?"

For a moment, Lady Jenny remained with her back to him. When he should have been plucking a book from one of the lower shelves, Elijah instead studied her perfect, downy nape.

And was still studying it when she turned. "Amanda and Fleur are Joseph's daughters from his first marriage, though Louisa dotes on them shamelessly, and they love her dearly."

"And Kesmore dotes on the lot of them."

He ought not to have said that, because all this doting and loving among Kesmore's brood put hurt in Lady Jenny's eyes.

"He does. And the baby. They all adore that infant. *We* all do."

She blinked, as if taken aback by the forlorn quality in her own voice.

Elijah slipped past her with the candle, took her

hand, and led her away from the shadows and all that intriguing erotica, back to the warmth of the fireplace. "The holidays make everything worse, don't they?"

She tugged her hand free and looked at him as if he'd recently escaped Bedlam. "I beg your pardon?"

"I beg *your* pardon. I am tired, and I have not yet done justice to all this scrumptious fare. I was asking if the holidays made being around family particularly difficult, but you will ignore this question. Tell me why Lord Kesmore's offspring think you will abet their Christmas schemes?"

Elijah Harrison was like a horse. His body mass was so great, the heat of it would dry out a damp blanket from the inside. He had the sleek musculature of a horse as well, all too evident beneath his damp shirt and breeches.

Jenny stopped herself from drawing any further equine analogies, though held against his body, her back to his chest, at least one more such comparison lurked in her awareness. "Shall we resume our meal?"

"Of course." He gestured toward the sofa, a gentleman in stocking feet and damp clothing, who posed difficult questions. "I take it you enjoy drawing?"

Very difficult questions. He settled on the sofa beside her, tucking into his food with unabashed enthusiasm, unaware of the havoc he wrought with her composure.

"I do like to draw, and you must like children."

He paused with a bite of yellow cheese halfway to his mouth. "I don't think one likes children or dislikes them. One rails against them or surrenders to them, surrender being the more prudent course. Aren't you going to eat?"

She was hungry—hungry to sketch him, hungry to know what he knew.

"Of course. What did you mean about the holidays making everything worse?"

He paused with a slice of apple in his hand. "I am from a large family, though I'm the oldest, which meant I could get free the soonest. My first objection to the Yuletide holidays is that they fall just as the worst of winter's weather is getting its grip on the land. Who would position a holiday thus? Travel is difficult; moving goods to the shops for holiday shopping is difficult. Absent gross extravagance, there are no fresh fruits or vegetables to facilitate holiday feasting. All in all, the timing is very poor."

While he spoke, he gestured with the apple slice, not grandly, but with the languid eloquence of a thoroughly Gallic wrist. He probably shrugged like a Frenchman too.

Jenny took a sip of her tea, but it was tepid and weak compared to the man beside her. "Have you other objections?"

"I do, but I would rather hear about your drawing, Lady Genevieve. Your nieces were convinced you had some skill."

Some skill. That was all she had—little training, and less hope of acquiring any unless she took very drastic measures indeed.

"I enjoy it."

He munched the apple slice into oblivion far

more tidily than a horse would have and reached for another. "You, my lady, are prevaricating."

On so many levels. "How do you know?"

"Your eyes. They truly are the window to the soul, and that window closes a little when we dissemble. Most people glance down and left, others—some women—acquire a particularly vapid expression when they lie. You aren't one of them."

He held the second apple slice up to her. "Tell me about your sketching."

Temptation loomed irresistibly. When Jenny had sneaked into Antoine's classes, she'd loved the time spent immersed in creation, but she'd loved just as much the discussions that followed.

"I dabble, though I love the dabbling. I can sketch for hours, and when I'm not sketching, I want to be painting. If I can't sketch or paint, then I can embroider. The tedium of the embroidery, the stitch-by-stitch pace of it, can be meditative, but it's frustrating too."

The entire time she'd spoken, he'd held the apple slice up before her and kept his gaze on her. Now he took a crunchy bite and held the half remaining before her again, his focus on her mouth.

She wanted to lean forward and take what he offered with her teeth; instead, she took it with her fingers, dodging whatever dare he'd posed.

"You're still holding back on me," he said, helping himself to the gingerbread. "You want nothing but to spend your days creating, studying the masters, or reading about their lives and works. You long to travel the Continent, I'm supposing, and feast your eyes on the treasures there—what treasures the Corsican didn't acquire for himself. Am I right?"

Jenny could not tell if he disapproved of the person he described or was merely familiar with such creatures.

"You have never been so afflicted?"

"I *was* so afflicted." He dispatched another crispy apple slice, followed it up with a few bites of ham, then set about buttering a slice of bread. "Inside every professional artist a passionate amateur lies entombed. Enjoy your frustration, my lady."

The arrogance, condescension, and lurking bitterness of his pronouncement made Jenny want to spit out the apple he'd just shared with her. "Are you mocking me?"

He paused with a dollop of butter on a wooden knife poised above the bread. No, not bread. They'd baked the year's first batch of stollen today, a holiday sweet bread made according to Jenny's German grandmother's recipe.

He set the stollen on her plate. "I am envying you, dear lady. I trust you enjoy butter."

"Of course." She did not precisely enjoy his company, though being around him made her feel more… more. "If you're unhappy with your art, why not give it up?"

The same question she'd asked herself countless times.

"I am not unhappy with my art, and now you are trying to distract me." His tone was gentle, coaxing, and implacable. "Tell me about your drawing. When did you become interested, and when did you become aware you were different from the other girls?"

Those who sat to him said Elijah Harrison was a comfortable fellow to spend hours with. Jenny had found the notion preposterous. Elijah Harrison was big, quiet, and self-assured. He moved through life with a knowing, confident quality that struck her as incompatible with comfortableness.

She'd come to that conclusion without ever having talked to the man, though, and here, late at night, over informal victuals, his coat gently steaming two yards away, he regarded her with such, such *compassion*, that she wanted to entrust him with all her silly secrets and dreams.

When she had sketched him, his eyes had been bored, lazy, and slightly mocking: *Here I stand, more confident in my nudity than you lot cowering in your fashionable attire behind your sketch pads.*

In hindsight, and with the passage of a few years, she had realized that in a room full of young men with varying degrees of artistic talent, he'd adopted that attitude more for their ease than his own.

"Genevieve?"

Zhenevieve? She ought to remonstrate him for his presumption, but the sound of her name on his lips was too lovely.

"I've always been different. I'm different still. Everything you said… that's who I want to be. I am a duke's daughter, though, and probably more significantly, the daughter of a duchess. Were I to give vent to my eccentricities, it would break my parents' hearts."

A quantity of food had disappeared, and now Mr. Harrison appeared content to feast on her silly notions. "So you choose instead to break your own heart?"

She left off staring at his hands and rose to tend the fire. His question had not been challenging, but worse—far worse—gently pitying.

"One can love others, Mr. Harrison, or one can love one's own ambitions. A woman who chooses the latter is not highly regarded in our society. A man who chooses the former is regarded as weak or possessed of a religious vocation."

He did not pop to his feet when she knelt before the hearth and arranged an oak log on top of the stack already burning. Oak was heavy, though, and the weight of the additional log collapsed the half-burnt ones beneath it, sending a shower of sparks in all directions.

"Careful. Your skirts might catch."

He'd seized her under the arms and hauled her away from the hearth in one smooth, brute maneuver. When she ought to have been offended or unnerved, Jenny was impressed.

"Thank you. While you finish your meal, I'll check on your room."

She left him there by the fire for two reasons. First, she'd offered him quite enough of her confidences for one night and had failed utterly to wring any from him—professional or personal.

The second reason Jenny fled into the cold, dark corridor was that she liked standing close to Elijah Harrison far too much.

Two

As Elijah accompanied his hostess through the chilly, dimly lit house, fatigue hit him like a runaway freight wagon. This was what came of trying to make a winter's journey when sane people were holed up with one another, tippling brandy and making gingerbread.

No, not sane people. Sentimental people.

"Your room is here," Lady Jenny said, opening a door. She led him into a blessedly, gloriously cozy space, into a bit of heaven for a man who'd considered he might end both the day and his life shivering in a snowy ditch.

"Lady Kesmore takes her hospitality seriously," he said. The appointments were in a cheery blue and cream with green accents—again, not quite the green of Lady Jenny's eyes—giving the chamber a feminine air even by candlelight. A fat, black cat kitted out as if in formal evening attire—black fur tailcoat and knee breeches; white fur cravat, boots, and gloves—rose from the bed and strolled for the door, tail held high.

When a room was truly clean, light filled it easily. A beam of sunshine or flicker of candlelight could bounce from a sparkling mirror, to a gleaming hardwood floor, to a polished lamp chimney or sconce mirror.

The room was very clean, and in the hearth, a wood fire crackled merrily.

"I have never regarded the scent of wood smoke as a fragrance," he said, "though tonight, I certainly do."

"You were quite cold, weren't you?" she asked, lighting the candles by his bedside tables. "I forgot to get you a book."

"I would not read a single paragraph before succumbing to the charms of Morpheus." Where, if God were merciful, Elijah would dream of Lady Jenny illuminated by candlelight.

Another scent came to him as she moved around the room, a light, spicy perfume that started off with jasmine and ended with feminine mysteries.

"I'll have one of Lord Kesmore's dressing gowns brought to you," she said, peering into the pitcher on the hearth. "A footman remains on duty at the end of the hall until midnight, and then we rely on the porter through the night."

"I'm sure I won't waken in the night, and I might have to be roused to break my fast as well."

Small talk. She ought not to be in this room with him, though for present purposes, she was his hostess and had left the door a few inches ajar as a nod to propriety.

"I'll bid you pleasant dreams, then." She bobbed a curtsy and withdrew, leaving Elijah alone in his heaven.

Somebody had brought his things in from the stable and set his bag on the chest at the foot of the bed. Lest his worldly goods rot by morning, Elijah took out each damp, wrinkled article of clothing and draped it over the furniture, making sure at least a clean shirt and cravat were in proximity to the fire. As he saw to his wardrobe, he munched on one of the three pieces of gingerbread he'd filched from his supper.

The last order of business on this difficult and interesting day was to wash off before climbing into the fluffy blue-and cream-wonder that was his bed. He peeled his damp shirt and waistcoat from his body, hung them from the open doors of the wardrobe, and set about using the water left considerately near the hearth.

The water was scented with something bracing—lavender and rosemary?—and was small compensation for the lack of a steaming hot bath. Elijah had just finished with his ablutions when a knock sounded on his door.

That would be the footman with a nice, cozy dressing gown, no doubt, courtesy of the absent Lord Kesmore. "Come in."

"I've brought—"

Lady Jenny closed the door behind her and stood across the room, clutching a green velvet dressing robe that would probably wrap around her three times.

"My dressing gown."

He'd long since grown comfortable sporting about in the altogether for inspection by others, provided the surrounds were comfortably warm. Around Genevieve Windham, his state of partial undress slammed into him like *two* freight wagons galloping at each other from opposite directions.

The practical part of him spoke up: *She's seen you in less than this. You're exhausted. Take the bloody dressing gown and bid her good night.*

But that sensible, familiar voice could barely be heard for the greater din created by what he saw in her gaze.

She was visually consuming him, taking in every muscle and sinew, cataloguing joints and textures even as she clutched the dressing gown to her like a shield.

"Were I modeling," he said as he approached her, "my exposed skin would probably be oiled, or, when needs must, coated with butter, the better to catch the light, particularly if the scene depicted is dark. I apologize for the lack of attire, my lady."

He tugged on the dressing gown. She didn't give it up.

"What kind of oil?"

"I prefer…" His brain became befogged with… *her.* Yes, he wanted to sketch her, wanted to unearth all the artistic and female confidences she'd denied him, but he also wanted *her* to sketch *him.*

Though he'd have to keep his breeches on.

Bid her good night.

"What kind of oil?" she asked again.

"Fragrant, soothing scents." Jasmine appealed strongly. "When one must hold the same position for a length of time, the more relaxed one is, the more successful the exercise."

She ought to tell him she hadn't known he modeled—small talk relied heavily on polite untruths—and then he could tell her he hadn't provided that service to anybody for years, which was not an untruth. He no longer needed the money, and he no longer had the time.

More to the point, the woman ought to be running

from the room in high dudgeon or at least sporting a furious blush.

Lady Jenny handed over the dressing gown and watched him shrug into it with something like grief in her eyes.

"My lady, I bid you good night, and my compliments to Kesmore on the quality of his wardrobe." The garment was lined with silk, and yet, Elijah wanted to drop it to the floor so Lady Jenny might continue to regard him so ravenously.

"Will you model for me, Mr. Harrison?"

She might have challenged him to a duel, so fiercely had she thrown down the question. He'd once had the same kind of determination, willing to travel through war zones to see an obscure Caravaggio.

"My lady, you flatter me, but my journey will take me away..." No true gentleman would have obliged her request. No true artist who understood the limitations of her station and the relentless clamoring of her artistic inclination would refuse her. Among all the dilettantes and dabblers to pass through old Antoine's studios, Lady Jenny was one of few students to possess a germ of real talent.

"You said you had only a few more miles to go, Mr. Harrison. Give me half an hour in the morning—the nursery has excellent light, being at the top of the house."

"I cannot be private with you when I am *en dishabille*." He should not be private with her when in a coma, and they both knew it.

"I did not expect that you would be. Fleur and Amanda would find it most curious were you to appear unclothed. After breakfast, then?"

The prospect of traveling even a few more miles in miserable weather had no appeal, and she'd taken him in when he might have perished for his stubbornness. Then, too, given how fiercely she'd regarded Kesmore's daughters, Lady Jenny wouldn't be focusing for long on a sketch when the children were underfoot.

"A half hour then. My thanks for the dressing gown."

She left, and this time didn't bother with a curtsy, nor he with a bow. He ran the warmer over the sheets then hung the sumptuous dressing gown in the wardrobe, where the scent of jasmine was even stronger.

When he laid down on the lovely warm sheets, the same fragrance assailed him.

Elijah's last waking thought was that Lady Genevieve had given up her bed for him and taken a colder, more humble chamber elsewhere in the house. This eased his last, lingering hesitance about giving her a half hour of his time in the nursery.

A half hour lounging about in the morning sun was small recompense to the lady who'd provided a virtual stranger food, clothing, shelter, and a night surrounded by her fragrance.

While tossing and turning in a strange bed, Jenny had given considerable thought to which part of Elijah Harrison she'd capture for her own on paper. His hands appealed—his big, elegant, so talented hands. With those hands, he'd done a portrait of the regent even Prinny himself was said to like. She considered those hands as Fleur and Amanda galloped around the hearth rug in the nursery.

"And where shall you pose me, my lady?" Mr. Harrison asked.

Jenny glanced at the eight-day clock in the corner of the nursery. He'd be leaving soon…

"Will you pose me too?" Amanda asked.

"And me," Fleur chorused. The girls turned big, beseeching eyes on Jenny, eyes that promised best behavior for at least five entire—though not consecutive—minutes. The nursery maids had decamped for a spot of tea, which Jenny suspected would be chased with a headache powder or two.

"In the light," Jenny said, taking Mr. Harrison by the arm and directing him to a rocking chair by the windows. "Amanda, can you fetch your sketch pad, and, Fleur, yours too?"

They thundered off, while Jenny regarded her subject. "I'm going to focus on your hands, Mr. Harrison. Hands can be complicated."

He smiled as if she'd just explained to the Archbishop of Canterbury that Christmas often fell on the twenty-fifth of December.

"I like hands," he said, taking his seat. "They can be windows to the soul too. What shall I do with these hands you intend to immortalize?"

She hadn't thought that far ahead, it being sufficient challenge to choose a single aspect of him to sketch. Fleur and Amanda came skipping back into the room, each clutching a sketch pad.

"You will sketch the girls, and I will sketch you, while the girls sketch whomever they please." The plan was brilliant; everybody had an assigned task.

Amanda's little brows drew down. "I want to watch

Mr. Harrison. Fleur can sketch you, Aunt Jen. You have to sit very still, though."

"An unbroken chain of artistic indulgence," Mr. Harrison said, accepting a sketch pad and pencil from Fleur. "Miss Fleur, please seat yourself on the hearth, though you might want a pillow to make the ordeal more comfortable."

Amanda grabbed two burgundy brocade pillows off the settee, tossed one at Fleur, and dropped the other beside Elijah's rocker. Jenny took the second rocking chair and flipped open her sketch pad.

Her subject sat with the morning sun slanting over his shoulder, one knee crossed over the other, the sketch pad on his lap. Amanda watched from where she knelt at his elbow, and Fleur…

Fleur crossed one knee over the other—an unladylike pose, but effective for balancing a sketch pad—and glowered at Jenny as if to will Jenny's image onto the page by visual imperative.

"Your sister has beautiful eyebrows," Mr. Harrison said to his audience. "They have the most graceful curve. It's a family trait, I believe."

Amanda crouched closer. "Does that mean I have them too?"

He glanced over at her, his expression utterly serious. "You do, though yours are a touch more dramatic. When you make your bows, gentlemen will write sonnets to the Carrington sisters' eyebrows."

"Papa's horse is Sonnet. Tell me some more."

While he spoke, his pencil moved over the page in short, light bursts of activity. "Notice the way Miss Fleur's eyes, as beautiful as they are, aren't pitched at exactly the same angle. Nobody's face is perfectly symmetrical, not if you study them closely."

"What's symmet—that word you said?"

While Jenny sketched, and Fleur sat a little taller on her burgundy pillow, Mr. Harrison provided Amanda a concise, understandable explanation for symmetry, then went on and described the ways asymmetry made an image interesting.

"Have you ever drawn a crow?" Amanda asked. "Or a pitcher?"

"I'm sure I have. Crows are a challenge because they want you to think they're black, but in the sun, they're many colors."

From across the room, Jenny saw her nieces consider crows in a whole new manner, not as rough-voiced avian nuisances, but as peacocks in disguise.

"So what do you do when you want to draw a crow?" Amanda's nose was less than an inch from Mr. Harrison's sleeve.

His pencil did not stop moving, though Fleur was beginning to fidget now that her soon-to-be-legendary eyebrows were no longer under discussion.

"I try to draw the crow as he sees himself. They're curious fellows, flying about as if the entire world were available as their perch. I've seen a crow light on the back of a cow, for example, and the cow had nothing to say to it."

Amanda grinned, a child who might like to fly through the clouds and light on the back of a cow.

"I'm curious too," Fleur said. "I don't want to sit on a cow. I want to sit on a pony."

"What would you name your pony?" Mr. Harrison asked.

Jenny listened with half an ear to the earnest and protracted discussion that ensued. Naming a pony was apparently a holy undertaking in the opinion of her nieces, but then, their father was a former cavalry officer.

As Jenny's father was. Her pencil stopped moving, as her mind started a roll call of family members who'd served in the cavalry:

His Grace; her uncle Tony; her oldest brother, Devlin St. Just; her brothers-by-marriage, Kesmore and Deene; her *late* brother, Bartholomew… Thoughts of Bart brought both grief and anger.

And, of course, guilt.

The clock chimed the quarter hour, prodding Jenny out of her reverie. Across the room, Elijah Harrison had made two conquests by virtue of simply talking with Fleur and Amanda. He'd glanced over at Jenny occasionally, his gaze amused and patient.

While she had only fourteen more minutes to give vent to years of artistic frustration.

And yet, when she looked down at the page twenty minutes later—Fleur would remain still no longer, not even with a book on her lap—Jenny had not sketched Mr. Harrison's talented hands, or not just his hands.

"Shall we have a critique session?" he asked as he rose. "I'm sure the young ladies would be happy to assist us."

His hand settled on Fleur's dark curls, and the little girl went still beneath his touch—even Kesmore didn't have that effect on his daughter—while Jenny felt her insides take flight. A critique session with Elijah Harrison?

"I have used up my half hour and then some, Mr. Harrison. I would not impose further."

"Nonsense. My model has been very patient, as has my assistant, and I'm sure they'd be fascinated to see what we've created."

"I can show you my sketch," Fleur volunteered.

"What's a critique session?" Amanda asked.

A critique session was when you put your heart in the middle of a busy thoroughfare and hoped at least some of the passing traffic didn't roll directly over it.

Mr. Harrison smiled down at Amanda. "A critique session is when people who share a similar passion try to help each other improve their work. Like when you read your papa's poetry and suggest a better rhyme to him."

"Mama does that," Fleur said. "She makes Papa smile. I know a lot of rhymes. Do you want to see my sketch?"

He held out a hand. "Of course."

In one gesture and two words, he'd given Fleur a gift of confidence no one would take from her. Jenny envied her niece and understood now why people enjoyed sitting to Elijah Harrison.

He was quiet; he was reserved. He was not the most cheerful individual, and he could be brusque, but he was kind. She had not appreciated this about him when he'd joined in the critique sessions at Antoine's, though her recollection was of a man who'd offered suggestions and observations, not criticisms.

He appropriated the brocade pillows and arranged them on the hearth, then held out a hand to her. "Come, Lady Jenny. Let us assemble the jury."

His hand was warm, and he seated her as graciously as if they were at one of the Duchess of Moreland's entertainments. Fleur and Amanda each tucked themselves against an adult, and Jenny tried to quiet her nerves.

He would not laugh at her work in front of the children, would he?

"Miss Fleur, your work comes first, lest you burst with excitement and rain feathers all over the room." He took Fleur's proffered sketch pad and regarded her efforts in silence for some moments.

"You are an honest artist," he remarked. "You have chosen to present your aunt without even a hint of a smile. That was brave of you, but also accurate, given how hard Lady Jenny concentrates on her art. Lady Jenny, what can you add?"

Jenny took the little sketch, prepared to wax enthusiastic about some lines and squiggles, only to be brought up short.

"Fleur, you have a good eye." On the page, a lady sat hunched in a rocking chair, the composition a heap of dress, chin, and severe bun, as if crabbed with age. No particular features were evident, and proportion was a lost cause, as was perspective, and yet, the child had managed to catch something of an unhappy intensity about Jenny's posture. "I'm very impressed."

"Let me see," Amanda demanded. She plucked the sketch from Jenny's hands. "That's Aunt Jen. She loves to draw."

Jenny wanted to study Fleur's childish rendering at greater length, she wanted to draw Mr. Harrison forever, and she wanted him gone from the house.

"Lady Jenny, your turn."

She passed her sketch pad over to him, feeling a pang of sympathy for accused criminals as they stood in the dock. And yet, she'd asked for this. Gotten together all of her courage to ask for this one moment of artistic communion.

"Well," Mr. Harrison said, "isn't he a handsome fellow? What do you think, ladies?"

"You look like a papa," Fleur observed. "Though our papa doesn't sketch. He reads stories."

"And hates his ledgers," Amanda added. "Is my hair that long in back?"

"Yes," Jenny said, because she'd drawn not only Elijah Harrison's hands, but all of him, looking relaxed, elegant, and handsome, with Amanda crouched at his side, fascinated with what he created on the page.

"I look…" He regarded the sketch in silence, while Jenny heard a coach-and-four rumbling toward her vulnerable heart. "I look… a bit tired, slightly rumpled, but quite at home. You are very quick, Lady Genevieve, and quite good."

Quite good. Like saying a baby was adorable, a young gentleman well-mannered.

"The pose was simple," Jenny said, "the lighting uncomplicated, and the subject…"

"Yes?"

He was one of those men built in perfect proportion. Antoine had spent an entire class wielding a tailor's measure on Mr. Harrison's body, comparing his proportions to the Apollo Belvedere, and scoffing at the "mistakes" inherent in Michelangelo's David.

Jenny wanted to snatch her drawing from his hand. "The subject is conducive to a pleasing image."

He passed the sketch pad back, but Jenny had the sense that in some way, some not entirely artistic way, she'd displeased him. The disappointment was survivable. Her art had been displeasing men since she'd first neglected her Bible verses to sketch her brothers.

"You next, Mr. Harrison."

"Of course." He passed her a charming little study of Fleur perched on the hearth, the tip of her tongue peeking from her lips as she concentrated on sketching Jenny. Something in his portrait reminded Jenny of Fleur's sketch of her aunt.

"You made her hair tidier," Amanda noted. "Fleur hardly ever looks that serious, though."

"One takes a few liberties in the name of diplomacy," Mr. Harrison said. He aimed a look at Jenny, likely intended to give the words deeper meaning.

He *was* tired, and he *was* rumpled. Where was the harm in showing those things?

"He means," Jenny said in anticipation of Amanda's question, "that one needn't show every unflattering detail when trying to render a person's essence on the page."

"Like if the crow had some tattered feathers, you'd still try to show how shiny they were?"

"Yes, Amanda," Mr. Harrison said, though he was looking at Jenny as he spoke.

The nursery maids returned, looking somewhat restored, and Jenny's half hour—an hour in truth—with Polite Society's most in-demand portraitist was over.

And in that hour, she had not earned his respect for her art. This should be a relief, should give her ammunition to aim at the part of her that wanted nothing but to disgrace herself with an artistic life, and damn the consequences.

As he escorted her down through the house, Mr. Harrison stopped on the first landing. "Why so quiet, my lady?"

The daughter of a duchess was capable of great feats of diplomacy, also great feats of courage. Jenny would never have an opportunity to work with an instructor of Elijah Harrison's caliber again, or at least not for many years.

"You did not like my sketch."

The servants had been busy. In the foyer below, wreaths hung in the windows, cloved oranges in the middle of the wreaths. The scents were lovely and the light cheerful, but the space, being high ceilinged and windowed, was cold.

"I liked your sketch quite well."

"What did you like about it?" Because in five minutes, he'd be on his horse and disappearing into the winter landscape, and Jenny had to know what he'd seen in her work, even if he'd seen only trite, unprepossessing efforts.

"You are good, Lady Genevieve. Your accuracy is effortless, you're quick, and your technique very proficient for one who has likely had little professional instruction."

Those compliments would have distracted her, had she not been watching his eyes. His soul was not in those terse compliments, and he'd be gone in four minutes.

"But?"

He captured her hand and placed it on his arm, moving with her down the last flight of stairs. "But you rendered me tired and rumpled, when I was quite sure the fellow in that nursery was the most charming exponent of English artistry ever to aspire to membership in the Royal Academy. You also made me look…" He glanced around as they gained the empty foyer. "Lonely."

"Amanda said you looked like a papa. I tried to convey the affection with which you—"

"I miss…" He frowned, unwound his arm from Jenny's, and stepped back. "I have many younger siblings. It's natural I should miss them from time to time. That you saw in me something I'd ignored in myself confirms your talent rather than denies it."

Somewhere in that grudging admission was a true compliment, though likely one he hadn't intended.

"Thank you."

Which left nothing more to say. The footmen being derelict or preoccupied with decorating some other part of the house, Jenny took Mr. Harrison's greatcoat down from the hook and held it up to him. Next she passed him his scarf, then held his hat and gloves while he buttoned up.

And then their time together was over, and Jenny heard the sound of many heavy coaches rumbling, not toward her artistic inclinations, but more in the direction of her heart. "Safe journey, Mr. Harrison."

"My thanks for your hospitality." He tapped his hat onto his head and pulled on his gloves. "Have you considered corresponding with old Monsieur Antoine? He's very generous with his guidance, and not at all opposed to encouraging the talented amateur, regardless of gender."

His suggestion cut in several ways, though it

was intended as another compliment—to a talented amateur of the inconvenient feminine persuasion. "Monsieur is, as you say, very generous, but his eyes are failing."

Mr. Harrison tossed the ends of his scarf over his shoulders in a gesture more Continental than English. "I didn't know that."

"Few people do. He has been helpful, though now when I call at his gallery, we spend our conversations on his reminiscences. He's very proud of you."

Mr. Harrison glanced up, as if entreating the heavens, then grimaced. "The Yuletide season has officially started." He pointed to the crossbeam over the antechamber, where a swag of mistletoe had been hung.

"Louisa and Joseph are quite enamored of all things—"

Whatever nonsense Jenny had intended to spout one minute before Elijah Harrison trotted out of her life, she forgot as he put a gloved hand on her shoulder. "It's a harmless tradition," he said. "One I've had occasion to appreciate."

With that, he kissed her, and not on the cheek as a proper gentleman ought. He touched his mouth to hers softly, a lingering, gentle kiss that conveyed... something. Regret perhaps, at having to face the miserable winter day.

Before he drew back, he whispered, "You'll want to look at the sketchbook I used, and, Genevieve?"

He bore the scent of rosemary and lavender, and he was leaving.

"Mr. Harrison?"

"You draw wonderfully. Be proud of yourself."

He gave her cheek a quick buss and passed through the door.

Jenny held his compliment close to her heart—the real compliment, the one he'd whispered. She held his kisses closer.

Three

"Yon beast will not go sound." Joseph Carrington, Earl of Kesmore, scowled at Elijah's horse as the gelding was led from the Kesmore stables. "Listen to the footfalls, Harrison. Your hind end is off rhythm."

And people called artists eccentric.

"Kesmore, good morning. My hind end is traveling down the lane posthaste, though you have my thanks for providing shelter for the night in absentia."

Kesmore's frown—the man's dark features had an entire repertoire of frowns, scowls, glowers, and glares—turned affectionate. "You will forgive my countess for not greeting you here in the yard. She must see to our son's safe passage up to the house."

Lady Kesmore, accompanied by a maid, was wending her way from the coach house up a shoveled path toward the manor.

"Congratulations on the birth of an heir," Elijah said. "I thought you had only the two daughters."

Kesmore's affectionate scowl became a long-suffering affectionate scowl. "According to my wife, when the child's nappies want changing, that boy is my son. When he's charming every female in the shire, he's her ladyship's son. Weren't you to have immortalized my daughters on canvas at some point?"

He would recall that, and likely recall that Elijah had dodged the commission. Now, Elijah needed juvenile portraits in his portfolio if the Royal Academy was to look favorably upon him, else he wouldn't be ruralizing away his holidays.

"I apologize for not being here to receive you in person," Kesmore said as Elijah's horse was led away. "My lady and I had business in Surrey, and last night we tarried at her sister Sophie's household rather than push homeward in dirty weather. The womenfolk must disappear into the nursery and exchange maternal intelligence while my brother-in-law and I disappear into his study and say nothing of any consequence beyond, 'I'll have one more tot, thank you.'"

"I see." Marriage had turned the taciturn Kesmore into a chatterbox. The transformation was both disconcerting and… endearing.

"You don't, but should the Almighty bless you with children, you shall."

"If the Almighty would see fit to let me get to my next destination without further mishap, I will be most grateful."

As Kesmore's wife disappeared into the house, Kesmore resumed his perusal of Elijah. "I trust Lady Jenny made you welcome?"

"Very." Kesmore's eyes narrowed, and like an idiot, Elijah babbled on. "She is knowledgeable about art, and her company is enjoyable." Also a sore trial to his self-restraint, which was why departure this morning was a relief.

Mostly a relief.

The thwack of Kesmore's riding crop against his boot punctuated the soft whistle of the winter wind. "Lady Jenny can handle the hellions gracing my nursery, which ought to recommend her to half the bachelor princes in Europe. She talks horses with me, poetry with Louisa, politics with His Grace, recipes with—"

Kesmore broke off and waved one black-gloved hand in the direction of the house—a silly wave, hand up, fingers waggling madly. Elijah followed the man's gaze and saw a woman in a third-floor window with a child in her arms. In a gesture ubiquitous among mothers, she was waving the baby's tiny hand in Kesmore's direction.

"The child probably can't even see you, Kesmore, and he has no notion why you're fluttering your hand around."

"Neither do I, and someday, neither will you." This time Kesmore waved his riding crop at the mother and child, who waved right back. Beside Lady Kesmore, Lady Jenny appeared in the window, a feminine incandescence in an otherwise prosaic tableau.

Elijah did not wave. Not to the baby, not to the baby's mother, not to his aunt.

"Here comes your noble steed," Kesmore said. "This is Bacchus. He's a sensible lad once he gets the fidgets worked out, and he's not particular about the footing."

The sensible lad was about the size of an elephant, the same color as an elephant, and possessed of a hair coat worthy of a mastodon. The beast was also making shameless eyes at Kesmore.

"He looks sturdy enough."

"Much like you, Harrison, he's a treasure whose subtle gifts can only be appreciated over time. If you'll excuse me, I'm off to interrogate my sister-in-law regarding the offenses committed by my offspring in my absence. I will take on this thankless burden without my countess's fortifying presence, while her ladyship tends to obligations in the nursery I am biologically incapable of assisting with."

This was more married-man-papa blather about Elijah knew not what. To see what a short trip to the altar had done to a decorated veteran of the Peninsular Campaign, a bruising rider, and halfway friend was unnerving.

And yet, Kesmore was… happy. Scowlingly though radiantly happy.

"If you had to choose one of Aesop's fables as your favorite, Kesmore, which one would it be?"

Kesmore paused midstride toward the manor and turned a puzzled frown on Elijah. "In what regard? A favorite moral, a favorite story? A favorite because the tale is brief and will get my daughters most quickly into bed?"

"Your favorite. The one you liked best when you were a boy."

The frown disappeared, replaced by a half smile. "'The Cock and the Jewel,' I suppose. When a fellow is famished, all the gems in the world will not satisfy his craving for a simple crust of bread, no matter how others might value the pretty jewel."

Elijah felt a whiff of relief. Little girls could draw roosters and gemstones, particularly with some assistance from their aunt.

"Be off with you," Kesmore said with a flourish of his whip that had Bacchus looking nervous. "And you"—Kesmore pointed the whip at the horse—"no mischief, or Father Christmas will make you do pony rides all Christmas Day for both girls."

The horse stood docile as a lamb at the mounting block. Once Elijah was in the saddle, Bacchus turned down the snowy drive without an instant's hesitation, though Elijah cast one last glance back at the empty third-floor window.

"What is this?" Louisa, Countess of Kesmore, marched across the nursery and thrust a sketch pad under Jenny's nose. "It doesn't look like your work, Sister."

Louisa did not glide about the house. She did not make small talk. She appropriated neither the airs and graces of a countess nor those of a recently published author whose poetry was acclaimed by the most discerning of the literati. She was simply Louisa: blunt, beautiful, and unfailingly genuine. Jenny loved her for those qualities but was not so enamored of Louisa's unrelenting curiosity.

"It's a sketch pad, dearest. The girls leave them all over the house." With a brother underfoot, they'd learn, as Jenny had, to keep sketches under lock and key.

"I know it's a sketch pad, Genevieve Windham, but what's *this*?" Louisa held out the tablet, flipped open to a pencil drawing of… Jenny, sketching.

Jenny regarded the page with something between dread and fascination. Her hand closed around the sketch pad while her feet clamored to leave the room. "I suppose Mr. Harrison drew it. Some artists must draw compulsively."

"Like you." Louisa's expression held only sympathy. "He's good, though not as good as you are."

Louisa was loyal to a fault too.

"Elijah Harrison is the most sought-after portraitist in London, unless you count Sir Thomas Lawrence, who is flooded with commissions and at the regent's beck and call."

"Which you ought to be. His sketch of you is quite good." Louisa came closer to study the drawing. "He's caught how fiercely you concentrate, like a raptor focusing on her prey."

"Louisa, I know you are a poetess, but that image is hardly flattering to a lady."

"Elijah Harrison has also caught you as a woman, Jenny. He drew you full of curves and energy, a female body engaged in a passion, not some drawing-room artifact showing off her modiste's latest patterns. He sees that your beauty is not merely physical."

Was that why he'd kissed her, or had it been merely a passing holiday gesture? "You are fanciful, Louisa."

"I am honest."

Both could be true, but one didn't argue logic with Louisa and win unless one was Joseph. "Why do you say I'm better than Mr. Harrison?"

Louisa flipped back to the sketch of Fleur. "Look at this."

"It's very accurate, and if he had time to sketch me, as well, he drew both quickly."

And why had he sketched Jenny, and then told her specifically to examine this sketch pad as he'd trotted out of her life?

"Portraiture is not exclusively about rendering an accurate image," Louisa said. "Fleur is a happy little soul. She doesn't have Amanda's inquisitive nature or impulsivity; she likes to make others happy. Fleur is quick to sense others' feelings, like my Joseph, but she hasn't Joseph's analytical bent."

Louisa spoke with the assurance of a mother who knew her children. Fleur and Amanda were Louisa's stepchildren, and Louisa had only known them a year; and yet, by virtue of marital alchemy, Louisa was their mother too.

Jenny did not point out that Louisa's husband was quick to sense *Louisa's* feelings, and probably only Louisa's feelings.

"What is your point, dearest?" Louisa always had a point, sometimes arcane, sometimes irrelevant to anybody else, but she had a point. Jenny wanted to flip back to the sketch Mr. Harrison had done of her, to study it, to copy it, to see what he had seen when he'd drawn her. Maybe that sketch had a point too.

Louisa moved away, grabbing a receiving blanket from a pile folded near the hearth and shaking it out. "Mr. Harrison didn't sketch *Fleur*. He sketched some little girl who looks like Fleur trying to make a drawing. He sketched what he saw, not what he felt."

Jenny studied the drawing again, and admitted that Louisa's conclusion was… not invalid. The image was accurate and whimsical, but not… *Fleur.* Her little-girl eyes, so full of life and vulnerability, didn't stare up from the page. "He doesn't know Fleur."

This was true—it was also a defense of an artist who needed no defending.

"I suspect he doesn't know children, or he doesn't know a nature like Fleur's. She's purely sweet and easy to love, much like you."

"Gracious, Lou, you've gone from spouting poetry to spinning fiction. I'll leave you now and give your regards to dear Sophie."

"And Joseph's regards to Sindal too please, and keep the sketches, Jenny. I think Mr. Harrison meant them for you."

Louisa didn't smirk as she made that observation. Her green eyes held a touch of pity, though, the same pity Jenny bore lately from her aunt and uncle, her cousins, her siblings, and—she would swear to this—her very own cat.

As she drove the pony cart over the snowy lanes to her sister Sophie's domicile, Jenny tried not to consider that pity, and yet, it circled her awareness like a shark among shipwreck victims.

The pity rankled because Jenny was pouting over Elijah Harrison passing through her life, leaving her a sketch, and departing without a backward glance.

Pouting was for children, *which she would never have.* Her family was a group of perceptive, forthright people, and yet, they would not talk about a sister who wanted to pursue art instead of holy matrimony.

They would only pity her.

"For Christmas, I would like to be spared my siblings'

pity." The pony, a shaggy little scrapper by the name of Grendel, shook his harness bells as if in reply. "I would like to be appreciated for who I am, for my art, and yet..."

As she turned the little gray up the Sidling driveway, Jenny buttoned up her untoward resentments and longings. Paris was a dream, not a just desert.

Sophie, Baroness Sindal, was waiting in the foyer of her sprawling Tudor home, little Kit clinging to her skirts, and the baby—he wasn't really a baby anymore—perched on her hip.

"Jenny, welcome! Sindal, take the children and let me have a moment with my long-lost sister."

Sophie's tall, blond husband hoisted the younger child to his hip and took Kit by the hand. "Jenny, you see how it's to be. The menfolk banished to the nursery while temptation wafts up from the kitchen. I ask you, how are we to be good little boys when faced with such an ordeal?"

Sindal stood well over six feet, and yet around Sophie he was a very good boy indeed.

"Papa, pick me up!" Young Kit held his arms up and was obliged with a perch on Sindal's other hip. "'Lo, Aunt Jen Jen!"

Kit shouted everything. Jenny could not recall the last time she'd shouted *anything*, and silently applauded the boy's boisterous approach to life.

"Hello, Master Kit. When your mama and I have finished the stollen, will you come down and sample it for us?"

She reached a hand out to tousle his blond curls but stopped short of her goal, fingers outstretched, the child grinning at her. A queerish feeling came over her. Were she not a lady, she would have called it *excitement*. "Whose scarf is that?"

The scarf in question hung on a hook in the foyer, draped over a gentleman's greatcoat, the pattern an unusual plaid done mostly in dark purple. When she'd first beheld that scarf, Jenny had noticed the colors—a green stripe, a lavender stripe—because the scheme had been unusual but quite pretty.

"That would be mine."

Elijah Harrison emerged from the drawing room down the hallway and bowed in Jenny's direction. "Lady Genevieve, we meet again."

He was smiling. He was smiling, and he was *here*, and though she knew her sister, her nephews, and even Sindal were watching her, Jenny was helpless not to smile back.

Elijah was used to working in spaces not entirely conducive to producing good art, much less great art. He was used to manufacturing sunlight where none existed, opulence of setting where none had *ever* existed, and personality traits—charm, dignity, sagacity, even chastity—his sitters' own mothers would never have ascribed to them.

He was not, however, used to ignoring the scent of Christmas baking while he set up his studio. Worse yet, through some quirk of antique architecture, he could hear Lady Jenny's voice wafting up from the kitchen through the flue, hear her laughter and the lilt and rhythm of her speech, though he couldn't make out a single word she said.

Fortunately, the Evil Chimney of Distraction had fallen silent about a half hour ago.

Elijah moved furniture around to make window light more available. He organized stretched canvasses, pigments, linseed oil, walnut oil for the lightest colors, brushes, and the containers where he stored bladders of paint, then he moved the furniture around some more.

Where was she? Was she staying under the same roof as he?

"Mr. Harrison?"

At first he thought the chimney had spoken to him, then he realized Lady Jenny stood in the doorway to the guest room he was converting to artistic use.

He bowed. Not because she was a duke's daughter, not even because she was a lady. He bowed because something in him finally was able to focus now that he knew where she was—and because she was carrying a small tray. "Lady Jenny."

"I'm having tea sent up, and I brought you some stollen fresh from the kitchen. I gather this is where you are to work?" She hovered in the doorway, much as she had at Kesmore's house the previous night.

"My temporary studio, the most recent of many. Won't you come in?"

Won't you please come in?

He shoved two heavy chairs nearer the hearth, then realized he hadn't lit the fire. "I apologize for the cold. Moving furniture about warms one up."

She came closer, peering around as if in a curiosity shop. "You have some of the heat from the kitchens too, I think."

"Which we will lose if that door remains open." He

crossed the room to shut the door, and not because the room would get cold. "Shall I light a fire for you?"

She set the tray down on the raised hearth and sent him an unfathomable look. What had he said? What had she inferred? Why was she destined to find him in shirtsleeves, cuffs turned back, rumpled, and untidy? He cleaned up decently when he made the effort.

"The tea will be along presently. That will warm us up if needs must. You made a sketch of me."

She wanted to talk about art, and he wanted to eat whatever was on that tray and simply behold her.

"You made one of me. Artists often perform reciprocal courtesies for one another. For years, my anatomy was available to model for Antoine's students." He should *not* have said that.

"I know."

And she *really* should not have said that.

The knock on the door felt every bit as intrusive to Elijah as if they had been on the point of a kiss—another kiss—or perhaps on the point of issuing each other a challenge.

"That will be our tea." He hustled over to the door, took the tray from the maid in the hallway, and closed the door in the servant's face. "Shall you pour?"

"While you butter our bread." She smiled as if this informal, impromptu picnic were a delight to her. Her smile wasn't loud, and it wasn't particularly merry.

That smile—he was astonished to conclude—was a trifle *naughty*.

He dropped into one of the heavy chairs without asking her permission and lifted the linen from the small tray. The scent of yeast and sweet bread hit his nose, and in the chilly room, fragrant steam rose from the half loaf of bread.

"Cutting it when it's warm takes skill," she said. "You need a good sharp bread knife and a light touch. Don't mash it."

She stirred cream and sugar into his tea while he feathered slices of holiday bread from the loaf. "You don't skimp on the goodies." The loaf was liberally full of candied fruit and nuts, to the point that Elijah's mouth watered.

"My sister Sophie doesn't skimp on anything related to the comfort or pleasure of her family. This is her recipe, or her version of our grandmother's recipe."

"Your grandmamma was German?" The tea in his cup was steaming too. To make a painting of steam was difficult—probably better suited to watercolors than oils.

"We're German on Her Grace's mother's side. My father would call it the dam line, and he'd use that language in company too. About that sketch, Mr. Harrison?"

He passed her a thoroughly buttered slice of warm holiday bread. "First things first. I arrived here after luncheon was served because I detoured clear back to the posting inn to make sure my baggage had been sent on ahead."

"And like a man, you did not want to impose on the kitchen when you got here, and you forgot to see to your victualing at the inn because you had a task before you. When you arrived here, you denied my sister the pleasure of caring for an honored guest—and you went hungry."

She was scolding him, which made him want to miss more meals so she might scold him some more. Surely the cold was addling his wits? "You have no patience for the starving-artist mentality?"

She held up her slice of bread, regarding it as melted butter drizzled onto her plate. "Art should be joyful, so joyful it sustains its creator in ways that have nothing to do with physical nourishment."

He took a bite of bread rather than snort at her naïveté. He'd believed the same thing, once upon a long, silly time ago. "Art should be pretty and remunerative. You say I'm an honored guest, but in reality, I'm a tradesmen reluctantly admitted into houses above my station."

She took a dainty bite, chewed slowly, and turned an innocent pair of green eyes on him. "You are the heir to a marquess. By rights, you are the Earl of Bernward. You outrank most of your subjects, though I suspect you keep the title quiet because your patrons would be self-conscious in your presence otherwise. Commendable of you, from an artistic standpoint."

He hadn't seen that salvo coming, and so he reacted less carefully than he ought. "How do you know I modeled for Antoine?"

Her ladyship munched another bite of holiday bread, not a discernible care in the world. "Your tea is getting cold, Mr. Harrison. I attended those classes whenever I could. Your generosity as a model did much to improve my understanding of the male body."

He finished his tea in two swallows. "Women were not permitted into those classes. Not ever." And yet, he'd known she was there practically from the first.

She popped the last bite of her bread into her mouth and dusted her hands together. "I grew tired of drawing kittens and… flowers, much as you might occasionally grow tired of painting corpulent old lords, aging beauties, and strutting lordlings."

A Renaissance master would have known what to do with her. She was heartrendingly beautiful to the eye, more beautiful the longer he studied her, and yet—she was a minx too. On the order of a saint who prayed with her eyes turned heavenward and much of her cleavage exposed. She likely didn't appreciate this aspect of her own personality though, which created a conundrum.

"The lordlings are the worst, and I knew you were in Antoine's classes."

All the languor in her manner disappeared. While Elijah watched, a blush crept up her neck, turning her perfect complexion quite, quite rosy.

"I suspected you knew when you came to Joseph's door last night. May I ask how I was found out?"

Relief swept through him, odd but welcome. She'd been bluffing. Those looks, that thoughtful chewing, the "your tea will grow cold" nonsense had been her attempt at a sophisticated repartee foreign to her nature. He held out another piece of buttered sweet bread to her and wondered why she'd try to misrepresent herself.

"Your sketches were always the best," he said, helping himself to more tea. "And yet, you never asked many questions, never spoke much at all. You were one of few students who had the sense to move around the room, to change your perspective on the subject from week to week. You took risks. You got down to business as soon as Antoine had described the exercise, and Antoine always had a few words to say to you when he wandered among the students."

"From that you deduced my identity?"

"Drink your tea before it cools, my lady."

His words provoked her minx-smile, which hadn't been their intended effect. He buttered himself more bread rather than smile back. "I followed you home, except you didn't go directly home. You went in the back door of a modiste's establishment, and no matter how long I waited, the pale young man with so much dedication and talent never emerged."

"Though Lady Jenny Windham did."

"If it's any consolation, I needed several attempts to figure out your scheme."

She tore off a bite of bread but didn't eat it. Even her fingers were beautiful—slender, graceful, elegant. "Why concern yourself at all, Mr. Harrison? You are the darling of the Royal Academy, your talent beyond question. Why would you care about one casual art student?"

A clever reply would have served them both well. They could smile false smiles at each other, finish the tea and crumpets, and perhaps dance a minuet before his nightly nap in the card room if they ended up in the same ballroom next Season.

Half a secret exchanged for half a secret.

He watched the holiday bread crumble to bits in her fingers and chose a different path. "I worried for you."

She studied her buttery fingers while Elijah tried to

find something else to occupy his imagination. "You *worried* for me, for my safety perhaps?"

Did nobody ever worry for her? Or did she never allow her loved ones to know what she was really about?

"You were safe as houses on the streets of Mayfair in broad daylight, even when you went sauntering down St. James Street in your masculine regalia at midafternoon." That had been naughty of her—also brave.

"One wants to see more than candlelit ballrooms and sunny bridle paths, Mr. Harrison. What I saw was a clutch of dandies lounging in the windows of the men's clubs, pretending a perfectly prosaic street scene somehow merited their devoted study. They reminded me of the lions at the menagerie—tame, twitchy, bored, and helpless to address their own miseries."

Her description was deadly accurate. "I noticed you did it only the once."

"One need not... I wasn't doing it to be daring. I wanted to *see*. Why were you worried for me?"

Afternoon tea should have been an occasion for some flirtation, a little sustenance, and maybe—if he flirted well and she were receptive—a bit of sketching. Elijah wasn't sure what to call their exchange, but it was *not* flirting.

"You never fraternized with the other students, never arrived or left with them. You never joined in the stupid, self-conscious banter that ensues when young men are in the presence of nudity."

She was regarding him with carefully masked bewilderment. He forged on, driven by motivations he was not going to examine closely unless thoroughly drunk.

"When one is talented, particularly early in one's career, one can suffer doubts. In my experience, the doubts can be commensurate with the talent rather than inversely proportional to it. The myth of the sensitive artistic disposition is not entirely false, and I didn't want..."

What was he saying? What was he *babbling*?

She picked up his uneaten slice of bread and held it out to him. "You did not want the quiet, withdrawn, somewhat talented student to doubt himself—herself—to the point of loss of confidence or foolish actions."

He took the bread and stuffed a large bite into his idiot mouth. Lady Sindal's recipe was scrumptious, and it went down like so much sawdust.

Lady Jenny held up his teacup. He washed the sawdust down with bilge water.

"Thank you, Mr. Harrison. Nobody has ever worried for me like that, and I suspect nobody ever will. Instead, they pity me. I prefer your worry to their pity, though I must apologize for giving you concern. I thank you, but I apologize too."

The smile she offered him now was not that of a minx. They had shared secrets of a sort, it said—more secrets than she'd known—and she was pleased it was so. The silence that descended was profound. No clock ticked; no fire roared. Outside, the frightful weather had subsided to a cold, still winter day.

Inside, something expanded in Elijah's chest—relief, happiness, he cared not what the best description might be, because words did not move him, and yet, words were necessary too.

"Lady Jenny, may I sketch you?" Those words were close but not exactly right, so he tried again. "Genevieve Windham, may I please sketch you?"

Four

Jenny had spoken with her brother-in-law, Joseph, Lord Kesmore, about Elijah Harrison, and Joseph had been wonderfully forthcoming. Mr. Harrison was heir to a marquessate, had studied abroad before and after his years at university, and was known for napping among the potted palms at Society's evening gatherings.

She'd seen Elijah Harrison on occasion, through the door of the card room, and wondered how bored one had to be to sleep at a Society function—or how confident of oneself.

"You've already sketched me, Mr. Harrison, and a fine likeness it was. Why would you want to sketch me again?" A fine, passionate, curvaceous likeness, to hear Louisa tell it—and Louisa was seldom wrong.

He rose and took a candle from the branch on the mantel. "Darkness approaches while I stuff myself with your excellent holiday bread. It's time to light the fire, don't you think?"

In moments, he had a cheery blaze going, moments in which Jenny became preoccupied studying the curve of his haunch under his doeskin breeches. She'd seen those flanks in the buff and knew the way his back flowed into his hips, thighs, and buttocks in perfectly proportioned bones, muscles, and sinews.

She did not know what it felt like to caress that same part of his anatomy.

He resumed his seat, managing to look regal despite his dishabille and the makeshift surrounds. "You ask why I want to sketch you a second time, my lady, and I'll answer with a question. Would you like to sketch me again?"

"Of course."

She should not have said that. She should have traced the seam of the chair's upholstery, glanced out the window at the sinking sun, and otherwise affected a sophistication she didn't have.

Though her attempts at posturing hadn't worked well with him so far.

"You've already captured my likeness, so why bother sketching me again, Genevieve?"

He started his own fires, and he used her name without permission. He fell asleep in Society drawing rooms and saw her as a woman of curves and passion. She resented his self-assurance mortally, and she wanted to remain near him, for all manner of hopeless reasons.

"I would like to sketch you again, Mr. Harrison, because you have an unconventional beauty that I can understand better by sketching."

"If we are to pose for each other, you should call me Elijah."

"No, I should not." He was going to pose for her

again, though, which meant she smiled when she should have been shaking her finger at him.

He appeared oblivious to the cold, while Jenny wanted to move closer to the fire. "Antoine was old-fashioned. All of that Mr. Harrison this and Mr. Harrison that when I was lounging about in the altogether wasn't to protect my delicate sensibilities."

"I doubt you *have* delicate sensibilities."

He went on as if she hadn't spoken, though now *he* was also trying not to smile. "His insistence on manners toward a naked man was intended to ensure all those puppies treated their own models decently. Modeling is grueling, often chilly work. The pay is lousy, and there's an assumption…"

His almost-smile faded. A log fell in a shower of sparks.

"There's an assumption that models and prostitutes are interchangeable," Jenny said. If he could use words like "naked man" and "in the altogether," she could manage "prostitute."

Though not without blushing.

"Stay there," he said, springing to his feet, crossing the room, and rummaging on a table in the shadowed corner. "Sit there, just like that. I'll trade you double minutes, in fact, if you indulge me."

"Double minutes?"

He returned to the fire with a sketch pad, pencil, eraser, and knife. "I'll sit to you for an hour if you sit to me for thirty minutes." He dragged his chair closer. The chair was old-fashioned, the sort of carved monstrosity popular back before Cromwell's nonsense. It would have served better as a battering ram than an article of furniture, and Elijah Harrison moved it around one-handed. Easily.

"Do we have an agreement, Genevieve?" He dragged the chair another few inches closer, so they were sitting quite cozily indeed.

"If I get double minutes, then yes, Mr. Harrison, though I must warn you that inactivity is foreign to my nature."

Particularly when Elijah Harrison was sitting knee to knee with her, and the urge to jump up and leave the room battled with the more compelling urge to shape the contour of his knee with her bare hand.

Harold Buchanan gestured to the pile of documents on the table. "We have the usual assortment of dabblers, sycophants, and eccentrics among the predictable slate of Associates."

"Some of the Associates are very strong candidates."

Of course they were, or they wouldn't be Associates of the Royal Academy. One didn't make a fool of old Fotheringale though, not to his homely face.

With silent apologies to the old masters gracing the walls of Buchanan's offices, he aimed a smile at Foggy.

"Fotheringale is right, of course, but we have only the two slots, and not every Associate is bound to become an Academician."

The other three committee members glanced at one another, at the cherubs on the ceiling, or out the window, where night had fallen, without the committee making any headway at all. At this rate, they would not have their nominations ready before the holidays, and Buchanan's wife would kill him—slowly, painfully, with a dull, rusty palette knife—if he missed spending at least some of the Yule season in the country.

"Would anybody care for more tea?" Another round of glances, some of them impatient. "What about something stronger? We're growing pressed for time, and the Academy is relying on us to nominate people for the available openings."

"Spot of that cognac wouldn't go amiss." That from Henry West, said to be a distant relation of the current Academy chair. "Do we know who has Prinny's endorsement?"

Fotheringale sat forward, his considerable bulk making the chair creak. "Hang Prinny! It ain't his Academy, and all this talk don't change the logical choices. Pritchett does fine work, and Hamlin even better. All those others"—he waved a pudgy white hand at the papers—"hacks, the lot of 'em."

As head of this little nominating committee, Buchanan knew better than to state a strong preference. He also knew if he didn't speak up, Pritchett, Hamlin, and any other hack who toadied to Fotheringale would soon grace the Academy's ranks. "Elijah Harrison's reputation is growing, and Sir Thomas considers him his heir apparent."

Fotheringale's fist banged down on the table, making the candle flames dance. "I'll not have it! He's taken his clothes off for money! Ask anybody who studied under that old Frog, Antoine. The day Elijah Harrison is elected as an Academician is the day I withdraw my support entirely from the school."

At least Fotheringale was predictable. "No one would like to see that, but West has a point: it is the *Royal* Academy. I'll have a word with the regent, not because he will ever dictate our membership to us, but because his taste is excellent and his support unceasing."

In other words, Fotheringale's money was important, but not as important as the prince's favor.

"Meet with whomever you damned please," Fotheringale said, sitting back and tugging his waistcoat down over his belly. "Won't make a damned bit of difference. Harrison will not do. Next thing, you'll be nominating women again."

Dear God, not that old argument. Buchanan scraped back his chair, trying to signal that the meeting was over, but Alywin Moser spoke up.

"Two of our founding members were ladies, I'll remind you. The ladies exhibit wonderful work as amateurs, and artistic talent doesn't—"

"Bother that." Fotheringale heaved himself to his feet. "Mary Moser drew flowers. That made her hardly more than a drawing-room talent, but her father wedged her into the Academy at a time when judgment was lacking and enthusiasm high."

Moser, who was not *officially* related to the late lady artist, was on his feet too. "Angelica Kaufman traded portraits with Sir Joshua himself, and Mary Moser's flowers were worth the notice of Her Majesty!"

"Gentlemen." Buchanan did not stand. "We can agree that Frogmore is lovely, and that there are not any ladies among this year's candidates, so perhaps we might adjourn to the drawing room, where a bottle of excellent cognac will fortify us against the night's chill."

Or against the committee's inane pettifogging and posturing.

"Cognac's one thing the damned Frenchies do right," Fotheringale grumbled. "But the only thing worse than admitting that Harrison to the Academy—a man who has done no academic work and not a single juvenile portrait, may I remind you—would be admitting a female. I trust I make my meaning clear."

Behind Fotheringale's broad back, Henry West sent Buchanan a sympathetic gaze. Harrison was talented, titled, congenial, and had done a number of academic subjects earlier in his career, though portraits were of course more lucrative. Harrison had offended nobody except, apparently, old Fotheringale—the deepest pockets on the Academy's board.

Buchanan gestured West closer. "Have we ascertained why old Foggy is so set against Harrison?"

West glanced at the rest of the party as they shuffled from the room. "Something to do with a woman."

Well, of course. The good news was Mr. Harrison wasn't prone to inconvenient left-handed tendencies. The bad news was Prinny could turn up prudish with all the zeal of a true hypocrite.

Then, too, Harrison had not done a single juvenile portrait.

"Keep digging. We have only a few weeks, and I, for one, do not want to celebrate the holidays listening to Fotheringale's bile, nor do I want to listen to the hue and cry if Pritchett and Hamlin are elevated to Academician status."

Elijah used two fingers to shift Genevieve's chin a half inch to the right, wanting the firelight to catch her at three-quarter angle.

His model flinched minutely. "I've never done this before."

Urgency pulsed through him, an urgency to capture her, and yet, experience came to his rescue. One must put the subject at ease. If one was going to take a true likeness from a subject, one had to make the experience comfortable.

"Yes, you have." He adjusted the tilt of her head as if handling beautiful women with transcendently soft skin were an everyday occurrence for him. And because he was a man who so rarely handled anything at all beautiful, he also traced his fingers back along her hairline, indulging in yet another pleasure as if it were of no moment. "You regularly sit in chairs before fires, thinking about…"

He rose to move the candle on the mantel so it would cast a touch of back light. "What is it you do think about, my lady?"

"I'm supposed to think about paying calls, stitching samplers, and reading the Society pages."

He resumed his seat, close enough that his knee bumped hers, and still not close enough. "And none of that bears any interest for you. Stay just like that."

Where to start?

Old lessons, lessons from his first boyhood ventures into sketching came into his head. *One begins by paying attention.*

"I was under the impression that rendering a

sketch involved moving the pencil across the paper, Mr. Harrison."

Still, he did not make the first mark on the pristine page. "You're nervous. I should think a woman with your looks would be used to men gawking at her, and you've dodged my question, so I'll ask another. You said my interest was preferable to your family's pity. Why should they pity you?"

Though her position did not shift, her expression did, and now—*now*—the sketch he would make took shape in his mind.

"I'm not quite on the shelf, and yet my fate has taken on an inevitable quality, like a prisoner awaiting sentencing when there were no witnesses for the defense."

His pencil began to move, long, curving strokes first. The outline of her came first: graceful, pensive, and full of passion dammed up by a massive, determined reserve.

"You don't want a husband and children? I can't believe you haven't had offers." He tossed the question out to keep that infinitesimal furrow to her brow, also to establish that between him and his subject, there need not be any secrets. He would be as a blank page to her—no judgments, no opinions, nothing but a sympathetic ear. When he completed her sketch, he would still be a blank page, while every line and shadow on the paper would be imbued with her secrets.

"My sisters are the ones who've gotten the offers, usually. There was a bishop last year, old enough to be my father."

"Bishops can usually provide well." And were

known to have large families. The idea nudged unhappily at his concentration.

"My family can provide well. If I must be a doting maiden aunt, then a doting maiden aunt I shall be."

Her features were rife with the small imperfections that made beauty interesting: Her mouth was not perfectly symmetrical, which gave her the appearance of considering a smile moment by moment, even when her eyes were serious. Her brows were a trifle darker than her hair, and her chin, upon close examination, bore a hint of stubbornness.

She hadn't answered his question about why she was unmarried; she hadn't answered his question about what filled her pretty head. He focused on her jawline and forgot all about putting the subject at ease.

His downfall as a boy had been Albrecht Dürer's watercolor of a young hare, a rendering so precise, the animal's nose practically twitched as one beheld it. How did so much life, so much vitality, fit into a simple two-dimensional rendering? And not even an oil, but a watercolor?

Elijah had become desperate to comprehend Dürer's genius. Somewhere along the way—Rome, maybe, or Vienna, possibly Copenhagen—he'd acquired technique and lost sight of the desperation.

"You are very quiet, Mr. Harrison."

He was supposed to say that she was a very absorbing subject, then smile and compliment a particular feature.

"I'm busy. What are you thinking?"

She wouldn't tell him, that was clear by now.

Genevieve Windham was a master at keeping her cards out of sight.

"I want to go to Paris."

The ear was a curious organ, more complicated than most people thought, like a horse's hoof. Lots of angles and shadows to the typical ear, but an ear could also be beautiful. "Paris in spring is lovely."

"I want to go *now*."

The point of his pencil broke, and he muttered an oath. Still her features did not shift from the serene, contemplative, secret-veiling expression she'd worn for long moments. Da Vinci would have been desperate to sketch her—nobody did justice to a sensual madonna like he had.

"A crossing this time of year can be quite rough, my lady." He feathered his eraser over the slight flaw in the line made by his infernal pencil, reshaped the point, and paused. "You want to go to Paris *now*?"

"Directly after the holidays, and I would not go to shop, hear the opera, or polish my French."

"Your eyes hold a wealth of determination." Also sadness. How to sketch both so they didn't overshadow the beauty? "*Why* do you want to go to Paris?"

Her gaze measured him. He could feel her studying him even as he concentrated on the image taking shape on the page.

"I want to sit someplace besides Gunter's and eat a pastry in public without it being a scandal. I want to have my pastry without a maid and a footman, as well as an immediate family member—preferably male, but at least married—within two yards of me at all times."

The determination in her eyes flared hotter. God in

heaven, *Wellington* had eyes like that. Calm, unstoppable, capable of banking a world of grief behind a slight smile—and this over a *pastry*?

"Do you think to acquire that freedom by outlasting all the bachelors on the marriage mart, Genevieve?" This was worse than the randy bishop, the idea that she might be purposely seeking spinsterhood—and it made no sense at all.

He sat back, feeling winded as a disconcerting notion rendered his pencil still. "Do you prefer *women*?"

Her lips twitched. "I love my sisters, of course, and my brothers' wives are lovely too—" Those slightly darker than perfect brows rose. "That's not what you meant."

She'd attended Antoine's classes. In every batch there was at least one pair of young sprigs who fancied themselves classically Greek in their lust for each other. They'd sat practically in each other's laps, called each other *cher*, and tossed languid, calf-eyed gazes at Elijah as he'd lounged about in his birthday attire.

He'd found it amusing and vaguely irritating. If young men brought to their art the same focus they brought to their breeding organs, the world would have many more works like Dürer's hare.

"I did not mean to offend, my lady. I see the Sapphic preferences aren't entirely unknown to you." Her family would be scandalized that she even knew of such things.

Her family would be scandalized if they knew how closely he was sitting to her, and yet, he wasn't about to shove his chair back to a decorous distance in the shadows and chill farther from the fire.

"I want to go to Paris to study art. I shall go, eventually." She did not gird her words with determination; she clad them in certainty, though Elijah had the sense it was a newfound certainty—very newfound.

Two thoughts collided in Elijah's mind, one sane, the other demented. The sane thought was: *She jolly well could study art in Paris.* Genevieve Windham was abundantly talented enough. Then, too, in Elijah's lifetime, the French had lost all gallantry toward their womenfolk.

French ladies managed commercial establishments, strolled about unescorted, and took unseemly interest in the nation's ongoing political debacle. Rational Englishmen had long stopped trying to explain the French, and look where France's democratic impulses had gotten her: her aristocracy butchered, her land beggared, her almighty, plundering emperor going slowly mad on some island.

Bugger France, even if Paris was lovely.

The second thought, the demented one, was so raw Elijah rated it more as a stirring of instinct: *He could not let her go.*

And then, more raw still: *He could not stop her*, not unless he were her husband or her guardian.

"Paris smells like cat piss."

His observation made her laugh, a merry, surprised sound that warmed him every bit as much as the fire, and yet he'd spoken the perfect truth. The whole damned city had a pissy stench in certain weather, worse even than Rome—though London had a prodigious stench of its own, especially near the river in summer.

"I daresay parts of the Morelands stable bear the same distinctive scent. One is told it keeps the mice down."

He dreaded to dim that smile, and yet he had to know the truth. "Does your family pity you because they regard this ambition as folly?"

Any reasonable ducal English family ought to.

Her smile didn't fade; it winked out like a snuffed candle. "I am not so stupid as to confide such a thing to people who think only in terms of when the next Windham baby will come along. These are the same relations who will not allow me to be alone at Morelands with thirty servants in attendance if my parents tarry in London. I am shuffled about, a spinster in training, because even thirty servants and the very gates of Morelands itself cannot guard my antique and pointless virtue."

Elijah was studying her still, his pencil re-creating the clean line of her nose, so he saw that these babies born in such numbers to her siblings made her sad too. He also saw that she likely didn't know this herself. She protected herself from sadness with a silent, determined anger, and that made him sad too—*for her.*

And none of these insights, the insights every portraitist resigned himself to and tried to leave behind when a commission was complete, were cheering in the least.

A clock chimed down the hall, and outside, the full darkness of a winter's night had fallen.

"You've had your thirty minutes, Mr. Harrison, and I must change for dinner." And yet, she did not move, and Elijah's pencil sketched more quickly. She might flee the honesty of their exchange, but she'd manage her retreat with dignity.

"Another moment." Now that he knew of her

hare-brained scheme to exile herself to the land of cat piss and flirtatious republicans, he was more determined to get her likeness on the page. "Your family doesn't know about your ambition to travel, so I must conclude they pity you because you have no babies coming along."

She turned her head, and it was as if the shutter on a lighthouse signal had opened. Her glare was ferocious, wounded, and magnificent, as was her silence.

He caught *her* then, in that single moment of genuine ire—all the ducal drive in her, the female passion, the thwarted artistic sensibility. His hand went still so he might behold her glory, and his mouth made words because he could not stand her heartache.

"Genevieve, I'm sorry. I'm sorry you've had to dance with spotty boys when you wanted to be sketching in the British Museum. I'm sorry you were not allowed to make a grand tour of the Continent. I'm sorry you stopped attending Antoine's classes."

Though he'd been relieved too. And then last winter, when he'd thought that strutting puppy Honiton had decided to snatch up an unmarried Windham daughter, he'd been rabid to warn the man off.

The battle light in her eyes dimmed to a mere spark, a spark Elijah suspected her family never noted. "Will you let me assist you while you're working here, Mr. Harrison? Even if I could merely observe, or distract the boys as you sketched them…?"

The humility with which she made her request walloped his senses, which was the only explanation for what came out of his mouth.

When he should have told her that the age of

tolerance toward women in the ranks of professional artists had passed, when he should have lectured her about the gratification of the true amateur's calling… he instead said, "Yes, of course. I would never turn down an artistically knowledgeable assistant. You must join me here whenever you like, to observe, assist, or critique. I'll enjoy the company."

Though God help him, how was he to concentrate on a pair of wiggling, sticky little boys, how was he to concentrate on *anything*, when she was in the room?

"You could ask him."

Tristan Leopold Harrison, Marquess of Flint, and father to more children than a sane man could manage, took a sip of holiday libation. The wassail bowl came out earlier and earlier each year as more and more of those children approached adulthood.

His lordship kept his voice down when addressing the second oldest of those children. "I am not asking your brother to come home for Christmas. A man doesn't need an invitation to come to his own home for the holidays, much less home to the estate he's going to inherit ere long."

Across the family parlor from where the gentlemen sat, Lady Charlotte Elizabette's lips pursed in an expression that presaged a telling silence when her husband escorted her above stairs later. She never scolded, never ranted, and yet, the marchioness always made her opinions known.

"Perhaps I'll invite him, then." Joshua suggested this possibility with the casualness of a grown man who knew exactly how to taunt his aging papa. "Or maybe I'll offer to join him in Town, and take Abner, Silas, Pru, and Solomon with me."

And like a seasoned papa, his lordship leaned back in his chair and contemplated his drink rather than the prospect of the holidays in exclusively female company. "Any invitation to remove Prudholm from the premises has a strong appeal. Teaching your sisters how to smoke cigars was bad enough, but experimenting with fireworks should have seen him brought up before the assizes for the toll he's taken on your mother's nerves."

At sixteen, Prudholm had spent one term at Cambridge and now considered himself quite the brilliant scientist. Thank God he was the youngest boy, and his older brothers mostly kept him in line.

"Don't you miss Elijah, Papa?"

Joshua was the family barrister. He'd been arguing with all and sundry since he'd been in dresses, but this tactic—an agile descent into pleading and sentiment—was dastardly.

"I miss your brother every day, and I pray for his well-being every night, as does your mother, who will not thank you for pressing me on this."

"She *would* thank me. Mama's too soft-spoken by half."

If the boy only knew… except Joshua wasn't a boy. He was a respected member of the legal profession—to the extent any member of that gang of rogues could be respected—and he was going to raise the next Marquess of Flint if Elijah continued to turn his back on his patrimony.

"Your brother and I exchange regular letters in which he asks after and I report upon the well-being of each sibling and relation in our vast and busy family," Flint said. "He also gets copies of the steward's reports, though I'm not supposed to know about that, and neither are you. Elijah has had many opportunities to announce that he will join us for Christmas and has not indicated a willingness to do so. I must respect his wishes in this regard."

Joshua took on the thoughtful expression that made him most closely resemble his older brother. "You, my lord, miss him until you're cross-eyed with it. The girls hardly recall what he looks like, and if you make good on your perennial threats to die of exasperation with your offspring, he'll become their guardian."

"He is heir to the title. Of course he'll become their guardian."

Joshua crossed long booted legs and ran a hand through the dark wavy hair her ladyship had bequeathed to all the children. "Little Gwynn makes her bow this Season."

A man who took stewardship of his acres seriously, a man who had no patience with the ordeal of the social Season, needed another sip of stout potation before he parsed out the ramifications of this half-yawned, diabolical aside.

"You're saying Elijah will run into his sister at some Society gathering, and there will be awkwardness."

And dear little Gwynn—all nearly six feet of her—would be mortified not to be recognized by her brother, which was a sorry, sorry possibility given how quickly and recently she'd acquired her statuesque proportions.

"I don't foresee any difficulty, Papa, unless she recognizes him first, which grows increasingly unlikely when she hasn't seen him to speak of for what… ten years?"

"Nine." And eight months, except for some chance sightings or cordial visits in Town. Where in all of creation had Elijah come by such stubbornness?

Joshua eased to his feet and ambled over to the punch bowl. The twins had pleaded a cold and gone above stairs, there to no doubt devour a lurid novel provided by their indulgent elders. The older girls were playing cards over in the corner, cheating shamelessly and gambling like sailors on shore leave—for hairpins. Pru, Abner, Silas, and Solomon were drinking more punch than they ought to and playing their own version of whist for God knew what stakes, while her ladyship presided over the whole with a serene beauty that never dimmed in her husband's eyes.

And yet, Charlotte was sad. Damn that stubborn boy; he was making his mama sad.

His lordship rose, snatched up his empty glass, and joined Joshua at the punch bowl. "You are a rapscallion and a pestilence, Joshua Harrison."

Joshua took his father's cup and ladled more of the Brew of Misrule into it. "Those qualities can be inherited, Papa. Excellent punch."

"It's my father's recipe, and while I will not invite Elijah to join his own family at his own home over the holidays, where any proper fellow would know *he's welcome unconditionally at any time*, I can hardly take exception to correspondence between siblings that extends felicitations of the season, can I?"

Her ladyship's needle momentarily paused over her embroidery hoop then resumed stitching. She was a demon with her needle, was her ladyship. She could conjure any scene in fabric and thread, and some of her creations were quite fanciful. Even a man whose art was limited to pen-and-ink sketches could tell that much.

Joshua took a hefty swallow of a mixture that well deserved the appellation "punch." He tossed it back so easily his lordship felt a spike of pride.

"Elijah has eleven siblings, your lordship. That would be a lot of felicitations, if I knew where to send them."

"Include your mother's, and it will be a veritable deluge. I always know where your brother is, and I always have."

The barrister's eyebrows rose, and his lordship had the satisfaction of seeing Joshua for once looking flummoxed. To eliminate any lingering confusion, the marquess touched his glass to Joshua's and winked.

"Here's to a happy Christmas, Joshua, for every member of my family." His lordship offered the words not only as a toast, but also as a prayer, the same prayer he'd been sending up for nine long years.

Five

PEOPLE LIED.

Jenny assured herself of this as she joined her sister and brother-in-law in the breakfast parlor. All the people who said sitting to Elijah Harrison was a pleasant experience were perishing liars.

Sophie beamed a smile from her place at Sindal's elbow. "Good morning, Jenny! I hope you slept well."

Jenny had tossed and turned for most of the night, wondering how—and *why*—a wish to see Paris had been announced to Elijah Harrison as something far more permanent and binding. "I slept splendidly, dearest, and you?"

"Well enough." Sophie cast a speaking glance at her husband. "Sindal, be a love and fix Jenny a plate. We must fortify her against the ordeal of the holidays at Morelands."

Sindal rose to his blond, golden height. "Jenny, prepare to be stuffed like a goose, though the boys would have me remind you that sanctuary always awaits you here. What is your pleasure?"

To be sketched the livelong day by Elijah Harrison,

even if it did leave her feeling… emotionally ravished. Wonderfully, exhilaratingly, emotionally ravished. The things she'd said to him…

"Some toast will do."

He set a plate before her laden with toast, omelet, crispy bacon, and several sections of a Spanish orange. "Sindal, I am not going a-Viking. If I eat all of this, I'll have to let out my seams."

Sindal paused to kiss his wife's crown. "One can never have too much of a good thing, and you *are* going a-Viking. Sophie says you've agreed to help with the boys' sittings, which I'm sure Sven Forkbeard himself would shudder to attempt."

Sindal's people had come from the North, as was evident in his height, blue eyes, and the intrepid courage with which he'd taken on marriage to Sophie Windham. Jenny liked him tremendously, and yet, the way he regarded Sophie was hard to watch so early in the day.

"Children are sometimes more themselves when parents are not in evidence," Jenny replied, touching a dab of strawberry jam to her toast.

Another look passed between Sindal and his lady, reminding Jenny that they'd met and fallen in love when Sophie had maneuvered a few days of solitude one fine Christmastide—a few days of freedom from the loving eyes of the duke and duchess.

"Good morning, my ladies, Sindal."

Elijah Harrison stood in the doorway in informal morning attire. At the sight of him, Jenny's hunger skittered sideways, into a bodily longing that had nothing to do with food.

"So, Harrison, any last wishes before you take on the Vandal horde?" Sindal pushed the teapot down the table as he spoke. His smile was friendly, though Jenny sensed an element of challenge to it as well.

"Tell my brother Joshua not to put up with any of his lordship's nonsense, and never to underestimate her ladyship." Elijah poured for himself and passed the pot to Jenny. "Though I'm sure your sons are delightful."

They were—also complete hellions.

"Jenny will be on hand to ensure nobody is seriously hurt," Sophie said. "You must help yourself to whatever appeals at the sideboard, Mr. Harrison. Cook is in alt to have company, though there will be more directly, based on Her Grace's last letter."

An alarm sounded through the fog created in Jenny's mind by the sight of Elijah Harrison's hands in morning light. "Mama has sent along some news?"

"She has. Papa has decreed that we're all to gather for Christmas at Morelands this year. Her Grace is vexed because Papa will not remove to the country yet, and such a large house party will require significant preparation."

Sindal winked at his wife. "His Grace is not done with his holiday shopping."

Mr. Harrison stirred cream into his tea, apparently used to marital glances and winks over breakfast. "I thought shopping was the province of the ladies. I have six sisters whose letters—when they bother to write—are filled with dispatches about this and that shopping sortie. Even the two youngest like shopping for books."

He stirred his tea counterclockwise then clockwise,

a slow dragging of the spoon along the bottom of the teacup. Jenny wondered if he stirred his paints with the same symmetry—first one direction then the other.

"Papa must find Mama the perfect Christmas present every year," Jenny explained. "Some years, we don't know what he gives her, but we know a gift was bestowed in private. One year it was new chandeliers for the ballroom in Town, another year he found her a Shakespeare folio. Another year, he borrowed the regent's chef for a private meal of Her Grace's favorite dishes. Papa can be ingenious, and he's very determined."

Mr. Harrison rose, aiming a smile at Jenny. "Determination is a fine quality. Would my ladies like anything else from the sideboard?"

Sophie came to her feet. "I am quite finished, thank you. I'll have the boys brought up to you in an hour, Mr. Harrison. Sindal, come along. A paternal lecture about decorum wouldn't go amiss."

Sindal was on his feet in an instant. "Of course, my love. The children can always use practice ignoring their father's advice."

And thus, Jenny was alone with the man who'd kept her up most of the night.

"Do you mind if I sit beside you?" Mr. Harrison asked. "The sun is in my eyes on the other side of the table."

He didn't wait for her reply, but took a seat to Jenny's left. No footman stood guard over the sideboard—or the proprieties—but the door was open, and Viscount Rothgreb or his lady might come down at any time. Rothgreb was Sindal's uncle, the one responsible for commissioning the boys' portraits, but a very elderly fellow who likely took a breakfast tray above stairs.

"You're going to eat all of that, Mr. Harrison?"

He glanced at his plate, which held steaming eggs, ham, bacon, and toast. "I'll have some oranges and stollen on the next pass. What can you tell me about your nephews? And please be honest. Once Rothgreb joins us, diplomacy will be the order of the day, unless I miss my guess."

"His lordship is a late riser, but he'd be the first to tell you the boys are very active little fellows."

Mr. Harrison grimaced and tucked into his eggs. "I thought one was yet a baby."

"He's fifteen months. He walks, he talks after a fashion." He also put all manner of inappropriate objects into his little mouth, cried piteously at the least sign of injury, had not one iota of sense, and could illuminate the world with his smile.

The disappearing pile of eggs suffered another grimace. "And the other boy?"

"About twice as old. He runs everywhere, yells everything, and is a prodigious good climber." Kit was also very gentle with Timothy, who'd been known to take a swipe at Sindal on a bad day.

The grimace became a scowl, the first Jenny had seen from Mr. Harrison. "I suppose they abet each other's mischief?"

"Siblings generally do." To wit, sisters abandoned one with handsome, interesting men at the breakfast table. Sophie had either failed to note Mr. Harrison's abundant charms, or she trusted that all in her ambit were as virtuous as she.

The wages of successfully appearing virtuous were constant temptation to behave at variance with those appearances.

Mr. Harrison sat back, his hands braced on the arms of his chair as if he'd rise and leave.

"Is there a problem with your meal, Mr. Harrison?"

"Yes." He reached for his teacup then dropped his hand without taking a sip. "No… there is a problem with my digestion."

Gracious heavens. "Is it the company? I would not impose on Sophie and Sindal above stairs, but I have correspondence—"

He shook his head and glanced at his plate, then at the plaster molding of disporting cupids above them, then at Sindal's vacant place at the head of the table. "I've never done a juvenile portrait."

His tone was a blank page. Jenny could not tell if he dreaded the task before him, resented it, was bored by it, was challenged by it, or… feared it. She could, however, hazard a guess he wasn't looking forward to spending days painting two small boys.

"Painting is painting, Mr. Harrison. Shapes, colors, light—the process doesn't change based on the subject. As children go, these two are attractive, and Rothgreb will be pleased with any reasonable effort."

He shifted to focus on her, his expression fierce the way a raptor was fierce. "*I* will not be pleased with any reasonable effort."

The conversation became more and more fraught, and Jenny had no clue as to why. "You are reported to have high expectations of yourself. You once burned a portrait of Princess Charlotte with her dog because it did not meet with your approval. Such standards have earned you significant respect."

And what might the regent give now to have that likeness of his late daughter?

"This portrait will determine whether I gain acceptance to the Royal Academy. Nobody puts it in such blunt terms, because there's always a vote involved, but ever since Reynolds made painting children so popular, it's like a tacit requirement. One must paint royalty and near-royalty, academic subjects, and even the occasional landscape, but one must also paint children."

"You do not like children?"

Something flickered through his eyes, something sad and bewildered. "I was a child once. That is the extent of my understanding when it comes to children."

Jenny considered him as he sat beside her, a plate of food growing cold in front of him, his finger tracing the rim of a blue jasperware teacup.

She was going to take advantage of him, shameless, wanton advantage. The knowledge was wicked, scary, and exhilarating—like the notion that she'd remove to Paris, with or without her family's blessing. "I will make a bargain with you, Mr. Harrison. You give me eight hours of your time sitting, and I'll assist you with the children for as long as it takes to complete their portrait."

His reply was immediate. "I already owe you an hour, and I don't see how you'll collect an entire day of my time without drawing the notice of our host and hostess. This time of year, there's hardly eight hours of proper light on a good day."

"I'll work with you by candlelight, and you will

instruct me." She reached over and stopped his finger as it circled the rim of the cup, this way then that way. "You will be brutally honest with me, and you will not spare my feelings. You will criticize every flaw, every mistake, every bad judgment you see in my work. Those are my terms, or we have no bargain."

She kept her hand over his, as if she'd trap him with a single touch.

Though he didn't pull away. "You cannot go to Paris, so you seek to bring Paris to you here."

She did—the part of Paris that had to do with improving her art, though the part about living her own life, indulging her own passions, and escaping her family would have to wait. She said nothing to him about all of that, because he could refuse her even what she'd asked for.

Mr. Harrison turned his hand up and laced his fingers with hers. "My lady, you have a bargain. Now, what else can you tell me about the children?"

The holidays had an inexorable quality, the way a blight on the crops took over the countryside or a plague transformed a city into a morass of mourning. Holiday offerings crept onto menus, an innocuous initial step, like a few old men falling ill. Servants busied themselves swagging the eaves with greens, and even that wasn't something a man need take notice of when his occupation kept him indoors during daylight hours.

Then, like an advancing illness, wreaths appeared on windows, cloved oranges were hung in public rooms, and table trees appeared in family parlors. Those of Germanic inclinations, which was to say a substantial portion of the aristocracy, might even have larger Christmas trees.

"The house is looking quite festive," Elijah said as he escorted Lady Genevieve to his makeshift studio.

She glanced about, no doubt taking in the red and green ribbons wrapped around the oak banister and the tapestry of Father Christmas hung over the main staircase like a heraldic banner.

"Sophie and her baron have fond memories of Christmas. My parents are of the same ilk, and Louisa and Joseph are falling into the same camp. Surely your family has some Christmas traditions?"

"They indulge in much silliness." Or they had, ten years ago. A change of subject was in order. "Am I to understand that you enjoy your sister's hospitality because Their Graces are still in Town?"

"Nobody states it quite so plainly, but every time my parents leave Morelands, I am invited somewhere on a cheerful pretext. I am to assist Sophie with her baking. I was to keep Louisa and Joseph's daughters company because they'd be simply too much for Aunt Gladys. Earlier this fall, Westhaven's wife, Anna, needed my artistic flair to help her redecorate their nursery for the new baby."

Elijah's spirits inched upward. "This makes you furious, being shuffled about."

She paused at the intersection of the main upper corridors and closed her eyes. "One can't be angry at people who are trying their best to *love* one, *but my artistic flair*?" She was quietly, beautifully incensed.

"They do acknowledge your talent."

"They denigrate it in the same breath. Hold still, Mr. Harrison."

He was so bemused with her ire, he didn't understand what she was about until she'd gone up on her toes and slid a hand to his nape. Her other hand rested on his chest, and a whiff of jasmine came to him on the thought: *She's going to kiss me.*

And I'm going to let her.

Soft, soft lips pressed not against his cheek—Lady Genevieve was no coward—but to his mouth. The kiss was chaste—no tongues, no expressing the groan that lodged in his chest, no plunging his hands into her hair and desperately clutching her to him. And yet, he could taste anger on her and a frustration that wasn't entirely artistic.

When she might have eased away, he settled his arms around her and brushed his mouth over hers. Kisses could be about anger, but they could be about so much more too: joy, pleasure, comfort… *lust.*

He dropped his arms. "Happy Christmas, Lady Genevieve."

She smiled up at him, her anger nowhere to be seen. "My father says the traditions should be upheld where they don't interfere with good sense, and *you* said mistletoe was a harmless tradition."

He glanced up. "In this house, it appears to be a much-respected harmless tradition. Would you like me to sit to you while we're waiting for the children?"

Because for the first time in years of sketching, painting, drawing, and otherwise rendering artistic images, it occurred to Elijah that the sitter was in an excellent position to study the artist.

"No, thank you."

"No? But I owe you hours, my lady." Eight long, lovely hours when he might study her chin, the curve of her shoulders, the way light shifted in her green eyes.

She stopped outside the door of his studio. "By candlelight, that was my condition. All of Antoine's classes were by daylight."

What was she about, and did he want to stop her?

"Some days were gloomy. You've sketched by candlelight, haven't you? I'm sure you've had other subjects oblige you in this regard."

She passed through the door, and Elijah was pleased to see somebody had started the fire. A tea tray sat near the hearth, the teapot swaddled in thick white toweling. Morning light, fresh and bright, came streaming in the windows.

Lady Genevieve turned in a slow circle. "We will need to make some adjustments, Mr. Harrison."

Please God she wanted to hang some mistletoe in his studio. Elijah watched the sunbeams dance along the gold of her hair and realized he'd just had his first holiday-minded impulse in ten years.

"In what regard must we make adjustments, and you never answered my question." She was forever dodging his questions.

She crossed her arms. "What question?"

"Have you sketched by candlelight?" And what would she look like, sketching by candlelight?

"I've sketched my dear sisters, though they aren't particularly obliging about holding a pose. I've painted enough still lifes to cover every surface in Carlton House." She aimed a glare at the hearth. "I've sketched Timothy in every position imaginable from every possible angle."

Dislike for this Timothy fellow rose up, ranking nearly equal with dislike for holiday folderol—most holiday folderol. "Who is Timothy?"

Her glower shifted, taking on a hint of despair. "My blasted cat."

He might have laughed, out of relief, but the image of her relegated to depending on the patience of a mute beast was not amusing. "Try something for me, Genevieve."

"We need to find some toys," she said as if she hadn't heard him. "The boys will be here directly, and if we don't entertain them, they'll entertain themselves."

Dreadful thought. "This won't take but a moment. I want you to curse."

Not only were her arms crossed, but she'd drawn herself up, aligned herself with some invisible, invincible posture board such as Helen of Troy might have relied upon to get all those ships launched in a single day. "I beg your pardon?"

"Curse. Call him your blasted, damned cat."

Her brows knitted, making her look like one of Kesmore's daughters. "I love Timothy."

"Of course you do." Lucky cat. "But you do not *love* having to rely on his good offices for your candlelit sketches." He prowled closer. "You do not *love* being shuffled about from family member to family member." Another step, so he was almost nose to nose with her. "I daresay you do not *love* baking."

"I rather don't."

He unwrapped her arms and kept her hands in his. "Genevieve."

"I do not enjoy baking in the least."

He waited, certain if he were patient, she'd rise to the challenge.

The corners of her mouth quivered. "I perishing hate all the mess and heat."

"Of course you do."

"It's a dashed nuisance, and one gets sticky." A smile started, turning up her lips, lighting her eyes.

"How sticky?

"Blasted, damned sticky."

"Say it again."

She beamed at him. "Perishing, blasted, damned, *damned* sticky."

He wrapped his arms around her. "Well done. You must curse for me more often, Genevieve. It makes your eyes dance."

And her cursing made him happy too. As she hugged him back, it occurred to Elijah that Christmas was touted as the season for giving, though in recent years, the occasion hadn't arisen for him to do much of that.

He'd give to her. He'd give her a safe place to curse, a place to draw as she pleased, and some kisses. If he counted his approval of the mistletoe tradition, that was two holiday sentiments in one morning.

Elijah dropped his arms and stepped back. Two sentiments signified nothing.

"You said something about toys?"

She blinked, though the smile did not entirely leave her countenance. "Toys. Yes, for the children."

"So I might pose them with their familiar objects?"

"Why, no, Elijah. We need toys because we're going to spend the next hour playing."

Myriad prurient connotations danced in his head in the instant he stared down at her. He mentally nudged them aside when he should have taken a cricket bat to them. "Playing?"

"I assumed you'd take Sir Joshua's approach to children as subjects."

She had gold flecks in those green eyes, and Elijah didn't know any Sir Josh— "Sir Joshua Reynolds. He played with the children he painted."

"Of course." She took a step back, looking self-conscious. "Not everybody ascribes to the same method, but these are very young children. I assumed you'd—"

"Of course. The children will have to be comfortable with me if I'm to spend hours taking their likeness. Toys are a given."

He'd dreaded this aspect of the commission. Dreaded the notion of getting down on the floor and playing at jacks or Patience or some inane, juvenile pastime. The dread had faded to a mild distaste. "What do you recommend?"

She prattled on about playing cards and spinning tops, toy soldiers, and jumping ropes, while Elijah thought back through their short, unusual conversation. He did not want to spend the morning playing with children, but he'd manage that.

Something she'd said had pleased him, pleased him even more than her hesitant, polite cursing.

Something she'd said rivaled even that kiss, which he took as a perfunctory nod to holiday protocol on her part, one that had turned pleasurable and sweet despite its origins in seasonal nonsense.

Something...

He lit upon it with the glee of a boy opening a holiday present, absolutely certain his heart's desire lay under the pretty paper.

He'd called her Genevieve, and she hadn't objected. Again, she hadn't objected, and better still, she had called him Elijah.

Jenny had a list of questions for her mother, questions she'd never ask. One of those questions was about grief: Does one keep having babies because the little ones grow up and get too big to cuddle in one's arms or sit in one's lap? Does one keep having babies—a dangerous, messy, uncomfortable proposition—because it's the only way to keep one's heart from breaking?

And then a question Jenny had barely let herself acknowledge: How did one cope when two beloved children had died as young men and no baby, no grandchild, no *anything* would ever bring them back?

Her thoughts were interrupted when William came barreling toward her on his chubby legs, Kit right behind and a harried nursemaid bringing up the rear. Jenny scooped up the smaller child and held out her hand to his older brother.

"My very best boys! How glad I am to see you!"

"You saw us last night," Kit said. "Is that the painter man?"

Mr. Harrison's brows rose at this rudeness. "I am Elijah Harrison, and I am here to make a painting of you and your brother."

"Can I paint too?"

"May I," Jenny murmured.

Little William chose that moment to swat her nose. "Paint!"

Mr. Harrison marched up to her and took William from her arms. "Draw first, with pastels, which have no sharp points. And you, sir, are not to be raising your hand to the ladies."

William made a grab for Mr. Harrison's chin. "Down! Paint!"

"He wants to get down and paint," Kit volunteered. "I want a scone."

"Later. You just had your porridge," Jenny said.

Mr. Harrison brushed a finger down William's little nose. "You're going to turn your nose blue, like some warrior of old with his woad, and try the same thing on your brother. I have five little brothers at home just like you. Then you'll eat my pastels, and I'll have to limit my landscapes to cloudy days with no pretty skies."

William was a fickle child. He was very shy of his uncles Benjamin and Valentine, and had a shrieking, unrelenting loathing for two of the footmen. He loved his uncles Gayle and Devlin, and the cat Timothy as well—most days. He was also, the little wretch, instantly enthralled with Mr. Harrison.

"Down!"

Mr. Harrison did not turn loose of his captive. "My lady, I think it best to put that tea service up where it will not tempt small boys."

"Of course." Jenny put the tray with its steaming blue teapot on the corner table, among the pigments, tablets, pens, and pencils. "Did you intend to get out the pastels?"

Mr. Harrison's expression was resigned, while on his hip, William beamed cherubically. "He really will try to eat them."

"We are not outnumbered, Mr. Harrison, and you outweigh him by a good twelve stone. We will dissuade him."

Kit tugged on her skirts. "Can I have a scone now?"

"May I, and no, you may not. Mr. Harrison has some wonderful things to show you, but you must hold very still for a time too."

"I can hold still." The little boy stiffened up, like some pagan figure carved in stone, breath held, arms at his sides, teeth clenched.

"Very impressive," Mr. Harrison said. He crossed to the table with William, and retrieved a sketch pad and box of colored chalks. "If I render your image thus, your parents will hound me from the shores of England. I will be lucky to earn my ale sketching caricatures at posting inns on the Continent."

Kit looked up at Jenny. "What did he say?"

"He said he'll do a better job taking your likeness if you're comfortable and having fun."

Mr. Harrison sent Jenny a look over William's head. His mouth conveyed humor, while his eyes conveyed… trepidation? He jostled William higher on his hip. "I suppose it's time we boarded our magic carpet?"

Never had a handsome prince sounded less enthusiastic about starting his enchanted voyage, and never had William been so content to remain in one place for so long.

"I'm coming too!" Kit caroled. He darted to the hearth rug and plopped down, landing by chance in the direct path of an early morning sunbeam. Jenny took a place beside him, though her skirts made boarding the carpet a somewhat undignified business.

"Shall I take William?" she asked.

"My first mate is content where he is," Mr. Harrison said, lowering himself so his back was braced against the raised hearth. "Though he's plotting the downfall of our expedition, lest you be fooled by his handsome visage."

"What's a visage?" Kit asked, crawling closer.

"I'll show you what a visage is, if you'll challenge your aunt at Patience."

At Kit's age, Patience was an exercise in flipping cards face up, making quite the fuss over any random matches. Nobody won, nobody lost, and nobody tried to keep track of where any cards might lie.

Jenny, however, kept track of Mr. Harrison. He sat against the hearthstone, legs splayed before him. William contentedly straddled one muscular thigh, while the sketch pad was propped on the other. Mr. Harrison's left hand absently braced William against his body as the right moved the colored chalk across the page.

Both of them, man and boy, looked at ease.

William was examining a red pastel, dashing it against Mr. Harrison's dark wool trousers and leaving jots of red powder. Mr. Harrison was dashing his colors against the page in more fluid motions, though his expression bore the same concentration as William's.

"Your turn, Aunt Jen."

Jenny flipped over two cards, the queen of hearts and the queen of spades. "A match. Where shall we put their highnesses?"

"Give them to me!" Kit propped the queens face out against Mr. Harrison's outstretched leg and soon had a family of royal spectators aligned there.

Mr. Harrison suggested that the twos might also enjoy the view from the gallery and could serve as footmen to the royal family. He offered this casually, an aside murmured between glances at Kit, glances at the page, and glances at Jenny.

When William started bouncing on Mr. Harrison's thigh, Mr. Harrison passed the child another color and put the red aside. "Nobody stays with the monochrome studies for long, but five minutes must be a record," he muttered to the child.

While Kit flipped over one card after another in search of a match, Jenny's heart turned over in her chest. The sensation was physical, painful and sweet, also entirely the fault of the man casually holding one of her nephews and sketching the other.

She'd resigned herself to never having children, and her art, paltry and amateurish though it was, was some consolation. Watching Elijah Harrison casually tuck William closer and retrieve the blue pastel from its trajectory toward the child's mouth, her resignation came into sharper focus.

The children she'd never have might have been Elijah Harrison's, or belonged to somebody like him—a talented, handsome man, capable of whimsy and patience. A man willing to sit on the floor and see his trousers attacked by a ferocious, pastel-wielding infant, even as he kept that infant safe and content.

"I found a match, Aunt Jen!" Kit waved the six of clubs and the nine of clubs around. "They can be coachmen!"

It was on the tip of Jenny's tongue to point out the child's error. A six and a nine were not a match, not even if they were of the same suit.

"Let me see those." Mr. Harrison set aside his sketch to pluck the cards from Kit's hand. While Jenny watched, the artist launched into another little homily about reflections—symmetry by any other name—and Kit forgot all about playing the matching game with his aunt.

Jenny picked up the discarded sketch pad, slid the box of pastels closer, and began to sketch, while William enthusiastically drew green streaks on Mr. Harrison's trousers.

Six

The Earl of Westhaven steered his horse around a frozen mud puddle, while the Duke of Moreland's bay gelding splashed right through, indifferent to the breaking ice or cold, muddy water. Westhaven, like his horse, was more of a Town fellow, while the duke longed for the countryside.

"Her Grace is growing restless, sir. I trust you are aware of this?"

Meddling adult children were a loving father's cross to bear. The duke glanced over at the handsome fellow who was his son and heir. "How is your wife, Westhaven?"

Westhaven rode bareheaded, so His Grace could see his son's expression take on the sweet, distracted air of a man contemplating the woman about whom he was head over ears. "Anna thrives. She is completely over the birth of our second son, and completely in love with the boy. He's a quiet little fellow, but sturdy and very alert. Anna says he takes after me."

"She's in good health then?"

"As good health as a woman can be when she's the

sole sustenance of a growing boy. It helps that this is not our first. We're no longer raw recruits to the ranks of parenting."

With two children still in dresses, Westhaven could wax parental, as if he'd invented the occupation himself upon the birth of his firstborn.

"How many siblings do you have, Westhaven?"

"Seven extant, two deceased, an increasing variety of siblings by marriage. What has this to do with my mother's discontent, Your Grace?"

Westhaven was a plodder, not given to leaps of intuition but incapable of missing a detail or failing to notice a pattern. When he took his seat in Parliament, England would be the better for it.

Though as a son, he could try the patience of a far more saintly papa than His Grace.

"I have raised ten children with Her Grace and been privileged to partner her in holy matrimony for more than three decades. Do you think I wouldn't know if the woman were growing restless?"

Westhaven's lips quirked up in a smile his lady likely found irresistible. As a young husband, His Grace had possessed such a smile, though ten children had rather dimmed its efficacy with their mother.

"I suppose not, sir. I could escort her to Morelands, if that would help."

"You will do no such thing, Westhaven, nor will you intimate to my duchess that you'll spirit her away from my side. You will caution your brothers and brothers-in-law not to make any such offer either."

A rabbit nibbling on a patch of brown winter grass looked up as the horses ambled along the path. Nose twitching, the little beast seemed to weigh the pleasures of filling its belly against the danger of remaining in sight of humans. It snatched another few bites then loped away.

"I confess myself puzzled, Your Grace. You are usually Mama's slave in all things, and the entire family is to gather at Morelands for the holidays. I don't know why you'd deny her the pleasure of preparing for our arrival, when she's so anxious to quit Town and return to Morelands."

His Grace was not above dissembling when it came to his family, though he'd learned that dissembling was a fraught undertaking where his duchess was concerned. So with his firstborn, he dissembled only a little.

"I haven't found Her Grace's Christmas present yet."

Westhaven's expression softened. "Your Christmas presents put the rest of us fellows in the shade, you know. Anna won't even hint what I might give her. If His Grace can come up with such inspired gifts, then surely a small token shouldn't be beyond me?"

Balderdash. Anna, Countess of Westhaven, was likely already hinting about a little sister for her pair of boys.

"Each year, it becomes more difficult to find something original, something unique. The challenge is to think of a gift your mother hasn't even admitted to herself she longs for."

Though she longed to have her family gathered together for the holidays. His Grace could be stone-blind and still see that.

"So you'll tarry in Town until inspiration strikes?"

"If I must." And because Westhaven would be Moreland someday, His Grace went on in the most casual of tones. "I don't think Jenny minds keeping Sophie company while your mother and I are in Town, particularly not when Harrison also bides at Sidling, doing portraits of the little ones."

Westhaven brought his horse to a halt at a fork in the bridle path. "Harrison? Elijah Harrison? The painter?"

His Grace's bay came to a halt as well. "Harrison is Flint's oldest boy, though he's likely close to your age by now. Fancies himself a portraitist, and when old Rothgreb was grumbling about children growing up too soon, I might have mentioned Harrison to him."

"Elijah Harrison served as Kesmore's second at last year's duel," Westhaven said. He stroked a hand over his horse's crest. Westhaven had inherited shrewdness from both sire and dam lines, so His Grace said no more but let his son ponder the puzzle pieces. "Seemed a decent sort. There's been no gossip about the duel, in any case."

"I wouldn't know anything about that, just as I have no idea what I'll get your mother for Christmas, though I'm scouring the shops until something comes to mind. I trust you'll pass along any worthy ideas?"

"Of course." Westhaven looked like he might have a question brewing in his handsome head.

His Grace lifted a hand in parting accordingly. "My regards to your family, Westhaven, and I'll look forward to seeing you out at Morelands ere long."

Westhaven saluted with his riding crop and trotted off in the direction of that wife and family, while His Grace considered whether and how best to explain this latest parental gambit to his dear wife. Perhaps she'd have some idea how long two artists might be thrust into each other's company before the creative passions took over.

❧

Reading Reynolds's *Discourses* was getting Elijah nowhere. The grand old style of portraiture—an approach that flattered subjects, carefully posed them, and surrounded them with heroic symbols of great deeds—was fading.

Children had no heroic deeds, in any case. They had sticky fingers, silky curls, and a particular scent, of soap and innocence, that Elijah had forgotten.

The door to Elijah's sitting room creaked open. His first thought was that a footman, presuming the occupant to be abed, had come to douse the lights and bank the fire.

His second thought... evaporated from his mind when he saw Genevieve Windham standing inside his door in her nightgown and robe, a sketchbook clutched in her hand.

"I want to do you in oils," she said, advancing into the room. "I will content myself with some sketches first. I trust you can remain awake for another hour."

"Awake will not be a problem." Sane, however, became questionable. "Genevieve, you cannot remain in my rooms with me unchaperoned when the rest of the house is abed."

She flipped a fat golden braid over her shoulder. "I was unchaperoned with you at breakfast; I was unchaperoned with you in your studio before the boys arrived. I was unchaperoned with you in the library when the children went for their nap after luncheon. How did you expect to pose for me, Mr. Harrison, if not privately?"

"You are—*we are*—not properly clothed."

Her gaze ran over him assessingly, as dispassionately as if this Mr. Harrison fellow were some minor foreign diplomat with little English.

"Had I been accosted in the corridor by my sister, Sophie would have taken greater notice were I not in nightclothes. Besides"—a pink wash rose over her cheeks—"I have seen you without a single stitch and memorialized the sight by the hour with pen, pencil, and paper. Perhaps you'd like to take a seat?"

He would like to run screaming from the room, and nearly did just that when a quiet scratching came from the door.

"This will be our chaperone," Lady Jenny said.

To be found alone, after dark, with a lady in dishabille could also be his downfall. The Academy would quietly pass him by, his father's worst accusations would be justified, and the example he was supposed to set for all those younger siblings would become a cautionary tale.

As he watched Genevieve stride across the room to the door, Elijah realized being found with him could be her downfall too, the loss of all the reputation and dignity she'd cultivated carefully for years. The Royal Academy might admit him in another ten years, despite some scandal in his past—Sir Thomas had been accused of dallying with no less than the regent's wife—but Jenny's reputation would not recover.

"Genevieve—"

She opened the door a few inches, and a sizable exponent of the feline species strutted into the room, tail held high. This was the same dignified, liveried fellow who'd shared a bed with Elijah at Carrington's. "And here we have Timothy?"

"None other. He can hold a pose for hours and all the while look like he's contemplating the secrets of the universe."

"While we contemplate folly. Genevieve, you take a great risk for a few sketches."

She moved closer to the fire and tried to shift his reading chair.

"Let me." He moved it rather than pick her up bodily and deposit her in the corridor. "Will that do?"

"Turn it a bit this way." She gestured with a finger, a clockwise swirl. He moved the chair as quietly as he could. "Now sit, as if you're lord of all you survey."

Elijah surveyed a looming disaster, on several fronts, and one very determined woman. "You have one hour, my lady, and then you and your familiar will go back to whatever dungeon you sprang from. A few sketches could get you married to me for the rest of your life, should we be discovered."

She made no indication she'd heard him. Instead, she was frowning at the chair, the fire, the *Discourses*, while her cat stropped itself against her nightclothes.

"I've never had the nerve to get myself ruined," she said, moving a branch of candles on the mantel. "I've had the opportunity, in case you've wondered. Take your seat, Mr. Harrison."

More and more dangerous, but at least she was

observing propriety in her form of address, which was how one was supposed to treat a model.

Drat the woman.

He sat, feeling like a prisoner about to be shackled. "What constitutes an opportunity to be ruined, if not the present circumstances?"

She took a position cross-legged on the floor near his feet, the firelight finding every shade of highlight in her hair—red, gold, white, wheat, bronze, and indescribable combinations thereof.

"His name was Jeffrey Denby, and he was my drawing master when I turned sixteen. He was charming, handsome, and had just enough talent to fool my parents for a summer."

Elijah abruptly forgot about career interests, looming scandal, and the frustrations of trying to sketch small children who could not hold still. "Did he fool *you*, Genevieve?"

She flipped open her sketch pad and stared at the blank page. "Twice. I did not consider the first encounter a fair measure of the experience, novelty being an issue, but the second time..."

Blessed, blasted saints. She should not be telling him this. She should not tell *anybody* of this, ever.

"The second time?"

"I was mortally disappointed. One reads poetry and overhears the maids giggling and one's brothers boasting, and one develops expectations." She produced a penknife and sharpened her pencil to a lethal point. "I am not as ignorant as you and the rest of the world might think. Lift your chin."

He obliged, when what he wanted to do was hunt

down this sketch-pad-toting Lothario, shake the man's teeth loose, and break his untalented, presuming fingers. "Are you trying to make me look imposing by sketching me from below?"

"I'm trying to find a position where I can be comfortable for an hour." *At his feet,* of all places. "Hold still."

She set her sketch pad aside and rose up on her knees. Elijah was obediently staring straight ahead, so he didn't divine her intention until deft fingers undid his cravat. That was bad enough, but then—merciful deities preserve him—she stroked her hand over his throat.

"The textures of a man's skin are a challenge," she said, stroking him again. "Your cheeks are roughened with a day's growth of whiskers, but your throat is smooth, and your chest..."

She unbuttoned his shirt, revealing a chest sprinkled with dark hair, a chest trying not to rise and fall rapidly.

"If you spend much more time posing your subject, Genevieve, you'll not have an opportunity to sketch the poor devil."

With one finger, she nudged the placket of his shirt aside, off center, baring some muscle to the light of the fire. "Like that," she said as she drew the finger down over his heart, moving the shirt aside another inch. "Now do that off-in-the-distance look you have. Contemplate deep things."

She sank back on the hearth rug and took up her sketch pad.

He could contemplate *nothing*, because all thoughts led to her and to the sorrow and surprise of finding out that she'd broken the rules while still a girl. Many did. Many broke the rules only to redeem themselves by marrying their partner in mischief.

The cat jumped into Elijah's lap, a heavy, purring mass of fur and warmth.

"Leave him," Jenny muttered. "He'll keep leaping on you until you give up attempting to deport him. Timothy becomes fixed on his goals."

Elijah shifted slightly as the cat settled in and commenced washing itself.

"With your drawing master, Genevieve…?" How did he ask an impossible question?

"Mr. Denby. Louisa called him the pulchritudinous Mr. Denby."

"Of course he would have been beautiful, and he would have known how to use his beauty on young girls, but *why him*? You are the daughter of a duke, lovely to behold, well dowered, and notably agreeable in disposition. Why risk your entire future for disappointment in some dusty attic or stable?"

Her pencil paused on the page. "He preferred the minstrel's gallery in the ballroom, which was dusty enough, but bore little risk of discovery."

Not even a cot, no candlelight, no fragrant, leafy bower with the murmur of a stream nearby. No sensation of the soft summer breeze or gentle summer sun on naked, eager young flesh. No place to drowse in a lover's arms, no intimacy about such a setting at all.

"Stop making a fist, Elijah. It was a long time ago, and hardly memorable."

And yet, she hadn't resumed drawing.

"You haven't told me why." He needed to

know, needed to understand. "Sixteen is a legendarily confused age."

"When Louisa turned sixteen, she threatened to go up to university as Mr. Louis Windham. His Grace found someone knowledgeable to tutor her in maths then, some formidable old fellow who spouted Newton in the original Latin."

"While you planned an escapade of a different nature. Was it merely curiosity, Genevieve?" God knew, boys were curious at that age—boys at sixteen were nothing but curiosity, most, if not all of it, sexual.

She peered up at him, her posture and expression by firelight making her look young and bewildered. "I fancied myself an artist, and artists understand passion. I wanted to understand passion too."

As if some fumbling, itinerant bounder would have bothered to teach her about passion? *About pleasure?* In her innocence, she could not have comprehended the folly of her choice.

"You understand passion as well as anybody I know, Genevieve."

She gave him a confused look, and he saw that she had yet to make the distinction between simple sexual desire, to which even the birds and beasts were prone, and a passionate nature. He wanted to throttle Denby all over again.

"I am determined, Elijah, which is not the same thing as being ruled by impulses. Please face forward, and do be quiet."

Her tone made plain that being ruled by impulses was a sorry condition.

Elijah wanted to argue, wanted to shake her for her

erroneous conclusions and dangerous experiments, but he remained quiet, as she had remained quiet about her lascivious drawing master.

Sitting motionless, the cat in his lap, Elijah did not contemplate deep things. He contemplated a good girl, a pretty girl, but an innocent trying to slip through the bars of propriety's cage out of passionate curiosity. She'd been experimenting with shadows at the age of sixteen.

She'd been experimenting with social damnation too, an experiment she'd apparently resumed, though with a different aim. She sought answers now not in the minstrel's gallery, not in Antoine's drawing classes, but—if she had her way—in blighted, stinking Paris.

In her pigheadedness, she might have been telling the story of his own adolescence. "Let me see what you've got there."

"Not yet."

For another fifteen minutes, Elijah petted the cat and endured the animal's stentorian purr. In the face of such audible contentment, it was difficult to sustain agitation, and yet, Elijah did.

She'd been sixteen, curious, desperate for some recognition of her talent—of *her*—and buried under a pile of rambunctious, confident, older siblings. She'd had nothing she trusted to differentiate herself from that pile but a love of art.

How well, how bitterly and how well, Elijah understood her motivations, and yet, Genevieve Windham had remained on good terms with her family and was on good terms with them still.

For now.

"Your time's up, Genevieve. Time to pay the piper."

Uncertainty flashed through her eyes. "You needn't bother with a critique. I insisted on ruthlessness and that other whatnot, but it's getting late, and you've had to put up with Timothy, and tomorrow there will be more sittings with the boys—"

He extended a hand down to her while she recited her excuses. Perhaps in the last decade she'd learned some prudence after all, for she fell silent. "Come sit by me and prepare for your fifty lashes."

She passed him her sketch pad, put her hand in his, and let him assist her to a place on the hearthstones beside his chair. She brought with her a whiff of jasmine. All day her fragrance had haunted the edges of Elijah's awareness, a teasing pleasure lurking right beneath his notice.

"A good critique always starts with something positive," he told her. "This raises the critic in the esteem of his victim, and lowers the victim's guard. When the bad news inevitably follows, the victim will be paying attention, you see, and will have no choice but to hear at least some of the difficult things hurled his way."

His tone was teasing; his warning was in earnest.

"I will clap my hands over my ears at this rate, Mr. Harrison. Please get on with it."

He studied her sketch for some minutes while the cat purred and Genevieve radiated tension beside him. She took her art seriously, so it was fortunate she was genuinely talented.

"You are accurate, your command of perspective is solid, and you've learned a lot about how to suggest details quickly since last I saw your work at Antoine's."

He liked having her leaning close to him, liked bending his head near to hers to torment himself with her scent. He did not like her handling of the shadows though.

"You give up too soon on the darker areas. My face has two halves, one in light, one in shadow, and yet, because you moved those candles on the mantel, both are illuminated to some degree. Attend me."

He took up her pencil and traced in some details on the darker side of his face. "Even if you can't see them with your eyes, your mind adds these features in dim lighting, doubly so if the face is familiar to you."

"So you're suggesting them. How does that differ from the shadow created by your beard?"

"A beard is a texture more than shadow. On a man who is blond or red-haired, you must render it without making it a shadow."

If the cat hadn't sprung out of Elijah's lap with an uncomfortable push from powerful back legs some minutes later, Elijah would likely have discussed that sketch until dawn, drunk on the scent of jasmine and the image of his features as she saw them.

And the entire time, arousal would have been stirring in the same stratum of his mind that took notice of Genevieve Windham's curves, of the highlights in her hair, and the guarded tenacity in her green eyes.

"It's time you were leaving, Genevieve. We'll need the morning light if we're to make any progress with the children."

She reached down to pet her cat. "You've been helpful. May I impose on you again tomorrow night?"

"I have given my word." He rose and assisted her

to her feet, then picked up the cat and moved toward the door. "You are due seven more hours of ruthlessness from me, but I see little point in spending them all sketching. Nobody will take it amiss if I set up an easel here, or if we set up a pair of easels in the studio."

He'd never made a more foolish or a more genuine offer, and his punishment was her naughty-madonna smile, a brilliant, blinding version of its previous incarnations.

"You will paint with me?"

"You will paint *for* me," he replied.

The cat hung in Elijah's hands like a great, purring muff. This turned out to be fortunate when Genevieve went up on her toes and kissed Elijah near the closed door. Because he held the cat, he could not wrap his arms around her and abet her efforts to turn the kiss into a conflagration of all good sense.

He bore it, instead, like a martyr. Bore the feel of her coming close in all her soft, warm nightclothes, bore the scent of her skin, bore the sensation of her hands framing his jaw, holding him still for a meeting of mouths that had nothing of Christmas about it and everything of Misrule.

She must have known he was trapped by the cat, by the moment, by lust itself, and worse, by a yearning to show her what desire ought to be. She took liberties. Her tongue swiped against his mouth, a little taste of sin and insanity that he returned as delicately as greed and longing would allow.

Genevieve Windham was so sweet, so wickedly, unbearably—

Timothy sprang from between them on an indignant

yowl, his back claws raking Elijah's belly through the fabric of his shirt.

Thank God for the blasted cat. "Leave now, Genevieve, else you will not get your sittings." He'd never used that desperate, raw tone before, much less on a woman, a lady.

She kissed his cheek and slipped away, closing the door quietly in her wake.

I desire Elijah Harrison.

Jenny had deprived herself of much sleep, marveling at this revelation, one she did not even speak aloud to her cat. She woke in the morning, still pondering the notion: for the first time in nearly ten years, she wanted a man.

As she rebraided her hair and wound it up in a tidy bun, she paused, a hairpin in one hand, a greater insight in the other.

For the first time *in her life*, she wanted a man, a specific man. With Denby, she'd wanted... *something*, an experience, a sin, a memory, relief from the presumption of unworldliness that chastity implied. She'd been disappointed but not devastated by what had transpired with him.

With Elijah, she wanted *him*, all of him, nothing less, and nobody else would scratch the itch that had started years ago in Antoine's drawing classes. She wanted intimate knowledge of his body, his art, his mind, his *everything*.

Though she could allow none of her desire to show, not before the rest of the household.

"Good morning, my lady." Elijah rose as Jenny entered the breakfast parlor, his expression genial, his eyes… watchful.

As badly as she itched to be erotically intimate with him, she itched to capture those eyes on canvas too. Itched, longed, desired… She was becoming a different woman, a more interesting woman altogether.

A woman who could carry off living in Paris, with or without her family's blessing. The notion stunned her, like strong summer sunlight stunned senses left too long in shadows. Joy and anxiety filled her in equal measure, her soul teetering between "Don't be ridiculous" and "If I don't at least try, I will regret it for the rest of my sweet-natured-maiden-aunt life."

Neither Victor nor Bart would have discouraged her from trying, and that insight freed her from a good portion of her doubts.

"Good morning, Mr. Harrison. Is Jock your only company this morning?"

Rothgreb's old hound dozed by the fire, the beast likely craving warmth even more than he longed for a snitch of bacon.

"He's agreeable company, if lacking in conversation. I trust you slept well?"

The watchfulness was still in Elijah's gaze, and something else, something… fierce, and yet…

He was worried about her.

Outside, the day was dreary, a winter morning making little effort to shrug off a blanket of clouds. Inside Jenny's heart, a rainbow sprang up, bright and warm. This was not Denby's you're-not-going-to-cry-on-me-are-you sort of male anxiety, which in truth had hidden the more genuine you're-not-going-to-peach-on-me-are-you worry.

Thoughts of Paris fled as Jenny realized what she saw in Elijah's eyes was *caring*.

"I slept wonderfully, Mr. Harrison, and now I am famished." For the sight of him, for that slight easing behind his eyes when she turned a smile on him. The food she could take or leave.

"Allow me to fix you a plate." He came around the parlor, stepped over the sleeping hound, and moved to the sideboard. "What would you like?"

He lifted the lids of the warming trays, served her eggs, bacon, toast, and some forced strawberries. He would have buttered her toast had they been guaranteed privacy, his solicitude putting Jenny in mind of her parents.

"Some tea, my lady?"

He'd know how she took her tea, just as His Grace knew exactly how Mama took hers. Jenny hazarded a guess that the tea the duke prepared for the duchess tasted better to her than those cups the duchess fixed for herself.

"I'm in more of a chocolate mood this morning," Jenny replied. The words were no more out of her mouth than Elijah was swirling the little pot, this way then that, and pouring her a steaming cup.

His plate was empty, and the parlor was empty save for the old hound. As Jenny picked up her first forkful of eggs, she realized Mr. Elijah Harrison had been waiting for her.

The eggs were ambrosially seasoned, the chocolate rich, the butter on the toast superbly creamy.

"Have you any ideas for working with the children today?" Elijah asked. He poured himself another cup of tea, while Jenny wished she'd thought to offer him the pot.

She was being ridiculous, but as long as she didn't *act* ridiculous, where was the harm?

"I'll distract them while you sketch, if you like. Cards seemed to go over well."

"Which suggests they'll be bored with them today. Kit isn't quite old enough to learn how to cheat."

"I forget, you're an older brother. I owe my older brothers an entire education that had nothing to do with deportment or elocution."

He paused while stirring sugar into his tea. "Such as?"

"How to fend off a bully, where to apply perfume." She'd also learned that she could trust her brothers to have her best interests at heart, even if they were complete dunderheads about it.

And she had learned that even her boisterous, indestructible brothers could die.

"They *told* you where to apply perfume?"

"Not willingly, of course. Little sisters eavesdrop and pick up on these things. Bartholomew remarked to Devlin that the nape of a certain chambermaid's neck bore the scent of lavender water when he kissed her there. Bart sounded bemused to note it, as if the woman wore her scent that way exclusively to lure him closer." Bartholomew had sounded besotted, but then he'd been besotted with life in all its fascinating details.

"God help me if my little sisters take their education from my brothers."

Jenny put a strawberry on his otherwise empty plate

and wondered where Sophie and Sindal had gotten off to. "Why not take their education from you?"

He sat back, as if something noxious had floated to the surface of his teacup. "Will the hound be as agreeable as your cat about sitting for a portrait?"

"Jock will bide anywhere there's a decent fire, and he's very patient with the children."

"We'll impress him into service then. I saw your sketches, by the way."

Jenny was so busy studying the way the blue of the parlor's wallpaper compared with the blue of Elijah's waistcoat that she had to think before answering.

"Which sketches?"

He peered into his teacup, his expression disgruntled. "The ones you made of the children, the pastels. They're brilliant."

"Pastels can't be brilliant." And yet he'd sounded so puzzled by his own compliment, Jenny couldn't help but be pleased. "I do enjoy children though, very much."

He glanced up from his teacup, as if he'd heard the reservation in her tone. She enjoyed everybody else's children, and that hurt like blazes.

A footman paused just inside the doorway. "Post for his lordship."

Jenny didn't think Sindal would appreciate his correspondence being left about for all to peruse. "Cornelius, the baron is likely—"

Elijah rose. "I believe Cornelius means me." He retrieved a single epistle from the footman and resumed his place beside Jenny.

Jenny finished her eggs, toast, and chocolate, trying

to decipher Elijah's expression. He looked bemused now too, and the script on the letter was pretty.

A word came to Jenny's mind, the perfect word for the feelings curdling the meal she'd just consumed: *damn.* Damn and blast. Elijah was handsome, charming, well liked, and never in want of commissions. Why shouldn't some pretty widow correspond with him about a portrait of her children or about renewing her acquaintance with him over the holidays?

Damn and… damn. *Double damn.*

Seven

"It's from my sister. My youngest sister." Beside Jenny, Elijah popped a strawberry into his mouth and chewed mechanically.

A sister? Jenny had the sense he was liberally blessed with same. "Are you concerned for her?"

"Sarah has never written to me before. She's the youngest by three minutes, though our mother claims they were a memorable three minutes."

Sitting right there beside her, so close Jenny could catch a hint of his scent, he'd gone away to some familial place in his mind.

"Open the letter, Elijah," Jenny said, passing him another strawberry.

He cast her one glance—a gentleman did not read correspondence at table—then slit the epistle with an unused knife.

If this sister called Elijah home before Jenny had pried from him just how those pastels merited the term "brilliant," she'd hunt Lady Sarah down and ensure that a lump of coal for Christmas would be the least of the young woman's problems.

"She's well," Elijah said, "and uses a fine vocabulary for somebody who doesn't yet put up her hair consistently."

"A bookworm, possibly. Louisa was the same way. I learned many a term from her that impressed our elders."

He peered at Jenny over his letter. "She and Ruth are both mad for books. I always know what to send them for their birthday and Christmas."

Twin sisters, then, which was common enough in large families. Two more strawberries disappeared while Elijah finished reading his letter, and Jenny stifled the urge to pace.

She was not ready to have him snatched from her. She needed these days with him, artistically and… otherwise. All too soon Their Graces would return from Town, the children's portraits would be completed, and Jenny would be heading off for Paris.

If she'd doubted her resolve on that goal before, she didn't now.

Come fire, flood, or famine, as His Grace would say. Jenny was more determined on her destination than ever, and Elijah Harrison was part of the reason for her conviction.

"Sarah misses me." He got up and crossed to the window, where bleak winter light did little to brighten the parlor.

Jenny glanced at the epistle long enough to see *"Greetings, dear and long lost brother…"* in the salutation.

Jenny had two long lost—forever lost—brothers, and would have given her right hand, the hand with which she painted, not to have it so. "You'll see her at the holidays, won't you?"

He remained facing away. "She can't possibly miss me. She hardly knows me."

Jenny rose and went to him, wanting to see what he saw out that cold window. "She *can* miss you. I barely recall my grandparents, but because most of my memories of them came from holiday gatherings, I do miss them."

Missing loved ones at the holidays was always part of the season. How could he not know that?

"I left when Sarah was little more than a toddler. I used to read her stories, her on one knee, Ruth on the other."

Jenny slipped her hand into his, because he seemed not simply gone away, but lost. "You'll be with them at Christmas, won't you?"

He let out a sigh of sufficient depth that the window fogged before him. "*After* Christmas, and then only if I'm made a member of the Academy."

"They often don't announce the results of their votes until the New Year, when the honors list comes out." And what had membership in the Academy to do with sisters who missed him?

"Then I'll wait until the vote is cast, but I will not go home until I can do so with sufficient standing that my father will have to admit he was wrong."

Jenny had been raised with five brothers and four sisters, each sibling a living tribute to their parents' legendary stubbornness. She recognized foolish pride when confronted with it, and recognized as well that to the person displaying it, it wasn't foolishness and never would be.

"What was your father wrong about?"

Elijah glanced down at her, then at their joined hands. He kissed Jenny's knuckles and gave her back her hand. "Very little, as it turns out. He told me I lacked the fortitude necessary to succeed as an artist, told me I was turning my back on my birthright out of laziness and self-indulgence, not because I had an artistic vocation. He told me I wasn't prepared for what my artistic inclinations could cost me."

"And you think he was right?" The hound stirred at the sharpness of Jenny's tone, but Elijah smiled.

"He was spot on about much of it, but not all of it. I'll admit that when I go home with an Academician's status. I'll admit I had no notion of the cost and effort involved in pursuing an artist's life, that I was a spoiled lordling with no understanding of the greater world—provided my father rescinds his judgment of my character."

So Jenny could blame this familial drama on honor, the worst of the crotchets male pride was prone to, and not just Elijah's honor, but the marquess's honor as well. She linked her arm through Elijah's and led him around the table, lest they disturb old Jock at his slumbers.

"The regent sings your praises. Sir Thomas sings your praises. Surely you don't need the Academy's imprimatur to prove your father wrong?"

"The last thing I said as I tossed my brushes and spare shirts into a traveling bag was that I would come back as an Academician or not at all. I knew I had enough talent, and I was determined he should admit it."

Jenny wanted to tell him he was an idiot. She wanted to tell him that young men rode off, full of themselves, their talent, and their invincible honor, and they came back in coffins. When they were dead, one couldn't write them letters, couldn't apologize, couldn't explain what had driven one to sharp words and stupid taunts.

"Tell your sister you'll see her at Christmas," Jenny said. "Or shortly thereafter. She really does miss you, Elijah."

Just as Jenny would miss him, even as she boarded her packet for Calais.

Elijah had a reputation for completing commissions quickly. He'd learned the necessity for speed early in his career, when his fees were modest and a gap in work meant a gap in coin.

Though in truth, he wasn't all that quick. He was organized and disciplined, and work tended to get done when a man rose early and spent time in his studio rather than at the numerous distractions available in London Towne.

Then, too, he'd cultivated the social nap, using fashionable Society's evening gatherings to catch up on his rest, fill his belly, and remind all and sundry that artistic talent was near to hand.

"My ability has gone begging today," he said. "I can render the dog down to every wrinkle and hair, but the children are beyond me."

Jenny glanced up at him from where she was building a house of cards with Kit. Wee William was astride old Jock, who dozed on the hearth rug at Elijah's feet.

"Come down here, Mr. Harrison. Your perspective from that chair has to be awkward."

She had a point, and she had a way with children, both on the page and on the thick carpet before the fire. Elijah gave up his seat and stretched out on his side on the floor. William dismounted from his perch on the dog and came careening into Elijah.

"Go for a ride!"

Elijah caught the boy with two hands on his chubby middle. "He is a solid fellow, is William."

Jenny balanced cards in a carefully inverted V. "He'll take after his parents and soon be as big as Kit."

Elijah rolled to his back and lifted William straight up above him.

"Weeee! Ride!"

"Won't Kit take after his parents too?"

"Kit is a foundling," Jenny said, helping the older boy to make his own inverted V. "Sophie and Vim took him into their household when he was less than a year old." She took the card from Kit's little mitts, where it would soon be bent beyond use. "Like this, my man. Gently and slowly."

When, all odds to the contrary, Kit managed to lean the two cards against each other, Jenny made a great fuss over her amazing, exceptional, clever nephew.

Elijah blew against the top of William's head, making a rude sound and feeling not in the least amazing, exceptional, or clever. He couldn't sketch worth a damn today because of his blasted sister's note, a bit of familial sand thrown into the gears of a morning that ought to be taken up with professional concerns… and with Genevieve Windham.

"You caught something of William's solidness in your pastels," Elijah said, lifting the gigging child up again. "You conveyed that he's a healthy, substantial young fellow."

"Because I've carried him around on my hip, and he is substantial." Jenny carefully, carefully placed a card crosswise over the two supports she and her amazing nephew had constructed.

"I-unt-up!"

Elijah lifted William straight up, realizing he'd forgotten this about youngsters. They were insistent and tenacious in their play, persevering at their fun when sense, strength, and adults had long since had enough.

"William is training me, like a bear at the circus."

"William is enjoying himself," Jenny countered. She had constructed another V, and was trying to show Kit how two cards had to balance perfectly together to become stable.

"You caught that too," Elijah said. "The fixity of purpose common to the young at their play." Whereas he had focused on rendering an accurate impression of little William's curls and Kit's small fingers.

"You have the same fixity of purpose," Jenny said. "Careful, Kit-my-love."

She sat, serene and graceful, with her legs tucked under her, and yet Elijah knew that Genevieve Windham's determination likely eclipsed that of all the males in the room combined, including the hound. He rolled to his side, the better to behold his stubborn lady, and settled William astride his ribs.

"You have it too, Genevieve. Your determination is one of your defining accomplishments."

She peered at the card in her hand, maybe wondering if he meant his words as a compliment, which he did. "I come by it honestly. My parents are strong willed."

"Ride!" William bounced hard on Elijah's ribs to emphasis the command, while Jenny smiled at her younger nephew.

"Vim takes them both up frequently, though lately it has been too cold. I looked at your pastels, you know."

Elijah wrestled himself free of his rider and came to a sitting position, legs crossed, William ensconced on his boots. "And will you render a critique?"

To ask her was an odd relief. She would not be brutal for the fun of it, as old Antoine could be in the presence of dilettantes, but neither would she be timid.

"Something in you does not want to see the essential nature of your subject when you look at these children, Elijah. With your other portraits, there's a compassion about what you render. You see the best in people. A peer might be elderly, too fond of his drink, portly, and forgetful, but you capture the humor in him, the fondness he has for his hounds or grandbabies."

She had studied his work, and that pleased him. "I have bills, the same as everybody else. The flattery inherent in the grand style is commercially sensible, for all the *Discourses* would have it artistically imperative too."

William grabbed for a card and captured the knave of hearts. Elijah took it from him and tried to balance it on the child's crown. The card came sliding down over William's nose, which resulted in much squealing and bouncing about.

"Sarah liked this game, though she got so she could hold quite still. Ruth never had the patience for it."

Jenny sent him a look, a look that included but was not limited to pity. "You miss them too, Elijah."

The second time, William purposely bounced on his little bottom to make the card slide off his head. "Maybe some."

Jenny passed Kit a card, then another, and sat back as the boy tried to balance them against each other. "How long has it been since you've been home, Elijah?"

"A while." He tousled Kit's curls, then William's. "What do you think the essential nature of these subjects is, Genevieve, the thing I wasn't able to capture in my sketches?"

"How long is a while?"

The knave went sliding for a third time, and William was just as delighted. Elijah wrapped his arms around the small, ecstatic boy and kissed his ear. "Nine years and eight months since I've been home. My mother sees to it I run into my siblings occasionally, as if by chance. I call on her when we're both in Town. My father and I meet at his club—it's all very cordial."

Nine years, eight months, and eleven days, but who was counting?

"You'll go home soon," Jenny said. "I'll go to Paris, and you'll go home to see your family."

Her tone held an ominous sense of resolution, and while Elijah didn't want to think of sweet, quiet Sarah and the more boisterous Ruth missing him, the notion of Jenny removing to Paris made him positively ill.

"Go!" William kicked out this time as he bounced, and the little house of cards went sailing in all directions. Elijah braced himself for a burst of outrage from Kit, but the boy clapped his hands.

"Let's do it again," Kit said. "This time I can be a wolf who blows the house down!"

Elijah Harrison could see the truth in others. He could find something attractive in a gouty old squire, a schoolgirl who hadn't yet put up her hair, or a princess expected to one day effectively rule a nation when she'd never seen peace between her own parents.

Elijah had no idea, not the first inkling, how attractive he was, lounging on the rug with William, scratching the ear of an old hound, or giving Jenny a crooked smile and asking for a critique.

She would show this attractiveness to him, just as he had shown her how much art she was leaving in the shadows of her sketches.

"You were expecting me," she said as he stepped back to allow her into his sitting room.

"The way Wellington expected the Corsican at Waterloo." He closed the door behind her, locked it, then leaned back against the door. "That was rude. I apologize. I am out of sorts."

"You are tired." So she would sketch him tired, but she would not, not even for the sake of his rest, give up her hour. "Let's begin then, shall we?"

He scrubbed a hand over his face then glanced around the room, as if looking for his wayward manners. "I'm imbibing. Would you care to join me?"

Parisians drank at all hours, and the ladies indulged in spirits there too. "Yes, please."

He prowled over to the sideboard, his blue velvet dressing gown making a beautiful line of his back. "Have you ever taken spirits before, Genevieve?"

"Of course."

He turned, a glass stopper in the shape of a winged lion in his right hand. "Don't lie to me, my lady. I'll find you out."

He could too. He could look her in the eyes and know all her secrets—or at least paint them.

"When we're ill or ailing, Her Grace advises the medicinal tot. She says one learns to appreciate medicinal tots as a function of marriage and children."

"Does she say that within the duke's hearing?"

Jenny accepted a glass with about an inch of amber liquid in the bottom. "She smiles directly at him when she says it, and he generally smiles back and toasts her."

Jenny smiled at them both, pretending the prospect of others' marital bliss, even in its mellowed and subtle forms, did not hurt. She lifted the glass to her mouth but was prevented from drinking by Elijah's hand wrapped around hers.

"Slowly. Bad enough you're secreted with me in dishabille at a late hour. If you're found tipsy or worse, I will not forgive myself."

The scent hit her nose before the liquid touched her lips—peat smoke, apples, oak wood, and a complex of things… botanical. Almost a perfume, and not the same as brandy.

She took a modest sip, which bloomed like a small firework in her mouth, the streams of glory trailing down to her belly. "What is it?"

"A fine old Scottish whisky. I travel with it, packed with my paints and frames and easels. Where will you pose me tonight?"

She wanted him stretched out, as he had been on the floor with William. Relaxed, a little preoccupied, and not very clothed. Her nerve deserted her, though, when she considered he'd probably balk at posing as her odalisque.

"Have you written to your sisters?"

He paused with a glass halfway to his mouth. "I'm to write to all six? I'd be at my desk the entire night, and that would mean an unproductive day tomorrow."

He *had* been drinking. The Jenny who'd been secretly relieved to see the last of Denby, the Jenny who'd made a perfect bow before the Queen, the Jenny known and loved by every Windham of every age—and their pets—would have pled a headache, set her drink down, and bid Mr. Harrison good night.

This Jenny, who was going to study art in Paris, took another sip of her whisky—lovely stuff, whisky, no wonder her brothers partook regularly—and considered her subject.

"Write to your sister, then. Just the one, at your desk."

He took a swallow of his drink and eyed the desk like a martyr beheld the lions' den. The escritoire was pretty and French, japanned and decorated with inlaid gold scrollwork more feminine than masculine, but Jenny liked the elegance of it.

He sat. She moved candles, positioned his drink to catch the light, passed him a white quill pen, shifted the inkwell, moved his drink again, and then considered how to position herself. She couldn't very well stand when she sketched him, but she wanted his face in shadows again, the better to apply what she'd learned the previous night.

"I have an easel," he said, rising and disappearing into the bedroom. He emerged a moment later with a sturdy wooden frame, one sporting clamps at the corners for holding paper if one were not inclined to work on a canvas.

"How did you know?"

He set it up a few feet from the desk, exactly where Jenny would have asked him to—after pondering all her choices and wasting half of her allotted hour.

"You don't want to be directly in my line of sight lest you distract me, and if you're doing a night study of me, you want a bit of distance and superiority, some detachment about the point of view."

No, actually, she wanted intimacy, but *he* wanted the distance, so she did not argue.

He resumed his seat, moving his drink a few inches closer to the blotter, which was where Jenny should have put it. She got her paper affixed to the board and regarded him, slouched back, brooding, vaguely dissolute and palpably annoyed, but at what?

"Is that how you want to remain for the next hour, Elijah?"

He glanced at the clock. "Forty-five minutes, Genevieve, and no. I might as well tend to my correspondence while you work."

Jenny said nothing, starting her composition with the structural elements—the mantel behind him, the flat plane of the heavily lacquered desk. Candlelight and firelight brought out the inlaid work, giving the surface the quality of a fish pond, the top a visual window to a different world.

Which would need oils, of course.

Elijah had assembled the requisite tools for correspondence: paper, pen, penknife, sand, ink, and a focused expression. While he stared at the blank page—assembling thoughts, perhaps—Jenny focused on his face.

An hour later, Elijah sat back and sprinkled a final quantity of sand over his letter, just as Jenny made a final appraisal of her study.

It would do. In fact, it would do nicely, and yet, she didn't want to show it to him. For a time, she wanted to revel in the notion that she'd applied what she'd learned the previous evening, and the result was impressive.

"You wrote only the one page," she said, unfastening her paper from the easel and laying the finished sketch on the table by the door.

He tossed the pen on the desk and capped the ink. "One doesn't want to be too loquacious. Females take their epistolary connections seriously, and I will be deluged with letters if my sisters decide I am a reliable correspondent."

"I dread hearing from my siblings for just that reason."

A hint of a smile scampered around his mouth. "You are teasing me. I deserve it."

"No, I am not. My siblings have lives, you see. This child cut a tooth. That husband is annoyed by some buffoon in the Lords. This wife is absorbed in a new project with the dame school—"

He rose and held out a hand to her, and Jenny hoped it wasn't the whisky inspiring Elijah's overture.

She gave him her hand and was tugged into an embrace, Elijah's cheek resting against her hair.

"While you sketch your cat, visit the sick with your mother, and seethe with frustrated artistic talent. Let's hear a curse, Genevieve. Let the drink, the lateness of hour, and the company inspire you, hmm?"

No cat came between them, no stays, no layers of proper attire. Held against Elijah's body, Jenny felt the implacable structure of a large, fit man. His person was as soft and giving as a sculptor's block of raw marble, but much, much warmer.

"The only curse I know is damn—double damn."

"That's a start, like a few lines on a page. Damn has promise, but it needs embellishment. Bloody double damn?" He spoke near her ear, his breath tickling her neck.

"Bloody is vulgar and graphic. Also quite naughty, and *daring*."

"All the better. Come, let's be vulgar and graphic on the subject of my sketches for the day."

He turned her under his arm, as if they were drinking companions, and Jenny felt a little more inclined to curse: she'd wanted him to kiss her, wanted a cat-free kiss, a whisky-flavored kiss that went further than a dose of foul language toward resolving what she felt when she got her sisters' chatty, conscientious, and unwittingly condescending letters.

"I like perishing damn," Jenny said as Elijah settled with her on a sofa. Like the desk, this was an elegant piece of furniture, and he seemed to take up more than his half of it.

"Bloody, perishing damn," he said, tucking his arm

more closely around her. "Say it. You're off to make war on France soon, like that We Happy Few fellow the Bard wrote about. Nobody will understand your English curses."

Jenny considered that Elijah might have been drinking for a while before she'd come upon him—except the bottle had been nearly full, so this whimsical crankiness on his part was not entirely fueled by drink.

"I won't *need* my curses in Paris, because I'll have something to write about besides… my bloody, perishing, damned cat." She'd surprised him—she'd surprised herself. "Now I feel I must apologize to Timothy."

"Timothy owes me an apology," Elijah said. "Damned beast about disemboweled me. I invite you to do the same." He took a breath, and because Jenny was sitting right next to him, she felt the whimsy go out of him. "I can't get Rothgreb's little fellows *right*, Genevieve. It's been two days, and nothing is… I should be half-finished by now."

He trailed off and scooped up a half-dozen sketches from the low table. These he deposited in her lap on a huff.

"Why don't you fetch our drinks," Jenny suggested, picking up the first drawing. She wanted him off that couch, wanted him wandering the periphery of the room or the coast of Wales while she examined these *nothing* sketches.

He obliged, and even detoured to poke up the fire before he set Jenny's drink before her. Thereafter, he took up a position leaning in the bedroom doorway, dressing gown gaping open, drink in hand.

The Artist Before Retiring. Jenny took in the

composition she'd make of him there, framed by the doorway, fatigue and frustration.

"These are technically stunning." For studies, for quick renderings used to work out details of composition and content, Elijah's sketches of Kit and William were masterly. She selected one and put the rest aside. "This is your best one. Let's discuss it."

He pushed away from the doorjamb and came down beside her without putting his arm around her. Jenny passed him the sketch and took another swallow of courage.

"This is technically adequate," Elijah said. "If I can't structure an adequate composition by now… The dog is truly amazing. Not my drawing of him, but that old hound. I've never seen a beast as tolerant of children."

The image on the page was William astride a recumbent Jock, the old dog somnolent in contrast to the child's gleeful countenance. Whereas Jock looked as if he would be found before that hearth until spring was well advanced, William's bare foot was raised, and his hand grasped one of Jock's floppy ears like a rein, as if to urge his canine steed to take flight.

"You've caught the trust between the dog and the child," Jenny said. "Jock would give his life for those boys, and in his eyes, they can do no wrong. He might chastise them with an admonitory growl, but only when they're older and ought to know better. I think that's what you drew."

"I drew a sleeping dog."

"You drew a sleeping dog who is also part guardian angel. Jock holds all of Rothgreb's confidences, you know. Lady Rothgreb says she had best die before the dog, so somebody adequate to the task can comfort his lordship in his bereavement."

Elijah set the drawing aside. "The elderly can take a morbid turn with their humor."

"The elderly have courage we can only guess at, like soldiers facing battle. That is a good sketch, Elijah. You should consider it for your portrait of William. Rothgreb would love it."

Jenny would love it, and as he grew up and prepared to step into his father's and Rothgreb's impressive shoes, William would love it most of all.

"I was commissioned to do one portrait of both boys."

He leaned forward to move the sketch to the bottom of the stack, and Jenny felt as if he was hiding her praise from view too. She turned to tell him as much when she caught sight of Elijah's chest, naked beneath the gaping dressing gown.

"You're not wearing a shirt or waistcoat."

The corners of his lips turned up, the first real humor she'd seen in him—and at her expense. "You spent a half hour sketching me, and you're only noticing this now?"

An hour sketching him, taking him apart visually and putting him back together on the page as a composition, a study. As he'd hunched over his letter, his chest had been a shadow she'd avoided.

"I noticed." Though she'd noticed by omission. Her gaze traveled down. "What is this?"

"The cat..." He didn't move, didn't leap off the couch and hold the door open for her.

Jenny pushed the dressing gown farther apart,

revealing two long, angry red welts running up Elijah's belly to his sternum. "*Timothy* did this?"

She touched the welts, surprised they weren't hot. Elijah's stomach went still beneath her fingers, as if he'd stopped breathing.

"Timothy was an uninvited guest at a kiss," he said. "An ill-advised kiss. He absented himself from the proceedings as best he could."

As Jenny would absent herself from England after the holidays. Abruptly, her travel plans loomed not as a daring response to impending spinsterhood and artistic suffocation, but as a parting from everyone she held dear.

And her family would not understand, though Elijah would understand. She wanted to kiss his bare, warm belly, kiss the hurt and make it go away. She settled for running her fingers over the lacerations, while Elijah finished off his drink in one swallow.

"Genevieve..." He sat directly beside her, his flat abdomen exposed to the firelight, his expression suggesting he'd welcome eagles tearing at his flesh rather than endure her touch.

"I wanted to sketch you without your shirt, but I was afraid to ask. I wanted to sketch you—"

The look he gave her was rueful and tender. "You will be the death of me, woman."

He sounded resigned to his fate, and Jenny liked it when he called her *woman* in that exasperated, affectionate tone. She did not like it quite as well when he hoisted her bodily over his lap, so she sat facing him and his exposed, lacerated torso.

"You will note the absence of any felines," Elijah

said, hands falling to his sides. "And yet, I must warn you, Genevieve, indulging your curiosity is still ill-advised."

He thought this was curiosity on her part, and some of it was, but not curiosity about what happened between women and men. Jenny's curiosity was far more specific, and more dangerous than he knew: she wanted to know about Elijah Harrison, and about Elijah Harrison and Genevieve Windham.

"My parents will be home in a few days, Elijah, possibly as soon as this weekend." The notion made her lungs feel tight and the whisky roil in her belly.

He trapped her hands and stopped her from tracing the muscles of his chest. "It's all right. I understand. Explore to your heart's content."

A pulse beat at the base of his throat. She touched two fingers to it. "It's late, you don't owe me—"

He kissed her, a gentle, admonitory kiss, like Jock's cautionary growl.

She took his meaning: no more trying to coax enthusiasm from Elijah for her company, no more trying to inspire him to reassurances that he felt something special for her. He would permit her curiosity and nothing more.

The perishing, damned man was going to model kisses for her.

Jenny rose up over him, pushed his dressing gown off his shoulders, shrugged out of her dressing gown, and framed his face between her hands. If it was curiosity he was prepared to indulge, then curiosity she would give him.

Eight

As a boy, Elijah had argued vociferously with his father that Christmas ought not to fall in the dead of winter. How was a fellow supposed to be good at the very time of year when keeping mud out of the house was an impossibility? How was he to avoid snitching a treat or two in that season when the kitchen was the only consistently warm room in the entire, cavernous Flint family seat?

How was a young man to avoid breaking the occasional vase when the weather was too cold to let off high spirits in the out of doors, and his younger brothers must plague him without ceasing and challenge him to a cricket match against their sisters in the portrait gallery?

As heat ignited in Genevieve Windham's eyes, Elijah felt the same sense of consternation, of temptation and reward colluding to foil a man's good intentions.

The devil was not some wrinkly old fellow savoring of brimstone and perdition. Eternal damnation came in a lavishly embroidered nightgown, had warm hands, and kissed like…

His mind went blank as Jenny brushed her mouth over his again. She'd trapped him with those warm hands, cradled his jaw in a grip both gentle and unbreakable. Her kisses were like brushstrokes, creating the contours and shadows of a yearning not entirely sexual.

Though sexual enough. Drink hadn't dulled Elijah's base urges one bit, but then, he'd barely opened the bottle when Jenny had come wafting into his room. Images of genies and odalisques went winging through his brain as Jenny took a kissing-tour of his features.

"I like your nose, Elijah. Were you teased about it as a boy?"

She teased him, kissed the indelicate feature that rendered him drunk on the scent of jasmine, then sat back as if to study her brushwork.

"I like your eyes too." She ran her tongue over his eyebrows, and Elijah groaned. He planted his hands on either side of her waist as if to steady himself, lost any semblance of balance as a result, and went on the offensive, lest the blighted woman part him from his reason.

He lashed his arms around her and covered her mouth with his own. She tasted of whisky and sin, of curiosity and all that was irresistible in a beautiful female late at night behind a locked door.

He'd checked that lock twice, and as Jenny's fingers tangled in his hair, Elijah was glad he had.

Dangerous, stupid thought. A bacon-brained enough scheme that Elijah broke off the kiss and rested his forehead on Jenny's heaving chest. "We have to stop, Genevieve. Did your brothers tell you to apply perfume to your breasts?"

He didn't realize the extent of his non sequitur until he beheld the confusion in her eyes.

"They did not."

"Your scent is stronger here." He nuzzled her throat. "Jasmine and insanity." A lovely combination. Her pulse raced at the base of her throat, matching the throbbing behind his falls.

"Genevieve." He swallowed and tried again. "Your nightgown sports a number of bows, my dear."

She smoothed her hands back through his hair, a caress that rippled over his skull, down his spine, and went right, straight to his bollocks. "Elijah, what—?"

He untied the first bow with his teeth, mostly in the hope that, because teeth were not as dexterous as fingers, some sanity might return between bows number one and six.

"Never, ever put the bows on your nightgown or your chemise in the front," he warned as he undid bows two and three in a similar fashion. "A man can take only so much temptation."

He glanced up at her, hoping for a cooling of the passion in her eyes.

God help them both, she was smiling a *smug* smile. Elijah stopped and canvassed his self-restraint. What she wanted, whether she knew it or not, was to be driven beyond the bounds of a self-discipline so ingrained she mistook it for her soul.

Obliging her would kill him, leave him to expire in a ditch of guilt, misery, regret, and plain old heartache.

These thoughts passed through his mind in the time it took Jenny to caress his hair again. "Elijah?"

He undid bows number four and five, exposing the

soft swell of luscious, jasmine-fragrant breasts. "Undo your hair, Genevieve. Undo it completely."

She reached up, making her breasts shift under the gossamer of her nightgown. Were he in his right mind, Elijah would probably have recognized the exact type of silk she'd used from the way it reflected and absorbed light. In his present condition, he had access to only small increments of vocabulary and reason.

Soft, sweet, hot, luscious. Dangerous.

He had full complements of determination, though. In that moment, he had more determination than Genevieve Windham could conceive of, because one more thought managed to materialize in his mind as she shook out the golden glory of her hair.

Genevieve Windham had experimented boldly with her drawing master nearly ten years ago. For years, she'd watched and waited, until she'd chosen Elijah for her next venture into self-exploration and intimate pleasures.

What's-his-name, the scapegrace itinerant Don Juan of the paint brush, had disappointed Genevieve Windham, *badly*. She'd even given the blighter a second chance, and he'd not improved his marks.

Elijah was not going to disappoint her. Though it might cost him his sanity and his soul, he would not suffer his Genevieve to be disappointed again.

"Percival Windham, *what are you up to*?"

His Grace's pen paused at the duchess's tone of voice. When he'd been a younger husband, that Wrath of the Goddess inflection had been enough to freeze his blood—or heat it. Coupled with Her Grace's posture—spine straight, arms crossed, fire flashing in her green eyes—that tone still made a prudent husband pay *close* attention.

He sat back but did not put the pen down. "In what regard, my love?"

She advanced across their private sitting room, nightgown and robe swishing, and appropriated the chair on the other side of his desk. "Do not think to dissemble, sir. I had tea with Lady Carruthers and Lady Hornby."

Percival twirled the quill pen, feeling both irritated and proud. The irritation was at having been found out so quickly; the pride was because Esther would always be able to unravel his small stratagems.

"And how are their ladyships?"

"They are leaving for the country tomorrow, and taking their spouses and offspring with them. Neither Hornby nor Carruthers will be underfoot to obstruct any of your bills in committee, contrary to all of your grumbling for the past week or more."

A duke didn't grumble, but a husband looking for excuses to bide in Town might.

"I suppose they're leaving the obstructing to Flint and Matheson, then."

"Flint has been at his family seat for more than a month. He's popped up to Town only to indulge her ladyship's holiday shopping."

"And is your holiday shopping complete, my love? My own is not."

Some of Esther's ire dimmed. She excelled at the quick rage, at least in private, but she also excelled at swift forgiveness.

Her mouth flattened in a way that suggested not full pardon but a commutation of sentence might be under consideration. "Percival, I do not need gifts from you. You are gift enough, when I think that I might have lost you..."

Percival well recalled the sensation of a horse sitting on his chest, the terror of being unable to breathe, and the twinges and aches that had preceded his heart seizure several years past. Not for anything would he want to relive those moments, nor would he want to inflict the worry and misery of them on his dear duchess.

And yet... That heart seizure had had positive consequences, one of which was the look in Her Grace's eyes at that very moment. Percival dropped the pen and reached for his wife's hand. "Esther, I am in grand good health. You would scold me to soundness were I not."

She smiled, she blinked, she squeezed his hand. "I would, and then I would let the children have a go, and even the grandchildren. I would let Westhaven's horse—"

Percival put a finger to his wife's lips. He would not linger about in the mortal sphere because of her scolds. He'd continue to enjoy a vigorous life because he loved her and she loved him. "Come sit with me."

He rose, drew her to her feet, and escorted her to their cuddling couch. Every ducal residence had at least one, usually in their private sitting room, with an auxiliary located in the duchess's private parlor. No argument was allowed on the cuddling couch, no scolding, no... prevarication.

On that thought, Percival seated his wife. "Are you

looking forward to the holidays, my dear? All of the children have confirmed that they'll be in attendance."

She tucked her legs up and curled into his side. "They had better be. Small children travel far more easily than the older variety, and a short visit from one's offspring at the holidays isn't too much to ask. But, Percival, have you counted heads?"

He had, but not like Her Grace would in anticipation of a family house party.

"Morelands can easily accommodate such a crowd."

She reviewed the numbers with him: seven married offspring, most with at least one child or in anticipation of a child. Kesmore had two extra from a previous marriage—darling little scapegraces who would lead their parents a merry dance in a few years—and if Rose were to consort with her cousins, then Amery, his lady, and Rose's small half brother would have to be included too.

"That's twenty-nine people, Percival, not including ourselves, and if I'm to have the least chance of maintaining peace and order over the holidays, then we must depart for Morelands posthaste."

Her Grace was a firm believer in peace and order, which was all well and good from Percival's perspective, provided a bit of mayhem and mischief came along to liven things up.

"You've forgotten somebody, dearest wife." The use of the word *dearest* would remind Her Grace of their sole remaining unmarried child.

"Jenny." Her Grace closed her eyes and leaned more heavily on Percival's shoulder. "She adores her siblings, but this gathering will be hard on her."

Percival adored all of his children, of course, but he'd always felt that in his daughter Genevieve he had a kindred spirit. This notion had little apparent basis in fact. Jenny was sweet, kind, dear, devoted to family, and in every observable way, a paragon—which His Grace was not.

Jenny was also, however, prodigiously stubborn, as evidenced by her ability to withstand any and all marital lures longer than her notably reluctant brothers or sisters.

"About our Jenny..."

Her Grace's head came up. "I've suspected you were up to something, Moreland. Out with it."

Percival occasionally ignored summonses from the regent, but never ignored that command from his wife when on their cuddling couch.

"Are you familiar with Elijah Harrison, Esther?"

She sat up but kept her hand in Percival's. "Flint's oldest, and the despair of his marchioness. The boy hared off years ago intent on his art, and there hasn't been a full reconciliation yet. Good-looking, said to be under consideration for the Academy, and not given to artistic excesses. The regent likes his work, and he's had commissions from the Continent."

In a few accurate sentences, she'd gone from a duchess peeved with her duke to a mama hound on the scent.

"Rothgreb is having Harrison paint a portrait of Sophie's little ones."

He felt the duchess snap the puzzle pieces into place. "Percival, that is... that is... diabolical. That is brilliant. That is magnificent." She bussed his cheek, the greatest prize he might win, short of securing a husband for his daughter. "Elijah Harrison is a handsome fellow too, and Kesmore speaks highly of him. Husband, truly you have outdone yourself. Jenny has been restless lately and has tried so hard to hide it."

Percival lived for such praise, and to make his duchess's eyes sparkle.

"So you understand why I need a few more days to shop for your present, Esther?"

"You need not give me a present, Percival, and I need more than ever to get back to Morelands. We can invite Mr. Harrison to call, and to the open house… what?"

"Jenny bides at Sidling as long as we're in Town, my love."

She drew in a breath, huffed it out, and settled against him. "You are ever more daring than I, Percival. Do you really think such drastic measures are called for?"

God, yes. If Jenny were to be ensnared, Harrison would likely have to strut his artistic wares—among others—directly under Jenny's dear, stubborn, discerning nose—again.

"It can't hurt. Jenny holds her art very dear."

Though, thank God, she no longer went sneaking out in male attire, risking scandal and disgrace every Tuesday morning for the sake of a few sketches. His Grace had nigh had an apoplexy to go with his heart seizure when his footmen had brought him that news.

And then there was that Denby rodent, now wielding his damned paintbrush in the wilds of Massachusetts, where bears and wolves might have the use of his talents with His Grace's blessing. Thank God, Bartholomew had caught on to the man's intentions before disaster struck.

His Grace set those thoughts on the scrap heap of paternal regrets and regarded his duchess, who—if Percival knew his wife—had on her considering cap.

"Can't Jenny remain with Sophie even when we return to Morelands?"

"Jenny hates to bake, my dear, and yet she's too nice to tell Sophie to leave her in peace. Then, too, I hear Flint and his marchioness will be up to Town on Thursday."

He'd made sure of it, in fact.

"Friday, then. We'll leave for Morelands on Friday."

His Grace made no protest, though he'd hoped for another week at least, but Harrison was a bright lad and a genuinely talented artist. Then, too, the season of miracles approached.

"Friday it shall be, and we'll collect Jenny on Saturday. Now, about your present..."

Elijah Harrison knew how to undress a woman with his *teeth*. Jenny watched as several bows came undone—more than three, fewer than she'd like—while he delivered a lecture to her on the ideal design of nightclothes.

Or something. Her brain was having difficulty extracting meaning from words, and the whisky was not to blame. The fault lay in Elijah Harrison's hands, in his voice, in his kisses.

"Your hair takes my breath away, Genevieve."

Not his words, but the look on his face—awestruck, reverent, *aroused*—made Jenny shake her head, letting her hair fall in disarray down her back.

He brought fistfuls of gold forward over her shoulders and buried his face in the abundance of it. "If I live to be a hundred, the scent of jasmine will bring me back to this moment."

If she lived to be a hundred, how would she recall the memory of straddling Elijah's lap, of learning his taste and scent, of wanting him so intensely that desire eclipsed all in her awareness?

"When I'm in Paris, I will miss you, Elijah. If I live to be a hundred, I will miss you."

Something passed through his eyes. Anger, maybe, that she'd remind them both their pleasures were stolen and temporary. That was good, that he'd be angry and not relieved.

"Let me give you something more to miss—or recall fondly."

As she had done the previous night, he used a single finger to nudge fabric aside and reveal flesh. He didn't touch her; he let the silk of her nightgown caress the slopes of her breasts until she was exposed to him.

She'd liked the position he'd put her in, once she'd gotten used to it. Sitting on his lap, facing him, astride him, she'd felt as if she had superior control and he was pinned to his fate.

He could not get away unless she allowed it, or so she'd thought.

But her position also meant he could study her breasts, trace blue veins with a fingertip, watch as her nipples ruched up in welcome—and she could watch him studying her.

"Thou art more lovely…"

He was quoting from somewhere; Jenny could not think where. His hands cupped her breasts, bringing warmth and wanting in equally generous measures.

"Before…" Jenny struggled for words. She put her hands over his, so he would not leave her bereft of his touch.

He leaned closer, ran his nose up her sternum. "When you were sixteen?"

Brilliant man, to read her thoughts so easily. She nodded. "I never… he never…"

He cast her a look full of sadness and understanding. "You remained clothed."

Another nod. Jenny closed her eyes, the better to savor Elijah's touch. That Denby hadn't seen her like this was cause for rejoicing, not regret, but that she hadn't known this… this *wonderment*, this cherishing caress, was a sorrow.

Elijah's hands left her. She did not open her eyes because Jenny could feel his gaze yet on her, and then… her nightgown drifted off her shoulders, leaving her entirely, wonderfully naked.

"You are glorious, Genevieve."

She *felt* glorious, not wanton, not wicked, but passionate and wholly, completely appreciated by the man who'd untied all of her remaining bows.

He anchored a hand in her hair and tilted her head for his kisses.

"*Yes…*" Kissing was a wonderful idea. Kissing let her revel in his hair, his lips, his tongue. She sank closer to Elijah, her sex coming against the ridge in his breeches that assured her he shared her wonder.

"Elijah, please…" She got a hand between them, groping the length of his erection. "You… naked… too."

She had missed the sight of his nudity. Missed the privilege of regarding him as God had made him, even as at each class, she'd wanted to cover him up and keep him for her private perusal.

"Genevieve, love, *no*."

"No" was just a sound made by a man who didn't understand what was needful. "No" was a syllable, a pair of random letters… Elijah's hand over Jenny's was not as easily ignored.

"No? Elijah? No? I'm sitting here without a stitch on—"

He stopped an incredulous tirade as well as a shameless spate of begging by the simple expedient of closing his fingers around her nipples. "Trust me, Genevieve. I'm saying 'yes' to your passion, but 'no' to complete folly."

She had not the first idea what he was nattering on about, for the term "struck by Cupid's arrow" had only at that moment become clear in her mind—and in her body. Animal need bolted from her breasts to her womb, swifter than arrows and more piercing.

Jenny arched into his hands. "Do that again."

He obliged, slowly closing his grip on her nipples, as if the dratted man had eons to explore her responses… which thought made her a little less desperate. "Again, please."

While Jenny tried not to pant, Elijah experimented with rhythm and pressure, and then—she did pant—with his mouth. She hung over him, helpless, as he teethed, suckled, soothed, and inflamed by turns.

And somewhere amid this conflagration, Elijah had slipped both hands down to cup her derriere and abetted her in establishing a slow rocking of her hips.

"I hate your damned breeches," she muttered against his teeth. "But I love the feel of you."

Yes, she had spoken those words aloud, and Elijah had comprehended them, because he lifted up, pushing his cock against her sex in a manner that astonished for the havoc it created, even through his damned, dratted, perishing, *bloody* breeches.

"Let go, Genevieve. Stop trying to manage everything. Trust me, and let go."

Even last night, when he'd all but pushed her from his rooms, he hadn't sounded that desperate, that... passionate. The threat in his voice of unbearable pleasure reverberated through Jenny's body and gave her permission to obey him.

She took shameless advantage of his generosity, grinding down on him, pushing her breast into his hand, consuming him in a kiss turned wet and devouringly voluptuous.

His hand stroked over her thigh, another first—nobody touched her there; she didn't even touch herself—

That big, warm hand moved higher, until the backs of his fingers brushed against the curls at the juncture of her legs. Jenny didn't stop moving, but she shifted her hips to leave Elijah room to maneuver, to brush his thumb down, and down some more.

"Elijah..." She hissed his name as a bonfire of tension lit inside her at his caress.

"Let. Go."

He did it again, just right, then again and again harder, better than just right, and the bonfire became a lightning strike of wrenching, white-hot, consuming, inescapable pleasure. When it ebbed, Jenny was draped over Elijah's shoulders, her lungs heaving, and her body that of a stranger.

He shifted, moved a leg, then an arm. Jenny was desperate for him not to set her aside, but could not bestir herself even to cling to him.

"Not yet." She whimpered this plea—she'd intended a stout command—to the muscles of his shoulder.

Her dressing gown wafted around her shoulders, cool, soft, and comforting. Elijah pulled it close, and thus pulled her close too. "Hush. Settle."

One could not settle a puzzle whose pieces were cast to the winds. One could not settle a heart fractured along cracks both old and new. One could not…

Elijah's hand landed in her hair, a smooth, sweet caress, and Jenny found she could settle her breathing. When she woke up, Elijah was still stroking her hair, but the world, the entire universe had shifted off its axis.

Her siblings' marriages took on a different hue. Procreation became a matter of more than biblical duty. The way the duke smiled at his duchess took on a sharper focus.

And years and years in Paris, even years painting any subject she pleased, became a lonelier and even bewildering prospect.

Nine

Genevieve Windham was brilliant.

She'd seen promise in the sketch of the boy with the old hound, while Elijah had dismissed the effort as unorthodox and off balance. The issue became how to get both boys into the hound's ambit, and create an image so perfectly composed it appeared spontaneous.

"We wondered if you might start without us." The lady herself appeared in Elijah's studio, William affixed to her hip, Kit grasping her hand.

She'd brought the children herself, no harried nursemaid in tow, and the tableau of Genevieve with the children did something queer to Elijah's insides.

"Good morning, my lady." He offered her as cordial a bow as he knew how to give, which was cordial indeed. Considering her lack of intimate experience, he hadn't expected her to risk his company over the breakfast table, but he had wondered if she'd brave the studio today. "You are looking exceptionally well this morning."

She set William down, and the boy predictably charged over to the hound dozing by the hearth. "Jock! Ride!"

The dog sighed. Kit dropped his aunt's hand. "Can we wreck the card houses today, Aunt Jen?"

"We'll see." She watched Elijah as if he were about to pounce on her, which would have served nicely had the children not been present.

"I missed you at breakfast, my lady." He could not have told her what he'd eaten, because he'd been so busy staring at the doorway and willing her to appear in it.

The light in her eyes shifted, became less guarded. "I missed breakfast. I slept late, so I took a tray."

Last night, she'd said she'd miss him too, when she went to blasted, bedamned Paris. Her ambition had apparently coalesced into determination, and yet, he could not allow her to go to Paris.

This thought—this *fact*—had crystallized in his mind before he'd drifted off to sleep. He'd escorted her to her room—a mere three doors down the guest wing corridor—taken himself to bed, then tended to his own needs within five minutes of kissing her good night.

The relief had been temporary and inadequate, and as he lay among the pillows and covers, he'd come to the conclusion that Jenny Windham had nowhere near the sophistication needed to manage the predators lurking among the artists of Paris.

And yet, she'd hate him did he thwart her scheme.

"Maybe I could take a turn building the house of cards," Elijah suggested. "Though I would, of course, need an assistant."

"Me!" Kit yodeled.

Lady Jenny was indeed an experienced aunt. She affected a pout. "And then what am I to do? You fellows will have your fun, and I shall be left to sit by myself, with nothing to do, all alone, not even Jock to play with—"

"C'mon, Aunt Jen. I'll help you too."

Elijah suggested Kit choose the cards, making sure that knaves were paired with knaves, and queens with queens, and Jenny was to build the structure. William mounted up on his sleeping canine steed and sang a happy-little-boy tune no composer would recognize and no parent would mistake.

As William took up the reins of Jock's ears, Elijah sat on the raised hearthstones and sketched. Excitement hummed along in his veins, a visceral recognition that he'd found the arrangement that would make a worthy portrait.

The point of view was only slightly from above, so that the shining crown of Jenny's head was in evidence as she bent to peer over Kit's shoulder. The feel of the angle was intimate, though, a child's-level view of a relaxed morning.

Lines and shadows arranged themselves into a small boy's smile and a sleeping dog's contentment. While the fire crackled cheerily, the house of cards steadily grew, and Genevieve Windham's hands became a subtle point of interest in the sketch.

When she sat back to admire her little card palace, Elijah caught her smile—loving, but always a bit wistful when in company with the children. He caught the way the boys looked at her too. They adored this relation who was as pretty as their mama, and never quite so stern. They adored her humor and affection, her gentleness, and her abiding regard for them.

The house of cards rose higher. Jock's back leg twitched as he dreamed his doggy dreams, and William left off riding his gallant steed long enough to accept the knave of spades from his brother.

"Careful," Jenny cautioned. "William is going to want to—"

On a gleeful cry from William, the knave went sailing into the upper stories of the palace, destroying twenty minutes of careful work.

William clapped his chubby hands then turned to Elijah, arms outstretched. "I-unt-up!"

The palace rose and fell several more times, Jock rolled over, and Elijah completed a detailed sketch of Jenny with her nephews. William occasionally supervised from Elijah's side, then toddled forth to wreak destruction like a one-boy Vandal horde.

Jenny presided over it all from her spot on the rug, a serene, smiling presence with endless patience for busy little boys and their portraitist.

She would be wasted on Paris. Elijah started another sketch on the strength of that conclusion, a study of Jenny's face as she regarded Kit's efforts to find "an ace with a blood-colored diamond" on it.

Her smile, indulgent, tender, and yearning, said she even loved the child's choice of words.

The door opened, something Elijah perceived with the part of his brain set aside for keeping track of matters not related to his sketch, like a porter's nook in the front chamber of a grand house.

"Beg pardon, your ladyship. Shall I be taking the boys now?"

The nursemaid's arrival would have been cause

for much relief the day or two previous. "Another moment," Elijah muttered, pencil flying.

"Soon, Norquist," Lady Jenny said. "We were about to finish up."

As he forced himself to retreat from the world of his sketch, Elijah realized the boys were trying to start a squabble over some lower order of card—a three?

"I-unts" became increasingly vocal, interspersed with "It's not your *turn*," until Elijah had to set his drawing aside and scoop William up in his arms.

"What you want," he informed the child, "is a stout tickling." He scratched lightly at the boy's round tummy, provoking peals of merriment. William's laughter, surprisingly hearty coming from so small a body, sounded to Elijah exactly as Prudholm's had when that worthy was still small enough to tease and tickle like this.

"Elijah..." Jenny's tone bore patience and a warning.

Don't get the little ones all wound up, Elijah. You're the oldest, and they look to you for an example of proper decorum.

He lifted the happy little fellow up over his head and slowly lowered him. "Enough, my lad. Time to go with nurse and have some bread and jam. You'd like that, wouldn't you? Or maybe some of your mama's delicious stollen. Mmmm."

"I want some of Mama's Christmas bread too," Kit announced. "Come along, Aunt Jen. We'll share."

Elijah stood, passed Sweet William off to his nurse, and took Aunt Jen by the hand. "I'm sure your aunt longs to accompany you, Kit, but she must stay here and *help me clean up this awful mess*."

Kit's gaze darted to the scattering of cards on the rug. To a small child, a deck held thousands of cards, none of which little hands found easy to stack. Such a pity, that.

"I'll save you a piece of stollen, Aunt Jen." Kit took his nurse's hand and towed her toward the door. "'Bye, Aunt, 'bye, Mr. Harrison."

"Au revoir," Elijah murmured. When the door closed, he still had Genevieve firmly by the hand lest she attempt an independent retreat.

"The cards," she began, turning away.

He swung her back to face him—"Hang the perishing, damned cards"—and kissed her.

"Elijah Harrison!"

He kissed her again, more soundly. "That's for thinking you needed those children to protect you from me this morning. Which gave you more worry, Genevieve, the idea that I might take liberties, or the notion I could possibly look upon you with indifference by the broad light of day?"

She peered up at him. "Both?"

One syllable held a world of uncertainty, a world of feminine anxiety that Elijah could not bear for her to suffer. He wrapped her in his embrace. "Neither, you daft creature."

Those words were no kind of reassurance, so Elijah cast around for others while he restored himself in some regard with lungfuls of jasmine scent. "I prosper as an artist, in part, Genevieve, because I'm a sober, hardworking fellow. I make no silly wagers. I rise early and tend to my work. I deliver on every commission I accept. You know this."

Her arms came around him; her cheek rested against his chest. "I know you are a man."

If she wasn't convinced of *that* by now...

"I am a gentleman. I would not take liberties before others." He fell silent as he realized the door—the very door not ten feet distant—was unlocked. Then, too, a gentleman would not take liberties *at all.*

Perishing, damned inconvenient business, being a gentleman. He turned her face up to him by virtue of kissing her cheek. "And as for indifference, my dear, I am not capable of it where you are concerned. I rarely show intimate attentions to others, and do not share yours lightly."

Those were still not the words a woman wanted to hear the morning after encountering the second man with whom she'd been intimate. Elijah knew this. He also knew she was determined to go to Paris, and more effusive sentiments would not be appreciated.

"You did not make love with me, not truly."

She'd spoken softly, though Elijah heard the bewilderment in her voice—the hurt.

"I wanted to." He stepped back, because making love with her right here and now was, in the opinion of his breeding organs, an increasingly fine notion. "I went back to my rooms, blew out the candles, thought of you, and committed the sin of Onan."

The lady knew her Bible, as evidenced by the smile tipping up the corners of her mouth. "You thought of *me*?"

"I could not get the image of you out of my mind, Genevieve. By firelight, your skin is luminous, and your hair..."

She sank onto the hearthstone while Elijah dropped to his knees and started picking up cards. "You have to know you are beautiful. Shall I make a list of your features?"

"I think you already have. Elijah, this is a wonderful picture."

His morning's work was in her hands. "It will do, I think. Something about the boys having fun in the same space, but not exactly playing together, works. It's a brotherly composition."

Whatever that meant. He was on his hands and knees, turning low cards face up, and pretending not to hang on the next words out of her mouth. His artistic soul teetered between destruction and glory on the strength of her next pronouncements.

"You've somehow caught the love, Elijah. I cannot wait to see the finished work."

He sat back, relief lifting through him in mind and body. "You like it?"

She looked right at him. "I adore this."

Elijah's next youngest brother, Joshua, had once careened into him as they skated across a frozen pond. Faster than thought, faster than anything in Elijah's experience, he'd seen his own skates silhouetted against a blue winter sky, a strange, incomprehensible image. He'd absorbed the perfect blue of the sky in the barest instant before finding himself flat on his back, unable to breathe.

Genevieve's three little words, fired straight at him—*I adore this*—had the same effect. She adored their shared passion, she adored his painting, she quite possibly—he reached a shaking hand for the last card—adored *him*.

He passed her the full deck, rose, and collected his sketch. "I must thank you for all of your patience this morning with the boys. I could never have caught that little tableau were you not in the center of it."

She took his proffered hand and rose. Whatever she might have said was lost to Elijah when somebody tapped on the door.

He dropped her hand and stepped back. "Come in."

"Greetings, you two." Vim, Baron Sindal, stood in the door in all his blond, Viking glory. If he thought it odd the room held neither children nor nursemaid, he did not remark it. "I come with a summons from my baroness. Luncheon is served, and then we're to hitch up the sleigh and invade Louisa and Joseph's peace for the afternoon."

Perhaps that was for the best. Perhaps breathing room was a good idea all around. "Lady Genevieve, enjoy your outing. I'll make a start on a canvas of this morning's sketch."

Sindal winged his arm at Jenny. "There's a letter waiting for you down in the library, Harrison, and your painting will have to wait. Sophie was very clear that you're to join us on the outing. She was sure you'd enjoy renewing your acquaintance with Kesmore, and I wouldn't dream of sparing you my sons' company when they're in high spirits."

He sauntered out with Jenny on his arm, a gracious host about his daily quotient of mischief. When the door clicked shut, Elijah lowered himself to the floor beside the old hound.

"I am not a stupid man, I'll have you know."

The dog thumped its tail once.

"I understand what Sindal was saying. He was warning me that no footmen were allowed up here to interrupt our morning's work with anything so distracting as delivery of the post."

Another thump, and amid the dog's wrinkles, two sad, sagacious brown eyes opened.

"He was telling me he's on to us, which probably equates to a warning that he'll break my fingers if I trifle with his wife's sister. He did not ask about the portrait. Neither he nor his lady nor old Rothgreb himself have inquired once about the portrait."

In which, according to Genevieve, Elijah had "caught the love."

He picked up his sketch. "She adores me. Said almost as much in plain English."

Saying the words out loud sent warmth cascading through Elijah's chest. He studied his work more closely, relieved to find that even on a deliberate critical inspection, the sketch still struck him as having that ineffable *something* that made an image art, and an accurate likeness a portrait.

The boys were the dominant elements of the sketch, and yet, there was Genevieve Windham in all her beauty at the center of it.

Her words came back to him as he noted details he didn't recall sketching. *You've caught the love*. Like he'd contracted a rare, untreatable condition.

Which… he… had. His first commission of a juvenile portrait was going to be a resounding success because he'd caught the love. Lady Genevieve adored his work, him, and the pleasure they could share, and looking at the image he'd rendered of her, Elijah realized he adored her right back.

Alas for him, she adored Paris more.

"You must tell me how my son goes on." Lady Flint accepted a second cup of tea from Her Grace, the picture of a gracious caller enjoying her hostess's company, and yet, Esther saw the shadow in her guest's eyes.

"I will report faithfully, you may depend upon it, Charlotte, but doesn't the boy correspond?"

If Esther's sons failed to write regularly, they knew a visit from their mama might well result—and from their papa. Then, too, the duke was an excellent correspondent—like any competent commanding officer—and set his sons a good example in this regard.

Lady Flint grimaced at her teacup. "Elijah is nothing if not dutiful. He writes to his father at least quarterly, and by some tacit understanding among their men of business, each always knows where the other is, but the letters..."

Esther put a pair of tea cakes on a plate and set them in front of her guest. She'd received Lady Flint in her private parlor, an airy, gilded space done in blue, gold, and cream. Esther kept sketches of her children on the walls, and considered this, rather than any of the formal parlors, her Presence Chamber.

Or perhaps her confessional. "When our boys write, their letters are like dispatches, particularly St. Just's. They report crops and calves and nothing of any importance. The ladies must keep me informed of what matters—is everybody in good health? Is the baby walking yet? What were the child's first words? When might a visit be forthcoming?"

"Dispatches—yes. Elijah should hire out as a

weather observer. I know the propensity for rainfall in nearly every shire, know when the first frost is likely, and when the lavender blooms. But I do not know…"

Esther pushed the tea cakes closer to her guest. Percival would have polished both off by now. "You do not know how your child fares." And now came the delicate part. "Does he enjoy travel, your Elijah?"

Charlotte picked up the little plate with the tea cakes on it, and regarded the contents as if they might reveal the future. As a young woman, Charlotte had never wanted for beaus, and it was her hands they all wrote sonnets to. French hands, maybe, graceful even in repose, hands Esther had envied at the time but did not envy now.

"Of all my boys, Elijah was the one least inclined to leave Flint. He loved the place, knew it as only a boy can know his home. He would harangue his father about which field ought to fallow, which ought to be planted in hops, and he was often right."

Esther took a nibble of a vanilla tea cake with lemon icing—the chocolate ones being reserved for His Grace. "And yet one hears your son hasn't been home for quite some time."

This was offered as a puzzled observation, and a mild judgment on the foolishness of young men. In no way did Esther intend her words as an accusation, though she knew they would be perceived as such.

"Elijah is as stubborn as Flint." Charlotte set the cakes down uneaten. "They had words years ago as only a young man and his father can, and Elijah galloped off in high dudgeon, determined to pursue his art. Flint maintains our son will come home—that

Elijah is too dutiful not to—but when, I ask you, will Elijah come home, if in ten years he's not set foot on the property even once?"

Esther wanted to hug her guest, for this sorrow was something one mother might share only with another, and yet, Charlotte had her pride too.

"Shall I lecture your son, Charlotte? I've had some practice at it, and not just with my boys. You will sympathize with me, I know, when I say that dear Percival occasionally benefits from his wife's gentle admonitions."

The moment lightened, as Esther had hoped it would.

Charlotte picked up the plate of cakes and took a dainty nibble of an almond and cherry confection. That a woman who'd borne twelve children had any daintiness left in her was a testament to significant fortitude.

"Matters are likely to come to the sticking point here directly," she said when she'd munched her cake. "Elijah is under consideration as a full member of the Royal Academy. He vowed—young men are so dramatic—he vowed he would not set foot on Flint soil again until he'd gained full membership, and he will not be voted in."

"Flint would do such a thing to his own son?"

"Flint would dearly love to see Elijah gain Academician status, but it isn't meant to be. The nominating committee includes old Fotheringale, and he will never allow it."

The worst problems were those created by a confluence of stubbornness and pride. "Mortimer Fotheringale wouldn't know a decent portrait if it fell off the wall and hit him on his fundament."

They shared a look, a look possible only when two ladies had made their bow the same year, and that year was three-and-a-half decades past.

"His arse," Charlotte rejoined, starting on the second tea cake. "Back in the day, Mortimer fancied me, and I chose Flint. Flint was a dab hand with the caricatures, and I preferred a fellow who could make me laugh to a man who'd lecture me. Mortimer was always going on about the proper helmet for this or that naked Roman god when portrayed at an obscure moment in some unhappy myth."

"If the Roman were naked, and as a young woman you *could* focus on his helmet, I would worry for you, Charlotte."

An impish, Gallic smile flitted over Charlotte's face, then faded. "Worry for me anyway. Fotheringale is wealthy and respected now, and he will sway many votes. I cannot blame him for wanting a wife of good fortune and good standing—marriage was not a sentimental undertaking thirty-some years ago—but he very much holds it against Flint for turning my head."

"Have some more cakes. My husband claims tea cakes can solve many ills, and Percival is considered a wise man." By most, anyway. Hearing this tale of masculine stubbornness and grudges, Esther wasn't at all sure Percival had been a wise papa where Jenny was concerned.

Charlotte accepted two more cakes, one vanilla with orange frosting, the other vanilla with lavender frosting. "We should serve tea cakes in the Lords."

"We should lock your son and his father in a room

and not let them have any cakes or let them out until they've reconciled."

Thank God her own boys hadn't gone haring off in a snit—except Bartholomew had to some extent, and the army had been the best thing for him, up to a point.

"You must not interfere, Esther. Flint claims Elijah will find his own way home, but their situation is complicated by Elijah's art and Flint's lack of recognition in artistic spheres. I've promised my husband I won't intercede, though I've often regretted that promise."

As well she should. When a man misstepped with his children, who was to set him back on a proper course if not his dear wife?

"I will not interfere, then. I give you my word on that, but tell me, Charlotte, is it interfering to write to your son and remind him of all the holiday revels he'll miss yet again? Is it interfering to send him a few holiday tokens? To admit that you respect his decision and can understand why his honor might require that he *never lay eyes on you again*?"

Charlotte's gaze narrowed on her tea cake. "I *am* in Town much less frequently—I used to at least be able to count on Elijah being home to me from time to time, but his commissions mean he hares all over the realm. Flint crosses paths with him in the clubs..." She fell silent, her mouth flattening. "I still have daughters to launch, but Elijah won't necessarily understand that."

Esther remained silent, having planted what seeds she could. "Christmas approaches," Esther said, squeezing her friend's hand. "We can hope your menfolk recall their senses over the holidays."

"Esther, you're not to turn up duchess on me, please. Promise me you will not take the boy to task. He's really very much like his father, and Flint is a fine man."

A world of uxorial understatement lay in Charlotte's modest appraisal of his lordship. Esther recognized a well-loved woman when she beheld one.

"I have given my word not to interfere, though you may release me from that promise at any time. Now, shall I ring for more cakes, and what is Flint getting you for Christmas? Percival positively torments himself over this each year, and all for naught, I can assure you."

They ordered more cakes, and swilled another pot of gunpowder before His Grace and his lordship returned from luncheon at their club. Percival and Flint each stole a kiss from the other's spouse under the mistletoe, and Their Graces saw their guests bundled back into a crested town coach.

When all the seasonal good wishes, waving, and smiling was done, His Grace led his wife by the hand back to the nearest spray of mistletoe and kissed her cheek.

"Your plan was brilliant, Esther. Ply a man with enough steak, commiseration, and seasonal libation, and all his troubles come galloping forth. Flint is miserable over the state of things with his oldest boy, and more miserable yet because his wife does not reproach him for it."

Esther slipped her hand around Percival's arm and let him escort her to their personal sitting room. She kept the fire going in here all day, because one never knew when one's husband might want a few minutes of one's time, say when the fate of nations or a little holiday scheming merited discussion.

"If her ladyship took Flint to task, his pride would have the fig leaf it needed to seek a rapprochement with their son," Esther reasoned, "and yet Charlotte gave her word she would not gainsay Flint on this matter. I gave my word too."

His Grace seated her on their cuddling couch, flipped out his tails, and settled beside her. "You rarely make promises, Esther. You are a duchess, need I remind you, and your word should be bond enough for anybody. What were you about?"

She was *about* being his duchess, and the mother of his children.

"I gave my word I would not interfere, Percival. Charlotte should know I certainly cannot speak for my husband's queer starts."

A smile lit His Grace's delphinium-blue eyes. "A stubborn old curmudgeon, is he, your husband? Given to queer starts and wild hares?"

Esther winked at him. "My husband is the dearest man in the world, and the most devoted papa on earth. Now, shall I have some chocolate and some cakes brought up?" Because a rare steak and a half-cooked potato often passed for sustenance in the men's clubs—that and copious amounts of spirits.

"You shall, you darling woman, and if these queer starts have to do with Fotheringale's nonsense, then you will lament over them in detail, because I confess the entire mess seems impossible to me."

The cakes and chocolate arrived, the cakes and the

chocolate disappeared, and—telling herself it was all in aid of dear Jenny's happiness—Esther did indeed lament her husband's meddling ways at length and in detail.

At least the letter was not from a sibling lamenting Elijah's protracted absence from Flint Hall, though in some ways, it was worse.

Harrison,

For a man seeking full Academician status, you've chosen a deuced inconvenient time to absent yourself from Town. Buchannon dreads the admission of Pritchett and Hamlin, but Fotheringale is adamant that their talent exceeds yours. In my opinion, Fotheringale's position presages the aerial perambulations of pigs. It is nonetheless true you have no juvenile portraits to your name.

Can one hope you're rectifying that oversight in the hinterlands of Kent?

If not, my only hope for seeing you join the Academy would be to reveal Pritchett and Hamlin to be women in disguise. If there's one thing Old Foggy despises more than your portraits, it's the idea of women contributing anything of substance to the world of art.

I'm having the committee to dinner this Saturday, and you must tear yourself away from the charms of country life to join us—hopefully with a juvenile portrait or two in hand.

West

The journey to London would take much of the day, but would allow Elijah to meet with his man of business and show the flag before the nominating committee. Fotheringale was stubborn, but not without artistic sensibilities. Some charm, some diplomacy, some…

Elijah paused in the midst of sorting his brushes as a wretchedly inconvenient thought popped into his head. Fotheringale would want assurances that Elijah could not countenance the admission of women to the Academy, not as associates, not as RAs.

The old dog, Jock, still sprawled before the studio hearth, let out a slow, hissing fart. A gloriously foul stench wafted up.

"My sentiments exactly, though what will Lady Jenny care? She'll be in Paris, where she'll be fêted and flirted with."

Where her gender would not hold back her art, and conversely.

Resenting the French was never difficult for an Englishman. Sitting on the hearthstones, a half-dozen brushes in his hands and a flatulent dog for company, Elijah resented the French, Mortimer Fotheringale, and… his life.

"I was an idiot," he informed the dog. "Everybody is an idiot when they're young. My father was an idiot too, but he's not the one begging at the Academy's door just so he can put in an appearance at the family seat."

Which did not explain why, ten years later, Elijah was still an idiot.

He banked the fire and evicted the dog, lest a foul

miasma render the studio uninhabitable by morning. Tomorrow might be Lady Jenny's last day at Sidling, which was a sufficiently dolorous thought that it drove Elijah through the darkened house and up to his rooms.

When he beheld Jenny Windham asleep in his bed, he revised his status from idiot to lunatic.

Ten

"Genevieve Windham, get out of my bed."

In keeping with his new status as lunatic, Elijah had whispered those words, not shouted them. The lady was asleep, probably worn out from chasing Kesmore's daughters, helping them build a snow fort, and bellowing instructions to them for how to best thwart their father's and Elijah's efforts to steal the precious bag of carrots that had been declared the afternoon's prize.

The ladies had soundly trounced the gentlemen. Kesmore's poor aim was in part to blame—at least half the time his snowballs had pelted Elijah instead of the opposing team, and much merriment had ensued as a result.

Elijah brushed a strand of golden hair from Jenny's cheek. "I had fun today."

He'd also ended up with a sorry case of holiday heartache, that particular brand of homesickness that afflicted him when in company with happy families this time of year.

Jenny's eyes fluttered open. "You're here." The sleep faded from her gaze as a smile rose in its place.

"And you, my lady, are leaving." When had he taken a seat at her hip?

The smile ebbed, though she made no move to obey him. "I *am* leaving. Louisa told me Their Graces left Town today and will likely be by to collect me tomorrow."

She rolled away from him, which meant Elijah could see she wore nothing—not her frothy nightgown, not a robe, nothing—beneath the covers.

He shook off a fascination with her bare nape and focused on her words. "Your parents' arrival means you must help yourself to my bed?"

Her parents' arrival meant he would never see her like this again. The artistic grief of that reality was eclipsed only by the sexual frustration of it. She said nothing for a moment, then rolled back to face him. Her hair was in a thick braid, one he could wrap around his wrist several times.

If he were fool enough to touch her now that she'd awakened.

"Our paths are not likely to cross again, Elijah. Not unless you travel to Paris, or I come back here to visit family."

Elijah turned his back on her and pulled off a boot. "I have had a bellyful of Paris. It stinks, and the French are mean, though in fairness to them, they're as mean to each other as they are to the rest of the world, and I miss—"

The French were not mean—practical was not at all the same thing as mean—and Elijah's mother had been born in France. Elijah was grousing because he missed his brothers and sisters. He missed Flint Hall.

He missed his parents, and he hated Christmas more each year as a result.

"What do you miss, Elijah?"

He yanked off the second boot and draped his stockings over the tops. In some regard, this casual disrobing was more personal than all the kissing and petting he'd indulged in with Jenny previously.

"I am missing my wits, if what I'm contemplating is any indication."

The covers rustled, and the bed bounced beneath him. "I want it to be you, Elijah."

He knew exactly what she meant and nearly strangled himself getting his cravat off as a result. "No, you do not. You do not want it to be anybody. Can't you save yourself for your art?" His favorite waistcoat went sailing across the room to land in a rumpled heap near his easel.

"Now you are being mean." She'd trotted out her Aunt Jenny voice, the same tone she might have used to convey disappointment in one of her nephews.

"I do apologize." Elijah got two buttons undone before wrenching his shirt over his head and tossing it toward the nearest chair—and missing. "I am not in the habit of finding naked women in my bed, particularly not women who regard a second deflowering as an item to attend to before taking ship."

One cannot be deflowered a second time. He knew she was thinking those very words even when he could not see her. He could smell her, smell jasmine and soap and a hint of peppermint tooth powder.

"You weren't like this last night."

Only his breeches remained on his person as evidence that he possessed a shred of honor or sense.

"Last night, I set limits, if you'll recall. I indulged your whims and dealt with, with—" He'd brought himself off. How did one discuss vulgar realities with a near virgin who happened to be naked in one's bed?

"You denied yourself."

Elijah felt a hand stroke over his shoulders. Jenny's caress was gentle and platonic, and yet, he felt it directly behind his falls.

"I expect you deny yourself often, Elijah, and think little of it, but must you deny me?"

Curses started piling up in his head. How was a man to know what honor required when a naked woman—a lonely, innocent, determined naked woman—turned the thumbscrews of guilt so easily?

"Do you want more pleasure, Genevieve?" He turned on the bed to face her, hoping he might placate his guilt and her determination with more half measures. "You can bring such pleasure to yourself, you know. There's no reason a woman—"

The rest of his homily on female self-gratification flew from his head. Jenny reclined against the headboard, the sheet draped across her lap. Her braid fell over one pale shoulder and her breasts…

The artist in him noted that her left breast was ever so slightly lower and boasted a bit more fullness than the right, and yet both were beautiful and perfect, and both rosy nipples were puckered, though his room was warm.

The man in him cast anything approaching scruples far out into the Channel and frankly stared at the bounty before him. He'd seen her before, seen her nude, spent, and gloriously happy with it in his arms.

But he'd not taken even a moment to *behold* her, to caress the glory of her with his gaze, and to savor the way firelight cherished each curve and hollow of her naked body.

"Genevieve Windham..." He raised a hand, then let it drop before he'd cradled her jaw against his palm.

"I want it to be you, but a lady can't do the asking." The determination was still there in her voice, but she was pleading too, for him to capitulate, to comprehend—

The gentlemen in him, the perishing, damned, inconvenient gentleman in him grasped both the plea and the solution. So simple and so wondrous, to give her what she sought and what Elijah needed.

"I want it to be me too. It shall be me, and for me, it shall be you." He leaned forward and kissed her, not touching her anywhere else, so he might savor the kiss sealing that vow.

"Elijah—" She sank a hand in his hair and hauled herself closer. "Yes, please and please again." She became a woman possessed, dragging herself up to her knees, locking her arms behind his neck, and devouring him with her kisses.

"Genevieve, slow down. Slow—" His hand curved around her flank and pulled her closer, and yet, the angle was awkward. He was half-turned toward her on the bed, she was clamped around him, and the damned covers were so much linen seaweed, dragging about them in all the wrong directions.

"I want you so, Elijah. I could not have borne to leave here in the morning without—"

He rose off the bed, turned, and stepped away.

"I could not either, but if I don't get my damned breeches off, I will not answer for the consequences."

She knelt among the blankets, rosy, naked, and smiling as if she'd just landed her snowball directly on his arse, which in a metaphorical sense, she had. Marriage to this woman was going to be wildly delightful.

"Let me get my breeches off, Genevieve, for both our sakes."

She said nothing, her gaze riveted on his chest. From somewhere, Elijah found the strength of will to slow *himself* down. This night would mark a beginning for them, and Jenny relied on him to make it the best beginning they could share.

"You do it," he said.

Innocent that she was, she blinked at him in bewilderment.

"My falls, love. I want not a stitch between us." He wanted to give her summer sunshine on naked flesh, he wanted soft breezes, and he wanted long, sweet nights full of pleasure for them both.

She knee-walked to the edge of the bed, studying his falls. "I've never done this before."

"I should hope not." He couldn't hide his amusement, but he did manage to stand there, hands relaxed at his sides, when her mouth made him think of things vulgar, naughty, and—with Genevieve, he dared to hope—within the realm of possibility in the not-too-distant future.

Her hands shook minutely as she unfastened the buttons to his falls. He could feel the tremor as well as see it as the flap gradually draped open.

Genevieve dropped her hands, sat back on her

haunches, and worried a nail between her teeth. "Now what?"

Now came the time when the man, the artist, and gentleman would collude to make this experience everything the lady had ever dreamed it might be. "Now I bring you pleasure."

Her smile was lovely, naughty, and a little worried. She moved to the center of the bed and scooted down beneath the covers.

"She hides her treasures," Elijah grumbled to no one in particular as he shucked out of his breeches. He heard her draw in her breath, and in a fit of spontaneous martyrdom, readjusted his immediate plans.

Rather than launch himself onto the bed, he stooped to pick up his clothes. She braced herself on her elbows and watched while he gathered up the sartorial casualties of his earlier haste and folded them one by one on the clothes press.

"Elijah?"

"Tidiness is a habit," he explained, though when a man's cock was bobbing against his belly, tidiness was a ridiculous habit. The idea that Jenny would one day tease him for his comment pleased him.

He moved behind the privacy screen, used his tooth powder, and prayed for fortitude.

And stamina. A determined woman deserved stamina in her prospective spouse.

"I have missed seeing you like this," Jenny said.

She would be seeing a great deal of him like this, and soon, if he could talk her into a special license. "Scandalous woman."

"I am, aren't I? My favorite session was when

you took Mr. Jackson's pose for *Satan Summoning His Legions*."

A pose that illuminated the subject's genitals nearly as well as his face, because all the light in Sir Thomas's painting was from the netherworld at the bottom of the image. Then, too, Satan's upraised arms required a pose that made the model's arms ache abominably.

Elijah approached the bed, noting when Jenny's gaze fell on his upthrust cock. She ran her tongue over her top lip, and he nearly vaulted onto the mattress.

"Shall I come to bed, Genevieve?"

A small, sensible part of him wanted her to fling back the covers, snatch up her dressing gown, and announce that she'd changed her mind. They were going about things backward, though many couples did. As much as Elijah wanted her, and wanted to please her, he also wanted her to know he'd wait for her.

For the three weeks necessary to cry the banns, he could wait for her.

She did not take her gaze from his cock. "Please, come to bed."

He climbed onto the mattress. "You use the word 'please' a lot."

"When I'm around you, and yet… often I want to holler it at you, Elijah. I want you to pause as you climb onto the bed, so I can capture the combination of eagerness and wariness I see in your eyes. I want you to hold a position over by the clothes press, because your body makes a perfect *contrapposto* pose angled to the firelight. I want to draw what I feel of your lips when we kiss—"

He remained on all fours on the bed and kissed

her to shut her up. "And to think you couldn't even ask me to remove my shirt." Their marriage was not going to suffer from an abundance of clothing. The artist, the man, and even that other fellow were cheered by the notion.

She slid down farther beneath the covers, and that meant Elijah had to follow her, until he was crouching over her, the covers between them.

"You are an indecently good kisser, Elijah Harrison."

"One grows inspired by the company. I have a title, you know." This was a paltry gift laid at the feet of a woman who'd been Lady Jenny since she emerged from the womb.

She squeezed his biceps, testing the resilience of his muscles, maybe, artist fashion. "Earl of Bernward. You ought to use it." She did it again, then levered up to press her face to his throat. "Elijah, I'm nervous."

He loved her. The knowledge came to him like a whiff of her jasmine—unmistakable no matter how faint or subtle. This was not mere affection, not infatuation, not a passing preoccupation. He'd caught the love, well and truly. He loved her for entrusting him not only with her beauty and with her past disappointments, but also with her nerves and her future.

He cradled the back of her head with one hand and braced himself over her with the other. "Nervousness is to be expected with a new experience. Give your nervousness to me, Genevieve." He was *not* nervous—this was the most right thing he'd ever done. He was aroused, though, and impatient to win her trust.

She angled her head to peer up at him. "This is a new experience, isn't it?"

"Completely, for both of us." The first of many.

He let her subside onto the mattress, then climbed under the blankets with her.

"You are warm, Elijah."

He wrapped an arm around her shoulders and drew her closer. "I'm on fire."

In less than a minute, he'd ignited his lady's passions too. He denied himself the pleasure of covering her, needing the check on his self-restraint to withstand another spate of kissing from his lover as they lay facing each other on their sides.

"I will forever associate tongues and paintbrushes when I'm around you, Elijah. I want to paint *you*."

"You have." He dipped his head and nuzzled her breast. "You shall."

She hiked a leg over his hips and pulled herself closer. "I mean I want to apply paint to your naked body, put colors on you *everywhere*—" Elijah felt a soft, female hand trace down his midline, then close around his shaft.

"Wicked, passionate, *imaginative* woman." He rolled to his back and prepared to be tortured. Of course she would want to see him. Male artists could inspect themselves in the mirror or gawk at models when they were working with nudes.

And yet, she surprised him by straddling him instead.

"We can do it this way, can't we? I've studied those exotic prints in Louisa's library, and last night—"

Marriage to her was going to be a scantily clad, glorious, exhausting undertaking.

Elijah treated himself to the feel of her breasts against his palms. "We can make love any way you please, Genevieve." Though, pray God, let it be soon.

"I like that." She closed her eyes and let her head fall back, her braid tickling Elijah's thighs. He pulled it over her shoulder and dabbed the end around her right nipple.

"Do you like that too?"

She opened her eyes, expression puzzled. "I like your hands better. I love your hands, whether they're sketching, painting, holding William, or touching me."

He trapped her fingers and brought them to his mouth. He would take her to Paris. He would take her there as often as she liked, and stay for weeks at a time. When he might have shared these sentiments with her, she tipped forward as if to kiss him, and Elijah thwarted her by taking a luscious nipple into his mouth.

"E-li-jah Har-ri-son." Her hand wrapped around the back of his head as he drew on her, and the heat of her sex so very near his cock burned at his self-restraint.

Because words were moving beyond his reach, he anchored a hand on Jenny's derriere and urged her down. She obliged, her damp, warm, lovely sex sighing onto his erection.

"That... That makes me want to kiss you, Elijah."

He switched breasts rather than tell her what it made him want to do. Without him asking, she started moving on him, a slow, wet drag and return that stole his breath and sent arousal spiraling out through his body.

She would not describe herself as a virgin, though to Elijah she was more deserving of consideration than if she had been. He gave up the pleasure of her nipple in his mouth and watched her face.

"Genevieve." He had to say her name, so absorbed was she in the stroke of her sex over his cock. "Genevieve, take me inside you."

Jenny stared at him, as if she groped for the sense of his words.

Elijah took her hand and wrapped it around his cock. "Take me inside you, now. *Please.*"

He fitted his hand around hers and positioned himself at the entrance to her body, then nudged up and went still. Her expression was fierce, aroused, and in some regard holy, like Lawrence's rendering of the dark prince. In a dim corner of Elijah's awareness, he wanted to paint her thus, poised on the brink of accepting both him and the pleasure that was her due, and yet he knew such an image exceeded his talent by leaps.

She snugged her body down enough to start their joining. "There? Like that?"

"Exactly like that. Kiss me."

She folded forward carefully, close enough that Elijah could fill one hand with the abundance of her breast and sink the other into the hair at her nape. "Like this."

He synchronized his tongue and his cock in slow undulations, until her body was moving smoothly over him, taking him deeper and deeper into bliss, deeper and deeper into *her.*

He felt her arousal welling up, felt her slowing her movements as if she'd cower away from the pleasure—and that he could not allow.

"Be brave, Genevieve. Be greedy and strong. Be *mine.*" He took control of their joining, anchoring an arm low on her back, thrusting into her hard, and watching her face.

"Elijah—" She arched her back, her throat gleaming white in the firelight as her body gave itself up to pleasure. Elijah had to close his eyes lest the sight of her surrender send him past control. In some ways, that decision was ill advised, for he could feel her fisting around him, feel the one, endless spasm that wrenched a groan from her throat, and feel when desire eased its grip on her and let her sprawl in a boneless heap on his chest.

A boneless, satisfied heap.

For long minutes, he contented himself with stroking her hair, her back, her derriere. His passion was not sated, and yet he was content. As he drew a queen of hearts on her back with the tip of her braid, Elijah debated telling Genevieve Windham that he loved her.

Such a declaration might be better saved for their wedding night, or for when he presented her with an engagement ring. Or perhaps—

Along with the lust throbbing gently in his veins, along with affection for the lady in his arms and pride in her fearless passion, a quiet thread of joy coursed through Elijah.

He'd take her to Flint Hall after the New Year—after he'd been officially admitted to the Academy—and tell her there that he loved her, for even a stubborn, idiot man who'd wandered in a wilderness of pride for ten years was entitled—was *required*—to show his bride off to his family.

Jenny shifted on his chest, nuzzled his sternum, then settled again.

He was a better man for loving her, he was a better artist for loving her, and he would tell her that too when he brought her to their home.

"Elijah?"

"Love?"

She kissed him and peered at him with the sort of intensity Elijah suspected had to do with questions a newly engaged woman found difficult to keep to herself.

How many children did he want?

A special license or St. George's or a wedding in the Morelands chapel?

Would they reside with his family at Flint Hall, or live for a time at Bernward Manor?

When would he speak to her father?

She brushed his hair back from his forehead, a wifely caress if Elijah had ever felt one.

"When I go to Paris, I will miss my family, but I will also miss… this." She kissed him again, sweetly, gently. "I will miss you so very much."

Elijah's hands stopped moving on her back; his lungs stopped drawing in air.

When *she* went to *Paris*…

When she went to Paris, exactly as planned, as if this night, as if *he,* meant nothing more than a passing whim.

As if he'd completely misconstrued her words, her glances, her intentions, and seen them through a haze of lust and longing that had obliterated his judgment.

But not his pride.

Anger welled up, at her, at himself, at Paris, and following immediately after, like an undertow follows a wave, despair surged—for himself and for her. He did not want to go to Paris, much less in the company of a woman whose view of their dealings was radically different from his own.

Jenny would go to Paris, though he was coming to suspect something more than artistic compulsion drove her there, perhaps something she did not understand herself.

For the past ten years, he had wanted to go *home*, and home he would go.

Allowing intimacies with Denby had been stupid and disappointing but not tragic. Marriage to Denby would have been tragic. These thoughts, along with both satisfaction and loss, coursed through Jenny as she sprawled on Elijah's chest.

Denby had been a selfish, inept boy, just as Jenny had been a selfish, inept girl, while Elijah was… a man, a skilled, generous, passionate, caring, talented…

Jenny very much feared that intimacies with Elijah Harrison were going to have consequences tragic for her, though she couldn't quite fathom how. She could still feel him, feel the pleasurable fullness of him inside her body, and suspected she'd feel him in her heart for far longer than was prudent.

"Elijah?" She could not say these things to him, and yet she wanted to say something.

"Love?"

The sensation of him using her braid like a paintbrush on her back was peculiar and soothing. He gathered her closer, and she kissed him, kissed him with all the regret and longing in her, with all the sorrow and loss too.

"When I go to Paris, I will miss my family, but I will also miss… this." She kissed him again, because the missing had already started. "I will miss you so very much."

His hands went still on her back, and Jenny's heart stopped beating.

He smoothed her hair back from her forehead and studied her, guardedness replacing the tenderness in his eyes. "You said you wanted it to be me, Genevieve."

"I did, and it was, and I thank you for that." One did not thank a man for indulging one's passions. Jenny realized that as she watched the guardedness cool yet more.

"You're pleased then, with this night's work?"

Work? He'd emphasized the word slightly, or maybe Jenny had heard emphasis where none had been intended.

"I am—I was. I'm not now." Their bodies were still joined—she was more or less lying on *him*—and yet, something was off, something was terribly, terribly off, and she was desperate to right it.

He closed his eyes, heaving up a sigh that Jenny felt bodily. "Why are you going to Paris?"

To study art. That was what she was supposed to say to him. Jenny folded down against his chest, relieved beyond measure when his arms came around her.

"I cannot bear…" She tried to stuff the words back into her mind, back so far under propriety and familial regard even she didn't have to acknowledge them. "I can no longer tolerate the company of my family. They don't know me, you see, and yet they love me."

This was as honest as she knew how to be, and yet, the answer didn't feel complete.

His hand moved on her back, no braid-paintbrush in his fingers, just his hand, slow and warm. "They know you. Our families know us even when we wander off for years, Genevieve."

He sounded so sad and faraway, and yet he was holding her close too.

"My family thinks I'm good, and when I see them gather together every Christmas, I'm reminded that I'm not good at all. I don't want the things I should want, and I do want things I shouldn't—selfish things." The feel of him inside her was diminishing, and Jenny gave up any notion that he'd indulge her in yet more passion. The pain of that loss helped dilute the pain of the topic she'd raised.

"My sentiments regarding you lie near your family's, Genevieve, and under most circumstances, I am not accounted a foolish man. You are a good woman. Headstrong, passionate, and misguided, but good."

Her brothers called her pigheaded, her sisters made her the subject of despairing looks, and her parents smiled and expected her to grow old in their keeping, and yet, they were all convinced of her goodness too.

Of them all, she could be honest only with Elijah.

"I hate them sometimes, with their cozy glances and knowing smiles. My sisters and brothers never used to nap, and now it has become something of a family institution. Mama and Papa are in some ways the worst. The grandchildren—"

Elijah kissed her temple, a small gesture full of encouragement.

"Their Graces see their own children through the grandchildren. Westhaven is father to the next heir, St. Just dotes on his daughters, Valentine dedicates sonatas to his, while I… I want to paint. I have to paint and sketch."

"Has nobody offered for you, Genevieve? A woman can paint and sketch while married and raising children. My mother certainly did."

His question was reasonable. She hated that his question was reasonable, and yet she could never hate him.

"I've had a few offers, but they all put me in mind of—"

Two fingers pressed themselves to her lips. "Don't say his name."

Elijah was right. That name did not belong in this bed. "Those men wanted a Windham daughter, a lady, a pretty, sweet, proper, well-dowered, biddable—I'm getting angry just thinking about it. If I'd told any one of my suitors I'd sneaked into drawing classes, if I'd told them I went to the workhouses to sketch the children, if I'd told them I still want to sketch those children, they would run shrieking in horror."

Elijah was silent for a time, his hands moving more slowly. "Don't go to the workhouses alone, Genevieve. Promise me that."

His tone was uncompromising, though his touch remained gentle. How Jenny wished she'd gone to those bleak, diseased, miserable places alone. "I promise. One need not frequent such locations to see poverty in London, and besides, I'll be in Paris."

Where there would be no indulgent, blissfully

married, surviving siblings, but where—according to Elijah—the stench was miserable. How could a woman enjoy her croissant and coffee on a street corner that stank?

"Where in Paris, Genevieve?"

The same uncompromising note underlay his question, and entwined with him bodily, Jenny did not even consider dissembling. "I don't know exactly. I was hoping you might have some suggestions."

"Of where to live?"

Something else lurked in his question, but Jenny had nobody else to ask.

"That, and other things. Antoine said his friends are all dead or no longer teaching. I'm sure there are galleries and shops—"

She went still, very much aware that Elijah had left off stroking her back.

"Genevieve, Antoine has been teaching in London since my father came down from university. He knows everybody with artistic aspirations here, on the Continent, and probably in darkest Africa. If he did not offer to aid you in establishing yourself in Paris, then it's because he chooses not to. Very likely his patrons and familiars would be offended to learn of it if he did, to say nothing of what your parents could do to him."

Gone was the tender lover, and in his place was a fierce, frustrated stranger. One who spoke aloud the conclusions Jenny had tried to spare herself.

"You could help me."

The words cost her, particularly when she could feel something shift in Elijah's body. Beneath her, he was no longer a warm, relaxed, naked man, he was

Satan Summoning His Legions, full of ire and power though he had not moved.

"I would be more comfortable with that observation, Genevieve, had you made it fully clothed and somewhere other than my bed." His body might have been that of a ferocious, dark prince; his tone was colder than the ninth circle of hell.

"You think I'd—" Offer sexual favors in exchange for his connections and knowledge of the Paris art world. The thinking part of Jenny, the part that had come up with Paris as a solution in the first place, saw how he might reach such a conclusion.

He lifted her away from his body and arranged her against his side. "I do not think that. I *would* not think that, and I *shall* not think that of you, particularly if you desist in your importuning. Many fashionable women have seen Paris since the Corsican's defeat. I'm sure you've asked them what they know."

Jenny was leaving in the morning, and that inspired boldness sufficient to overcome her dread of his disapproval.

"You know more than they do, more than probably anybody but Antoine knows. The rumors are you were in Paris even during the war."

He remained silent, and something bright and brave in Jenny's heart sank. "Shall I leave, Elijah?"

His chest heaved up, then down, a sea of male emotion beneath her cheek. "You shall not."

"Will you make love to me again?" Of all the questions she'd asked him, that one was the most difficult, and yet she wanted more of his warmth and tenderness, more of *him*.

"You've exorcised your ghosts, Genevieve, and it's late. Go to sleep."

He tucked her closer and closed his eyes, ending the conversation as effectively as if he'd left the room, the manor, and the shire.

As Jenny drifted off to sleep, the last thing her thinking mind registered was that though Elijah had not offered her his help and had refused her any further lovemaking, when the fire had burned down to coals and a winter wind whistled around the old house, deep in the night, he still held her close.

Eleven

Breakfast was trial by tea and toast. Elijah's host and hostess bid him safe journey to London, then drifted off to whatever business would fill their day. Elijah took his customary place, back to the windows, and prayed Jenny would have the wisdom to remain above stairs until his departure.

Then he prayed that she'd come down early and spend every possible minute with him before he rode out of her life.

Then he prayed that a blizzard might start up and prevent them both from leaving, because the developments of the previous night had been too complicated and overwhelming to allow a man to think them through clearly.

"My lady." He rose as Jenny paused in the doorway, a vision in holiday green. "Good morning."

Her smile was hesitant. "My—Mr. Harrison."

He'd told her about the title. He'd very nearly told her he loved her. "Won't you sit with me? There's a little sun to be had at this end of the table. May I fix you a plate?"

May I tell you that despite the fact that I thought we were to be married, and you did not, I will always treasure the hours you spent in my arms?

He'd told her that much when he'd deposited her fast asleep in her own bed not two hours past and kissed her cheek in parting. *How brave of me.*

Her smile became more confident. "I'd like that. The day looks encouraging."

No, it did not. The day looked all too well suited to travel. Her smile, though, looked encouraging. "What will you have?"

He heaped up a plate for her, knowing she'd never eat that much but wanting to give her something, even if it wasn't what she'd asked him for last night. When they were seated at the end of the room nearest the hearth, Elijah filled her teacup with strong, fragrant tea and added cream and sugar.

This was the last bit of solitude they might have. "Are you well, Genevieve?"

"Quite, thank you. These strawberries are particularly good."

He tried again. "You know there might be consequences from last night?"

She went still, a succulent berry halfway to her equally succulent mouth. "Consequences?" The word came out care-ful-ly, as if she hadn't realized any such thing. "But you didn't… I thought… Heavens."

She'd blushed nearly as red as the strawberry.

"I did not." Thank a merciful, benign, forgiving Deity. Elijah had not spent his seed in her body. "There can still be consequences, and you will not bear them alone." He passed her a folded piece of foolscap. "My man of business always knows where to reach me. If there's need, you will contact me immediately. Promise me, Genevieve."

She took the paper, stuffed it in some secret female pocket in her skirts, and nodded.

A tension in Elijah's chest eased. "Butter?"

"Please."

Ah, God, not *that* word. He buttered a slice from the toast rack in the center of the table. "What will you do with yourself today, Genevieve?"

"My parents will collect me shortly, and I'll probably spend the morning planning the house party with Her Grace."

He chose a toast point for himself and tried to memorize the curve of her cheek. "House party?"

"My entire family is gathering for the holidays. Morelands can hold such a crowd, but it's quite an undertaking. When did you stop putting butter on your toast, Elijah?"

He stopped chewing and stopped trying to pretend. "I'll miss you, Genevieve, and I'll worry about you. Will you come see the children's portrait when it's complete?"

"If I'm still here, of course. I'll miss you too. Very, very much."

Two verys. The tension eased more, which was no help. Without anxiety to mask other emotions, Elijah felt a welling sense of loss, as if leaving Sidling was another leg in the long and ill-advised journey away from Flint Hall.

"Ah, there's my darling girl!"

His Grace the Duke of Moreland came striding into the breakfast parlor, cheeks ruddy from the cold, smile warm, blue eyes merry. "Jenny, my dear, I have missed you this age."

She went into her father's arms, while Elijah got to his feet.

Her family should not have her back yet, please, not just, quite, already… *yet*. "Your Grace, good morning."

The duke hugged his daughter, clearly a man who need not stand on ceremony, and a papa glad to be reunited with his offspring. And then, with an arm still around Jenny's shoulders, His Grace turned that smile on Elijah.

"Bernward, felicitations of the season. I hope my girl hasn't been pestering you too awfully. She does take her little pictures seriously." He winked at Elijah and kissed Jenny's temple, while Elijah wanted to tear her from the older man's side.

Little pictures.

"Lady Jenny and her considerable artistic talent have been an inspiration, Your Grace. I could not have achieved what I did here, much less in so short a time, without your daughter's assistance and insight." Too short a time.

"Right. Jenny, are you ready to go, or can you spare your old papa time to visit the nursery?"

The relief in Jenny's eyes was subtle, too subtle for a blustery old duke to comprehend. "You can visit upstairs for as long as you like, Papa. I'll finish my breakfast."

"Bernward, good day. I'm off to corrupt the youth of England." His Grace wrapped several slices of stollen in a napkin and strode off, and not a moment too soon.

"They're not little pictures, Genevieve. You have talent. Never doubt that."

She sat with the air of a convict whose petition for a royal pardon had just been denied. "Papa loves me. He loves all of his children. Mama does too."

And their love was choking her. Jenny consumed her breakfast in silence, while Elijah sensed he'd underestimated the depths to which she dreaded her return to Morelands.

"You will take Paris by storm, Genevieve." Another nod, and Elijah felt despair wash over him, because how was she to take Paris by storm when she hadn't yet secured decent lodgings? When she had no clue where to begin with the gallery owners and shopkeepers?

Rather than offer her more hollow assurances, he offered her relief from his company. "Will you see me to my horse?"

"Of course."

They traveled through the house until Elijah paused with her in the entry hall. "Which cloak is yours?"

She passed him a pretty green wool cloak with cream trim, the buttonholes elaborately embroidered in a gold fleur-de-lis pattern.

"You've been planning your escape for a long time, haven't you, Genevieve?"

"Years. More dreaming than planning. I'm planning now. This is your scarf." She wrapped soft purple wool around his neck, and almost as if they were married, they dressed each other for the chill beyond the door. "You'll show the nominating committee the sketch of the boys' portrait?"

"Of course." He did not tell her he might come

back for a few more sittings, because French dragoons couldn't have marched him back at gunpoint. Until she left for Paris, he'd be wise not to set foot anywhere in Kent. "You won't lose the direction for my man of business?"

She stroked an ungloved hand over his scarf. "I promise, Elijah. Good-bye." Without warning, she went up on her toes and kissed him. "Safe journeys, and Elijah?"

Somewhere nearby, a sprig of mistletoe hung—or should be hanging. Elijah kissed her back. "What?"

"Go home. Reconcile with your family. I'm leaving my family behind, but I'll also take them with me in a sense, if they'll allow it. You can't racket around forever, pretending you're an orphan when you're a titled lord with a family you love, and who loves you."

This was not what he'd expected from her in parting. He escorted her from the house, lest he be tempted to kiss her again. "Is that advice my Christmas token from you?"

"No." She fumbled about beneath her cloak and produced a small packet wrapped in red paper and tied with a green bow. "This is."

"Thank you." Whatever it was, it was small enough that Elijah could tuck it into his pocket. "I have something for you as well. You must open it in private."

He led her to his horse, opened the leather tube he used for keeping sketches safe in transport, and passed her a small paper rolled up with a red ribbon. "In private, Genevieve. Happy Christmas."

Mistletoe bedamned, waiting groom bedamned, and whatever eyes were watching their parting from the house be double damned, he wrapped his arms around her and kissed her full on the mouth.

"I wish things could be different, Genevieve Windham. I wish it with my whole heart."

She rubbed her cheek against his scarf as if drawing in his scent one last time. "I double damned, perishing wish they could too, Elijah Harrison."

He stepped back, relieved to see she was smiling, because then he could smile too. The groom was busily studying the snowy driveway, which was fortunate, because those smiles—and the pain they held—said worlds about what might have been, what should have been, and what would never be.

Louisa, Countess of Kesmore, paused to admire her son, who gurgled up at his mother happily. "I believe this child will have his father's nose."

Jenny looked away from the mutual admiration society that was mother and son, to yet another gray winter day beyond the window—the third such day she'd spent under her sister's roof. This time.

"Joseph has a lovely nose. A nose suited to his character." The child, however, had his mother's nose. Any fool could see that.

Louisa tucked the infant against her shoulder. "One forgets you study things like noses. Was it so awful at Morelands?"

Yes, it had been. More awful than usual, which Jenny blamed on Elijah Harrison, Lord Bernward, painter of portraits and stealer of hearts.

"Just the usual: Her Grace could not decide which

suite should be assigned to which family, though we went through the same exercise last year and nobody complained regarding their quarters. She couldn't decide whether to assign the children a separate breakfast parlor, make up a children's parlor in the nursery wing, or have everybody share the usual breakfast parlor closest to the kitchens." Jenny rose to pace Louisa's private sitting room, lest she start shouting. "Mama thought perhaps the open house should start earlier, then decided that no, the family should have an hour or so to gather before the guests arrive. And then the menus..."

The duchess could spend days dithering over menus, when she knew down to the smallest grandchild what each individual's preferences were.

Louisa sat the child in her lap, holding his tiny hands in hers. "When was the last time you painted something, Jenny?"

"I haven't been one place long enough to set up my easel." And she'd been drafting chatty, curious notes to her aunt Arabella, who'd often traveled to Paris early in her marriage.

Louisa's mouth quirked, suggesting Jenny's usual talent for dissembling wasn't going to meet with success. "I thought you'd cobbled together a studio of sorts in the east wing at Morelands, near the nursery suite."

This was why Jenny had sent a desperate request to her sister, begging an invitation to visit, why she'd fled—*fled*—her own home.

"Her Grace decided paint fumes would be harmful to the children and instructed the footmen to pack up my 'artistic whatnot' until after the holidays."

Louisa paused in the entertainment of the chubby little fellow on her lap. "Unpack your whatnot. Tell Her Grace that, of the seventy-three private rooms at Morelands, you need one for your art. That's not too much to ask, Sister mine."

Louisa would have asked. She would have done so at a family meal, debated with her own mother until she'd gotten the room of her choice, and then had it set up exactly to her liking before sunset on the same day.

"I did ask. She said she'd think about which room she could spare for my little hobby, and, Sister, I wanted to perishing shriek at her." Bloody, perishing, damned shriek, at her own mother.

"Don't we all, occasionally?"

Jenny had paced half the length of the parlor before Louisa's words registered. "You want to shriek at *Her Grace*?"

"This is the selfsame Her Grace who gave me *Fordyce's Sermons* for my sixteenth birthday and sent my Greek tutor packing in the name of establishing economies."

"I'm sorry." And this was exactly the kind of sibling support Jenny was going to miss terribly when she moved to Paris. "I hadn't realized she'd done that. What was she trying to accomplish?"

"Take this baby, please. One cannot drink tea and hold Kesmore's heir, lest one's clothing comes to grief."

Jenny obediently took custody of her nephew, a stout, cheerful infant who would be crawling ere long—which she would not be on English soil to see.

"Her Grace sent the tutor packing because I had exceeded his abilities, I'm guessing, but he was still somebody with whom I could discuss my translations, and that was…"

"Important to you. This child has gotten heavier since I was here barely a week ago."

"They do that, rather like men get handsomer when you fall in love with them. I received a note from Her Grace this morning, Jenny."

Louisa's voice had lost its typical brisk, pragmatic inflection. Jenny cuddled the child closer and braced herself accordingly. "And?"

"Your parole is at an end. She must have you back before next week's guests arrive, but don't worry." Louisa patted Jenny's hand. "When I take you home, I'll make sure your studio is reestablished, and not in some priest's hole or butler's pantry, either."

You have talent, Genevieve. Never doubt that.

"A butler's pantry might do, Louisa, if it were entirely mine and had at least one decent window."

Louisa set down her teacup and scooped her first-born away from Jenny. "That's the problem with you, Genevieve. You are too nice. You ought to have a fit of the sulks, grumble to Papa, and pick at your food until Her Grace realizes she's blundered—Papa is very obliging about these things when he thinks he's being clever. Mama is proud, but she does love us."

Louisa understood cause and effect the way Jenny understood images and light, and yet the idea of sulking, grumbling, and dissembling in this fashion was… exhausting. "If you're to return me to my dungeon, I'd best gather my things."

Louisa rose with the child on her hip. "Yes, you had. Joseph had a note from Mr. Harrison."

Jenny rose too, hoping the weakness in her knees was momentary. "I trust he fares well?"

"He's considering some commissions in Northumbria. Said he's taken an interest in juvenile portraits, of all things, and that the Academy's nominating committee was very encouraging when they saw his sketches of Sophie's boys. What do you suppose Papa has gotten Her Grace for Christmas this year?"

"I haven't the least notion what His Grace has gotten for Mama. Northumbria is lovely this time of year, and Mr. Harrison's composition was quite good."

Louisa paused in her march toward the door and gave Jenny a look that suggested Bedlam might be lovely this time of year as well—if one enjoyed subarctic climates in winter. "We'll restore your studio, Genevieve, and when the grandchildren arrive, Her Grace will be too busy managing His Grace to trouble you over it much."

Elijah used the entire journey from London to consider his latest of several dinners with the nominating committee.

He'd had Buchannon's butler announce him as Lord Bernward; he'd dressed to the very teeth in sober evening attire; for the first time in years, he'd shown the Harrison family crest on his town coach.

Even old Fotheringale had been impressed with the sketches of Sindal's sons. The composition was good art, as evidenced by the fact that it became more interesting the longer one studied it. West had muttered that the portrait harked back to Sir

Joshua's skill with juvenile subjects, and no one had contradicted him.

Elijah's gelding slipped on a deceptive patch of ground, more ice than road. He let the beast right itself, scanned the horizon, and wrapped his scarf more snugly around his chin.

The evening had had two sour points.

The first was when Fotheringale had harrumphed into his port that one unfinished portrait hardly demonstrated depth of skill or range of ability. Anybody could pull off one pleasing portrait of *children*, for pity's sake.

The second was when Fotheringale had gone off on a tangent about the Academy finally being free of the pernicious influence of dabbling females. He'd squinted at Elijah, as if his tirade ought to have particular meaning, and Elijah had remained quiet.

Which had been a mistake. A prudent man seeking a well-supported nomination would have chimed in with ringing endorsements of Fotheringale's sentiments, except in his mind, Elijah kept seeing Genevieve Windham sitting at the breakfast table and eating strawberries she could not taste while her dear, doting Papa casually tromped all over his daughter's dreams.

Mindful of the lowering clouds and the increasing wind, Elijah pushed those thoughts aside and asked his horse for a faster pace.

"There, you see?" Louisa pulled on her gloves with the same confidence she did everything. "Ten minutes of asking Mama's opinion, thirty minutes of overseeing the footmen as they moved your easels and *whatnot*, and twenty minutes of setting things to rights, and you have your studio back, better than ever. Now I had best leave you, or my daughters will have fed the cloved oranges to Lady Ophelia."

Jenny fastened the frogs of Louisa's cape, wishing her sister could stay longer. "I thought Joseph's pig preferred lurid novels."

Louisa's smile was wicked and gleeful. "Lady Opie doesn't get a crack at those until Joseph has read them to me first. I threatened to name our firstborn Radcliffe, and oh, the lengths Kesmore traveled to bribe me from that notion."

"You are so happy."

Jenny hadn't meant to speak the words aloud, much less sound forlorn when she did. Louisa paused with a red merino scarf half-wrapped around her neck, her smile fading. "I am. You will be too, Jenny. Christmas is the season of miracles, and surely, with all the holiday socializing, the mistletoe, the wassail... Did you know Eve and Deene exchanged their first kiss under the mistletoe?"

"I am not Eve." And Elijah Harrison was not Deene. Elijah Harrison was on his way to Northumbria, where winter was very cold, and mistletoe likely hung from every rafter.

"Joseph and I kissed under the mistletoe too, before we were engaged. I daresay mistletoe had something to do with Sophie and Sindal's initial dealings."

Jenny glanced around at the soaring entrance hall to the Morelands mansion. Mistletoe was in evidence, of course. She wanted to burn every sprig and branch of it.

"I'm going to Paris, Lou. After the holidays." The packet schedules were up in her room, and four days ago, Jenny had sneaked into the attics and set a pair of cedar-lined trunks to airing.

Louisa stopped fussing with her bonnet strings. "To Paris? Are you going to shop? With Their Graces?"

"No, I'm going to Paris to study art. They do that there—allow women to study art, not simply dabble with watercolor still lifes. I've had seven Seasons, and I cannot... I have no interest... Victor once said..." Louisa was studying her with what looked like understanding—or pity. "Will you write to me, Lou?"

"For God's sake, of course I'll write to you, but Paris? St. Just would cheerfully take you North with him, or Valentine would welcome you to Oxford—"

"No more damned racketing about as the doting maiden aunt. An artistic calling requires sacrifices, and it's time I started making a few in the right direction."

There. Jenny had put the situation into words any sibling could comprehend. Victor and Bart would both have approved.

Louisa left her bonnet strings trailing. "You just cursed, and now that I think on it, you haven't called me dearest... I can't recall the last time you called me dearest. Are you sickening for something, Genevieve?"

You have talent, Genevieve. Yes, she was sickening, and that was Elijah Harrison's fault too. "I beg your pardon for my language, and I am not sickening for anything. I do not relish telling Their Graces that I am eloping. If I tell them, the holidays will be most difficult."

Louisa studied her for an uncomfortably long moment. "If you don't tell them, you'll break their hearts. They need time to grow accustomed to this, Jenny. You'll regret ambushing them and leaving them no time to adjust."

Yes, she would. She'd also regret giving them time to change her mind about it.

"I reached my majority years ago, Louisa, and I have a competence from Grandmother Himmelfarb. Their Graces cannot deny my heart's desire indef—"

The row of coat hooks along the wall by the porter's nook caught Jenny's eye.

"Think about this, Jenny. A step like this cannot be untaken, and you've never even visited Paris. You might hate it. Joseph says the stench on rainy days is horrendous." Louisa treated Jenny to a fierce hug, kissed her cheek, and took her leave.

While Jenny ran her hand over a purple scarf of very soft wool with a subtle tartan print woven into it. She lifted it off its hook and brought it to her nose.

"Elijah."

"I have a dozen grandchildren, counting various stepgrandchildren and works in progress. If you want subjects for juvenile portraits, we've a full supply. More brandy?"

Elijah passed his host an empty glass. "My thanks, Your Grace. Perhaps we could focus first on the painting for Her Grace that you mentioned in your note?"

In his summons, more accurately. The epistle had been three sentences long, and every word had savored of imperatives.

His Grace handed Elijah back a half-full glass, topped up his own drink, and resumed a seat on a blue velvet sofa near the fire. The blue of the velvet brought out the blue of Moreland's eyes, something Lady Jenny had probably often noted.

"I still managed to look distinguished," His Grace said. He wasn't smiling, and the words bore no humorous inflection, and yet Elijah had the sense the man was poking fun at himself. "I'd like to memorialize myself for Her Grace before old age transmogrifies dignity into stubbornness and ducal consequence into pomposity."

A towering need to search the premises for Genevieve Windham receded—but did not disappear—as Elijah considered his host's words. A portraitist often became a repository for confidences, a consequence of time spent in close proximity to people who could not camouflage their thoughts and emotions with activity.

"This is not a public portrait, then?" And how did one convey on canvas the essence of a man who could use the word transmogrify convincingly?

His Grace considered his drink. "This is a gift for my duchess, not a statement of Moreland power and influence. The woman I love deserves such a token, but it's one I've neglected over the years. To sit for a portrait has always seemed… arrogant, to me. Her Grace would have it otherwise, and so you see before you a willing subject, as it were."

To Elijah, His Grace's casual use of the word "love"

was more impressive than all the polysyllabic blather Moreland had at his command. "My recent work at Sidling notwithstanding, I do not make a credible holiday guest under your roof, Your Grace. Her Grace will have to know the portrait is being done."

"Young man, do you think I'm going to sit still for hours with only your company to occupy me? Of course Her Grace will know. She will supervise the entire undertaking, making sure I behave myself adequately to see the painting completed. You will consult her on every detail of the composition, and thwart her wishes at your mortal peril."

This was beyond an imperative; this was Moreland Holy Writ, perhaps Windham family Holy Writ as well.

"Of course, Your Grace, though to finish the portrait between now and the first of the year will be difficult. I haven't yet completed Sindal's commission, and I'm sure you'll have holiday duties that interfere with your sittings."

"You are a bachelor, so allowances must be made." His Grace rose, took up the poker, and jabbed at the fire. Elijah studied the duke's movement, the way he hunkered before the hearth, the confidence with which he wielded a substantial length of wrought iron.

His Grace was not merely spry, as that adjective was applied to old men who yet managed to dodder around unaided. The duke was limber, lithe, and strong, full of energy and… determination.

"When you wed," Moreland said as he replaced the poker in its stand, "you will understand that he who fails to make proper gifts at the proper time where his lady is concerned risks disappointing that lady, and living with the shame of his failure well beyond the end of the occasion. Do you know why I maintain a conservatory here, Bernward?"

"To protect delicate plants over the winter and conserve them for the next year's spring."

"To give my duchess flowers when she's in need of them. You're here for the same purpose, to give my duchess a portrait when she's in need of one."

No, Elijah was at Morelands because he could not get out of his mind that sketch Genevieve had done of him when he'd been trying to write to his sister. The rendering had been accurate, but it had been another image of a lonely man—also a man bewildered by a simple bit of correspondence to a younger sibling.

And in some dim corner of his brain, Elijah perceived that the answer to his loneliness lay in Genevieve Windham's hands—or at least the temporary relief of it.

"I'll need some help if I'm to be done before Christmas, Your Grace. Perhaps Lady Jenny might again assist me?" He took the last sip of his drink in hopes that request might come across as casual.

"What says you have to be done before Christmas?"

Lady Jenny's travel plans said it plainly enough. "The Academy announces its new members along with the honors list, Your Grace. I'd like to be back in London to congratulate the new Academicians."

And he did not want to be here when Jenny went on her wrongheaded, misguided, unnecessary pilgrimage to Paris. For it was a pilgrimage, though Elijah had yet to determine what transgression on Jenny's part necessitated such a penance.

"You will not disappoint my duchess, Bernward. The portrait will be done in time for our open house on Christmas Eve."

"As you wish, Your Grace."

"Then be off with you. Any footman can see you to your quarters. Jenny's about somewhere, unless her sisters have impressed her into doting on their offspring again. Ask the footmen. Put off dwelling at the family seat as long as you can, Bernward. One loses track of one's family in these old mausoleums."

Bernward. The title didn't feel as awkward coming from Moreland as it might from many others. "Thank you, Your Grace. Am I to join the family at meals?"

One could wait above stairs in evening attire for a summons that never came, or one could plainly ask.

"For God's sake, of course you will dine with us. Her Grace would never forgive me if I suffered Charlotte Beauvais Harrison's darling boy to shiver away his meals in a garret. And you have some correspondence."

The duke stalked over to the mantel and swiped up no less than three letters, which he shoved at Elijah. "Your womenfolk are after you, and spying on my house, no doubt. Never underestimate the espionage of females, Bernward. You will tell your sisters Morelands is gracious, snug, and majestic—regardless of drafty corridors, tipsy maids, or footmen who linger near the mistletoe."

The tone was gruff; the wink was charming. Elijah took the letters, feeling as if the Earl of Bernward had just been welcomed into some benevolent protective society of males who must endure the holidays without cursing before the womenfolk.

"My thanks, Your Grace."

Elijah took his leave, and had spotted no less than eight fat sprigs of mistletoe before he paused to wonder how his family had known he'd be at Morelands, when four days past Elijah himself had been convinced his next destination was Northumbria.

Twelve

"So tell me, my lady, do you like it?"

Jenny looked up to see Elijah Harrison standing in the doorway of her newly christened studio. Had she not been studying his parting gift to her, she would no doubt have sensed his presence.

"You came back." She could not help but smile as she spoke.

"One does not refuse a ducal commission. It's said Moreland has influence in every corner of government, and his duchess in every corner of Society. Then, too, as the duke himself informed me, any number of juvenile subjects are expected here over the holidays, and I'm intrigued by that potential."

These words constituted a credible, if *wrong* answer. The heat and tenderness in Elijah's gaze as he prowled across the room gave Jenny far more cause for rejoicing. "You've closed the door, Mr. Harrison."

"Elijah to you, though it seems I'm becoming Bernward to the rest of the world." He stood very close to her, so close she could catch his sweet lavender scent. "Happy Christmas, my lady. Did you like the sketch?"

He did not kiss her, and the frustration of that was profound.

"I cannot show this sketch to anybody, Mr. Harrison. No one but my lady's maid has seen my hair down for years."

His eyebrows spoke volumes: *he'd* seen her hair down, her body naked, her face suffused with arousal. Thank God he'd sketched her in the grip of other emotions: pensiveness, a hint of humor, and something else she couldn't name.

"You've caught a resemblance between me and His Grace. I can't say I've noticed that before, but the likeness is genuine."

"You have much of your father in you. Will you lend me your studio?"

He moved off, and Jenny wanted to grab him by the hand and drag him down to the carpet, there to renew his acquaintance with her unbound hair until spring.

"Who is to sit to you? I'm fond of my nieces and nephews. I assume you'll allow me to assist again?"

He paced to the windows, which looked out over the stables and paddocks, toward Kesmore's estate and Eve's little manor at Lavender Corner. "My sitter is more fractious than any juvenile subject. His Grace has taken a notion to present his duchess with a portrait for the Christmas Eve open house. The light here is good."

"I'm having a parlor stove brought up too. Her Grace will love a portrait of Himself." *Why haven't you kissed me? Do you carry the lock of hair I gave you?*

He turned and propped his backside against the

windowsill, a pose Jenny's brothers often adopted. "We never had a chance to paint together at Sidling, Genevieve. Would you enjoy that?"

Zhenevieve. "Yes. And you will critique my work." Not better than kissing, but some consolation.

"And you will critique mine. I'll have my equipment set up here." He sauntered toward the door, and while that view was agreeable, his departure without even touching her was maddening.

"Elijah?"

He half turned, a listening pose as opposed to one that focused on her visually. "My lady?"

"I'm glad you're back. Very glad." So glad, her chest had developed a peculiar ache, and her hands had balled into fists.

"I'm glad too, Genevieve."

He sauntered back to her, kissed her cheek, and left.

Elijah tried to read the letters sent by his remaining sisters—they'd shared paper, the better to economize—and he'd barely comprehended anything except that they missed him and hoped to see him at Christmas.

Perhaps they would, if the Academy had given him the nod by then.

And perhaps they wouldn't.

"I should not have kissed her," Elijah informed a cat that looked very like the one he'd seen at Kesmore's and Sindal's. This beast also occupied Elijah's bed, a green-eyed feline stare tracking Elijah as he unpacked his clothes and hung them in the wardrobe. Against the green, gold, and cream appointments of the room, a black-and-white cat commanded attention.

"I could not help but kiss her. When she saw me, she just stood there, a serene smile on her face, and me, not knowing—"

Not knowing if he'd made a small mistake by coming here, or a huge mistake.

"I am here to fulfill a ducal commission."

The cat lifted a paw and commenced to tongue-wash between its claws.

"I am here because I could not hang about London, waiting for word from the nominating committee. The other fellows would stop by, the Christmas invitations would come. I wouldn't get any work done." Though he was caught up on his commissions, all except for the portrait of Sindal's boys.

The cat rose to sitting and turned its back on Elijah, then tended to its ears with particular assiduousness.

"I am here because it's someplace my family will not casually drop by and leave hints the size of elephants that this year, I ought to join the revelry at Flint Hall."

Though they'd stooped to letters, which was beyond hinting. The cat glanced over its shoulder at Elijah then started licking its own belly.

"I am here because Moreland's holiday hospitality is legendary. The regent himself recommends Her Grace's recipe for punch."

At this, the cat started licking its privy parts. Elijah sat on the bed and put the damned beast on the floor. "Dignity, cat. At the very least set me an example of dignity."

The cat leapt onto the bed, appropriated Elijah's

lap, and once settled in, began purring without any dignity whatsoever.

"Right. I am here because I want to spend whatever time I can around Genevieve Windham, even if it's only a few weeks amid paint fumes and under her parents' watchful eyes. I am here to share with her whatever support and insight I might render regarding her art before she leaves for damned France. I am here"—he brushed his nose along the top of the cat's head—"because I could not resist the opportunity to see her, to kiss her, even once more."

The cat appeared to consider this, then bopped Elijah's chin.

"I am here because I am a fool."

A knock on the door cut short these pathetic confessions. Elijah set the cat aside and opened his door to behold a mature version of Genevieve Windham.

"Your Grace." He bowed to the duchess then stepped back, hoping he'd put his stockings and under-linen out of sight.

"Bernward, welcome. I am remiss for not being here when you arrived, but I needed a recipe from my daughter at Sidling." She came into the room, a woman whose very posture could teach lionesses about dignity and presence. "Your mother and I made our bows together, you know."

Though she offered him a smile that likely dazzled men half her age, she was warning him of something. His Grace's words about the womenfolk and their espionage came back to him.

"Mother has mentioned this, as did His Grace. I enjoyed a drink with His Grace upon my arrival."

"Timothy is welcoming you too, I see. Jenny's cat is as particular as most of his breed. I hope you aren't given to sneezing around cats?"

"He's a friendly sort, and I like cats, generally."

"Gracious, Bernward. You aren't seeing to your own clothing, I hope?" She considered the open wardrobe and his traveling bag, where—thank ye gods—no stockings or linen were in evidence.

"My things are damp from the weather, Your Grace, and the sooner they're hung up, the less objectionable my attire will be at dinner."

Her inspection landed on him. "You have your mother's pragmatism, though I'll send along a footman posthaste. Tell me, Bernward, do you paint quickly?"

This was the woman for whom Elijah would be rendering a portrait of the duke, and so her interest in his art made some sense. And yet… the cat had stopped purring.

"Fairly quickly. Mostly, I'm disciplined. I spend hours in the studio, as any laborer spends at his work. His Grace says the portrait must be completed for your Christmas Eve open house."

She peered into the water pitcher on his nightstand, putting Elijah in mind of Lady Jenny doing the same thing when he'd spent a night at Kesmore's.

"Can you do two portraits between now and Christmas Eve?" While her tone was merely curious, the hairs on the back of Elijah's neck prickled.

"I… can, if my sitters cooperate and I'm left undisturbed for most of each day." That she might be requesting a portrait of Genevieve made his blood churn and ideas racket about in his brain—Genevieve in green or blue? With her cat? Sketching? Genevieve merry or pensive? Genevieve looking regal or slightly mussed? A portrait of Genevieve absorbed in her art?

"I assure you, Bernward, you will have full cooperation, for you see it's my portrait I'd like you to paint."

The disappointment this news engendered was hard to keep off his face. "It will be my pleasure and my privilege, Your Grace. Will this portrait be a surprise to His Grace?"

Her smile was mischievous, a smile he'd seen Jenny wear under circumstances her mother would not approve of. "If possible. Can you manage that?"

"I can, as long as it's understood nobody sees what I'm working on until it's complete—nobody except Lady Jenny."

Fine blond brows drew down. "Sophie said you would never have gotten such a wonderful rendering of her boys without Jenny's assistance."

The espionage of females, His Grace had called it. "Lady Sindal misstates the case, Your Grace. I would never have gotten *any* rendering of those children without their aunt's patient and clever intervention."

The duchess's smile turned maternal. "Jenny is very good with children. Her siblings, nieces, and nephews adore her."

Genevieve was equally good with a sketchbook, though Elijah doubted her mother would smile if he said as much. He tried anyway. "Her assistance was also artistic, Your Grace, having to do with both composition and execution of the portrait. Your daughter has a great deal of artistic talent. I've asked

His Grace's leave to call on Lady Jenny's assistance while I'm here."

While he watched, the duchess crossed to the wardrobe and withdrew a sachet bound in cream muslin with a green ribbon. She held it up to her nose—neither the lady nor her nose would qualify as dainty—and sniffed. "These need to be replaced. We've a large gathering descending in a few days, all of it family, Bernward. Your late addition to the party means the staff might not have been as attentive to your accommodations, for which I apologize. Please don't hesitate to ask for anything at all that will make your stay with us more enjoyable."

"My thanks, Your Grace. The duke made it clear I am to consult you regarding all aspects of his portrait. When would you like to begin on our project?"

She left off running her finger down the mantel above his fireplace. "Tomorrow morning. You will meet with me first, and then we'll summon His Grace and make haste before the rest of the family arrives at week's end, if that suits?"

She was as accomplished at issuing orders as her husband was. "That will suit perfectly." Particularly if he was to complete two portraits in less time than many would need for one.

"I'll wish you good day, then, Bernward. If you've any correspondence to send, you can leave it on the desk in the library. We do not dress for dinner except on Christmas Day and Sundays, and of course for the open house. You will attend services with us, weather permitting."

"Of course, Your Grace." He bowed to her in

parting, feeling as if a military fanfare should have started up as she swept from the room.

She was a gracious hostess and a woman intent on securing a holiday gift for her husband, but that she was more worried about the sage hanging near his clothes or the dust on the mantel than about a compliment to her daughter's talent made Elijah want to… pitch his stockings at her.

Elijah Harrison was a demon, a slave-driving fiend.

"You have once again neglected the shadows, Genevieve. Here"—he gestured to the folds of the curtains in her sketch—"and here. Whether they are crisp folds or soft, whether they hang exactly straight or a trifle rumpled, it all makes a difference to the image you convey."

She was going to clobber him with her sketchbook then dance a gavotte on his elegant, talented fingers while wearing her riding boots.

"This is a *sketch*, Mr. Harrison. This is not the finished portrait of my mother. Your shadows are no better defined than my own."

Dark eyebrows rose up, and he stepped away from the table where their day's work was displayed side by side. "What do you mean?"

She pointed to the hearth beside Her Grace's seat in his drawing. "That is a gesture, not a rendering. The light sources in any painting are of a paramount importance, and you've barely hinted at the dimensions of the fireplace."

His hands went to his hips, and he seemed to grow

not just taller, but larger. "I *know* that, Genevieve, but having painted several hundred portraits, I also *know* that wasting my time in pencil on an object that can be rendered accurately only with paint is dithering."

She closed the space between them. "And your carping on my perishing, damned shadows is the same!"

That felt good. The consternation in his eyes when she used foul language felt very good indeed, almost as good as kissing him.

"We're tired," he said, his gaze on their sketches. "All of this will be here in the morning. We can shout at each other further then. Better still we'll get out the paints and inspire you to more cursing. Please promise me, however, that you won't curse in front of your parents."

As if she could.

She *was* tired, tired from spending most of the day in this room with Elijah Harrison, being close enough to catch his lavender scent, to see the way he studied his sketch as if composing a sermon for its betterment, to watch how his beautiful lips firmed when he was concentrating most closely on his work.

Jenny was also tired from trying to see her parents not as the people she'd known and loved since birth, but as subjects for portraits.

Mostly, she was tired of exercising the discipline necessary to not touch him.

"I don't want to shout at you, Elijah." She wanted to put her arms around him and feel his arms around her. With him in his shirtsleeves and waistcoat, his cuffs turned back to reveal his wrists and forearms, she wanted very much to touch him.

He moved the sketches aside and used the table as a bench, scooting back to sit on it. "The French shout, Genevieve. They are a pugnacious, articulate people, and not without prejudices where women are concerned, for all their talk to the contrary."

She took the place beside him. "You are telling me Paris will not be a bed of roses. I know that. Are you hungry?"

Clearly, the question surprised him. "I am. It's late, though. Shall I escort you to your room?"

This was not an offer to accompany her to bed. This was Elijah being proper, and Jenny nearly hated him for it.

"Come with me." She hopped off the table and grabbed him by the wrist. "Papa is always testy when he's peckish, and I'm no different."

She didn't turn loose of his wrist, but towed him along through the darkened house. The cloved oranges lent the corridors a holiday fragrance, while mistletoe dangled from the rafters.

"Is there a reason you're not having a late-night tea tray sent up to your room?" Elijah asked.

"The staff is exhausted from the preparations for all the arrivals tomorrow. The larder is full to bursting though, and nobody will miss what we help ourselves to now."

The kitchen was in a lower corner of the house, where access to water was assured by an ancient well in the cellars, and where the pantries and gardens were close by.

"I have always liked kitchens," Elijah said as they gained the darkened main kitchen. "They are warm in winter, and they say a lot about a family."

"I should have pried you loose from that studio earlier." Jenny dropped his wrist and took a candle into the cook's pantry. She appropriated butter, bread, an apple, and a wedge of cheese.

"You can slice us some ham," she said when she emerged with her platter. "I'm going to make chocolate."

She expected an argument, because for the past three days, they'd mostly argued. Twice she'd caught Elijah regarding her with an expression she could not fathom, but both times, he'd dropped right back into his art.

His damnable, excellent art.

"Who were today's letters from?" She fetched the pitcher of milk from the window box and stirred up the coals in the hearth.

"My two middle brothers. There's an epistolary siege underway. Is this enough ham?"

"You could eat twice that amount yourself. What is the objective of the siege?"

The knife came down on the cutting board loud enough to make a "thwack!" in the shadowed kitchen. "My pride is being besieged. I made a vow I would not return to Flint Hall until I'd gained entry into the Royal Academy. My dear siblings"—Thwack!—"would have me violate that oath."

Jenny snitched a bite of ham. "So would I."

"Watch your fingers, Genevieve. What do you mean?"

She held up a bite of cheese, wanting him to nibble it from those fingers. He instead took it from her and held it, his posture expectant.

"How old were you when you made your infernal vow?"

He popped the cheese in his mouth and chewed slowly. "I'd gone up to university. I wasn't a child."

She moved away, to the hearth, where the pan of milk was beginning to steam over the coals. "The chocolate is in that tin on the counter and the grater is right beside it."

Elijah had made hot chocolate before, apparently. He ground off an appropriate portion of chocolate and sprinkled it into the heated milk while Jenny stirred briskly. Next came a dash of salt, some spices, and a bit of sugar.

"I've never had it with cinnamon before," Elijah said, setting two mugs on the table near the fire. "Why do you think I should go home this Christmas, Genevieve?"

She followed with the tray, thinking this was a meal designed to nourish more than the belly.

"You know what folly I got up to at an age when most boys go off to university. I wanted to marry Denby."

He took the tray from her, pausing for a moment so they were both holding it. "You wanted to *marry* him?" His tone suggested that a desire to contract the plague and pass it along to the regent would have been easier to fathom.

"I was sixteen, Elijah. I was even younger when I sent my brother Bartholomew off to war."

He gestured with the tray. "Sit and explain yourself before the chocolate gets cold. You did not send your brother off to war."

She sat at the head of the table, so they would

be neither beside each other nor directly across. "I love the scent of cinnamon. Bart liked it in his chocolate too."

"He would be your late older brother?"

Late—a euphemism for dead, but not much of a euphemism. "*One* of my late older brothers."

Elijah slathered butter on a piece of bread, added ham and cheese, and passed it to her. "And you *sent* him off to war?"

She studied the food, studied her mug, and took a fortifying whiff of cinnamon and nutmeg. Elijah ought to go home; she knew this as clearly as she knew her destiny lay in Paris.

"Adolescents are prone to righteousness. Bart made the mistake of teasing me about my drawing once too often, and I—I suspect my female humors were in part to blame—I came at him with guns blazing."

"You could not aim a gun at a living creature to save yourself." He made himself a sandwich twice the thickness of Jenny's.

"I have a temper."

He munched a bite of sandwich. "You are passionate where your art is concerned."

Only her art? Jenny's hands tightened around her mug, because the idiot man was humoring her. "I appropriated my mother's tactics. His Grace rants and blusters when he's in a temper, but his words are not intended as weapons. Her Grace's artillery is much quieter. She sniffs, she frowns, she mentions, she lets a quiet question hang in the air, and one is devastated."

Elijah took up a knife and the apple. "What did you mention to your brother?"

Jenny set her mug aside, the scent of spices no longer appealing. "I *mentioned* that I was ashamed of him. He'd finished his studies and was idling about, getting his younger brothers into trouble, making Mama worry, and starting up horrible rows with His Grace. He drank excessively, at least by my juvenile standards, and he terrorized the maids."

"If you knew that and you were his lady sister and little more than a child, then he should have been ashamed. Have a bite of apple."

Elijah held out his hand with four eighths of an apple in his palm. She took two.

"You aren't going to tell me young men are full of high spirits? That a young man needs to learn to hold his drink? That a ducal heir should have lived long enough to outgrow those high spirits? To produce the next heir?"

Elijah crunched off a bite of apple, the sound healthy and… reassuring. "If he'd finished his education, Genevieve, Lord Bart had had three years in that expensive conservatory of spoiled young manhood known as Oxford. He'd had years to lark about, chase the tavern wenches, learn to hold his liquor, and acquire the knack of living within an allowance. By the end of my first year there, I was serving as banker to the older boys, and had taught one of the chambermaids the rudiments of reading."

The notion that not all heirs to titles had a misspent youth was novel. "Why?"

He passed her sandwich to her. "Because I am the oldest of twelve. I could not do otherwise. The cost of educating six boys and launching six girls is substantial, even for a man as wealthy as my father. I could not countenance squandering my education or setting an example that would allow any of my brothers to squander theirs. Eat your sandwich."

She took a bite and chewed, finding both the food and the conversation fortifying. "Bart was not the oldest, not really."

"He was the heir to a much-respected dukedom, which is responsibility enough. He was also likely at or near his majority by the time you took him to task, and I say it was high time somebody did."

The sandwich was good, much better than cheese, bread, butter, and ham had a right to be. "He and Papa reconciled. Papa bought commissions for Bart and Devlin, though it made Mama cry."

He passed her two more apple quarters, though she hadn't touched the first two. "Mothers cry. I suspect fathers do too, but not when anybody's looking."

"That's why you should go home."

He paused while stacking together the ingredients for a second sandwich. "I assure you, the Marquess of Flint is not crying over my absence. We're quite cordial. I meet him for dinner at his club at least once a quarter unless I'm traveling. I take tea with my mother. I entertain my younger brothers when they're in Town."

Idiot. Buffoon. Imbecile. Jenny posed her question sweetly. "And your younger sisters?"

He sat back. "You wield your mother's weapons quite skillfully."

"How long, Elijah?"

"I haven't seen the twins since… for quite a while."

"And they miss you, and when you persist in

this foolishness, they will miss you yet more and think they've done something to make it easy for you to stay away. If you're thrown from your horse tomorrow, Elijah, if you should sicken from bad fish and die, what are they to make of the example you set for them?"

He took a bite of his second sandwich and chewed slowly while Genevieve took a swallow of chocolate.

"I've written to them."

She snorted and bit into an apple quarter rather than cry. When Elijah patted her knuckles, she nearly jumped in surprise.

"We'll start painting tomorrow afternoon."

Jenny rose and took her mug to the sink. By the time she came back to the table, she'd decided to allow the change in topic. "*You* will start painting. I will greet my siblings and their various spouses and offspring. Her Grace has made it plain that my presence will not be excused merely so I can look over your shoulder while you paint."

"Then I'll work on finishing up Sindal's commission, and your parents' portraits can wait their turns. Sometimes a project turns out better when I'm given a day or so to think about it."

"You are doing this so you don't get ahead of me. I expect you to be much faster than I am, Elijah." He'd challenged Jenny to paint two portraits, one of each parent based on the same sittings he was using, and then they'd compare their efforts.

"I am not particularly fast, Genevieve, but I apply myself to my commissions in a disciplined fashion. Are you going to eat that cheese?"

She pushed the tray closer to him, realizing he had to have been famished before they'd come down here—and she was still famished.

"Why haven't you kissed me, Elijah?"

He paused with a slice of ham and a slice of cheese rolled together in his fingers. "I kissed you the day I arrived here."

"Hah. My brothers kiss their horses with more mischief than you allowed in that kiss."

"Your brothers, all three of whom are reputed to be dead shots, dead shots who will arrive tomorrow. Then there's Kesmore, whose aim is legendary, while Sindal looks like he might enjoy breaking my knuckles for his casual entertainment."

She plucked the food from his grasp and took a bite, then handed it back. "Your point?"

He set it down uneaten and rose, his chair scraping back loudly in the otherwise quiet kitchen.

"Genevieve, we are under your parents' roof. You are *going to Paris*, need I remind you, and while I understand a lady might need to lay a ghost or a regret to rest, kissing can lead to… to folly. To the type of folly that will remove Paris from your future, if it hasn't already."

He looked exasperated and… dear.

Jenny took a considering bite of her apple and wondered what it meant that she tempted him to folly—with mere kisses, she tempted him to folly. She took another bite of apple and realized that lurking at the edges of his rejection was a lovely consolation that had to do with chivalry and respect.

"So I'm to content myself by painting with you instead?"

"You want to go to Paris. Painting with me seems a good use of your time while you're making arrangements for your travel."

His words reminded her that she still hadn't read the packet schedules, or started filling those trunks. "Come sit."

He obliged, but he would not look at her. Instead, he interrogated the last bites of ham. "When will you know?"

He would not write letters of introduction for her, but he'd provide her as much artistic instruction as he could before her departure. Jenny was trying to decide whether to be pleased or disappointed when his question registered.

"When will I know what?"

He looked around, as if her brothers and brothers-in-law might have been hiding in the kitchen's deep shadows. "Know if you are *with child*."

For an instant, she thought she'd heard hope in his voice, but then common sense asserted itself. Hope and anxiety were close relations—she'd heard nothing more romantic than an unmarried, honorable man's worry.

The next instant was spent grieving that she did not carry his child and would not ever have with him the domestic riches the rest of her family enjoyed in such abundance.

In the very next instant after that, she vowed it was time and past she made those travel arrangements he'd alluded to.

"I'm sorry, Elijah. I should have told you when I laid eyes on you several days ago. You have no need to worry about impending fatherhood. Finish the ham."

His expression gave away nothing. Not relief, not disappointment, not irritation. Nothing.

"Was this why you came back to Kent, Elijah? Because you were concerned about a child and you did not trust me?"

His lips quirked up. "I trust you, Genevieve. I came out to Kent to accept a ducal commission, and now it has turned into a double commission with the possibility of an entire gallery of juvenile portraits to follow. I do not regret my decision, but it's late. Let me escort you to your room."

She wanted to argue, but he hadn't given her anything to argue about. Her entire family would descend tomorrow, and even the thought of their noise and activity was wearying.

Elijah took the tray to the counter. Jenny rinsed out his mug and let him hold the candle as they walked through the house.

"You don't need to see me to my room, Elijah. I've been sleeping in the same place for nearly a decade, and I know where it is."

He said nothing, but rather, winged his arm at her. Jenny wanted to slap him on the elbow. She wrapped her hand around his sleeve instead and let him lead her through the chilly house.

"You'll miss your room when you're in Paris." His tone was regretful rather than taunting, and he was right. She would miss her room.

Even her room.

"I expect Timothy will have abandoned me again tonight," Jenny said. She'd miss Timothy too.

"He does keep one's feet warm. This is your room?"

She dropped his arm. "My very own. Good night, then. You're going back to the studio?"

"Perhaps. Sleep well, my lady."

"You too."

When she should have turned and slipped into her room, Jenny instead indulged in a spot of folly—necessary folly. She wrapped her arms around Elijah's waist and held on. For a moment, he held still. Then, he set the candle down on the side table and returned her embrace.

He gave her no words, but he did hold her until she stepped back, kissed him on the mouth, and withdrew into her room. She stood on her side of the closed door, listening to his footsteps fade, not in the direction of his room but back toward the studio.

And, of course, there was no sign of Timothy anywhere in Jenny's room.

"Elijah Harrison is the only person who takes my art as seriously as I do," she announced to the room she would miss.

Jenny lay awake for some time, wondering why she wished it were not so, and trying to get her feet warm.

Thirteen

Genevieve Windham was an unscrupulous, lovely, audacious fiend who also happened to be a genius with paint. Elijah leaned closer to her and tried not to inhale jasmine and folly through his nose.

He gestured at her canvas, toward the beginnings of a fire in the hearth. "How did you do this?"

"You put yours closer to the corner of the canvas, where it won't be structural," Jenny said. "I wanted mine to anchor the illumination in Her Grace's expression as she listens to her husband's voice."

"Your father reads Shakespeare very well."

She stepped back from the paintings just as Elijah's hand—without any communication with his common sense—came up as if to touch her hair.

"I'm sure Papa has Her Grace's favorite sonnets memorized by now, just as I'm sure Her Grace will send a footman up any moment to fetch me. The hordes will start arriving ere long."

"Then let her send a footman, Genevieve. Let her be the one to think, 'Jenny certainly is intent on her painting.'"

She studied the beginning of her portrait, which was like no work Elijah had ever begun. Her use of color vaulted over the rules—rules for the oil medium she'd likely never been taught—to achieve results that stunned, intrigued, and pleased.

"If Her Grace were going to get the message that I'm intent on my painting—if anybody in this family yet living were—they might have gotten it when I was sixteen. I've managed to knot my smock..."

She turned around, presenting Elijah with temptation in the form of her exposed nape. He knew how that skin tasted, knew the warmth and sweetness of it against his tongue.

He stepped closer. "Are you doing this on purpose, Genevieve?"

She sent him a cross look over her shoulder. "Yes. I typically knot up all my smocks so I'm held prisoner in them until a passing stranger rescues me."

She *had* made a knot, probably because she'd been too proud to ask him to tie her a simple bow. He had to bend down to study it. "Hold still." The thing was stubborn, so stubborn that when Elijah gave it a stout yank, Jenny stumbled back against him.

"Oh, damn." He used his nose first, drew it along the top of her collar where warmth and fragrance threatened to annihilate his balance. "Your painting is a wonder."

So was her hair, so soft against his cheek. So was the place beneath her ear, where a man was doomed to kiss her. So was—

A tap sounded on the door. Had it been the deferential scratching of a servant, Elijah might have missed it, but it was a stout tap, more of a loud knock.

"It's stuck," he said, stepping back. "Perhaps it will have to be cut off."

Cut off, indeed.

She gave him a curious look and went to the door. The squealing when she opened it was deafening.

"Maggie! Oh, my dearest, dearest Mags! I'll get paint all over you. I'm so glad to *see* you!"

And at the same time: "Jenny! Oh, you're painting. Of course you are. Hang the paint and tell me everything. Let me *see* you. Oh, I've missed you so!"

Elijah had been forgotten, relegated to such insignificance he might as well have never existed, and yet he listened to Jenny and her oldest sister greeting each other and felt the sweetness of it like a punch to the chest.

His sisters carried on in exactly the same way, every time they ran into him. The twins would likely squeal him halfway to Surrey.

Jenny gestured awkwardly behind her back with one hand. "Help me with this stupid knot, and you must greet Lord Bernward."

Elijah pulled his thoughts away from the notion that an artist need not have good hearing, and smiled at Jenny's sister. Maggie Windham, now Maggie, Countess of Hazelton, was taller than Jenny, red-haired, and lushly curved. Her beauty was more grand and severe than Jenny's, and Elijah would have bet his Associate Academician status that Jenny could do a phenomenal portrait of her.

"Your ladyship, good day." He did not pick her hand up because his fingers sported splatters of brown and white paint.

"Lord Bernwood." Her smile was cool, her green eyes full of mischief. "Good day. You will wish Jenny a Happy Christmas now, because I must have her all to myself for the duration. We have much, *much* to catch up on. Jenny, get out of that old winding sheet and come along. St. Just got a later start from Town than we did, but I'm sure he's right behind us."

The espionage of women had started up already.

"Turn around, Genevieve." Elijah saw the countess's eyebrows rise at his tone, but Jenny—biddable, sweet Jenny, now that her family was in evidence—turned around and swept tendrils of golden hair off her neck. The pose was incendiary, it had such erotic overtones.

Elijah picked up a penknife and sliced through her knot. "You're free. Enjoy visiting with your sister."

Jenny shot a fleeting glance at her just-begun portrait, a glance of such longing Elijah nearly wished the countess Happy Christmas before pitching her into the corridor on her pretty bum.

"I'll tidy up here, my ladies. Lady Hazelton, a pleasure."

The women linked arms as Elijah closed the door behind them, the countess's head bent close to Jenny's. "Jenny, what on earth has gotten into Their Graces? I've never seen so much mistletoe in my life!"

While Elijah could no longer see the mistletoe, because his vision was consumed with Jenny Windham. The New Year could not arrive soon enough, but as Elijah studied Jenny's painting, his unease on her behalf grew.

The French took their art seriously, and Jenny's unconventional approach might draw their fire. Bad enough she was a woman, and worse yet she was a talented woman. If some of the established portraitists perceived that she was a *brilliant*, talented woman, the result could well be savage. Was that what she sought in France? Persecution rather than freedom?

Jenny's cat, who had taken to following Elijah about in the secret way of cats, stropped itself against his shins. "She's not taking you either, old boy. Best find some other lady to dote on you."

Another rap on the door interrupted Elijah's study of Jenny's handling of fire.

A tall, dark-haired, green-eyed man stood there, looking fierce and disgruntled. "You're not Jenny." He had the same angle to his chin as Jenny, and eyes that had seen the world at less than its best.

"You must be her brother. Elijah, Earl of Bernward, at your service."

"Rosecroft. It being Christmas, you address me as St. Just or suffer dire consequences." The man's bow was the merest gesture. "Where is my little sister?"

A small, dark-haired girl came galloping down the corridor. Timothy shot through Elijah's feet and made it to the mantel in a single determined bound. "Papa! Papa, Mama says to tell you she and Baby Belle are with the aunties in the library. The aunties want to kiss you hello. They already kissed me on *both* cheeks, and so did Grandpapa and Grandmama!"

The fierce expression became fiercer yet. "If you value your life or your sanity, Bernward, remain above stairs until dinner." St. Just's daughter led him away, a man facing inescapable doom—a man who also hadn't even glanced at the paintings.

Elijah had barely collected Jenny's brushes for cleaning when yet another rap sounded on the door. When Elijah glanced at the mantel, Timothy was nowhere in sight.

A liveried footman held out a silver tray. "The post, your lordship."

Elijah took the letters—three again—with a sense of foreboding that had nothing to do with the servant's use of his title. Three letters meant his siblings were doubling up, or the cousins and aunties had been recruited for the siege, which was a drastic tactic indeed. Pru in particular hated putting pen to paper, being more a man of action—or impulse, which amounted to the same thing at his age.

Elijah tidied up thoroughly, cleaned every brush and palette knife, stacked sketches neatly in several piles, and generally procrastinated as long as he could. The portrait for Sindal was coming along nicely. He considered starting on a session with it, decided that would be rank cowardice, and opened his letters instead.

By the time he'd finished reading the third one, he looked up to find Joseph Carrington, Earl of Kesmore, standing in the doorway, Timothy in his arms. "I thought I'd find you here."

"Are you going to kiss me? I have declared this space a kiss-free zone." The declaration was recent but well intended.

Kesmore sauntered into the room and paused to study the portraits. Elijah could hear the cat purring and tried not to feel betrayed. "No mistletoe here, God be thanked. Downstairs, it's a veritable gauntlet. His Grace must have appointed himself Lord of Misrule early this year. How goes the painting?"

Joseph Carrington was the closest thing Elijah had to a friend on the premises, so Elijah understood the question was not about painting per se.

"My family has taken a notion to bludgeon me into submission."

Kesmore settled into one of the rocking chairs, the cat curling up in his lap. "You have a deal of family. I gather from the various lamentations of my in-laws that sisters are the worst."

Sisters were bad enough. Brothers were bad enough.

Elijah brought a fragrant, single-page missive to his nose, set it aside, and took the second seat. "My mother has explained to me—ten years after it might have done some good—that I will never gain admittance to the Royal Academy."

"Mothers, even your mother, can be wrong. Her Grace's judgment was not infallible where Louisa was concerned, and His Grace knew not how to intervene between two such strong-willed and dear ladies."

"You are a good friend, Kesmore, but my mother's logic is unassailable. She not only turned down the suit of one Mortimer Fotheringale, she told him at the time he had not one-tenth of my father's artistic talent, no imagination, and no respect for what women could contribute to art. Mind you, my father was an amateur caricaturist only—though I gather Fotheringale was among his targets, and Papa must rely on his marchioness to match his coats and waistcoats. According to my mother, the only way I might meet with more enmity from Fotheringale is if I were her daughter rather than her son."

Kesmore scratched the beast's white chin. "Who

is this Fotheringale person? Shall I shoot him for you?"

Tempting thought, because Kesmore was only half jesting. "Dear Mortimer is the wealthiest member of the Academy's nominating committee, though Mother was right about his talent. He paints only academic subjects, takes forever to do them, and then gives them away, probably because nobody would pay money for them. The assassination offer is appreciated but hardly in keeping with the spirit of the holidays."

The door opened, and Sindal slipped through, closing it quickly behind him. "I thought it might be safe in here. It's Bedlam downstairs—children, dogs, His Grace producing sweets for the little ones at every turn, mistletoe everywhere. I've brought fortification."

He held up a bottle as if it were the price of admission to the studio.

"Come join us," Kesmore said. "Bernward here is not going to get into the Academy, and, of course, true love is to blame. He wants cheering up."

Sindal pulled up a hassock and uncorked the bottle. "What academy?"

Hazelton came next, though how such a big man moved without making a sound was a mystery. He too brought fortification and had dragooned a passing footman into supplying more of same at regular intervals, as well as quantities of sweet breads with butter.

The cat made the round of various laps; the bottles made the rounds. Stories of Christmases past came out, and Elijah even offered a few of his own—cricket in the portrait gallery, freezing his arse off with two of his brothers to see if the animals spoke at midnight on

Christmas Eve, hitting his granddame with a snowball by accident and having to visit her as penance thereafter.

"Bet she spoiled you rotten," Hazelton groused. "Old women know best how to spoil a little fellow. My son's nurse is eighty if she's a day."

Sindal took exception. "She is not. She just looks eighty so she'll be safe from you."

"I'll have you know…" Hazelton began, while Elijah's attention wandered to his brothers' letters. His mother's news was disturbing, because Fotheringale had no motivation for giving up his various grudges. Artistic insecurity had a prodigious memory, one that typically magnified slights and forgot praise.

Hazleton left off defending his manly honor, or his eyesight, or something. "Bernward's brooding. Pass him the bottle."

Kesmore passed Elijah the cat instead. Timothy's claws went to work directly on Elijah's thigh. "Come, young man. Tell us what afflicts you, and we'll ridicule you for it accordingly."

How inchoate inebriation had added years to Kesmore's standing, Elijah did not know. "My brothers miss me."

Looks were exchanged all around, and then the door opened. Jenny's brother, St. Just, slid through. "I've brought more refugees. The carnage on the battlefield is terrible. My own dear wife kissed the butler and was sizing up the senior footmen when I escaped."

St. Just opened the door widely enough that two more men could scurry in behind him. They both had what Elijah was coming to think of as Windham chins—a trait from the sire's line. They had green eyes, and those green eyes looked harried if not haunted.

Kesmore gestured with the bottle. "Bernward, some introductions: The mean-looking one is St. Just. Around his mama we call him Rosecroft. The prissy one is Lord Valentine, and the sniffy one is Westhaven. Cowards, the lot of them. Afraid of a few shrieking children, a bowl of wassail, and some holiday decorations."

"I don't see you down there," Westhaven said, taking a place on the raised hearth and looking, indeed, sniffy about it.

"I have *three* children, and I am married to *Louisa*," Kesmore said. His smile was fatuous. "And don't be fooled, Bernward. St. Just is a dear, Lord Valentine more stubborn than the other two put together, and Westhaven only looks sniffy when he's not beholding his countess. I say this with the authority of a man who loves them sincerely and is only a bit the worse for drink."

Lord Valentine took the place beside Kesmore; St. Just simply sat on the floor.

"Your brothers might miss you, Bernward," Sindal said, "but we've a few brothers to spare. In the spirit of holiday generosity, we'll lend them to you. You may have Westhaven here on indefinite loan, for starters."

By the time they'd gotten around to wondering how His Grace not merely endured but thrived on the holiday mayhem, Elijah had reached an insight that did not provide even as much comfort as the four-ton cat contentedly shredding his breeches.

His sisters missed him, and his mother was threatening essentially to cut him off if he remained "as stubborn as his father." She might make good on her threats, though Elijah could ambush her in Town and wear her down over the next few years. That prospect was daunting, much like facing the melee below stairs daunted these happy, tipsy men who were delighted to spend time with one another.

Elijah's brothers missed him too. He'd known that.

What he hadn't known was how badly he missed his family—the entire lot of them—and how difficult it was going to be to ever gain entrance to the Academy. The latter realization didn't disturb him nearly as much as it ought to, while the former disturbed him far more than it should have.

"Look at me."

Elijah muttered the words, as if the effort of speaking had been snatched from the orts and leavings of his ability to concentrate. He got like this when he painted—gruff, absorbed, and to Jenny, fascinating.

She looked directly at him. "I am not my mother."

He studied her for perhaps ten consecutive, silent seconds then went back to scowling at the image taking shape on his canvas. "You have the same shade of green in your eyes, you have the same—" His brush paused, and he fired another glance at her. "Almost the same shape of upper lip."

He would not have heard anything she said in reply, so Jenny resumed work on her own effort, which was His Grace's portrait. Without planning it, she and Elijah never worked on the same subject at the same time.

And thank goodness her brothers had appropriated

the studio yesterday afternoon, or Elijah would have been much further ahead.

"You are displeased about something. I can feel it." Elijah spoke without shifting his focus from his canvas.

"Not displeased. I'm glad you got nothing done yesterday. I like to watch you work."

He wrinkled his nose then added a touch of paint to Her Grace's shoulder. "You're daft."

"Look at me."

He obliged. He had a smear of white near his chin, his hair was sticking out in all directions, and his eyes were not the same blue as His Grace's, but Jenny studied them as if they might be.

"I know you spied on us yesterday," he said, touching his brush to his palette.

"I came in the same door as everybody else, Elijah. How can you call that spying?"

"Nobody noticed you. They were all too absorbed with Sindal's tale of winning the fair maid over a pile of dirty nappies."

They had been, the sentimental, kissable, happy lot of them. Jenny had eavesdropped in a quiet corner, wondering why Sophie—her own sister—had never shared so much of her courtship.

"I believe there was mistletoe involved, and my brothers claim to have had a hand in matters."

They fell silent. Fifteen minutes from now, Elijah might reply to her comment, or he might curse the fact that he'd run out of green paint, or he might decide he'd reached a place to pause in his own efforts and rip up at her morning's work.

Jenny had listened to Sindal's tale yesterday, then

listened to Joseph add his Christmas recollections, but she'd also used the time to study her brothers. Each man bore the stamp of His Grace's paternity, in the eyes, in the chin, and oddly enough, in the way their hands joined their wrists.

His Grace had beautiful wrists, and he'd passed that trait down to his progeny.

"Why are you staring at your wrists, Genevieve? The portrait won't paint itself."

"I have my father's wrists. I wonder if His Grace ever had artistic aspirations. I can't imagine he did." And why had she never noticed this?

"My father did—amateur aspirations, from what my mother has said, though his sense of color is abominable. I need to mix up more brown. Why must all wood be brown?"

Wood was not brown. It was red, blond, black, sable, and many other colors that only looked brown. Jenny did not correct Elijah. She'd realized, in the first hour they'd painted together, that she sometimes disagreed with him for the... *spark* of it.

Minor tiffs and spats formed some kind of verbal mistletoe, having to do with the way Elijah's eyebrows rose, his nostrils flared, and his chin turned an inch to the right.

"Have you ever seen your father's work, Elijah?"

He stepped back from his canvas and wiped his hands on a rag. "A few caricatures only. My mother has talent, though. What on earth are you doing with His Grace's boots?"

The duke had chosen to wear riding attire, which Jenny thought showed his excellent figure to good advantage and helped with the informal nature of the rendering.

"He wore his favorite pair," she said. "They are comfortable rather than impressive, so don't start in with your dratted lectures again."

To Elijah, a portrait was not a likeness, so much as a commentary on the subject—and a flattering commentary, at that. He propped his fists on his hips, sails clearly filling.

"Genevieve, do you *know* why the grand manner of portraiture found favor for more than half a century? Do you have any *idea* the problems that result when a sitter does not like your work? Can you *imagine* how limited your commissions will be if you—?"

He could go on like that for eternities. Jenny shut him up by the simple expedient of setting aside her palette and brush and kissing him.

His arms came around her, but then the dratted man lifted his head. "Somebody could come in, Genevieve."

At least he'd muttered that with his lips against her temple. "Nonsense. As much as this place was a madhouse yesterday, this morning it's quiet as a tomb." A tomb where the shades were much in need of headache powders.

Her logic must have appeased his overactive conscience—his worries were for her, she knew that—because he commenced kissing her back.

And oh, the pleasure of it. Elijah was never a frantic, pushy kisser, and yet in the very deliberation of his attentions there was passion.

"I wasn't going to *do* this," he informed her earlobe. "We were to have a footman in here, to—"

"Kiss me."

"Not to—"

He kissed her. He kissed her with a building heat and banked desperation, such that when Jenny realized she might be getting paint all over his shirt and waistcoat, she also realized it was already too late.

In so many ways, it was already too late.

She subsided against his chest. "We need to clean up. Luncheon will be served soon."

This was a pretext. Her Grace kept a buffet with varying selections available in the breakfast parlor from dawn until midafternoon. People would wander in and out as their appetites and overindulgences dictated.

"You're hungry. I'm sorry. I should have realized—" He glanced at the clock. "You would let me starve you, woman."

Elijah, when not painting, could also be gruff. Jenny particularly liked that about him. She slipped her arms from his waist, knowing he'd tolerated as much kissing as the moment would allow. "Your portrait is coming along very well."

He didn't take that bait, but instead studied *her*, rather than the color of her eyes.

"You looked lonely yesterday, sitting in your dark corner, eavesdropping on the men like a tired tavern wench."

"I will miss my brothers." Miss them with an ache of much greater proportions than she'd realized. Miss their wrists and chins, miss the way any two of them smiled together over some complaint made by the third. Miss the way each of them had known she was there, and none of them had given her away.

Elijah continued to study her. "Let's clean up, then. I wanted to ask you about something."

Jenny gathered up her brushes, hoping he meant to ask her about something artistic. He argued with her, he exhorted, he lectured, and he explained, but he seldom asked her opinion regarding anything artistic, and usually took issue with the ideas she did express.

She was unschooled, he said, and he wasn't wrong.

They set their canvases across the room from the fire. Jenny took off her smock; Elijah rolled down his cuffs. He tolerated her doing up his sleeve buttons, just as she held still while he wiped a dab of paint off her nose, and then allowed her to wipe off his chin.

These small intimacies were a consolation of sorts, though Jenny thought kissing would have consoled her rather more.

"What did you want to ask me?"

Before he answered, he turned a full circle, hands on hips, inspecting their work space. She saw his gaze light on a sketchbook lying near where the cat sat in sphinxlike repose on the mantel.

"When the regiment decamped yesterday to take their wives in hand, I spent some time in here getting organized, and I found yonder feline sitting on this." He passed her the sketchbook. "It has to be one of yours—the style is yours—but the subjects are unusual. I don't recall seeing it before."

Jenny opened the book and knew at one glance exactly what folly Timothy had led him to, the wretched beast. "These are just some old sketches. Are you hungry?"

"Those are not just some old sketches, Genevieve."

"They are juvenilia, Elijah, not even worth your criticism." Which would be considerable, she was sure. She folded the sketchbook against her chest, unwilling to watch him examine the contents. If he tore into these sketches the way he carped at and criticized everything else, she would cry.

"Come here, Genevieve."

She followed him over to the sofa and watched with foreboding as he tossed more fuel on the fire. Was he preparing for a long harangue? "If you want me to sit beside you on that sofa, Elijah, I might fall prey to an impulse to kiss you again."

"I delight in your impulses, Genevieve." He offered this with a crooked, pained smile, suggesting his delight was tempered with regret.

She took a place beside him on the sofa. "What did you want to discuss?"

"Give me that." He took the sketchbook from her and opened it on his lap. Timothy leaped onto the sofa and settled into a perfect, feline circle at Jenny's hip. "These sketches are brilliant."

Brilliant. Now, when he'd found a book Jenny never wanted to see again, he pronounced her work brilliant.

"I had no sense of the rules. I had no judgment about what was a suitable subject. I had no business sketching those children." Many of whom had likely perished.

"You're wrong. You're more wrong about that than about anything you've been wrong about since you first sketched me at Kesmore's."

Timothy began a rumbling purr against Jenny's body, as if Elijah's pronouncements were so much small talk, not arrows aimed at Jenny's conscience. "Can we put this book away, Elijah? I find I'm really quite peckish, and by now even my brothers ought to be stirring. They'll want me in the breakfast parlor to help with the little—"

He shut her up by virtue of his lips applied lingeringly to her cheek. "These are your best work. Tell me about them."

His buss to her cheek was the first kiss he'd initiated since his speech about babies and folly, which Jenny could probably have recited to him verbatim but for the lump in her throat.

"I sneaked out to the poorhouses when I was supposed to go shopping for the holidays. I went to the poorhouses in winter, when it was so cold I had to sketch with gloves on. The children had no gloves."

They'd had no gloves, no coats, no food, no coal, no health, no hope. Every time, her brother Victor had forbidden her to go, and every time, he'd waited right beside her, until she could bear the scent of death and despair no more.

Elijah's arm came around her shoulders. "What was a duke's daughter doing in the poorhouses?"

"I don't know. Trying to understand, I suppose, as adolescents must understand everything, as they must rebel against everything. Why do I have so much, why do others—equally valuable in the eyes of God, we're told—have nothing? Why do some children have only five years of life on earth, and every day of that five years is miserable with illness, starvation, and vermin? And I have loving family, health… everything, in abundance?"

He turned a page, to an image of a small child huddled near a puny, smoldering fire. Gender was not apparent, so huge were the eyes, so pronounced the facial bones, and shapeless the rags that passed for clothing. The child's expression was vacant to the point of death, death at least of the soul.

"As a gently bred young lady, you should not have seen these things."

"My brother Victor said the same thing. He said when I was older, perhaps, and in a position to take on charitable works. He always brought money for us to leave, but those places are corrupt."

Elijah turned the page again, the scene a cozy parlor, the fire blazing in the hearth, rugs thick on the floor, and heavy curtains over the windows. A portly fellow stood beside a desk, his attire that of a prosperous burgher, his smile genial—though in their coldness, his eyes had something in common with that of the child on the previous page.

Examining the sketch now, Jenny realized she'd used the idea of illumination from below to imbue a cozy scene with lurid, satanic shadows. The choice had not been conscious, but it had been effective.

Now, Jenny could barely stand to glance at the sketch. "I noticed that the people who tend to the poorhouses were always well fed, always comfortable. It drove me mad to see that. I gave away all my pin money for years, until Westhaven remarked that I wasn't wearing new frocks—or perhaps Victor peached on me. As sick as he was, he fretted for me and encouraged my art without ceasing."

Elijah set the sketchbook aside and angled his

body to wrap both arms around her. "Victor died of consumption?"

She nodded against his throat. "The poorhouses are breeding grounds for all manner of disease. When Victor fell ill, he forbade me to go back lest I suffer the same fate, and I was"—the lump in her throat was going to choke her—"I was relieved. I was relieved never to go back."

"You still give your pin money to charity."

Another nod, because she was weeping now and burrowed so closely against Elijah, they might have been making love.

He said nothing more, and for long moments, Jenny cried like she hadn't cried since Victor's death. Cried without worrying that she sounded unladylike, cried without worrying that she'd never stop.

And throughout all of this tumult, Elijah held her close. She had the sense that if Their Graces had burst through the door, Elijah would not have moved unless and until Jenny had regained her composure.

"I m-miss him."

"Victor." Not a question.

"He could make me laugh. Even when he was *dying*, he could make me laugh, and he never protested when I sketched him." She'd filled pages of the same sketchbook with images of her brother, chronicled his long, miserable battle with an enemy nobody ever defeated. Another entire notebook held Bart, always laughing and smiling.

"Victor understood you."

Three words holding a world of insight. "He understood everybody. Victor was a charming man, but by the time he died, he was a wise man too."

"When did he die?"

Another quiet comment, but this one reverberated through Jenny bodily. She lifted her face, not caring that she looked a wreck. "Right before… Christmas. He died right before… I did not realize… It never occurred to me…"

When she settled against Elijah again, she felt less at the mercy of grief, and on the strength of the one simple insight. "The anniversary of his death is next week."

And her family would ignore it. Perhaps in the privacy of the ducal apartment, Their Graces would acknowledge the date somehow. Maybe some of the glances between her brothers would be about old loss, but in public, the past was not part of the upcoming holiday.

Elijah brushed her hair back from her face and said nothing, though his silence was comfortable, like Timothy purring right beside her.

"I want to look at those sketches," Jenny said. This was not entirely truthful. She dreaded looking at those sketches, but she also wanted to know what Elijah saw in them that was brilliant.

"Next week, when we've made more progress on Their Grace's portraits. For now, you need sustenance." He produced a handkerchief, which Jenny put to use and did not return to him.

"I need to compose myself."

He withdrew his arm but remained right beside her. "No, you needed to lose your composure. I think you also need to go to Paris."

An after-shudder hit her, though she was done with her tears. "You're concluding that only *now*?"

Timothy rose and stalked across Jenny's lap—why did such soft little paws land like jackboots?—to get to Elijah.

"I knew you *wanted* to go to Paris, that you *longed* to be there. Now I understand that you *need* to go. It will be hard, Genevieve. When you're starting out, there's competition from every quarter, and it won't help at all that your papa's an English duke."

She reached over and stroked Timothy's sleek, dark fur. He was not purring, which struck her as odd. "I know that. Will you write me some introductions?"

He hesitated a single instant. "You won't need them. Your talent will be your introduction, and the French have discernment, Genevieve. They can spot ability, regardless of how unconventionally it's presented, or how unusual the artist."

His refusal hurt, but his compliment was genuine. He had faith in her. The notion comforted wonderfully. She set aside the temptation to wheedle anyway. "I am famished. Shall we have our luncheon?"

"We shall." He picked Timothy up and rose to set him on the mantel. The cat looked about itself, clearly not pleased with the change of location.

"He's contrary," Jenny said. "That's exactly where he wanted to be earlier, but now he must find fault with it." Would she be equally fickle about Paris once she'd arrived there?

Elijah helped her to her feet then surprised her by pulling her into his arms. "We will look at those sketches, Genevieve. They are magnificent."

She did not question the embrace, but rather, closed her eyes and breathed in his scent. "Next week, then. I will hold you to it."

He surprised her yet again by kissing her. His lips on hers were warm, firm, and lovely—nothing fleeting or demanding. When he raised his head and did not step back, she tried to figure out what his kiss had been about. Respect, of course. Elijah was never disrespectful of her person.

But even more than respect, his kiss had tasted of awe, as if he were kissing a goddess come to earth. Jenny leaned against him, abruptly feeling fatigue to go along with her hunger.

"Come, my lady." Elijah shifted to link their arms, ballroom promenade-fashion. "We will fortify ourselves. Your brothers will likely be stirring, the mistletoe is still threatening from every corner, and if I understand aright, yet more family will be arriving today."

His smile said that amid all that mayhem and holiday nonsense, she would have an ally. She would have a quiet place to come and paint; she would have a handkerchief when she needed one.

She'd have a friend who would not risk any more folly with her, regardless of how badly she'd miss him once they parted.

The realization hurt with a whole new pain, particularly when she thought back to when he'd noticed her the previous afternoon as she'd sat quietly in her dim corner. She'd studied her brothers, with their wrists, chins, and glances, and she'd studied Elijah too.

He missed his family, missed them more deeply than he likely knew. She would go to Paris, but if there was any benevolence to the holiday season at all, Elijah would give in to a towering case of homesickness and take himself off to Flint Hall.

Fourteen

Marriages developed a language as sophisticated and subtle as any code devised by the War Office—more so, for being flexible. The better a man understood that code, the more peacefully his marriage would proceed.

Charlotte glanced up from her embroidery hoop in a manner that told Lord Flint she'd been patient long enough. "What does your son have to say for himself, Flint?"

He did not pass her the letter, not with Prudholm lurking by the window, gilding the shine on some adolescent sulk. "Elijah? Just the usual. His commission is coming along. He's in good health. Lady Jenny Windham has more than a bit of talent. He encloses Her Grace's recipe for wassail, along with a warning to imbibe it in moderation. He's having to keep his studio locked when not in use to keep all the Moreland progeny from coming to harm with the paints and such."

"Your son is a trial to a mother's heart, but he understands the little ones."

From a reading chair in the corner, Pru let loose a snort that might have resembled a cough.

"Moreland's letter is more interesting."

Her hand paused in midair, the needle drawn as far from the fabric as it would go without snapping the thread. "*His Grace* wrote to you?"

"Moreland has ever been a reliable correspondent. He says Her Grace has insisted that the artists be left to their work and disturbed as little as possible, lest her present not be completed by the Christmas Eve open house."

"I have eleven other children to look after, Flint. I am not spending my Christmas Eve in some bouncing sleigh, freezing my—" She fell silent, her French grasp of subtleties stealing the rest of her outburst. "Artist*s*?"

"Elijah has asked for Lady Jenny's aid in the studio, but His Grace says it has turned into some sort of art lesson for his daughter. She's handy with a paintbrush, according to her father."

Flint leaned closer to the candelabrum, as if to see the words more clearly. He was in fact thwarting his wife's impulse to snatch the letter from his hands.

Charlotte stabbed her fabric as if it were the villain in a bad farce. "Handy with a paintbrush? That is ridiculous. That is a man who does not comprehend portraiture. That is a papa who is not paying attention. If Elijah says the girl is talented, then she's likely a genius."

"Perhaps."

She looked over at him, arching a Gallic eyebrow that had captivated him across many a ballroom and every one of their bedrooms. "Flint, you try my patience worse than all your sons put together. What else does His Grace say?"

He chose his words carefully, because Prudholm had stopped shifting and sighing and using every other aggravating means to remind his parents of his presence. If Oxford was to continue benefiting from Flint's largesse, they'd give in to his pleading and start Hilary term on Boxing Day.

"He implies that his sons and daughters have a tacitly agreed-to schedule, upon which they routinely intrude on the studio—to look for missing children, to extend an invitation to tea, to inquire about the whereabouts of a particular cat."

His marchioness made an impatient wave with a graceful hand.

He got to the point, to the troubling, puzzling point. "They none of them report anything of a questionable nature when they drop in unannounced, though neither Elijah nor Lady Jenny is willing to let anyone inspect their works in progress."

For a moment, Lady Flint was silent, and this was exactly why Flint hadn't waited to bring matters to her attention. What could it mean that Elijah was closeted with an artistically talented, pretty, available young lady for hours at a time, and not one hint of impropriety could be discovered in his dealings with her? What did it mean that for the first time in nine years—nearly ten—their firstborn had mentioned a young, lovely, unmarried, well-dowered woman of suitable station in his correspondence?

"Elijah is probably preoccupied with whether to join us here this year for the holidays," her ladyship observed. She held her hoop at arm's length, studying a scene of snowflakes and pine trees so real, Flint expected it to reek of pine boughs.

Pru shifted on his chair and turned the page of a book. The first page he'd turned in more than fifteen minutes.

"Elijah will join us," Flint muttered. "I have every confidence he'll heed his mother's summons."

"I do not summon anybody, Flint."

Prudholm's book snapped closed, and he exited the room without a word to either parent. A subtle and wearying tension left with him.

"Your youngest son makes a poor spy for his siblings," her ladyship said. She glanced at the door through which their baby boy had just stalked. "Flint, you must not worry. That Elijah does not trouble the young lady means he respects her, and better still, he respects her art. The lady's siblings collude with her to keep any mention of longing glances and little touches from Their Graces' notice. All will be well."

Ah. When she explained it that way, it made perfect sense. As a younger man, Flint had been heedless with many a merry widow, willing chambermaid, and courtesan, but never again once he'd met his Charlotte.

"What is that you're embroidering, my dear?"

"A shroud for the fools at Oxford who think young men ought to be sent home for the holidays to stomp about the house, nip their papa's brandy, and tease their sisters."

"You love that scamp," Flint said.

She sent him a look, part parental commiseration, part exasperated wife.

"Pru reminds me of you, Flint. He makes the grand

gestures and is full of posturing, and it's all a diversion. The boy is plotting something. Elijah likely is too. The Harrison male is a crafty creature and determined on his goals, something I love about every one of them."

She counseled, she flattered, she pretended to inspect her embroidery. He would adore this woman until his dying day.

Flint passed her the letters and a pair of his reading glasses.

"I am going to heave this cat at the next Windham sibling who just happens to come through that door without knocking." Jenny kissed the top of Timothy's head, so the cat at least would know she was blustering.

Though only just.

Elijah glanced at the clock then resumed studying the side-by-side portraits of the duchess. "We have at least another twenty minutes before the next sneak inspection. Your portrait of Her Grace is superior to mine."

She put the cat up on the mantel, having realized the room's higher spaces were warmer than any place closer to the floor. When she turned back to the easels, Elijah was still before them, arms crossed, lips pursed.

What had he been—?

"I beg your pardon. What did you say, Elijah?"

He held out a hand. "I said, your portrait of Her Grace is superior to my own."

She did not take his hand. "You spend better than a week carping, criticizing, and sniping at my work then pronounce it better than yours?"

He dropped his hand. "I do not snipe."

"The Duke of Moreland is not a pair of old riding boots, Genevieve," she quoted, folding her arms.

"He's not. I'm trying to figure out *how* your portrait is better," he said. "I'm trying to find the technical terms, the details of execution, the subtle compositional differences, and I can't. It's simply… *better.*"

She wanted those details too, wanted him to enumerate them, write them down in triplicate. She wanted him to send a copy to *The Times*, give the second copy to her, and post the third copy on the door to the breakfast parlor. "Both portraits are fine likenesses, and I'm having more trouble with His Grace."

"I think most people have more trouble with your father." He stepped back. "Color is part of your secret. Your palette is more varied. You have different colors of shadow."

She was not going to let him start on her shadows. Not when he'd paid her such a fine, rare compliment. "It's time we took a walk."

"Yes. Because in"—another look at the clock—"seventeen minutes, one of your sisters will burst in here, all smiles, and ask if you'd like to take the children down to pet the horses' noses, or get up a game of hoodman-blind."

She gave Timothy a farewell caress. "I've always hated that game. Nothing about being without sight has ever struck me as enjoyable."

The door swung open, and a shaggy canine behemoth padded in, followed by a dark-haired little girl. "Hullo, Aunt Jen!"

"Bronwyn, hello. Please tell Scout not to knock anything over."

On the mantel, Timothy had come to attention, though he remained sitting. He hissed at the dog and added a low, menacing growl for good measure.

"Scout, come."

The dog ignored his owner, another Windham grandchild, this one down from the North with St. Just and his countess. The scent of Elijah's boots was apparently more compelling than the punishment for indifferent hearing.

"Scout, come here this instant." Bronwyn sounded like her papa, the former cavalry officer, but the dog had apparently never bought his colors.

Elijah nudged the beast in the direction of the door with his knee. "Miss Winnie, was there something you were looking for? Something you wanted to tell us?"

"Yes!" The dog walked over to the girl while Jenny steadied a jar of brushes his tail had nearly knocked to the floor. "I forget—oh, I remember. Aunt Eve is here. You have to come get kissed. She's going to have a baby, and Papa says from the size of her he thinks it will be a baby horse."

Jenny hoped St. Just hadn't said that within Eve's hearing—though he probably had. "We'll be along presently. You can tell everybody we're coming." The child whirled and darted from the room, and the dog trotted after her. "Elijah, do you have your key?"

He produced the key from his watch pocket. "Always. Yours is in the lock. If Lady Eve's arrival merits as much celebration as Rose's and her parents' did, then we won't get a thing done for the rest of the day."

He was right, and that was fine with Jenny. She wanted to treasure his judgment of her portrait for at least a few hours before she again tackled the challenge that was her dear papa.

Eve was, indeed, well along in her pregnancy. Deene, her husband, hovered like a mother cat, until Westhaven suggested the ladies might want their sister to themselves for a bit, and Deene was all but forcibly dragged off to the billiards room by the menfolk.

While Jenny and Elijah slipped out the door.

When Genevieve Windham was allowed to paint for hours, she became luminous, exhausted, and serene—as if she'd been well satisfied in bed. Observations like that were only one reason Elijah found it increasingly difficult to work beside her day after day.

As they crossed the back terrace, he wrapped her hand over his arm. "What do you find difficult about your father's portrait?"

"I find Papa difficult," Jenny said. "He's noisy, arrogant, absorbed with his bills and committees, and yet, he's devoted to Her Grace, well intended, and would cheerfully—cheerfully—endure endless torture or lay down his life for any member of his family."

That was all likely true, particularly the protective and devoted parts. "You're afraid he'll forbid you to go to France."

She tucked closer, and Elijah cast around for something comforting to say besides, "*So why the hell are you going?*" Particularly since he'd seen that sketchbook full of dying children and Jenny's departed brother, he'd understood why she was going, though she likely did not admit all of her motivations to herself. Unless he was very much mistaken, she had equally skilled sketches of her brother Bart secreted somewhere too.

"How do you like my portrait of Sindal's boys, Genevieve?"

"I adore it. Sophie and Sindal adore it, and Lord and Lady Rothgreb will be crowing to all of their neighbors about it. You made two busy, grubby, noisy little boys charming, and yet, it's them. It really is them."

He wanted to kiss her, and not for the usual reasons. He wanted to kiss her because something about having her on hand when he'd done those sittings had given him the courage to come out of some sort of artistic exile and enjoy his work again.

They left the terrace, moving across the snowy wasteland of the Moreland gardens. "That's what you have to do with His Grace. You have to be honest but compassionate, so your rendering really is him."

"Because the portrait is for Her Grace, I tell myself I must try to see Papa as she sees him. He is her dear Percival, and whatever there is about him to love, Her Grace focuses on that."

They were moving farther and farther from the house, far enough that Elijah let himself take Jenny's hand. "My parents are the same way. Her ladyship might seem like a manipulative, scheming French baggage to some. To Flint, she's charming, determined, and adept at managing a big family. He isn't some fellow who likes outlandish waistcoats, he's her dear Flint. I couldn't see that when I was younger, but they are a team in ways I could not appreciate then."

She paused before a gate in a tall wrought iron fence, her expression concerned. "You're going to go home, aren't you, Elijah?"

"Everybody goes home, eventually." He took her hand in his again. The snow was deeper here, more than a pretty dusting. "I miss my family, and they miss me. My mother claims the Academy will never allow me full membership."

"You think she's scheming?"

"I think I'm as talented as the next four contenders put together, and there are two vacancies." Though talent had never been necessary or sufficient to gain entrance. "I think a man, particularly an arrogant young man, should pay the consequences for giving his word."

And yet, how long were those consequences supposed to last, and upon whom were they to devolve?

"I will miss my family too. I know that."

Not the way she'd miss them when the winter wind on the Channel hit her in the face like a slap, and nobody and nothing could turn the boat around. "You'll be fine. You'll make new friends. You'll have your art."

And far from her family's benevolent meddling, she'd effectively eliminate any and all possibility of having children and a family of her own.

She said nothing until they reached their destination, and then she turned a slow circle, taking in each gravestone and marker. "You remembered. Oh, Elijah, you remembered."

He would remember this too, remember Jenny Windham wrapping her arms around him as the wind picked up and the flurries danced down. He'd remember that when he might have argued her away from her course, when he might have offered her marriage and frequent trips to Paris, he'd instead held her and held her and held her.

And then he'd let her go.

"Jenny has taken a daft notion to go to Paris." Louisa knew she sounded worried, but it couldn't be helped. The parlor door was closed, the syllabub had been served, and this was likely the only privacy the children, spouses, and parents would allow her with her sisters.

"Paris in springtime is supposed to be lovely," Sophie observed. "Sindal says he'll take me one of these years, but there always seems to be a baby on the way or one just arrived."

Petite, blond Eve, her feet up on a hassock, patted her belly. "Please, God, let one arrive before I explode or Deene frets himself into a decline. Lou wouldn't be worried if Jenny were making a quick shopping visit."

Maggie left off poking at the fire—no footmen would disturb this gathering—and took up a rocking chair. "Jenny told me the same thing. Told me not to be angry with her, but if she didn't leave now, she'd never go."

"She needs a fellow," Louisa said. "We all needed a fellow, and the boys needed their ladies."

Sophie considered her drink. "I don't know, Lou. Your fellow lets you write all the poetry you want, and has you dedicate the racy verses to him. Ladies have been writing poetry for eons. Jenny's art is a different matter."

"Deene let me ride King William," Eve said. "Before I got as big as King William. Maybe the right fellow will encourage Jenny's painting."

There was a point to be made here, and Louisa had not the patience to make it subtly. "It's not just that Jenny paints, it's that she paints well—better, I think, than half those buffoons in the Royal Academy. My poetry is all well and good, but it hardly ranks with Milton and Shakespeare. Joseph says Jenny is brilliant."

And Joseph, as anybody with any brains knew, was nigh infallible.

"Amateurs can be brilliant," Maggie said, though her tone suggested they seldom were.

Eve appeared to study her feet as if she hadn't seen them in some time. "I gather the difficulty is not only that Jenny is talented, it's that she's English. Frenchmen do not limit their ladies to dabbling in watercolors and lounging about like brainless ornaments. The Germans let their ladies paint too, as do the Italians."

Louisa glowered at her sisters. "Frenchmen no longer understand gallantry, what few Frenchman are left between the ages of five and fifty. They will pillory the daughter of an English duke on general principles, despite their convenient reversion to monarchy at the end of Wellington's sword."

A silence descended, not even the clink of a spoon disturbing it. Glances were exchanged. Eve, the most recently married, spoke up.

"Mr. Harrison is gallant, and he understands art.

Deene says the menfolk chatted away an entire afternoon while Jenny eavesdropped, and Mr. Harrison had eyes only for her."

Maggie picked up Timothy, though how he'd gotten into the room was a mystery. "Mr. Harrison insisted Jenny be free to help him complete his commissions, though when I pop into the studio, Jenny's always before her own easel, spattered in paint and looking..."

"Happy," Sophie said. "She looks happy when she paints."

The cat started purring in Maggie's lap, loud enough for all to hear.

"We're agreed, then," Louisa said. "Mr. Harrison makes Jenny happy, and Paris would make her miserable."

Eve yawned, Maggie stroked the cat, and Sophie picked up an embroidery hoop. "Paris would make her miserable, if she were allowed to go, which will never come to pass as long as Their Graces draw breath. Shall we order another syllabub?"

Tea was an occasion for parents to leave their offspring in the nursery and gather below stairs for some sustenance and conversation. Because Jenny and Mr. Harrison remained in their studio, it was also an opportunity to compare notes.

"So what will you do?" Joseph, Lord Kesmore, asked his brothers-by-marriage.

Westhaven glanced around and noted Their Graces were absent, and the ladies were gathered near the hearth on the opposite side of the large, comfortable family parlor.

"Do? I wasn't aware we were required to do anything besides eat and drink in quantities sufficient to tide us over until summer of next year," Westhaven said.

The Marquess of Deene patted his flat tummy. "Hear, hear. And make toasts. One must make holiday toasts."

St. Just shifted where he lounged against the mantel. "Make babies, you mean. My sister looks like she's expecting a foal, not a Windham grandchild, Deene."

Gentle ribbing ensued, which Westhaven knew was meant to alleviate the worry in Deene's eyes.

"The first baby is the worst," Westhaven said. "His Grace confirms this. Thereafter, one has a sense of what to expect, and one's lady is less anxious over the whole business."

"One's lady?" Lord Valentine scoffed. "You fool nobody, Westhaven, but Kesmore raises an excellent point. Every time I peek into the studio in search of my baroness, all I see is that Harrison and Jenny are painting or arguing."

"Arguing is good," Kesmore informed a glass that did not contain tea. "Louisa and I argue a great deal."

Respectful silence ensued before the Earl of Hazelton spoke up. "Maggie and I argue quite a bit as well. I daresay the consequences of one of our rousing donnybrooks will show up in midsummer."

Toasting followed, during which Lord Valentine admitted congratulations were also in order regarding his baroness, and St. Just allowed he suspected his countess was similarly blessed, but waiting until after Christmas to make her announcement.

When every unborn Windham grandchild had been recognized by the assemblage, Westhaven said what they'd all been avoiding.

"My countess tells me Genevieve has taken it into her head to remove to Paris. I suspect she wants to avoid being aunt-at-large, while her own situation admits of no change. We are Jenny's family, and Christmas is upon us. Harrison paints, he argues with her, and he has all his teeth. What say you, gentlemen?"

"Paris reeks," Lord Kesmore said. "Harrison's scent is rather pleasant by comparison."

"He smells of linseed oil," St. Just observed.

"A point in his favor," Hazelton murmured, "from Lady Jenny's perspective."

Westhaven glanced around the group. "Then we are agreed. Lady Jenny will have no need of the dubious sanctuary of France. None at all."

Paris began to loom like salvation for many reasons.

Jenny had checked the packet schedules. She'd made lists of what she'd take with her. She'd quietly packed up several boxes and stowed them in the bottom of her wardrobe, and just as quietly interrogated Aunt Gladys and Aunt Arabella about where a lady might find proper quarters in a decent part of town.

Gladys had given her a long, pitying look, but had shared what she'd known.

"You could do more with that necklace," Elijah said, peering at Jenny's portrait of Her Grace. "Pick up the highlights from the fire and Her Grace's hair. Make them resonate with the ring she wears and the candles."

Elijah was a great one for making things resonate. Jenny was tempted to make his skull resonate with her retort, but she kept her tone civil.

"I could tell *you* that your portrait is of a duchess, while mine is of a wife and mother. She doesn't even like jewels, Elijah, but wears them so as not to hurt His Grace's feelings."

Elijah wiped his hands on a rag and glanced around the room. "Your cat has abandoned us, and you're peckish. Tea came and went an hour ago, and you've hardly left this room since you took a luncheon tray some hours before that. I was making a suggestion, Genevieve, not a criticism."

Outside, darkness had fallen. Jenny had painted for hours, not in an attempt to keep up with Elijah, but simply to be near him.

"Is your portrait of Sindal's boys done?" she asked, stepping back from her easel.

Elijah used his rag to wipe paint from the handle of a brush, the way a soldier might wipe blood from a sword. "As done as it will be. West has written that Fotheringale harps on the lack of a completed juvenile portrait from me, though I showed them all the sketches."

Jenny passed him her brushes—Elijah was meticulous about tidying up at the end of each session—and took a seat by the hearth. "You can send them the completed portrait. Rothgreb wouldn't begrudge you that."

Instead of cleaning the brushes, Elijah dunked them

in a jar of turpentine—also across the room from the fire—and sat on the hearth beside Jenny. "Will you marry me, Genevieve?"

He kissed her cheek while Jenny flailed about for a response, any response at all. "The paint fumes are affecting you, Elijah, or you've spent too much time imbibing His Grace's wassail."

"*You* affect me. I paint better when you're near, and I was warned about His Grace's wassail—or Her Grace's—by the regent himself. Marry me."

She wanted to say yes, even if this declaration was not made out of an excess of romantic love. "If I marry you, I cannot go to Paris."

He leaned back, resting his head against the stones behind them, closing his eyes. "I'll take you to bloody Paris, and you can appreciate for yourself that the cats have ruined the place. Rome isn't much better, though I suppose you'll want to go there and sniff it for yourself too."

He'd promise to take her there, probably to Moscow as well if she asked.

"Babies put rather a cramp in one's travel plans." Because if she were married to him, and Windham proclivities ran true, babies would follow in the near, middle, and far terms, and all hope of painting professionally would be as dead as her late brothers.

"Your siblings all managed to travel with babies. What's the real reason, Genevieve? We're compatible in the ways that count, and you're dying on the vine here, trying to be your parents' devoted spinster daughter. Marry me."

He was tired, and he felt sorry for her. Of those

things, Jenny was certain, but not much else. She hadn't foreseen an offer from him that would ambush her best intentions and be so bewilderingly hard to refuse.

"You need to go home, Elijah. I need to go to Paris. Painting with you has only made me more certain of that. If I capitulate to your proposal, I will regret it for the rest of my days, and you will too. You feel sorry for me, and while I appreciate your sentiments, in Paris I will not be an object of pity."

Nor would she be the object of marital schemes, and that... that was important too, though exactly why it was important, Jenny could not fathom.

Elijah was silent for a moment, while beside him, Jenny tried to swallow around the lump in her throat, because she would *also* regret not capitulating to this proposal, even though giving up on a life's dream for a man who'd proposed out of pity wasn't prudent.

"Compassion is not pity, woman. I find it puzzling that a lady who's about to turn her back on all she's known—family, friends, and familiars—exhorts me so relentlessly to go home."

The paintings were coming along nicely, which Jenny suspected was symptomatic of her first brush with channeling one kind of frustration into another kind of creativity. She would likely paint masterpieces in Paris as a result of the same frustration.

Though in Paris, a woman could take a lover. The notion was incomprehensible—a procession of Denbys and glorified flirts who would only leave her feeling lonelier.

"We are not going to marry, Elijah. My family

stopped even pretending to chaperone us days ago, or hadn't you noticed?"

"I noticed, though I drew a different conclusion entirely." He took her hand, and she not only allowed it, she reveled in it. His touch was never presuming, but neither was it hesitant. "You will face challenges in Paris, Genevieve. When things go well, you'll tell yourself that's reason to stay longer. When things go poorly, you'll tell yourself you can never leave in disgrace, and you'll use even the setbacks and criticisms as justification for staying far from home."

He spoke from experience, and she hurt for him. Hurt for the very young man who'd taken on an unlikely profession and made himself successful at it.

"I am not you, Elijah. I have nothing to prove. I want only to paint and to be taken seriously. My brother Victor died—"

Jenny blinked, the lump in her throat turning painful and sharp without warning.

Elijah drew her close, wrapped an arm around her shoulders, and kissed her cheek again. "Let's not argue. We have a few days left, and then we'll part. What did you think of the green I added to the curtains, hmm? Did it pick up on the green in Her Grace's eyes? I can tone it down, but I think I like it."

Jenny fell asleep, cradled against his body. When she woke up, she was in her own bed, alone but for the cat curled up at her feet.

The cat whom she'd also miss when she went to Paris.

"I've come to let you know that your portrait is all but finished."

Elijah had much more he wanted to say to Moreland, but the old fellow was a whirlwind, taking a batch of grandchildren out for a sleigh ride, escorting his duchess on various calls, and then disappearing into this very study to wreak God knew what mischief-by-correspondence with his cronies in the Lords.

The stack of letters Elijah had sent in response to his siblings' pleadings was dwarfed by the volume of Moreland's epistles, and each was written in the duke's own hand.

His Grace sat back but didn't rise from the monstrosity of a desk at which he was ensconced. Mistletoe hung above the desk, only a few berries remaining among the leaves.

"Good work, Bernward. You'll stay long enough to see all and sundry admiring your handiwork, though. Her Grace delights in the Christmas open house, and I won't see her deprived of a chance to show you off."

Elijah turned his back on the duke, which was rude, but necessary if civilities were to be observed and His Grace's Christmas decorations admired. "Her Grace would do better to show off Lady Jenny's talents, my lord."

A chair scraped back. "Jenny enjoys her dabbling, but I was rather hoping she might enjoy your company more. Was I mistaken?"

Behind the genial bonhomie of a doting father and relaxed host, Elijah heard a thread of ducal steel.

A cloved orange was beginning to turn brown in the middle of a wreath on the back of the study door.

"We enjoy each other's company, Your Grace, but you have to know your daughter is not content."

Moreland came around the desk to stand beside Elijah at the window. "You're not going to ask my permission to court her, are you?"

The honesty was unexpected, also a relief, like the cold radiating from the window provided relief from the fire's cozy blast. "She would not welcome my suit. You underestimate your daughter's devotion to her art."

The duke snorted. "You've spent what, a couple of weeks with her, and you presume to tell me her priorities? I've known that girl since she first drew breath, Bernward. She's no better at hiding her discontent from me than is her mother. The holidays are hard on them both is the trouble. Come calling when spring is nigh, and you'll be well received. Both ladies are preoccupied now, with all the family underfoot and entertaining to be done."

His Grace's voice had dropped with that observation, revealing sadness and possibly bewilderment. The latter made him less a duke and more like a man who had many children to love but only a father's resources with which to solve their problems.

"I expect to leave on Christmas Day at the latest, Your Grace. It's time I went home to Flint Hall." Outside, in the sprawling back gardens, a snowball fight was in progress. One was probably under way at Flint Hall as well.

"Your mother will be pleased to see you."

His Grace had the most arrestingly blue eyes Elijah had ever beheld, also the most shrewd. "My father will not be glad to see me?"

"Oh, of course, though Flint will likely refer to it as relief rather than sheer joy—if he refers to it at all. You took Jenny out to the family plot the other day."

Moreland was reputed to leap about like a March hare in his conversation, but Elijah grasped that the duke did little without premeditation—witness the impact of a complete verbal ambush on Elijah's wits. "Lady Jenny and I went for a walk. I believe we were in view of the house for most of it."

Though not when they'd come to the graveyard and Jenny had wept silent tears against Elijah's chest.

"Her Grace and I remark the occasion of Victor's passing with a visit to his grave, and we do as much for Bartholomew, my parents, and late brothers too. You mustn't allow Jenny to feel obligated to make the same effort."

The footprints Elijah had seen in the snow made more sense. Not servants, not even a duke and duchess, but rather, two parents whose heartache would never entirely abate where two of their sons were concerned.

"I sought to get her away from the paint fumes, Your Grace." A lame answer, but the older man merely regarded the melee beyond the window, in which the women and children were administering a sound drubbing to the gentlemen.

"Jenny is lonely, Bernward. With all her family around her, she is yet lonely. To the extent your painting afforded her a distraction, you have my thanks."

For a moment, Elijah considered the possibility that he'd been commissioned to paint the duke and duchess solely to distract Lady Jenny as the holiday approached and the Windham horde descended.

Not even Moreland could be that calculating, could he?

"You're in correspondence with my father, Your Grace."

"I am. He and I do not see eye to eye on the Catholic question. I am a staunch Tory but cannot find much threat in allowing Catholics to vote when so few of them hold land or wealth adequate to qualify them for the privilege. Moreover, the entire debate has gone on too long and taken up far too many resources, and Wellington both agrees with me and has a grasp of Irish politics that eludes many an English lord. Your father's views are to the contrary."

And for ten years, Elijah had been allowed to breathe paint fumes, when as successor to the Flint title, he ought to have been paying attention to issues such as this.

"Do you have any artistic inclinations, Your Grace?"

The duke turned back to his desk. "Her Grace is in charge of sweetness and light in this household, if that's what you're asking. I cannot sing, draw, paint, or otherwise account for whatever airs and graces my children claim. I plot and scheme to safeguard the realm, and that suffices to justify my existence in Her Grace's eyes—also in the eyes of the Almighty, one hopes."

The duke was apologizing for Flint in some way, or distracting Elijah from the fact that Victor Windham's brothers had not remarked the anniversary of his death, but Jenny and Their Graces had.

And for that reason, because she still remarked her brother's death, Elijah owed Jenny one more charge on the citadel of His Grace's paternal obliviousness.

"I've enjoyed my time here, Your Grace, but I cannot caution you strongly enough that Lady Jenny's abilities should not be ignored. Talent such as hers deserves to be supported, not humored." Any more blunt than that, and His Grace would likely eject Elijah from the premises bodily.

Moreland resumed his seat, his expression amused. "My thanks for your words of advice, Bernward. Now hadn't you best be joining the battle outside or that game of nine pins in the portrait gallery? One hears the entire mad idea originated with you, though I caution you that the young ladies will find a way to cheat if they can."

Nine pins in the portrait gallery—how apt. "My thanks for your patience, Your Grace. I think you'll be pleased with the portrait you commissioned."

Though if Jenny's plans came to fruition, Moreland would probably burn the thing, and his duchess would send the ashes to the Academy's nominating committee.

Fifteen

"You look as if you've just lost your best friend." Eve took a place beside Jenny on this observation, which leavened Jenny's sense of desolation with a spike of resentment.

"With all my family around me, how could I possibly be in want of companionship?"

Eve watched their mutual siblings stepping through a minuet while their brother Valentine held forth at the piano. "The same way I can long to dance while the minuet plays all around me."

Marriage had settled Eve, and impending motherhood had only honed her already formidable instincts.

"You're admiring your husband, Lady Deene, even when you can't dance with him."

"He's promised me a waltz, though Valentine will probably find one to play at the speed of a dirge." She fell silent for a moment as the dancers one-two-three'd around the space created by the music room and an adjoining parlor. "You would make a wonderful mother, Jenny."

The worst pain was not in the words Eve offered,

but the combination of pleading and pity with which she offered them.

"Becoming a mother usually contemplates becoming a wife first, and I've no wish to wed some man for the sole purpose of bearing his babies." Not the sole purpose... As the dancers twirled and smiled, it occurred to Jenny that Victor had made her promise not to stop painting, but he hadn't said anything specific about eschewing motherhood.

Had he?

Another pause in the conversation, while the music played on. Eve, however, was notably tenacious, so Jenny waited for the next salvo, and Eve did not disappoint.

"You look at Bernward the way I look at Deene, the way Maggie looks at Benjamin, the way—"

"Louisa looks at Joseph, I suppose." And Sophie at her baron too, of course. They needn't start on how the Windham brothers regarded their respective wives.

"Louisa's gaze is a touch more voracious. I was going to say, the way Mama looks at Papa."

Ouch. Ouch, indeed. The duke and duchess turned down the room with the grace of a more elegant age, and yet, their gazes spoke volumes about the sheer pleasure of sharing a dance.

Jenny stated the obvious as matter-of-factly as possible. "Their Graces dance beautifully."

Eve's feet were propped on a hassock. She wiggled her toes in time with the music, the left and right foot partnering each other. "Bernward also dances quite well."

Elijah was dancing with Valentine's lady, Ellen's

preferred partner being ensconced at the keyboard, as usual. "Bernward is dancing carefully, lest Valentine take exception."

Eve twitched her skirts. "Bernward is dancing with one eye on you, you ninnyhammer, and with the certain knowledge that all three of our brothers are waiting for him to come over here and get you to stand up with him. How many more times do you think you can check on the punch bowl between sets without Bernward taking insult?"

Check on the full punch bowl, offer to turn pages for Valentine when he was playing from memory, or trim the wicks on the lamps that the footmen had trimmed not fifteen minutes earlier. This Christmas gathering was driving her mad.

"I'm going to Paris after the holidays."

Jenny hadn't planned on making the admission, but Eve's good intentions—her meddling—were enough to pluck confessions from a saint.

"Do you need money? My pin money is generous, and though one hears the Continent is affordable, I will worry about you."

Eve had been the second-to-last sibling to marry, and perhaps Jenny ought to have anticipated her reaction. Except she hadn't.

She absolutely had not. "You won't try to stop me?"

Eve's feet went still. "I know what it's like, Jenny, to be one of the few remaining Windham daughters without an offer, but I also know you could have had offers. I know you're afraid if you don't do something drastic, you'll compromise and accept a wrong offer. I could not live with myself—"

Eve's gaze went to her handsome husband, her expression conveying nothing short of besottedness.

"You feel guilty for abandoning me in favor of Deene's charms," Jenny concluded slowly. "Who is the ninnyhammer now, Lady Deene?" She couldn't make it a reproof. She was too grateful for her sister's concern.

"We love you," Eve said, keeping her voice down as the music came to a close. "Of course we're worried. Their Graces are challenge enough when one has reinforcements, but all you have is that dratted cat and the occasional sympathy visit from the rest of us."

"I'm not dead. I don't need condolence calls." But she did need Paris, if she wasn't to lapse into the very creature Eve described.

"Bernward has apparently taken the hint and given up on you."

Jenny watched as Elijah led Ellen off the dance floor and chatted up Valentine, who showed no signs of leaving the piano bench.

"Genevieve, it's time you obliged your old brother and took a turn down the room. Anna says I'm neglecting you."

Not Elijah, but Westhaven, the biggest, handsomest mother hen ever to stand in line for a ducal coronet—also the most meddling of older brothers.

"Might as well dance, Jenny. If you refuse, Westhaven will only nag you and send the rest of them over," Eve remarked. "I'll set Deene on you, and he is a very good dancer."

"Come." Westhaven held out his hand. "If you sneak off to your studio now, Her Grace will send one of us to retrieve you, and you'll end up right back here anyway. If you dance, you can plead fatigue then be credibly excused."

His green eyes held such understanding, Jenny wanted to flee the room. Her cat at least kept quiet and couldn't compel her to dance.

She took her brother's hand and rose. "The pleasure will be entirely mine."

True to Eve's prediction, Valentine chose a very decorous pace for the ensuing waltz.

"Jenny, what can I do to help?" Westhaven's expression was merely genial, but in his words, Jenny heard determination and that most dratted of holiday gifts, sibling concern.

"Help?"

"You're quiet as a dormouse. Maggie says you're chewing your nails. Louisa reports that you're taking odd notions, and Sophie won't say anything, but she's clearly worried. Her Grace muttered something about regretting all the time she's permitted you to spend among the paint fumes."

"What would Her Grace know of paint fumes?" What would the duchess know of anything relating to painting?

"She's our mother. Where knowledge fails, maternal instinct serves. Is Bernward troubling you?"

Westhaven was an excellent dancer, and if Jenny did not finish the dance with him, Her Grace would casually suggest that tomorrow be a day to rest from the activity in the studio. The idea made Jenny desperate.

"Westhaven, you must not involve yourself in anything to do with Elijah."

"Elijah." Westhaven's gaze shifted to a spot over Jenny's shoulder. "And does he call you Jenny?"

He calls me Genevieve, and sometimes he even calls me "woman."

"He calls me talented and brilliant but uneducated and unorthodox too. I've enjoyed working with him these past weeks more than anything—"

"Excuse me." Elijah had tapped Westhaven on the shoulder. "May I cut in?"

Westhaven's smile was diabolical. "Of course. Jenny would never decline an opportunity to dance with a family friend."

Family friend? Her blighted, interfering, perishing brother was laying it on quite thick.

Elijah bowed. "Lady Genevieve, may I have what remains of this dance?"

Two days remained. Two days and three nights. Jenny curtsied and assumed waltz position. As Elijah's hand settled on her back, his scent wafted to her, enveloping her in his presence.

"You're avoiding me," he said. "You needn't. I'll be leaving soon, and I hope we can at least part friends."

With her siblings, she could dissemble and maintain appearances, but with Elijah…

"I am honored you think me a friend, Elijah." And he danced wonderfully, with the same sense of assurance and mastery that he undertook painting… and lovemaking.

"I am your friend too, Genevieve. If you cursed right now, very softly, only I would hear you."

Cursing abruptly appealed more strongly than anything in the world—almost anything. Jenny gathered her courage on the next slow, sweeping turn, and leaned in close to her partner.

"I would like to be sharing your damned bed right now, Elijah. My family's kindness and concern make me want to perishing scream."

He did not falter in any regard but drew her a shade closer. "Swive, roger, bed, possess, lie with, copulate, fornicate… you can be explicit in your wishes, my lady. They're only wishes."

And he was warning her they'd only ever be wishes. Each word was rendered in a slightly different shade: daring, naughty, flirtatious, challenging, but none of them took her sentiment seriously.

The damned man was trying to jolly her past a sulk, for which she would not forgive him.

"You're leaving, Elijah Harrison, and I desire you. I still want it to be you."

He let more distance come between them as the music played on. "There are things you want more than you want me, Genevieve. Important things nobody else can give you, things you think you'll find in Paris. I would not deny you your heart's desire."

He spoke so gently, Jenny felt her throat constrict. "Damn you to rubbishing hell, Elijah."

Maybe he heard the desperation in her voice or saw the tears she blinked back, because he offered her no more flirtation or jollying. He danced with her until the music ended, then bowed and escorted her right back to her brother's side.

In Elijah's experience, fatigue came in two varieties. The primary colors of fatigue were an unsubtle indication that the body or mind sought rest. Ignoring this kind of tiredness came at a peril. Bad decisions, stupid pronouncements, inept paintings, ill-advised couplings, and inane arguments could all result from an unwillingness to accommodate the basic forms of fatigue.

Elijah's argument with his father had happened late at night, around yet another bowl of holiday wassail. He and his sire had both been tired, and unfortunate words had been exchanged.

So Elijah had learned to heed the signs of simple fatigue.

The more subtle fatigue was of the spirit, and like a secondary color, it had antecedents, and usually involved a blending of bodily weariness with something more. One grew overwhelmed observing the world in all its folly, overwhelmed by want and woe on a scale too great to be productively addressed. One grew weary of being good, of being kind, honest, hopeful, and civil.

He'd tempted Jenny into swearing the previous evening in hopes of alleviating some of her weariness of heart, more fool him.

For she'd passed beyond the common hues of fatigue into something more, some unassailable state of calm, which Elijah suspected resulted from his rejecting her intimate overtures on the impromptu dance floor.

She stood not two feet away, a monument of serenity in green velvet. "The portrait is lovely, Elijah. Rothgreb and his family will treasure it."

Jenny's smile was sweet, a bit tired, and to all appearances genuine.

She'd left for Paris already.

"It's a good effort. I suspect if I take on more juvenile commissions, I'll become more confident with them. I do like it." This portrait of Sindal's sons was the best thing Elijah had ever painted, in fact. Its temporary frame did not do it justice.

Jenny touched old Jock's ear, a bit of brushwork of which Elijah was particularly proud. "Will you display it at the open house?"

He resisted the urge to touch the lock of hair that wanted to curl over Jenny's ear. "I will not. Nothing will be allowed to overshadow Their Graces' portraits. The duchess was clear on that, as was her doting swain."

"You mean Papa. Shall I have this one packed up then? I'm sure Rothgreb will want to display it as soon as possible."

Did she have to be so blasted helpful? "I'm reluctant to lose sight of it."

She quirked an eyebrow, looking much like her father. "The joy is in the creation, Elijah, not in the possession."

Where was the polite, demure Lady Jenny who'd offered him shelter from a winter storm? Would he want her back if he could restore her? Was she any happier than this talented, determined, exhausted version of the same woman?

"There can be joy in creating *and* savoring, my lady. Pack it up and send it off. The painting belongs to the one who commissioned it, not to the fellow who merely happened to create it."

"Or to the lady who merely happened to create it."

She wanted an argument, and he was hard put not to oblige her. "Just so. I'd rather we spent this afternoon completing Their Graces' portraits instead of crating up finished business."

They had only this afternoon, after all. Tomorrow was the open house, when Elijah's ducal portraits would go on display before family and friends.

"A splendid notion," Jenny said, reaching for her smock. She looped it around her neck and reached behind herself to tie it in back.

"Allow me."

She turned her back to him and dipped her chin, so her nape was exposed to Elijah, a vulnerable, delectable pose, particularly when she wore a comfortable old dress and a simple painting smock. He tied a bow for her, and let his hands drop when what he wanted was to pull her close and hang the consequences.

Hang Paris.

"You're having trouble with the duke," he said. "Have you figured out why?"

She aimed a peevish look at him over her shoulder, and that was seductive too. "*You* didn't have any trouble with him. Your portrait catches all of his most appealing attributes."

Elijah slipped his sleeve buttons into a pocket and turned back his cuffs. "Which would be?"

Jenny studied their side-by-side paintings, her arms crossed, her expression disgruntled. "His Grace never fails to act, even when he ought to remain idle. He fires off letters, delivers speeches in the Lords, cozens the MPs, interferes wherever he must to see his ends achieved. You made that seem like leadership, or his responsibility, not busybodying."

Elijah laid out his brushes and wished his mouth was going to start humming some seasonal tune, though he knew it wouldn't. "You could not paint the duke as easily as you did Her Grace because he embodies the parts of yourself you are least comfortable with. Are you going to paint, or stare away the afternoon?"

Jenny turned, dropping her arms. "You think I'm like *His Grace*?"

She was fascinated, not horrified, which meant he was doomed to explain rather than defend his notions. He chose a small, fine finishing brush, took up his palette, and added a dot of green to the drapery behind the duke.

"When was the last time you had any instruction in art, Genevieve? Anyone to discuss your ideas with, anybody to trade criticisms with?"

She watched as he brought His Grace's curtains into harmony with the same drapes in Her Grace's portrait. "I tried for a while after my come-out to work with Antoine, but the subterfuge was too much, and he became… He humored me."

"And yet, you still painted. When you couldn't paint, you drew. When you couldn't draw, you embroidered." He turned to aim a glower at her. "You are relentless."

He'd all but growled the words, and yet, she was smiling a bemused smile. "After Victor died, I didn't want to paint, but he'd made me promise, and he was right. I am … relentless. His Grace is relentless too—so's Mama."

She started in painting, still not getting the duke

quite right in Elijah's opinion. The portrait was all but completed, and recasting the sitter's personality was not easily done in touch-ups and finishing work.

His Grace was relentless, and tireless in pursuit of his ends, but he was also a man capable of asking for what he wanted, even demanding what he wanted, and Jenny had far to go if she were to emulate her father.

He paused, his brush poised above the duke's heart. Jenny had been very forthright on the dance floor. Elijah considered the curtains, decided they needed more work, and allowed Jenny to paint away the afternoon in silence.

"Elijah didn't even suggest Sindal's portrait should be sent to the nominating committee." Jenny turned at the mantel and paced back across the parlor the ladies had taken over for the holidays. "He didn't mention the Academy at all. Just told me to pack the thing up and send it along to Sidling."

"Sit down," Louisa muttered. "If I only have an hour before the baby wakes, I don't want to spend it watching you careen about like a kite in the wind. Maggie, send that teapot over here."

Maggie rose from her rocker by the fire and set the teapot—a porcelain confection of green leaves and pink cabbages roses—down before Louisa. "Jenny is worried for her artist. If the committee doesn't see this portrait, then some old curmudgeon—Farthingdale?—will keep Bernward from being nominated to the Academy."

"Fotheringale," Jenny said, taking a seat next to Louisa. "He holds a grudge against Elijah's parents.

I believe Elijah has given up any hope of becoming an Academician."

Sophie glanced up from her embroidery hoop. "Men have been known to give up when they receive no encouragement whatsoever."

The door opened, admitting a flushed and flustered Lady Eve. "I have ruined Christmas!"

"Close the door," Louisa groused. "We can at least be cozy while we endure this ruined Christmas."

Eve flounced down onto the sofa on Louisa's other side. "I'm serious. Deene and I agreed to exchange our presents on Christmas Eve under the mistletoe, because we wanted a tradition, and that's today, and amid all the commotion and the coming and going, I left his p-present at L-lavender C-court!"

Louisa put an arm around Eve, who took to weeping, while Jenny exchanged looks with her sisters. Eve and Deene's first kiss had been beneath a sprig of mistletoe, just as Elijah and Jenny's had been.

"We'll send a footman," Maggie said.

"Can't," Eve replied, blotting her eyes with a handkerchief. "Mama has them running all about in preparation for the open house later today."

"A groom?" Louisa ventured.

"They're still decorating the ballroom," Eve wailed.

"I'd send Sindal, but he's gone off to fetch old Rothgreb," Sophie said.

Jenny rose, before her sisters could stop her. "I'll go. I'll be there and back in a trice, and Mama won't notice my absence, because you lot will distract her if the preparations don't suffice. You will not tell our brothers, either."

Another round of looks was exchanged: Louisa's thoughtful, Sophie's dubious. Eve looked hopeful—also quite gravid and in no condition for any upset—while Maggie looked… Maggie's expression was hard to discern.

"Go then," Louisa said. "Eve, describe this dratted present, and, Genevieve, you will not tarry or end up in a snowdrift, lest we're left explaining to Mama why she has a portrait to show off to the neighbors this evening but no Lady Jenny, hmm?"

Jenny listened with half an ear as Eve described an oblong box left on a sideboard. Lavender Court wasn't far at all—it adjoined the Morelands park on the other side of the woods—and far more important than Eve's sentimental intentions toward her husband, this errand would free Jenny from Morelands for the space of at least an hour.

❧

"Lady Maggie told me I'd find you here." Clearly, had Elijah tarried even another minute above stairs, he would have missed Jenny's departure.

Jenny paused as she fastened the frogs of her cloak. "And why would you be looking for me, my lord?"

He tugged her hands away and went to work on her cloak—*my lord, indeed.* "I wasn't looking for you. I was enjoying a comfortable spot of tea in the agreeable company of your feline familiar, when Lady Maggie said you were haring off across the countryside, intent on some errand for your younger sister."

The look she sent him gave away nothing, except

perhaps general displeasure. His mother had perfected that very expression early in his boyhood.

"It's snowing, my lady, and while you are yet in England, you will allow a gentleman to escort you on any cross-country *sorties*."

He frenchified the word but kept most of his exasperation behind his teeth.

She held his greatcoat out to him, which Elijah took for a compromise. He might walk by her side on this short outing, but only because a week or a month hence, she'd be free to dodge the offal on the streets of Paris without even a footman to attend her.

The notion was increasingly hard to tolerate. "Take my scarf."

"I have bonnets—"

He looped his scarf over her ears and around her neck, but did not wrap it right over her fool mouth. "Bonnets will not keep you warm, and bonnets do not fare well when snowed upon."

She fussed with the drape of the scarf but did not hand it back to him. "It's not snowing that hard."

"Not *yet*."

God help him, it felt good even to argue with his Genevieve. The duchess had been fretting over the weather all morning, though, worried that guests would not be able to attend her open house, worried they'd be snowed in if they did. Worried for her duke, who was serenely content to organize the loudest scavenger hunt in history for the children—or perhaps for his grown sons, who had apparently secreted bottles of French potation in various locations.

Lady Jenny pulled on gloves. "If it's going to

snow, then the sooner we're off, the less we'll have to contend with." She gestured at the door, her posture and tone reminiscent of her mother.

Elijah did not attempt to offer the lady his arm, but rather, accompanied her out the front door, down a shoveled path past the stables, and on toward the home wood. When he could tolerate her freezing silence no longer, Elijah opened a topic he thought safe. "Is the scavenger hunt a tradition?"

Jenny crunched through the snow beside him, her pace approximating a forced march with the enemy in mounted pursuit. "Yes."

"Do the ladies take part?"

"No. We enjoy some peace and quiet or we help Mama and the staff put the final touches on the public rooms for the open house." She came around a holly bush and stopped short. "This didn't use to be here. I could swear this wasn't here the last time I rode through these woods."

An oak of considerable proportions had fallen across the path ahead. "The way looks clear around to the—"

She was already scrambling over the horizontal trunk, despite the wet snow, despite the availability of a gentleman whose stated purpose was to provide escort.

Off to Paris, she was. She'd probably departed weeks ago—years ago, even. If Bartholomew's death hadn't purchased her a ticket for Calais, then Victor's certainly had.

Elijah vaulted across the trunk, turned, and pulled her the rest of the way over the fallen tree. "You've snow all over you. Hold still."

She tolerated his brushing at her cloak, stood still

like some martyr enduring blasphemy. "Will you tell me about Paris?"

A small, chilly question, though it lit a flame in him. He finished dusting her off. "Anything you want to know. Ask me anything."

To his relief, she wanted to know practical things: where to stay, where to procure food, where to never, ever go, even with an escort. To whom might she apply for instruction, where might she display finished works. How did one procure a horse and keep the beast and any conveyances, grooms, or coachmen? Where did one find domestics?

The last question comforted most, because it meant Jenny contemplated a cozy establishment, not some drafty garret where she'd enjoy only mice as companions.

Their pace slowed as they wound through the home wood, and at some point Elijah took Jenny's hand. When they emerged from the trees, she stopped again but kept her fingers laced with his.

"I want to paint this. I want to paint Eve's cozy little manor house, the snow coming down, the greenery adorning the windows. I want to paint it for myself."

Because she'd miss this too. Elijah let her look her fill, the wind whispering through the trees behind them, flurries dancing on the frigid air. Snowy days had a scent to them, a subtle, different feel to the air.

Jenny was talented enough that she could probably paint even the scent of snow.

"Come, my lady. You'll become an ice sculpture if we stand here long enough."

She turned the same regard she'd shown the house onto Elijah, a memorizing sort of look that conveyed both affection and impending loss. He marched away from her, intent on escaping her scrutiny and the longing it held.

"Have you any more questions about Paris?"

She huffed out a sigh that made a little cloud before her. "I have nothing but questions, though I didn't want to distract you from your painting. Have you ever come across a female sculptor?"

"I have not, thank God. Do you have a key?" The knocker was down, and staff likely let off for the holidays.

Jenny withdrew the key and handed it to him. "Why 'thank God'?"

He pushed the door open, admitting them to an entryway that on a sunny day would glow with the light of polished wood, but at present was gloomy and cold.

"Thank God, Genevieve, because you probably have some notion of becoming the first internationally renowned female sculptor. Do you favor the proportions of a stevedore on a duke's daughter? Bad enough you'll heft heavy canvases. Sculptors wrestle their art from stone, you know, and—"

She stared at the floor immediately inside the doorway, making no move to free herself from his scarf or her gloves. He'd probably driven her clear off to Moscow this time.

He unwrapped his scarf from her, shook the snow from it, and draped it over her shoulders. "You aren't listening to me." Her gloves came next. "If you want to become a sculptor, then you must, because you'll be brilliant at that too, but I cannot—hold still." He used his teeth to get his own gloves off and went to work on her frogs. "I cannot countenance that you will face difficulties and you will have no support. You will have *no one*. Your art must stand or fall on its own merit—such as merit can be subjectively determined—and as much as I want to, I cannot be there to temper the winds of fortune for you."

He stepped back and yanked at his buttons, lest he start shouting. She wasn't asking him to temper any winds of anything for her, and she never would.

She stood there, her cloak hanging open and his scarf adorning her shoulders like some bishop's stole. "That's why you've taken me to task so much over my painting? You've carped and criticized because you think that's what awaits me in Paris?"

The daft woman was smiling as if he'd given her some sort of holiday present.

"The French regard criticism as sport, Genevieve, and none are immune. Your gender, your birth, your looks—*nothing* will preserve you from their verbal violence if you cross the wrong Frenchmen in the wrong mood. They are utterly democratic in the sense that no one, not they themselves, not the masters of antiquity, and certainly not English aristos are spared when inspiration strikes—"

She stopped his ranting with two chilly fingers pressed to his lips. "Get your coat off, and let us find Eve's present."

So calm, and yet humor lurked in her green eyes. He was mad with worry for her, and she was amused. He pitched her cloak and his coat onto hooks, tossed his hat onto a sideboard, and let Jenny lead him through the gloom.

"This is a pretty little place. Was it part of your sister's dowry?" And why, even when barely heated, did it have to smell so wonderfully of pine, cedar, and something else, something comforting—lavender?

"It was. Our grandmother thought, as the youngest, Eve might be older when she settled down, having to wait for her sisters to wed first. Eve got property, and the rest of us got competences, which have been invested for us. Westhaven has agreed to continue handling my finances for me after..." She started up a wooden stair. "After the holidays."

Elijah followed her, resisting the urge to tackle her on the landing and make her say the words: After I leave everyone who loves me, and every comfort I've ever known, because I must be a martyr to my art.

She led him down a dim hallway then opened the door to a peculiarly cozy guest room.

"Ah, there it is." Jenny crossed the room and picked up a little box done up in green velvet with red ribbon. "Eve was beside herself. Whatever this is, Deene had best appreciate—why are you staring at me like that?"

He closed the door and stepped closer. The room was unusual, built with a small balcony overlooking a conservatory that might have been added as an afterthought, hence its relative warmth and humidity, and the lush scent of foliage blending with all the other fragrances wafting through the house. "Looking at you like what?"

"Like... you just lost your best friend? Won't it be wonderful to go home to Flint Hall, Elijah?"

Elijah was better than *my lord*, and because she seemed

to need it, he lied for her. "Wonderful, indeed. Have you told your parents yet that you're going to Paris?"

He had the sense she was waiting for him to leave Morelands first, unwilling to have his support even tacitly.

"Not… not yet." She set the perfect little gift down. "Louisa says I must, and she grasps tactics with an intuition I can only admire. I wish…" Her gaze went to the elegant little parcel. "I wish…"

While Elijah watched, Jenny lost some of that distant, preoccupied quality that had characterized her since they'd finished their paintings. She gazed on that parcel as if it held secrets and treats and even a happy ending or two.

Once they completed the twenty-minute walk back to Morelands, they'd have no more private moments *ever.* He'd leave for London at first light; she'd sail for Paris, probably before the New Year.

"What do you wish, Genevieve?" Because whatever it was, he'd give it to her. His heart, his soul, his hands, passage to Paris—passage *home* from Paris. How he wished she'd ask him for that, but passage home was something she could only give herself.

"Will you make love with me, Elijah? You're leaving tomorrow, I know that, and I shouldn't ask it. I shouldn't *want* it, but I do. I want you, so much. Please?"

Sixteen

Not touching Elijah Harrison over the past days had been the hardest thing Jenny had asked of herself, ever. Harder than admitting her mistake with Denby, harder than giving up Antoine's instruction, harder, even, than watching her siblings find true love, one by one.

She blinked at Eve's gift and expected to hear the sound of the door slamming. A lady would never proposition a gentleman, especially a gentleman who'd gently, even kindly, already rebuffed her advances.

A lady would never run off to the Continent and abandon every notion of familial support and love.

A lady would never curse, though if Elijah stalked away, Jenny was going to curse loudly and at length. Also weep, *damn it*.

A hand settled on her shoulder, bringing warmth and ineffable relief. "Woman, you will send me to Bedlam." He turned her into his embrace, just like that.

"You're always warm, Elijah. I love that you're warm." She also loved that he was never in a hurry—usually, she loved this—but she could not allow him to deliberate his way out of the last lovemaking she might ever experience. "You will indulge me, then? I didn't plan this, not even when I realized the staff—"

He cradled the back of her head in his palm and urged her to rest her cheek against his chest. She felt his mind come to a rest, felt him give up on common sense and gentlemanly scruples, felt him relinquish for a time the struggle of being both protective and proper.

"I will pleasure you. We'll let everybody think we traveled the lanes, and take our time with each other here instead."

"We left tracks."

"The wind and weather will obliterate them easily." He spoke so gently, Jenny felt tears threaten yet again. She wrapped her arms around him, holding him tightly and thanking the powers who looked after wayward spinsters that Eve had left her gift behind.

Jenny kissed him first, unable to tolerate the emotions washing around inside her. She wanted him, for Christmas, for herself, for her memories; this one last time, she wanted *him*.

And she wanted this stolen pleasure to last, so she kissed him slowly and gently, the way he often kissed her.

Gradually, his arms tightened around her. His fingers tunneled through her hair, and Jenny felt the solid, incontrovertible proof of his passion rising against her belly.

"Bed, Elijah. On the bed, please."

"Not *please*." He growled the words against her mouth. "You don't have to beg, only ask. Never beg."

With that, he heaved her up, boots and all, and

deposited her sitting on the edge of the bed. This was fortunate, because Jenny had abruptly become breathless and a little stupid with the fruits of her boldness. She ran a hand over Elijah's damp hair as he knelt at her feet. "I'm only being polite."

Foolish words, but they made him smile, and Jenny knew then that this interlude, this purloined hour of passion, was going to be wonderful.

"You're being insecure, rather, and you've no need to be." He eased a boot off her foot then started on the other. "France will be good for you. French women do not suffer fools. They know how to enjoy themselves without guilt and hypocrisy, and French men—"

He fell silent, his brow against Jenny's knee. She was certain he'd been about to say, "and French men know how to appreciate such women," or something along those lines. His silence was more of his worry, more of him being protective.

"French men could never appeal to me." She shifted, silently reminding him that she still wore a boot—and a great many other items of apparel.

The room wasn't warm, but neither was it as frigid as the rest of the house. Because of the balcony overlooking the conservatory, the little chamber had the feel of a bower—a marvelous trysting place for a lady who'd given up her virginity in a dusty minstrel's gallery nearly a decade ago.

Elijah soon had her down to her shift, and when Jenny would have assisted him to disrobe, he instead flopped back the covers. "You warm up the sheets. I cannot vouch for my restraint if you're the one undressing me."

How stern and unyielding he sounded as he wrenched off his cravat. Jenny scooted under the chilly covers and let herself watch.

This was Elijah Harrison in a hurry. With impressive dispatch, his boots, stockings, coat, shirt, waistcoat, and breeches ended up in a haphazard pile on a chair. Jenny had just a moment to admire the line of his spine, buttocks, and legs—a mere instant to long for her sketchbook—before he turned and revealed the impetus for his hurry.

"You are aroused, Elijah." The longing for her sketchbook evaporated in a longing for him. "You are quite, quite aroused."

His stride across the room blended a prowl and a swagger. Jenny wanted to ask him—not beg him, though—to do it again so she could watch more closely how his muscles and sinews moved.

Except she couldn't quite find the words. She instead reclined against the pillows, while Elijah climbed directly onto the bed and commenced kissing her.

Really, truly kissing her. Kissing her while he positioned himself on all fours over her, kissing her while she twined her arms around his neck and let herself kiss him back.

He pulled back, frowning down at her. "Your hair—"

Jenny tugged the covers up under her arms and wondered what it was about Elijah's kisses that addled her wits. "What about my hair?"

"I want it down, Genevieve, and you don't fool me. When you're about your pleasures, you're about as modest and demure as a tempest. Sit up."

Elijah, dear, reserved, composed Elijah, was very

managing when naked. Maybe that was the cause of her witlessness, because in this context, she quite liked him giving orders—and she sat up.

"How many pins does it take to hold up a single braid?"

"Twenty four." Twenty-two of which were piled up on the night table in an instant, and as for the other two, Jenny would find them when she went hunting for her wits—later.

Elijah lifted the covers and joined her beneath them, the bed rocking and bouncing with his movements like a heaving sea. "You are very bold, Genevieve, but you haven't let yourself acknowledge this yet. Make love with me." He wrestled her into his arms then rolled with her so she was straddling him, her hair streaming down around them like so much swagged Christmas greenery.

"Make love with you."

Splendid notion, particularly with his erect member very much in evidence against her sex. He traced her hairline, pushing her errant locks back, the movement slow and sweet.

Abruptly, sadness threaded through the glee and anticipation fueling Jenny's arousal. "You should not have taken down my hair. I'll be forever putting it back in order."

"You should not consign yourself to Paris. And as for your hair, I love it down. I love every single—" The look in his eyes shifted, as if Jenny's sadness were contagious. The sternness became tenderness. "I've loved every time I've seen it down. I've loved knowing that while others might see you only properly tucked up and pinned into place, I know the truth."

His hands cradled her breasts, and lest he embroider further on his metaphor—for it was a metaphor—Jenny closed her eyes and arched into his touch. "I love it that you know, Elijah, and I love it when you do that."

For he'd applied a sweet, steady pressure to her nipples, the exact right touch to illuminate her insides like one of her German grandmother's decorated Christmas trees—all candles and sparkle, sentiment and joy.

"Elijah—I love..."

He was wiser than she. Before she could let fly with her folly, he leaned up and kissed her, nothing tucked up or pinned into place about it. His tongue came calling, and one strong arm wrapped around her back while his free hand continued to tease at her breasts.

"Love me, Genevieve. You asked for what you wanted, and I intend to see that you get it."

When had she started to move? When had she begun to drag the slick, secret folds of her sex over him, to initiate the true prelude to their joining? Jenny curled forward, bracing herself over her lover on one hand. With the other, she positioned him for her pleasure, and paused.

Elijah's hands slid to her hips. "Minx. Tease. Siren. Houri. Mad woman. Brilliant, talented, daft, mad—"

He might have aired his vocabulary the livelong afternoon, but Jenny rolled her hips forward and took him inside her body in one slow, glorious slide.

"Holy, perishing—some warning might have been in order, Genevieve." He sounded dazed and witless.

She leaned down, resting her forehead on his. "Do I make you want to curse, Elijah?"

"Curse, sing, laugh, pray. Love me."

She did. She most assuredly, absolutely did love him. Because he did not stop her from following her dream, because he'd told her where his second cousin might let rooms to her, because he'd suggested she might find instruction with another second cousin who was cranky but very astute and well connected.

More than that, she loved him because he'd taken her seriously and he'd insisted that her family take her seriously.

Mostly, though, as her body began to sing with the joy of intimate congress with his, Jenny admitted to herself that she loved Elijah because she was leaving, and this was the last they would ever be together.

Elijah watched as pleasure suffused Genevieve Windham's features, watched as she shifted from beautiful to transfigured. Her body clutched at him, wrung every ounce of self-restraint from him, to the point that he had to close his eyes or lose control.

And that he could not do, not when she was so close to realizing her dream, and he was… a gentleman.

As Jenny subsided onto his chest, Elijah wrapped his arms around her and revised his word choice. No gentleman would take a lady other than his wife to bed, though he might take other women to bed under certain conditions.

And Elijah had, from time to time, but he could not recall their names, their faces, their scents, anything about them.

"Hold me, Elijah."

Always. He kissed her hair and snugged his arms more closely around her. "You're all right?"

"Mmm." Not even a word, but it conveyed profound contentment.

The moment was tender, dear, and for Elijah, not content at all. His cock throbbed with wanting, and while he could not recall his previous partners, he would not be able to forget Genevieve. He *could* follow her to Paris, of course, and she'd probably bestow more of such moments on him.

More crumbs for him, more risks to her safety, her reputation, and her dreams.

"I want more, sir." His sleepy, sweet tempest began to move.

"Then you shall have it."

He'd never intended to spend. He'd intended to let her have her pleasure of him, to stretch out this joining as long as he could, to make as many memories with her as she could bear to share with him.

A man in love treasures even the pain of his affliction, after all.

Jenny ambushed him, though, moving on him with increasing power and speed, her arms lashed around his shoulders, and then, without warning, she pitched off to the side, dragging him over her.

Exactly where he longed to be.

"Genevieve..."

She silenced his warning with kisses, with her body determined to shower pleasure upon them both, with her hand gripping his hair, and with—a curious, fierce sensation—her fingernails gripping his buttocks. "Don't beg, Elijah. Never beg. Love me. Love me *now.*"

He could not refuse his lady's command. He loved her, and he made love with her, and when she slept in his arms, sated and sweet, her hair in complete disarray, he only loved her more.

Jenny watched as Elijah tugged on his boots then paused while he examined his footwear. "If there's a baby—"

She cut him off with a look and a nod. "Of course. I wouldn't visit illegitimacy on my child. Our child."

The words, even the very words, *our child*, weakened her knees to the point that she had to sit on the bed. She might have just conceived a future Marquess of Flint. The notion was upsetting, for any number of reasons.

Paris had loomed like an artistic haven, of course, and like a sanctuary from her family's well-intended, smothering attentions. Paris was the antidote to everything stupid and backward about the present version of English chivalry too, and to all of Polite Society's idiot notions about a true lady being a useless, decorative, porcelain figurine.

Paris was where she could keep her promise to Victor and put her entire focus on her art.

At what point had Paris also acquired the lure of a coward's way out?

Elijah took the place on the bed beside her and extracted the brush from her limp fingers. "I'll do that."

He tended to her hair, just as he'd assisted her to dress, with brisk competence that suggested regret for what had passed between them.

"Elijah, are you angry?"

He tucked the last pin into her hair and drew her back against his chest. "If I am angry, I am angry for you and with myself, not with you. We'd best be going."

Not an answer she could comprehend, not with her body that of a sexually sated stranger, her mind in a complete muddle, and her heart…

Her heart breaking.

She let Elijah lead her through the house, sensing darkness gathering even earlier than usual.

"The snow has picked up," Elijah said as they donned coats, gloves, and scarves. "You will take my hand, Genevieve, damn the appearances, until we've reached a cleared path on Morelands property."

That he'd understand she needed some lingering connection with him was a relief. That he'd do her the further courtesy of making it a command was a blessing.

"I don't need to hold your hand to make my way through a few inches of snow."

He tucked the ends of his scarf under her chin. "Perhaps I need to hold yours."

She held his hand until they'd reached the very steps of the Morelands back terrace.

"Lovely. Lovely, lovely, lovely."

Jenny watched while His Grace the Duke of Moreland gushed—that was the word—gushed about the portraits on display, and the duchess quietly beamed her satisfaction with the duke's praise.

Also with His Grace's portrait, which, now that Jenny considered the image dispassionately, emphasized not only the man's ducal consequence but also his regard for his duchess. Percival Windham as rendered in oil on canvas was a man capable of humor and sternness, of loving his country fiercely and his duchess gently.

Elijah had caught that *heart*, and caught it wonderfully. He might also have caught a sudden case of lung fever, because the entire family had assembled in anticipation of the open house, while the artist in residence had yet to come downstairs.

"Both portraits are quite good," Her Grace said. "I am particularly pleased with how my surprise turned out."

Her surprise being the portrait of her, done for His Grace's holiday present.

When Elijah dared to venture down the steps, Jenny was going to ask him some pointed questions about that portrait, but for now, her siblings and their spouses were adding their choruses of appreciation for the art they beheld.

"I do think that portrait of Her Grace is better even than the one he did of the children," Sophie allowed. "Sindal, would you agree?"

Everybody agreed, and in the middle of all this smiling and agreeing, Louisa sidled up to Jenny, bringing a hint of cinnamon and clove with her. "Have you told them yet?"

"You are like the bad fairy, Louisa, insisting on difficult tidings when they'll easily keep for a day or two. I don't intend to leave until after the New Year. There's time yet."

Louisa's mouth flattened, but she kept her voice down. "You cannot hare off as if you're eloping with a disgraceful choice, Jenny. That's not fair to you. It's even less fair to Their Graces. They'll need time to adjust, to strike terms."

"I am going to move to Paris," Jenny said, just as firmly. "I do not expect you to understand, Lou, but I do expect you to keep my confidences, within reason."

Louisa opened her mouth to say something, likely something articulate, insightful, and painful—though not mean—when her expression shifted. "It's a bit late for that."

Jenny glanced over her shoulder to find both of her parents hovering only three feet away, the good cheer of the season apparent in the eyes of neither.

Elijah hustled as far as the first landing, then paused, took a deep breath, and came down the last set of stairs at a pace that befit a gentleman and a guest in a ducal household.

Though Jenny would likely skewer him for leaving her in the grand parlor alone amid the milling, smiling herd of her family, all decked out in their holiday finery, all blessedly ignorant that Lady Jenny had trysted away an hour of her afternoon.

With him.

As they'd left Lavender Corner, she'd seemed right enough, seemed composed, for all she'd gripped Elijah's hand the entire distance back to Morelands. And yet, he hadn't wanted to leave her, not when her undisclosed travel plans hung like the holiday equivalent of the sword of Damocles over the entire family gathering.

He came through the doorway at a pace halfway

between dignity and panic—an enthusiastic pace, perhaps. A holiday pace adopted when a man needed a clear shot at the punch bowl—only to stop short.

His Grace was glowering mightily at Jenny, who was resplendent in red velvet and white lace. Beside the duke, Her Grace looked concerned, and Jenny looked… determined. Mulishly determined.

"What is this tripe about moving to Paris?" His Grace asked.

God help them and their chances for a happy Christmas. Elijah sidled through a crowd of Windham lords and ladies, the women's expressions mirroring concern for their sister, the men's eyes guarded and their arms around their wives' waists.

"Mama, Papa, I'm moving to Paris to study art. I trust you'll wish me well."

She hadn't asked; she hadn't begged or prettied up a request with pleases and perhapses. Elijah had never been more proud of his Genevieve.

"Percival, talk to your daughter." That from Her Grace, whose tone conveyed bewilderment. "The strain of holiday entertaining has taken a toll on her."

"You, Genevieve, are distressing your mother," His Grace began. "I know not what wild start you're positing, but no daughter of mine is going to waste her youth and beauty getting her fingers dirty in some frozen French garret, when her proper place is here, among the family who loves her. A husband and children—"

"I beg Your Grace's pardon," Elijah cut in.

"Elijah," Jenny muttered. "Keep quiet."

Oh, of course. She must be a martyr in this too. "I

cannot keep quiet, my lady. You will say things you regret to people who love you, but I can speak reason to them."

Artistic heathen though they might be.

He could wallop them over the head with reason if necessary, or with truth, or with any other blunt object heavy enough to dent the legendary Windham pride, but he would not let Jenny rain down her frustration and ire on her own parents.

That way lay ten years of estrangement, and they would be long, cold years too.

"You are interfering, Bernward," His Grace spat. "I have no doubt you've abetted this rebellion in a girl who used to be the example I held up to her sisters of all that is admirable in a lady."

"Jenny is no longer a girl." Her Grace's soft observation suggested Jenny's mother was coming to this realization only as the words left her lips. Perhaps some feminine sympathy informed the duchess's thinking, or maternal prescience.

"Lady Genevieve has artistic talent beyond anything possessed by a mere girl," Elijah said. "The evidence lies right before your eyes."

He gestured to the portraits, sitting side by side in temporary frames on their easels. On canvas, the duke and duchess sat facing each other at a quarter angle, each work complete in itself, and yet the two together formed a greater composition. His Grace held a volume of Shakespeare sonnets, as if reading to his wife—which he had been for much of their sittings.

Her Grace worked a bit of embroidery, a peacock and a unicorn full of colors and soft textures.

"Which is the better work?" Elijah asked.

Her Grace's eyebrows rose, suggesting more of her intuition already grasped the problem.

"The portrait of Her Grace," said the duke without hesitation. "The subject is more pleasing, of course, but—from the perspective of one who knows nothing of art—the execution is flawless, Her Grace to the very teeth. You've outdone yourself, Bernward, and I am most pleased with the result, even if you've been fomenting insurrection while you paint." The portraits dismissed, the duke turned a blue-eyed glower on Jenny. "I am not at all pleased with a daughter who exhibits crackbrained notions about dabbling away her looks and youth when she ought to be about the business of finding a husband and setting up her nursery. What can possibly—?"

Elijah felt Jenny draw herself up, and he let her be the one to wield the only relevant truth.

"*I* painted that portrait of Her Grace, Papa. *I* did. Not the much-lauded associate to the Royal Academy, not the artistic heir apparent to Sir Thomas, not the man with years of training and experience. *I* did that painting of Mama, *and it is beautiful.*"

She'd spent her ammunition, fired off powder she'd been keeping dry for years, and her eyes were painfully bright as a result. Elijah twined his arm through hers, slipped her his handkerchief, and took up her cutlass for her.

"Lady Genevieve outpainted a much-vaunted professional portraitist, and she did it easily, without support from her family, without much training, without anything approximating true encouragement. She kept up with me when I worked hour after hour, then she turned around and endured more hours of hoodman-blind and whist, when all she wanted was to be back up in the studio, creating more beauty. She deserves to go to Paris, and I very much doubt you could stop her, in any case."

Which was a damned shame, because she needed to be stopped.

Someone cursed, someone else muttered a refrain about prophets and honor. The duke stood glowering for a moment then winged his arm at his duchess. "Genevieve, you will attend your mother and me in her private parlor at once. You, Bernward, come along too."

The duchess took her husband's arm. "Percival, the guests will start arriving any moment."

"Hang the guests. Our children can exert themselves to be charming to the neighbors while we sort through Jenny's contretemps."

Her Grace looked like she'd say more, but processed from the room with a dignity that reminded Elijah of his mother.

"You don't have to do this, Elijah," Jenny said as he moved her toward the door. "But I love what you did."

Her love, given in his direction in any sense, was reward enough.

"Blame the cat," he murmured as her brothers and sisters parted to let them leave the room. "Timothy rolled a paint brush off the mantel—one I'd not collected at the end of a session—and a dab of green splashed into the middle of the fire on my version of Her Grace's portrait. I could either display a wet canvas of my own or take the wiser course suggested by Providence."

"Jenny!" Westhaven was the last obstacle Elijah and his lady had to face before gaining the door. The earl stood looking much like his father, until his lips quirked, and his smile showed a resemblance to the duchess. "Well damned done, Sister!"

He slowly clapped his hands together, his countess joined in, and a cascade of sibling applause filled the room.

"Hear, hear," Sophie echoed as the din died away. Brothers, sisters, and in-laws raised their glasses, the good wishes ringing back and forth now that Their Graces had left the room.

"Don't back down," St. Just advised. "Not if painting is what you need to be happy."

Lord Valentine winked at his sister, looking… proud, unless Elijah missed his guess. "Windhams sometimes have to make their own way, and Ellen's been after me to take her to Paris."

"We'll all visit you," Lady Maggie added.

Lady Eve was positively beaming. "You won't be able to stop us. Nothing will stop us from making nuisances of ourselves on your doorstep."

Elijah wanted to ask where all this great good cheer had been previously, when Jenny had been so lonely for encouragement she had taken stupid risks and made even worse compromises, but he kept his silence and escorted her from the room.

They would visit her in Paris, the lot of them, and bring their children and stay for weeks. They wouldn't wait ten years to send a few letters, and leave the rest up to her.

Seventeen

Jenny felt as if she were dwelling a short distance from her body, as if a weight had been lifted from her shoulders and from her heart. Even Papa saw the quality of her art, and Elijah…

"You aren't subject to ducal decrees, Elijah. I can manage Mama and Papa."

He paused where two hallways intersected, one leading to the public rooms, one to the family chambers. "That's not just a mama and a papa you're facing, Genevieve, it's also a duke and duchess. They're used to ruling by divine right, and quelling insurrection merely by raising an eyebrow. I daresay their daughters don't defy them, though their sons likely have."

Jenny went up on her toes and kissed him—the happiness in her compelled it, as did the sadness. "You must not worry, Elijah. Papa himself admitted that I paint as well as you."

Better than Elijah—and that had been so, so sweet, though one painting did not an impressive body of works create.

"Admitting you paint well will not get you to

Paris." He took her hand and led her down the hallway, his grip firm, his stride determined.

Foreboding edged happiness away. "What are you about, Elijah? Papa himself vouched for my talent."

Elijah stopped outside the parlor door and dropped her hand. "If you get to Paris, it will be because your family loves you, and only because they love you. I'm counting on it."

He left her no time to argue or refine on his point—of course her family loved her—before he planted a swift, no-nonsense kiss on her lips, then opened the parlor door and ushered her through.

"Your Grace, if I might have a word with you privately?"

At Elijah's question, the duke stopped pacing and aimed a glacial stare at his guest. "A *word*? With *you*? Most assuredly." He bowed to his wife and left the room with Elijah, while Jenny regarded her mother.

"A medicinal tot is in order," the duchess declared. "For both of us, and, Jenny, you must not let your papa's temper dismay you. He's… he blames himself when I'm upset, and he's surprised."

Which was exactly what Louisa had warned Jenny against.

Jenny glanced at the door, foreboding expanding in her middle to the proportions of dread. When she accepted a drink from her mother, the duchess's fingers were cold.

"What can they be discussing?" Jenny asked nobody in particular.

"A marriage proposal?" the duchess suggested.

"I doubt it."

Her mother gave her a considering look from the sideboard. "If Bernward offered, Genevieve, would you choose Paris over him?"

Her Grace was a pragmatic woman, also a mother who would cheerfully kill for her children or for her dear Percival. Her instincts were not to be discounted, ever.

"I did."

"Oh, my dear, whatever could be more important than love?"

And now the dread moved up, north of Jenny's belly, into her throat, because that one question befuddled and hurt and made a hash of Jenny's ability to think.

The door opened, and His Grace rejoined them, though of Elijah there was no evidence. To Jenny's eye, the duke's paternal fire had been snuffed out, and where his blue eyes had held the promise of retribution for anyone fool enough to cross him, now he looked… sad.

"Ah, you're drinking. My love, might I have a tot as well?"

Something was wrong. When His Grace's temper was so completely replaced with what looked for all the world like regret, something was dreadfully wrong.

The duchess held her drink out to him. He brought it to his lips but kept his gaze on his wife, as if imbibing courage with the very sight of her.

"Bernward is a canny young man," the duke said. "Shall we sit?"

Jenny did not want to sit. She wanted to find Elijah and wring from him a recounting of what had aged the Duke of Moreland ten years in less than two minutes.

She wanted to take the worry from the duchess's eyes, and she wanted to go to Paris right that very instant.

Her Grace took one end of a small sofa and Jenny the other. The duke peered around the room as if he'd not spent many and many an hour reading to his wife in the very same location.

"Bernward claims you are not determined on Paris so much because you want to paint," the duke said. He set his little glass down on the sideboard and turned his back on Jenny and her mother.

That was rude, and His Grace was never intentionally rude to his duchess. Jenny's heart began to thump a slow, ominous tattoo in her chest. *Please rant and bellow, Papa. Please be in a magnificent temper and hurl a few thunderbolts, then tell me I can go with your blessing.*

The duchess's hand stroked over Jenny's shoulder, an it-will-be-all-right caress Jenny knew like she knew her own reflection, though it brought no comfort.

"Genevieve, Bernward claims..." The duke's shoulders heaved up and down, slowly, as if he were sorely fatigued. "Bernward is of the opinion that you seek the Continent not because your talent compels it, or not solely because of your talent, but because you blame yourself"—behind his back, the duke's hands were laced so tightly his knuckles showed white—"you blame *yourself* for the death of not one, but of both your brothers, Bartholomew and Victor."

The duchess's soft gasp sounded over a roaring in Jenny's ears.

"Bernward claims," the duke went on softly, "you must exile yourself out of guilt, because you are of the daft notion that only your happiness will atone for the loss of your brothers' lives, though he suspects you disguise these sentiments even from yourself, or you try to. I cannot credit this. I simply cannot, and yet… you are our daughter. We know you, and Bernward, God *damn* the man, is not wrong."

An ache grew and grew inside Jenny. An awful, choking, suffocating ache, an ache she thought she'd learned long ago how to manage. She wanted Elijah. She wanted to sprout wings and fly from the little parlor where she'd sat on her mother's lap and learned to embroider with her sisters. She wanted, in some way, to die rather than contain the pain pressing at her very organs.

When His Grace turned from the cold, dark window, Jenny did not look away quickly enough. Even through the sheen blurring her own eyes, she could see that tears had also gathered in the eyes of His Grace, the Duke of Moreland. She looked down, seeing nothing, while her misery increased without end.

"Oh, my child." The duchess enveloped Jenny in a ferocious embrace. "Oh, my dear, dear child. How could you think this of yourself? How could you possibly— Percival, more drinks and your handkerchief. *This instant.*"

Fortunate indeed was the man whose wife had the presence of mind to keep him busy when sentiment threatened to render him… heartbroken. His Grace poured himself a shot of whisky, downed it, and poured another. This one he considered, while across the room Her Grace held a quietly lachrymose daughter, a young lady exhausted by her emotional burdens and by a failure of trust in her parents' love.

And dear Esther… Percival fished out his second handkerchief—Windham menfolk were prepared for the occasional domestic affray, particularly around the holidays—and passed it to his duchess. She pressed it to her eyes while keeping an arm around the girl plastered to her mother's shoulder, then gestured toward the sideboard.

"Of course, my dear."

Brandy for the ladies. More brandy. Percival dallied by pouring just so, arranging the glasses just so on a tray, and opening and closing the drawers to the sideboard until he'd found two clean serviettes. When the weeping sounded as if it was subsiding, he brought the tray over to his womenfolk.

"Drink up, young lady, and prepare to explain yourself."

Over Jenny's head, Esther's slight smile indicated he'd gotten it right: brusque and unsentimental, but more papa than commanding officer or duke.

Jenny accepted a drink from her mother, but the poor girl's hand shook, and the duke had to make a significant inroad on his second whisky. At this rate, he would be drunk before the guests arrived, which was a fine idea all around.

"I think I can guess some of it," Her Grace said. *She* hadn't touched her drink. The woman had fortitude beyond description. "You blame yourself for Bart's joining up, because you had such a very great row with him before I finally relented."

Jenny stopped folding and unfolding her damp handkerchief to peer at her mother. "Relented?"

Oh, this was difficult. Percival pulled up a rocking chair and sat at his wife's elbow. "Lest you forget, missy, Windham men have a long and distinguished tradition of serving King and Country. Bart needed to work out the fidgets, so to speak. He was setting a terrible example for the younger boys, wreaking havoc with the domestics, and upsetting your mother. I'd started negotiating for a commission, but your mother could not…"

Could not put her son at risk of death. Percival met his duchess's gaze, thanking her silently yet again for never once blaming *him* for Bart's death.

"I could not let him go," Her Grace said quietly. "He was my firstborn, the child conceived as your father and I fell in love and married, a bright, shining symbol of so much that was good, but your father had the right of it: Bart was becoming spoiled, and if he was ever to make any sort of duke, he needed to grow up."

Grow up. Such a simple term for a complicated, fraught, difficult process that could challenge dukes well into their prime. His Grace marshaled his fortitude and said a few more simple words. "You were not responsible for Bartholomew's death. He died in a Portuguese tavern because the damned fool boy propositioned a decent woman with protective family. I've blamed myself, I've blamed Wellington, I've blamed the entire Portuguese nation for being so deucedly full of pretty girls, but in my wildest imaginings I never once blamed you."

His feeble attempt at levity went right past Jenny, but Her Grace gave him another small smile.

So he soldiered on.

"You are not responsible for Victor's death either."

Jenny's face disappeared into her blasted handkerchief. Her Grace tucked the girl closer, and the pain in the duchess's eyes…

Two sons buried, and this daughter nearly lost to an abundance of responsibility and a want of parental attention. It was enough to make a man plan the demolition of Paris. Percival served his wife a steadying look, because the woman would soon be blaming herself for the whole of it.

Truly, Genevieve was their daughter.

"V-Victor went with me to the worst p-places. To any poorhouse, any slum, and he stood by me while I drew and drew… And then he was sick, and I promised him I'd keep painting."

All no doubt true, also quite beside the point. "That, young lady, is complete twaddle. Everywhere your brother escorted you, two stout footmen followed. Her Grace insisted. You did not fall ill, the footmen did not fall ill, and yet Victor did."

Luckily for a papa's composure, this pronouncement got Jenny's attention "You knew?"

Her Grace pushed a lock of Jenny's hair over the girl's shoulder, not because Jenny was in any disarray, but because a mother never got over the need to cosset her babies—nor a duke the need to cosset his duchess.

"We knew," Her Grace said. "Victor made sure we knew, and said we ought to find you a better drawing master, one who'd cultivate your talent, because you couldn't stop drawing or painting if you wanted to."

"But he became so ill… He died, and all because I dragged him around with me, just so I could draw all those children and old people. I told Victor if I drew them, then death wouldn't entirely win. I was a selfish idiot." She balled up her handkerchief, and His Grace stifled the urge to duck. "Death won."

So young, and so burdened. So damned unnecessarily burdened. "Death ended Victor's suffering, but you, my girl, did not cause it. You never knew my brother Peter, a great strapping fellow who would have made a marvelous duke had he not been cursed with a weak constitution. By the age of thirty-five, he was no longer riding out."

Her Grace picked up the argument for the defense right on cue. "My younger sister, Ruth, succumbed to consumption before she was out of the schoolroom. Consumption is a scourge, and you did not invent it. I daresay Victor was exposed to disease in a number of unsavory locations about which I will not expound upon, lest I disgrace his memory."

Oh, excellent. A touch of maternal vinegar turned the moment for Jenny to one of thoughtful consideration rather than self-flagellation.

His Grace winked at his wife. Well done, indeed. She took a dainty sip of her drink, lifting the glass an inch in His Grace's direction. A certain duke was going to find some mistletoe when this dreary business was through, see if he didn't.

"You are not responsible for your brothers' deaths, Genevieve. That you could think it breaks my heart, and your dear mother will likely require much comforting as a result of the misperception you've labored under. I hope no more need be said on the topic?"

He prayed no more need be said, but any prisoner liberated from guilt needed time to relearn a world of freedom. While he leveled a glower at his daughter—a loving glower—His Grace had the thought that Genevieve would have made a good duke.

She understood responsibility and loyalty instinctively, but like her mother, she was not as comfortable with delegation of her assigned tasks. Perhaps Bernward might help her with that.

"No more need be said right now, Papa."

If only *that* were true.

"I need to say something." Her Grace glanced at Percival as she spoke, and he returned the look. Anything she wanted to say, or needed to say, could only add to the discussion and as always, cover the difficult ground her husband—*any* husband—would sprint across hotfoot.

"I need to say—Percival, would you hold my drink?—I need to say that I am proud of you, Genevieve. I am proud of the regard you hold for your siblings, proud of your talent, proud of your determination—you get that from your father—and so very proud of your courage."

Oh, damn. What was a man to do when confronted with a teary duchess and a weeping daughter? Percival set the bloody drinks aside, grabbed a serviette, and enveloped both crying females in a hug.

This had the advantage of ensuring he had the privacy to take a surreptitious swipe at his own eyes, but did not relieve him of the obligation—of the need—to reinforce Her Grace's words.

And to lay the groundwork for a bit of paternal strategy.

"Of course we're proud of you. We have always been proud of you, but I must tell you, Genevieve, Paris will not do. Not when there's the whole of the Continent full of art and drawing masters. Paris alone simply will not do."

"I cannot imagine what lies in London that requires you to abandon all sense, much less abandon the woman you love, and subject your horse to such a journey. My countess will worry about you, and that is a sore trial for the rest of the household."

Kesmore passed Elijah a flask as he scolded, and Elijah took a sip of smooth, fiery brew redolent of hazelnuts.

"I must pay a call on a member of the Academy's nominating committee then visit my family at Flint Hall. Your hospitality these past two days has been much appreciated."

Particularly when a foot of snow had fallen Christmas Eve into Christmas Day. Kesmore had offered to take Elijah home with him after the open house, and Elijah had left Morelands, bag and baggage, rather than remain where at least one duke and one duchess held him in mortal dislike.

As well they should, though not for the reasons they did.

Kesmore capped the flask. "Are you paying the least attention, Bernward?"

"No." Elijah tested the snugness of the horse's

girth, because he might have tightened it, and he might have not. Such were the mental faculties of a man with a broken heart, a man who'd waited in vain for Genevieve to leave the upper reaches of the house and join the party below on Christmas Eve.

"She leaves New Year's Day for the Continent," Kesmore mused, and abruptly the foggy, boggy morass that was Elijah's brain regained the ability to focus.

"Genevieve is going to Paris?"

His initial reaction was… a sentimental mix of gladness for her, pride in her resolve, and the certain knowledge that no amount of drinking or rumination was going to ferment those feelings into outright joy.

"Eventually. Seems a widowed aunt wants to visit relations in Vienna, though the itinerary will take them through Rome, Venice, Florence, a few other places known for their art treasures. Paris is on the list, I'm sure. When His Grace says a little travel broadens the mind, one had best start packing."

England without Genevieve would be a lonely place. Any studio without Genevieve would be a lonely place.

The back of Elijah's horse would be a very lonely place, particularly when that horse was pointed away from the lady. That she was achieving her heart's desire was much less comfort than Elijah had hoped it would be.

"Wish me safe journey, Kesmore, and thanks for all of your hospitality."

Kesmore shoved the flask at him. "Louisa says you are an idiot, but I must be patient because you are an idiot in love with an imbecile. She says that's the general case where tender sentiments are involved, and I am ever grateful for my countess's guidance. Safe journey."

Kesmore yanked him into a hug, walloped him once on the back, then let him go.

As Elijah swung down from his horse, long, weary, frigid miles later, the force of Kesmore's blow still reverberated in memory, almost as if the man had been trying to knock sense into him.

"Mr. Buchanan will see you now, my lord."

They all *my lorded* him now, the entire committee. He didn't like it from them any more than he'd liked it from Genevieve—for different reasons.

"Bernward, welcome, and what a pleasure!" Buchanan's face was wreathed with a smile that suggested he knew things Elijah did not. That smile went onto the growing list of things Elijah did not like.

"Buchanan. Apologies for the lack of notice, but I was passing through Town on my way to Flint Hall."

Those words dimmed the smile, blending it with consternation. "You're off to the family seat?"

"For what remains of the holidays, yes. My mother's wishes trump royal edicts, papal bulls, and likely the whims of the Almighty. I did, however, want to discuss with you—"

A footman appeared bearing a tray. Buchanan gestured the man into a room, the walls of which were crowded with old masters growing dark with age—and not a smile to be seen among them.

"You wanted to discuss the committee nominations," Buchanan said when the footman had withdrawn. "Shall we sit?"

No, they shall not sit. "Afraid I haven't the time,

sir. You will understand the urgency of keeping the Marchioness of Flint from a display of stubborn temper?" Mama would kill him for that prevarication. Her menfolk were the ones afflicted with stubborn temper.

Buchanan's expression became considering, the look of a politician rearranging his chess pieces. "If you're going to Flint Hall, perhaps you'd take a package for me to Lord Flint?"

"Of course, though the purpose for my call was to retrieve from you the sketches I'd passed along of a certain portrait." The best portrait he'd ever done, and the best likeness he'd rendered of a certain young lady.

Who was on her way to the bloody, sodding Continent in only a few days' time, there to kick up her heels, admire art, and be admired by not just Frenchmen—those were bad enough—but Germans, Austrians, Dutchmen, and *Italians*. Possibly Russians as well, and those dear chaps had burned three-quarters of Moscow in the dead of winter rather than allow Napoleon the satisfaction of sacking it. Genevieve would be right at home among them.

"So you don't want to discuss the committee's nominations?"

Turpentine and paint fumes could addle a man's wits, particularly when they were all he breathed for decades at a time. Elijah spoke gently. "I do not care that"—he snapped his fingers under Buchanan's sizable nose—"for the committee's nominations."

Plainer than that, he could not be. Not without lapsing into profanities, but what mattered the committee's blessing when Genevieve was packing for the

Continent, and the last coffin nail was being pounded into Elijah's relationship with his family?

Genevieve had told him to go home, so home he would go.

Buchanan regarded him for another moment, looking less like a politician and more like a man who'd once rendered portraits and had the knack of reading faces. "I'll get your father's package. It's in my study, and your drawing is with it."

Elijah followed him through a chilly, dank house—the damp could not be good for all the art displayed on the walls—into an equally chilly, damp, and cramped room toward the front.

Buchanan's study had good light, though. As Buchanan opened a cupboard and extracted a leather tube about thirty inches long, Elijah realized they were standing in what had once likely been a studio.

"Do you miss it?" Elijah asked.

Buchanan passed the leather case over, his eyes revealing comprehension of the question. "I do. I should not have stopped, but the Academy is a fine institution, and it wanted guidance. I was never as talented as some, but I miss the painting. I do miss it."

He let go of the case, and his lips quirked up. "I'll keep your sentiments regarding the committee to myself, for now. That is a fine, fine portrait, Bernward."

Elijah turned to follow Buchanan's line of sight, only to be gut-punched by the painting hanging against the far wall.

Genevieve and the busy, laughing little boys, old Jock snoozing happily, and everything Elijah had ever wanted summarized in one painting. Even as his mind comprehended that the portrait was good—better than he'd known—his brain was scrambling to make sense of the painting in its present context.

"What is that doing here?"

"I agree," Buchanan said, stepping closer to the painting. "If I'd commissioned this, I would never have let it out of my sight, but it arrived with a note from no less than His Grace the Duke of Moreland, with leave for the committee to consider it when deciding upon their nominations. Said his daughter, whose artistic sensibilities eclipse those of any academy member, required it of him. Even Fotheringale shut up for once. You apparently have a talent for rendering children."

Or for rendering any setting that included Genevieve Windham, and yet the committee's flattering reception of this one painting did not change anything—anything of consequence—one bit.

Though Elijah spared an internal sigh for Genevieve's generosity of spirit. Maybe a return to the Harrison family seat would help ease that ache—and maybe not. "I'm off to Flint Hall, Buchanan. You'll want to send that painting back to Kent with all due care."

Elijah snatched up the case of drawings and departed. When he'd traveled halfway to Flint Hall and had to stop to rest his weary horse, it occurred to him to wonder what was in the case.

Some of his mother's drawings? She was quite talented… and yet, the package was for his lordship. A gentleman did not open another gentleman's mail.

Though Elijah's drawing of Jenny and the children was in there, and Elijah was seized with an abrupt yearning to look upon that image. He wanted to indulge the impulse now, before he dealt with the drama of his arrival at Flint Hall, before Genevieve left the country for a journey that could go on for years, before anybody who knew him might observe his folly.

He appropriated the snug at a familiar posting inn, opened the case, and unrolled a thick sheaf of drawings. What they revealed had him cursing, laughing, and climbing back on his tired, muddy horse.

"So you're really going?" Louisa kept the question light, because Jenny was in love, and people in love were prone to inconvenient histrionics, as were people in expectation of interesting events.

"Aunt Arabella has agreed, so yes." Jenny held a boot in each hand, ordinary lace-up half boots, but they must have had some significance known only to her, because she held them as if they were… original poems penned by a beloved.

"And how long will you be gone?"

"I don't know." The boots went into a trunk, placed gently, like an infant's baptismal gown might have been stowed away. "Have you seen my—?" Jenny worried a nail then retrieved an embroidered bag hanging inside the door of her wardrobe.

From her seat at Jenny's escritoire, Louisa watched as the little bag got the same sentimental treatment. "What's in there?"

"Elijah's Christmas present to me. He left it on my pillow before he came downstairs on Christmas Eve. The embroidery is his mother's, and it's exquisite."

Embroidery, no matter how beautiful, was tedious as the devil, and Jenny could create more fantastic stitchery even than what graced that bag. "He gave you the bag?"

Jenny nodded, her gaze on the bag where it lay on top of the other contents of the trunk. She might have been regarding the mortal remains of a beloved pet, based on her expression. "He gave me sketches, I'm sure of it. I'm saving them for when I'm in Italy, or Austria. Possibly France."

Or maybe Bedlam. Louisa shoved to her feet and snatched the bag from the trunk. "You haven't even opened your Christmas present, and yet you won't leave the country without it. You, Sister, are in a state."

Jenny said nothing, and that gave Louisa pause. The old Jenny, the Jenny who called everybody dearest and had to have a sketchbook in her hands, was never in a state, much less one she admitted openly.

This Jenny had a softness about her, and while she was given to leaving rooms abruptly, and sometimes looked as if she'd been crying, she was an easy person to love.

Eve's brilliant ploy with Deene's supposed Christmas gift had not worked, or not worked well enough, and Their Graces were watching these travel preparations with worry in their eyes.

Worry for Jenny, who'd never given anybody cause to worry.

Louisa opened the bag and peered inside. "These are not sketches."

"They're not?"

Before Jenny could grab the bag back, Louisa

extracted a sheaf of letters. "Oh, good. Some are written in German, and I do enjoy German. This one's Italian, and there are several in French. This must be… I didn't know Elijah had a grasp of Russian."

"He spent a year in St. Petersburg. Let me see those."

Louisa handed over one, the first one in French, and watched while Jenny translated.

"Oh, that dear, dratted, man. That dear, dear…"

Rather than listen to Jenny prattle on, Louisa translated another of the French missives. "These are letters of introduction. Your dear, dratted man has written you letters of introduction all over the Continent. This one is written in French but addressed to some Polish count. This one is to some fellow on Sicily. Will I ever see you again?"

"There are ruins on Sicily. Greek, Roman, Norman… Beautiful ruins."

What that had to do with anything mattered little compared to the ruins Louisa beheld in her sister's eyes. "Was he *trying* to send you away?"

Jenny handed Louisa the letter, watching with a hungry gaze as Louisa tucked the epistles back into their traveling bag. "I didn't ask Elijah for those letters, and I won't use them."

"Why in blazes not?" Blazes was not quite profanity. When a woman became responsible for small children, her vocabulary learned all manner of detours.

"Because he'll never get into the Academy if he's seen promoting the career of a woman in the arts. The Academy has been his goal and his dream for years, and he's given up years of time among his family to pursue it. There's unfortunate history between one of the committee members and Elijah's mother, and it will obstruct Elijah's path if he's seen to further my artistic interests. I would not jeopardize Elijah's happiness for anything."

Elijah. Not Bernward, not his lordship, and certainly not Mr. Harrison. Perhaps Eve's pretty, empty box hadn't been entirely in vain.

Louisa pronounced sentence as gently as she could. "You love him. You're in love with him."

A young girl, a girl who'd never known real heartache, would have beamed hugely at this pronouncement and fluffed her hair or twitched her skirts. Jenny's smile as she regarded her nearly full trunk was that of a woman, a woman who'd endured both life's joys and its sorrows. "I love him."

Being a Windham, this was a life sentence without hope of parole or pardon. "Does he love you?"

The smile dimmed, went from soft to uncertain. "Elijah is very kind. He cares for me, but he gave up everything to pursue his painting professionally—home, family, social connections—and now he has a chance to have it all back and more. The regent has taken notice of him. His family is clamoring for him to return to Flint Hall. As a Royal Academician, Elijah can accept their invitation without causing injury to his pride."

Jenny's recitation made no sense, though it resembled the convoluted maunderings of people overcome by sentiment regarding a member of the opposite sex. Louisa attempted to apply logic to the situation anyway.

If Bernward returned Jenny's sentiments, he'd pop in at the ancestral pile, appease the family, then turn his horse right around and stop Jenny's mad flight. His chances of doing so were enhanced if somebody—say, the Earl of Kesmore—made certain the exact details of Jenny's departure and itinerary were put into Bernward's talented hands.

"I think you should read these," Louisa said, passing the bag of letters over to Jenny. "Bernward has lovely penmanship, and you should know which doors he's so graciously opened for you."

Also, how far away those doors were. Louisa led her sister to the escritoire then sent the footman in the hallway for tea and cakes. As much praise as Bernward had heaped on the talents of the woman whose aspirations he ought not support, it was going to take Jenny quite a while to read his letters.

The door banged open, but it was not one of the small Windham grandchildren charging into Jenny's sitting room, but rather, Their Graces—His Grace at a brisk pace, Her Grace following more decorously behind.

"Your father has come up with a wonderful addition to your itinerary." Her Grace sounded particularly pleased with His Grace. "You really must consider it, Jenny. Why, at this rate, we'll be sending you to darkest Peru and the Sandwich Islands!"

Eighteen

Louisa's expressions were not often hard to read, but Jenny's sister looked torn between humor and exasperation.

"Perhaps you're sending Jenny to Sicily now? She says there are wonderful ruins there. Greek, Roman, and what was that other?"

Such a helpful sister. "Norman," Jenny said. "Though we have Norman ruins aplenty here in England."

Her Grace beamed at the duke. "We can convince Arabella to nip down to Sicily, can't we, Percival?"

As if traveling half the length of Italy was on a par with tooling out to Richmond. Jenny felt something building inside, something she'd felt since Elijah had been nowhere to be found after the Christmas open house. Whatever it was, it was not ladylike or pretty, but rather, loud and maybe even profane.

"Of course," His Grace replied, looking equally pleased. "And then they can sail around to Venice. You cannot miss Venice, Jenny. They make glass there, and the place has canals. You like a pretty canal now and then, don't you? You could sketch—"

"Venice would make a nice stop off on the way to Vienna," Her Grace added. "And a respite from Florence. Florence will overwhelm you, I'm sure, with its basilicas and palaces. Florence ought to be pronounced the madonna capital of the world, according to your father."

"And the bridges, my love. Don't forget the bridges. Jenny can sketch those too."

Except Jenny hadn't sketched a single thing—not even Timothy—since Elijah had gone away. Timothy had been obliging, but Jenny's hands had lost the ability to render an image on a page.

"Bridges are pretty," Louisa noted. "I should think canals might tend to stink, particularly in summer."

"Not these canals," His Grace pronounced. "The sea tides keep them sparkling, or so the guidebooks say. So it's decided. Rome, Sicily, Florence, and Venice. Marvelous."

Louisa sent Jenny a look that had a hint of daring about it, and the loud, profane urge beating against Jenny's insides took on an edge of dread. Elijah had written those letters, and Louisa would open her big mouth and see every single letter put to use.

"You forgot Pompeii," Louisa said, as if mentioning a misplaced handkerchief. "Any trip to the Italian states surely ought to include Pompeii *and* Herculaneum. Is Jenny going to see the pyramids while she's larking about the Mediterranean?"

I will kill my sister, even though her husband is a flawless marksman.

Her Grace slowed in the act of clapping her hands, so what resulted was instead a prayerful pose. "Percival? Might Arabella—?"

In the years—the *decades*—of travel Jenny's family was planning for her, Elijah would find some other lady to become his marchioness. He'd find a woman without troublesome artistic inclinations, one who'd never ask him to pose for her or argue with him over the proper use of the color green.

Never need him to tell her she was brilliant, never smile at her as she built a house of cards any child might topple in an instant.

Jenny shot up from her seat at the escritoire. "*No.*"

Three heads turned toward her, as if noticing she was present for the first time. The duchess's hands fluttered to her sides. "No? You don't want to see Pompeii? I suppose it is a sad place, full of ruins and death—but very artistic too."

The place was full of naughty frescoes and *objets d'art* a lady wouldn't even be allowed to see—without a husband along to insist she be permitted.

"No Pompeii, no Rome, no Italy."

His Grace frowned. "Straight to Vienna, then? I suppose that makes sense, particularly if you're interested in seeing Moscow and—"

"No Vienna, no Moscow, No Buda, no Pest. No *anywhere.*"

A slow grin broke across Louisa's face, and Jenny's parents both, doubtless by coincidence, found it necessary to study the carpet.

"What about Paris?" Louisa asked. "Surely you don't intend to give up Paris?"

The duchess admired a wedding ring she'd likely worn every day for thirty-some years. His Grace said nothing.

But they were listening. Jenny had told them no, and they were listening to her every word.

"What I might have with Elijah is worth more than all the art in the entire world. Maybe Paris is in my future. I don't know. All I know is that I must take myself to Surrey before I go anywhere else."

Her Grace studied her for a moment, and Jenny braced herself for a lecture about being steadfast in pursuit of one's goals and travel arrangements having been made. Papa would chime in with comments about young ladies not knowing their own minds. He would profess to be confused, while dripping disapproval from every syllable, Her Grace having taught him a thing or two about raising daughters.

No matter. "Where I need to go isn't Italy or Russia or Paris. I need to go to Surrey. I'll walk there if I have to, but I must leave within the hour."

His Grace laced his hands behind his back, which signaled not a lecture but an entire speech in the offing. The duchess, however, slowly raised her arms and opened them wide.

Jenny was preparing to deliver a speech of her own when she noticed her mother was smiling. "I thought we were going to have to send you abroad for you to find your senses, Genevieve."

Jenny went into her mother's embrace, while the duke muttered something that sounded like "About damned time."

"Joseph says Bernward is headed off to York for another commission," Louisa said. "If you don't want to travel two hundred miles north in the dead of winter, you'd best make haste to Flint Hall."

"You, sir, are a fraud."

In the privacy of the Marquess of Flint's study, Elijah toasted his father as he made that accusation. His lordship looked pleased, though Elijah had spoken in complete earnest.

"Your mother accuses me of being a rumgumptious scalawag, which in a French accent sounds dire indeed, and now you promote me to the status of felon. It is wonderful to have you home, Elijah."

"And it is wonderful to be home." An understatement among understatements, also beside the point. "Explain these, if you please."

Elijah passed over the leather case Buchanan had given him and watched while the marquess unrolled the lot.

"Oh, my. I'd never thought to see these again. I suppose Buchanan passed them along?"

"He did. They've been collecting dust in some cupboard or other for the past few decades." And yet, the drawings were brilliant, each and every one a masterpiece in pen and ink. "I was told you were a skilled caricaturist, nothing more, and yet you can draw like this."

His lordship remained silent, gazing at a drawing of a much younger George III. His Royal Majesty had two small princesses on his lap, everybody attired for court, but the image was redolent of love and affection nonetheless.

"They say old George still asks for his dear little Amelia."

Such regret, such commiseration.

Such *talent.* "Papa, I do not understand. Your ability easily eclipses my own, and yet you put your art aside. What could have possessed you to stop creating when you have an eye like this?"

Every detail was superbly rendered, every nuance of expression carefully drawn. Elijah had spent half his trip down from London and a long night wondering why such skill had disappeared into a dusty cupboard. Through a joyous reunion with siblings, mother, and father, he'd kept that question to himself, but in the cold, bright light of day, he needed an answer.

He got another silence, though this time, his lordship directed his attention over the fireplace, where a lovely Reynolds portrait of her ladyship held pride of place. "They call it Daltonism now. Seems to afflict us fellows more than the ladies."

"I do not know what Daltonism is. You draw brilliantly."

"Your mother said as much, but you paint brilliantly, and hence your ambitions deserved support."

Support. Elijah tried to wrap his mind around the notion that years of living from commission to commission, of enduring a status that hovered between tradesman and guest, of missing his family was a form of support.

"What is this Daltonism?"

His lordship continued to study the portrait. "I cannot see colors, apparently, or at least some colors. Your mother says I lack a proper appreciation for red, and I must believe her. My attempts at portraits and even landscapes were disasters." Flint's gaze flicked over Elijah's face. "Hard to do a rendering of a lady's smile or her blushes, when a fellow doesn't understand the color red."

The words made no sense.

"How can you not understand a color, for God's sake?" And what a curse would that be, to perceive line, composition, and emotional content, *but not color*?

"Your mother asked me to paint a small study of flowers, using the colors I saw, and she explained to me that I'm using greens, browns, and oranges in places where I ought to use red. Red, she claims, is a color like the taste of a pomegranate, the scent of roses, or the feel of the flame between your fingers when you pinch out a candle. She says it's like orange without yellow, though I cannot imagine such a thing."

Elijah dipped them both out a glass of wassail, despite the early hour. "So you do not perceive even the blood in your veins as red?"

His lordship smiled. "What matters the color of my blood? It beats through my veins effectively enough, particularly when I regard your mother."

That smile was sweet and pleased. The smile of a man who'd made hard, correct choices. "This puts Mama's preference for you over Fotheringale in a somewhat different light."

His lordship's brows came down. "Fotheringale is blind to much more significant matters than whether a tree is red or green. He could not see your mother's talent, and he bitterly resented my little scribblings."

"He still does." Which also mattered not at all. "You all but dared me to try for the Academy, knowing he stood against me?"

His lordship let the top image roll up—sketches not

stored flat would do that—and regarded a picture of the royal couple with a few of their older children in adolescence. Again, attire was proper for an informal evening at court, but the queen was gazing at her king, husband, and the father of her children. A notably reserved woman, Her Majesty's eyes yet held admiration for her spouse as well as warmth and worry.

"Ten years ago, Fotheringale was only getting started as a patron, but you were… You were restless, Elijah, as all young men must be, and your mother could not watch your talent be smothered by the weight of a title and family obligations."

"A wanderjahr, then. You wanted me to have a year to wander, a time to fly free as an artist and to learn more of my craft."

His lordship let the remaining sketches roll up all at once. "I wanted you to stop trying to herd eleven younger siblings into order, to stop trying to outshine the very stewards with your knowledge of the land, to spend less time with your nose in a ledger book and more time where you were happy. All too soon, you will find Flint and its obligations around your neck like a millstone. Your mother and I agreed that your art deserved support."

Images of Jenny holding yarn for her sisters, playing hoodman-blind, dancing dutifully with her brothers flashed through Elijah's mind while he tried to absorb his father's words.

"You made the right choice," Elijah said slowly. "I know more of the greater world, more of human nature, and more of *myself* for having pursued my art. I thank you for that."

His father studied his drink for a moment then treated Elijah to a doting smile. "You will make a fine Marquess of Flint, and the Academy will be lucky to count you among their members."

His lordship's words held apology, but something more too: a paternal blessing Elijah would happily have wandered another ten years to earn.

"I rather doubt I'll ever see membership in that august body, nor will I seek it further. Fotheringale has deep pockets, but he's been allowed to elevate his sycophants regardless of lack of ability. He has been less than gentlemanly regarding Mama, and his antipathy toward women artists generally sets art back, rather than propels it forward."

His lordship picked up Elijah's glass and handed it to him. "I had not counted on your stubbornness when you took off to paint the world, but it sits well on you now. You will be called principled and a man of integrity. We are agreed Fotheringale is an ass, but your mother says he is to be pitied."

And Mama's opinion would always matter greatly to Flint. Elijah touched his glass to his father's. "To Mama and her stubbornness. Do you ever regret the choices you made?"

He asked because a man could love his wife and still be honest. Flint's answer was to leaf through the sketches and pull out one of a young couple from a bygone era, his evening attire nearly as resplendent as her ball gown—for all the image was in black and white.

"The fashion at one point was to have mirrors in ballrooms, the better to serve both light and vanity.

At our betrothal ball, I caught a particular glimpse of your mother's face as we danced, and it has been all the answer any husband should ever need."

The young marchioness gazed at her husband much as the queen had gazed at her king—with love and admiration, but without the worry. Clearly she had found her way into the arms of the one man in all the world who was right for her.

Flint picked up the sketch. "I would give up the ability to see any color, the ability to sketch, and several appendages as well to spend my life with your mother. She says Fotheringale is to be pitied, and she's right. The Academy needs fellows like yourself, who stand above old Foggy in both talent and consequence, but your mother would ask you to show some tolerance to a man who ended up without talent, title, or lady."

Without lady.

"About the lady."

The lady who was setting off on her own wanderjahr, which might easily turn into years, not of exploration but of exile, while Elijah… what?

While he missed her. While he looked at his drawing of her the same way his father gazed at the portrait of her ladyship. While he never got his greens quite right and had nobody to tell him so.

Elijah had been stubborn, but Genevieve Windham could hold onto things—guilt, goals, those sorts of things—more tightly than Elijah ever had. He'd given her all the letters of support he could, but he had not given her the one thing any artist needed to endure the privations of her trade, the one thing that might turn her steps in the direction of home and people who loved her.

"The lady? Are you inquiring about your mother?" Flint asked, taking a sip of his drink.

Elijah drank as well—somebody had made some sort of toast—and swallowed a bit of brew that kicked like a happy donkey.

"Not that lady. I must cut my visit short, your lordship. I must see about a lady who will wander for ten years, alone and far away, unless somebody offers her a different path. You cannot see a few paltry colors, but I cannot see my way home when it's staring me in the face."

Elijah turned to go, pulling Kesmore's letter from his pocket as he headed for the door. Today was Wednesday, which meant Jenny might leave as early as—

A knock sounded on the door.

Flint caught Elijah's eye. "Enter."

"Callers, your lordships. The Duchess of Moreland and Lady Genevieve Windham. The young lady said I was to interrupt you, and the marchioness agreed."

"See them in," Flint said, which was fortunate, because Elijah could not organize a single thought beyond a fleeting recollection of His Grace's reference to the espionage of women.

Flint Hall was every bit as imposing as Morelands, and far more grandly appointed. Jenny suspected much of the art was her ladyship's, though it wasn't quite as warm or detailed as Elijah's renderings.

"Their lordships will see you now." The liveried footman was all that was correct and courteous, without being friendly. Her Grace swept by Jenny and paused outside a door to greet another lady of mature years.

"Happy Christmas, Your Grace!"

"Charlotte! Happy Christmas!" The ladies touched cheeks, linked arms, and Jenny felt misgiving uncoil in her belly. Elijah's mother had that certain self-possession Jenny associated with émigrés and duchesses, a self-possession that might equate to impatience with a young lady seeking an audience with a son recently returned home. The marchioness turned a brilliant smile on Jenny, one that did not remind her of Elijah at all.

"Lady Genevieve, welcome. Elijah has told me much about you, and I confess I am most curious. Thomas, we'll be having tea and a tray, please."

As the ladies strolled into a roomy, paneled parlor, the marchioness bent her head close to Her Grace's. "Did you like the portrait of His Grace? I am dying to see it. Moreland has such presence, much like Flint."

Jenny did not hear the duchess's reply, because Elijah was standing across the room, illuminated by a shaft of sunlight that showed him both tired and handsome.

So very handsome.

"Ladies, welcome." An older fellow advanced, one who had Elijah's eyes and chin. He bowed over Her Grace's hand with old-fashioned courtliness, and still Elijah did not move from his spot by the window.

"And you must be Lady Genevieve. Elijah would no doubt enjoy showing you our portrait gallery, though we keep it chilly this time of year to discourage impromptu athletic competitions—to no avail, I might add." Lord Flint cleared his throat. "Elijah?"

"Yes, Elijah," the marchioness added. "The tea will take a moment, given the state of the kitchen of late. Show Lady Genevieve the portraits."

Elijah held out his hand, and Jenny stifled the urge to run to him. "Nothing would please me more. Lady Genevieve, welcome."

Still he did not smile. Jenny took his arm and processed from the room with him as if they were promenading around some ballroom before all of Polite Society.

"I should not have come."

"I'm so glad to see you."

They'd spoken at the same time, which caused Jenny to pause in her progress down a quiet, carpeted hallway. "I beg your pardon?"

Elijah glanced around. "My brothers are playing skittles in the portrait gallery, and it's bound to be freezing. Come. We'll have only a moment, and there are things I need to say to you." He took her hand in his and tugged her into a room near the end of the corridor.

And Jenny allowed it—there were things she needed to say to him. They might be the last words she ever exchanged with him, but she needed to say them more than she'd ever needed to paint, draw, or embroider.

More even than she needed to keep a promise extracted by a wily, if mortally ailing, brother.

Elijah closed the door behind them quietly, and Jenny found herself in a room much like what the Windham children called Her Grace's Presence Chamber. The walls were full of sketches, the furniture was as comfortable as it was elegant, and everywhere there was color. The upholstery was blue and cream, the gilding a mellow gold. Green pillows riotously embroidered with flowers added a comfy touch, and gold fleur-de-lis decorated the walls.

"There's no red," Elijah said.

"That's what you wanted to say to me?" Though he was right. The room sported neither red nor pink, even.

"This is my mother's parlor, and it has no red. But that is not what I wanted to say. What I wanted to say—"

He went to the door and locked it, which could presage either difficult words or—

He took her in his arms and brushed his mouth across hers. "We haven't any mistletoe, Genevieve, and I know you'll soon be on your way, but—"

Jenny went up on her toes and kissed him back, kissed him as if he were every destination on His Grace's splendid itinerary and the place she'd come home to all rolled into one. "Hang the red, hang the mistletoe, Elijah."

Hang Paris. She wanted to hang Paris, and yet she might still end up there. Jenny eased back, but did not leave Elijah's embrace. "Happy Christmas, Elijah."

His cheek rested on her hair. "That is your version of a holiday greeting now? I'll not be introducing you to my brothers, if that's the case."

Jenny inhaled the scent of him and closed her eyes. To be in Elijah's embrace was better than Paris, better than the world. "You left Morelands before I could give you my Christmas token."

"I don't need any tokens from you, Genevieve."

He also apparently did not need to let her go, which was a fine thing indeed. Jenny, however, needed to see his eyes when she bestowed her gift, so she eased away.

"I need to offer this to you anyway, Elijah."

He joined his hands behind his back, the same gesture His Grace had made when Jenny had announced a pressing need to add Surrey to the Itinerary from Hell. "If it's a farewell, Genevieve, then you may—"

She put her fingers to his lips. "My gift is a question. I want to give you a question."

He took her hand in his, his expression grave. "Ask, Genevieve. With me, you have ever only to ask."

His fingers were warm around Jenny's abruptly cold hand. Her heart thumped painfully against her ribs.

"Will you come to Paris with me?" That wasn't what she'd wanted to ask, but it was close.

Elijah's expression didn't change. "Paris stinks, it's full of Frenchmen, and they have addled notions of chivalry. Why do you want to go to Paris, Genevieve?"

He hadn't said no. Jenny clung to that and to his hand. "I don't want to go to Paris, and I'm not sure I ever did. I don't want to go anywhere that means I can't be with you."

"Do you want a travel companion, Genevieve? If that's what you're asking, then I must refuse the honor."

Pain threatened to buckle Jenny's knees. "Not a travel companion. Not just that."

"Somebody to paint with and appreciate art?"

"Not that either." Because she would set aside her artistic aspirations happily in favor of creating a life with him.

"Good, because as much as I admire your talent and dedication, as much as I would enjoy seeing all the great capitals and treasures of the Continent—of the world—with you, I would decline that invitation too."

It dawned on Jenny that he wanted her to ask a different question.

"What invitation would you accept? Tell me, Elijah, and I will extend it."

He took a step closer. "You already have. You have invited me to love you, and I do, Genevieve. I love your heart, I love your gentleness and determination, I love your concern for all around you, and I love your kisses."

He kissed her, a quick punctuation mark at the end of a lovely little list.

"But you won't travel with me?"

"I've seen the wonders of the Continent, Genevieve. Stared at them for so long I was blind to much else, such as the wonders of a loving family and a welcoming home. Marry me, and I will happily explore those more impressive wonders with you, regardless of what country we find ourselves in."

Marry me. The question she hadn't known how to ask him. Jenny bundled into Elijah's arms. "Yes. Yes to the family and the home, yes to becoming your wife. Nothing would make me happier."

In the small parlor curiously devoid of pink or red, Elijah held her close, which was very good indeed, because Jenny felt as if she'd fly apart if he let her go, so great was her happiness.

"We can make Paris our wedding journey," Elijah said, kissing her cheek. "Though I'd spare you a winter crossing if I could."

She aimed for his mouth and ended up kissing his chin. "A New Year's crossing, please."

His hand slid down her back to cup her derriere and draw her closer. "I can't wait a year."

"*This* New Year."

"Better," he growled against her mouth. "Nearly tolerable, in fact. Kiss me."

She did, and she was still kissing him when a tap sounded on the door.

Elijah smiled crookedly and eased away, pausing to tuck a lock of Jenny's hair behind her ear. When he opened the door, Jenny saw his parents and Her Grace in the hallway.

The marchioness led the parental parade into the parlor. "Excellent! You are showing Lady Jenny your sketches. Her Grace tells me she has a similar collection, most of them done by her daughter."

"Perhaps it will be a family tradition, then," Elijah said. He slipped his arm around Jenny's waist. "I am happy to inform the assemblage that Lady Genevieve has consented to be my wife. His Grace led me to believe my suit would be accepted, and Genevieve has indeed agreed."

His Grace? As Jenny accepted a hug from her mother, she spared a thought to wonder when His Grace-of-the-never-ending-journey might have said such a thing.

"Welcome to the family," Lord Flint said, bowing over Jenny's hand. "Elijah, I suggest you complete the ceremony before you allow your lady to meet your brothers."

"Flint, that is not funny." Her ladyship bussed both

of Jenny's cheeks. "Now that Elijah has found a lady willing to put up with him, his brothers might well see the blessings to be enjoyed in the state of holy matrimony. Genevieve, well done."

As Lord Flint led them back to the paneled parlor and poured generous cups of wassail, Jenny stayed by Elijah's side.

"Do you really want to see Paris, my dear?" Elijah had bent close to whisper his question, while their mamas debated the use of the Windham chapel or the facilities at Flint Hall.

"Paris can wait. There are other things I want to see more."

"Such as?"

Jenny gave him a very direct look. "If I'm to give up my art, then I expect certain consolations, Elijah."

He set his drink aside. "Papa's brew has addled your wits. What nonsense is this?"

"Someday you will become a Royal Academician, but not if your lady wife is showing up at Venetian breakfasts with paint on her fingers. I understand that."

He studied her for a moment, as if trying to puzzle out which pigments would accurately depict her hair in strong sunlight. "You would stop painting, stop drawing, stop even embroidering?"

She hesitated only an instant before nodding. "I expect that home and family you allude to will keep me adequately occupied."

"My mother bore twelve children, six of them boys."

What did that have to do with anything? "I look forward to meeting your brothers and sisters."

"Come with me, Genevieve. If you think a few

babies will excuse you from your art, then you have much to learn as a future marchioness of Flint."

He dragged her from the parlor, barely giving Jenny time to set her drink down, and hauled her up two flights of stairs and down a long hallway.

"This is the portrait gallery, also the cricket pitch, skittles hall, and pall-mall pitch, among others." He opened a carved door and ushered Jenny into a room at least ninety feet long. "It's cold. Take my coat."

Frigid was a better word, but as Jenny gathered Elijah's coat around her shoulders, she was content to endure the cold.

"You lot!" Elijah called to a group at one end of the room. "Clear out! I'm proposing to my prospective wife."

Hoots and whistles resulted, and smiles from the young ladies, two of whom looked exactly alike but for their attire. As Elijah's siblings filed past Jenny, the youngest fellow winked at her, and Elijah cuffed him on the back of the head.

"Pru is the worst," Elijah said as he closed the door. "You must not allow him to cozen you, ever."

Jenny made no reply, because she was too busy staring at the chamber before her. This was not a collection of a dozen or so renderings of the various Lords of Flint, but rather an exhibition, a room stacked as high as any in Carlton House with portraits, still lifes, landscapes, ensemble pieces, and the occasional academic study.

"Mother finds time to paint," Elijah said. "You will too."

Jenny turned a complete circle, taking in dozens upon dozens of completed works. They weren't all brilliant—some were clearly experiments, others were quick efforts more whimsical than beautiful—but they all showed talent.

"She hid her talent for you," Jenny said, hurting for the marchioness. "She did not want the Academy taking you into further dislike because she was so talented."

"You're wrong." Elijah laced his arm with Jenny's and started her on a tour of the room. "Mama has given away any number of paintings. She embroiders the most fantastic receiving blankets and christening gowns you'd ever want to see. What I've concluded is that she put aside the Academy's notice because it really did not matter. In her day, she might have lobbied for membership, but she chose to be my father's marchioness instead."

Jenny gazed at smiling children, doting ancestors, Lord Flint on a bay hunter, Elijah as a young boy—she was going to study that one at length. "She made the better choice. The wiser choice."

"She did, and we will too. There's an epistle downstairs bearing the seal of the Royal Academy, and it has my name on it. I'm going to decline the nomination."

As she had turned away from Paris?

"Accept it, Elijah. For your parents, for me, for yourself. You accept this gesture of recognition, and I will not give up my art." He sent her a look that revealed his uncertainty, and Jenny fell in love with him all over again.

"You're sure? I will never hide my wife's talents, Genevieve. Not for them, not even for you would I do such a thing."

Jenny wrapped her arms around him. "Your wife

would not ask it of you, nor would she allow you to hide yours. But, Elijah?"

"My love?"

"As much as I look forward to sharing a studio with you and arguing with you about the proper use of the color green, I suspect we're going to have a very large family."

Elijah's smile was devilish and sweet. "I suspect we will too."

They shared several wonderful studios thereafter—at Flint Hall, at Morelands, at their London residence, and in the homes of each of Jenny's siblings, Elijah having developed a preference for juvenile portraits and subjects being available in quantity.

They also argued over the proper use of every color in the rainbow, and over many other things besides.

And they had a very large, happy family, the first child—Rembrandt Joshua Harrison—making his appearance exactly nine months after the wedding.

Read on for an excerpt from Grace Burrowes's bestselling Scottish Victorian series

The MacGregor's Lady

Available February 2014 from Sourcebooks Casablanca

Hannah had been desperate to write to Gran, but three attempts at correspondence lay crumpled in the bottom of the waste bin, rather like Hannah's spirits.

The first letter had degenerated into a description of their host the Earl of Balfour. Or Asher, Mr. Lord Balfour. Or whatever. Aunt had waited until after Hannah had met the fellow to pass along a whole taxonomy of ways to refer to a titled gentleman, depending on social standing and the situation.

The Englishmen favored by Step-papa were blond, skinny, pale, blue-eyed and possessed of narrow chests. They spoke in haughty accents, and weren't the least concerned about surrendering rights to their monarch, be it a king who had lost his reason or a queen rumored to be more comfortable with German than English.

Balfour was neither blond, nor skinny, nor narrow-chested. He was quite tall, and as muscular and rangy as any backwoodsman. He did not declaim his pronouncements, but rather, his speech had a growl to it, as if he were part bear.

The second draft had made a valiant attempt to compare Boston's docks with those of Edinburgh, but had then doubled back to observe that Hannah had never seen such a dramatic countenance done in such a dark palette as she had beheld on Balfour. She'd put the pen down before prosing on about his nose. No Englishman ever sported such a noble feature, or at least not the Englishmen whom Step-papa forever paraded through the parlor.

The third draft had nearly admitted that she'd wanted to hate everything about this journey, and yet, in his hospitality, and in his failure to measure down to Hannah's expectations, Balfour and his household hinted that instead of banishment, a sojourn in Britain might have a bit of sanctuary about it too.

Rather than admit that in writing—even to Gran—that draft had followed its predecessors into the waste bin. What Hannah could convey was that Aunt had not fared well on the crossing. Confined and bored on the ship, Enid had been prone to frequent megrims and bellyaches and to absorbing her every waking hour with supervision of the care of her wardrobe.

Leaving Hannah no time to see to her own—not that she'd be trying to impress anybody with her wardrobe, her fashion sense, or her eligibility for the state of holy matrimony.

Her mission was, in fact, the very opposite.

Hannah sanded and sealed a short note mostly confirming their safe arrival, the earl having graciously given her the run of his library.

But how to post it?

Were she in Boston, she'd know such a simple

thing as how to post a letter, where to fetch more tincture of opium for her aunt, what money was needful for which purchases.

"Excuse me." The earl paused in the open doorway, then walked into the room. He had a sauntering quality to his gait, as if his hips were loose joints, his spine supple like a cat's, and his time entirely his own. Even his walk lacked the military bearing of the Englishmen Hannah had met.

Which was both subtly unnerving and... attractive.

"I'm finished with your desk, sir." My lord was probably the preferred form of address—though perhaps not preferred by him. "I've a letter to post to my grandmother, if you'll tell me how to accomplish such a thing?"

"You have to give me permission to sit." He did not smile, but something in his eyes suggested he was amused.

"You're not a child to need an adult's permission." Though even as a boy, those green eyes of his would have been arresting.

"I'm a gentleman and you're a lady, so I do need your permission." He gestured to a chair on the other side of a desk. "May I?"

"Of course."

"How are you faring here?"

He crossed an ankle over his knee and sat back, his big body filling the chair with long limbs and excellent tailoring.

"Your household has done a great deal to make us comfortable and welcome, for which you have my thanks." His maids in particular had Hannah's gratitude, for much of Aunt's carping and fretting had landed on their uncomplaining shoulders.

"Is there anything you need?" His gaze no longer reflected amusement. The question was polite, but the man was studying her, and Hannah felt herself bristle at his scrutiny. She'd come here to get away from the looks, the whispers, the gossip.

"I need to post my letter. When do we depart for London?"

He picked up an old-fashioned quill pen, making his big hands look curiously elegant, as if he might render art with them, or music, or delicate surgeries.

"Give me your letter, Miss Hannah. I've business interests in Boston and correspond frequently with my offices there. As for London, we'll give Miss Enid Cooper another week or so to recuperate, and if the weather is promising, strike out for London then." He paused and the humor was again lurking in his eyes. "If that suits?"

She left off studying his hands, hands which sported neither a wedding ring nor a signet ring. What exactly was he asking?

"I am appreciative of your generosity, but I was not asking you to mail my letter for me. I was asking how one goes about mailing a letter, any letter, bound for Boston." Hannah did not like revealing her ignorance to Balfour, but if she was to go on with him as she intended, then his role was not to make her dependent upon him for something as simple as mailing letters, but rather, to show her how to manage for herself.

He laughed, a low warm sound that crinkled his eyes and had him uncrossing his leg to sit forward.

"Put up your guns, Boston. I know what it is to be

a stranger in a strange land. I'll walk you to the nearest posting inn and show you how we shuffle our mail around here. If you still want to wait for the HMS Next-to-Sail, you are welcome to, but I can assure you my ships will see your correspondence delivered sooner by a margin of days if not weeks."

"Your ships?" *Plural.* Hannah made a surreptitious inspection of the library, seeing hundreds of books, a dozen fragrant beeswax candles in addition to gas lamps, and thick, spotless Turkey carpets.

"When one is in trade with the New World, one should be in control of the means of distribution as well as the products, though you aren't to mention to a soul that you know I've mercantile interests. Shall we find that posting inn?" He rose, something that apparently did not require her permission, and came around the desk to take her hand.

"I can stand without assistance," she said, getting to her feet. "But thank you, some fresh air would be appreciated."

They'd had a dusting of snow the night before, though the sun had come out and the eaves were dripping. Just like in Boston, the new snow and the sunshine created a winter brightness more piercing than the summer sun.

"We should tell your aunt we're leaving the premises."

This was perhaps another rule, or his idea of what manners required. "She's resting." Aunt was sleeping off her latest headache remedy.

His earlship peered down at her—he was even taller up close—but Hannah did not return his gaze lest she see contempt—or worse, pity—in his eyes.

"We'll leave a note, then. Fetch your cape and bonnet while I write the note."

How easily he gave orders. Too easily, but Hannah wanted to be out of this quiet, cozy house of stout gray granite, and into the sunshine and fresh air. She met him in the vestibule, her half boots snugly laced, her gloves clutched in her hand.

"Perhaps you'll want to wear your bonnet," he said as a footman swung a greatcoat over his shoulders. Hannah counted multiple capes, which made his wide shoulders even more impressive. Though how such a robust fellow tolerated being fussed over was what Gran would call a fair puzzlement.

The bonnet had spontaneously migrated from whatever dark closet it deserved to rot in to the sideboard in the house's entryway. "Why would I want to be seen in such an ugly thing?"

"I don't know. Why would you?"

Propriety alone required a bonnet for most occasions, but she wouldn't concede that, not when the only bonnet she'd packed was a milliner's abomination. And yet, when they gained the street, she wished she had worn her ugly bonnet, so bright was the sun. Sun meant spring was coming—not a cheering thought.

"A gentleman would not comment on this," her escort said as he tucked her hand over his arm, "but I notice you limp."

That arm was not a mere courtesy, as it might have been from Hannah's beaus in Boston, but rather, a masculine bulwark against losses of balance of the physical kind.

"A blind man could tell I limped from the cadence

of my steps. You needn't apologize." The only people in Boston solicitous of Hannah's limp were fellows equally solicitous of her unmarried state and private fortune, but the earl could not know that.

Silence stretched, while they meandered along walks shoveled clean of snow. Hannah knew she limped, but she forgot she knew most of the time. She forgot the ache in her hip that went with it, and forgot all the times her stepfather had told her to stand up straight lest her shoulders become as crooked as her leg.

"Does it pain you?" This handsome, wealthy man was to be Hannah's escort for the next several months, for reasons she could not fathom. His tone was pleasant, his arm a sturdy support, and his question unexpectedly genuine.

Her reply was unexpectedly honest as a result. "It rarely hurts. Not unless I overdo."

"We will have to see you do not overdo, then. Shall we sit? The sun is really quite lovely, and the less time I spend cooped up behind stone walls, the happier I am."

With that startling little revelation, he directed her to a bench in a widening in the walkway. Somebody had dusted the thing free of snow early enough that it was dry, or perhaps the February sun was that strong here in Edinburgh.

He seated her, then took a seat beside her—without permission. "Why are you in Great Britain, Miss Hannah Cooper?"

She'd wanted to resent Balfour, whose job it was to deliver her to London, like a federal marshal might deliver a felon for trial. And yet, she shared with the earl an appreciation for the out of doors, for plain speaking, and for a sunny bench. Hannah shouldn't derive a sense of kinship with Balfour on such meager footing, and yet, she did.

"I am to find a husband," she said, reciting the litany that had been shouted at her. "I am an American heiress and only a little long in the tooth, and it shouldn't be too hard to find a willing baronet's son or an aging knight."

"I see."

"What do you see?"

"You are a mendacious American heiress." The amusement was back, and maybe a hint of approval.

"And you are an overly observant English gentleman."

Another silence, while Hannah studied her bare hands and tried not to smile. Her escort was wearing soft kidskin gloves likely made to fit his big hands. Gloves like that would feel heavenly next to the skin. Supple, warm, soft…she'd bet his were even lined with silk.

"I am not your enemy, Boston, and I am not English." His tone was gentle, but not apologetic.

"You are the instrument of my enemy, though. You are to squire me about the ballrooms and so forth, and quietly let it be known I come with a fat dowry."

He eyed her sidewise while Hannah pretended not to notice that the brilliant winter sun turned his dark hair nearly auburn.

"You honestly don't want to find yourself some minor title and swan about on his arm for the next several decades? Have a few babies to show off to your friends and relations while casually flashing a vulgar diamond or two at them as well?"

"I have never swanned in my life and I hope to die without the experience befalling me."

Swan, indeed. But the babies… Oh, damn him for mentioning the babies.

"I see."

"What do you think you see?"

"I see why the ugly bonnet," he said, rising. "Come, the posting inn is several blocks off and I promised to show you how we go about our mails here. We should stop at a grog shop too, so you can see how we do our toddies and rum buns."

That was all he said, no lecture, no lambasting her for her unnatural inclinations, her ingratitude. The lack of resistance made Hannah uncertain, like the bright sunshine, and she leaned him on a little with the disorientation of his response. Perhaps he simply didn't care what she was about—he'd get to fritter away his spring in any case, and she really didn't intend to be much of a bother to him.

Not much.

As they walked the streets of the neighborhood, Hannah found differences between Edinburgh and Boston in the details, like tea with scones instead of bread and butter, and gas lamps taller than those at home. And were she home, she'd be accompanied by a maid and not this great, strapping man in his beautiful, warm clothing.

He walked slowly, as if he had all the time in the world, as if he hadn't seen these streets over and over in all seasons.

"You are being patient with me," Hannah said.

"I am avoiding the mountain of paperwork waiting

for me back in the library. It's a pleasure to share a pint of grog with somebody who hasn't had the experience—also a bit naughty. Ladies do not usually partake of strong spirits, but cold weather provides the exception to the rule and we're not as mindful of strictest propriety here in the north. And truly, our rum buns are not to be missed."

"A bit naughty" sounded *fun* when rendered in those soft, dark tones, as if the earl were as much need of a treat as Hannah might be.

Or in need of a friend?

Acknowledgments

Lady Jenny's story brings us to the end of the Windham family series proper. I would have been content with stories for Westhaven, St. Just, and Valentine, but somebody in the Sourcebooks, Inc., marketing department got the notion I should write a Christmas story, and *Lady Sophie's Christmas Wish* appeared. Having written a tale for one Windham sister, sibling relations—and my editor's suggestion—resulted in stories for the remaining sisters, of whom, some genius who shall remain nameless (whose initials rhyme with Grace Burrowes) had already decided there would be four.

I don't know of any other author whose debut work has turned into an eight-book series, plus a few novellas. This represents prodigious commitment on the part of a publisher, and a Herculean effort on the part of my editor, Deb Werksman, marketing, public relations, art, production, and sales folks. If a book does well, the writing may have something to do with it, but most assuredly, the efforts of these people to brand the book, raise its visibility, and position it where readers can find it are indispensable.

So thanks, to Madam Editor and Madam Publisher, to marketing, to art, to sales, to public relations (this means you, Danielle), and to production (waving at Skye) for working your part of the magic that makes a manuscript into not just a book, but a book that finds its way into the hands of many happy readers.

And for those of you anticipating Windham-withdrawal, don't worry. The Windhams have many friends, relations, and offspring. I have a few ideas…

About the Author

New York Times and *USA Today* bestselling author Grace Burrowes's bestsellers include *The Heir*, *The Soldier*, *Lady Maggie's Secret Scandal*, *Lady Sophie's Christmas Wish*, and *Lady Eve's Indiscretion*. *The Heir* was a *Publishers Weekly* Best Book of 2010, *The Soldier* was a *Publishers Weekly* Best Spring Romance of 2011, *Lady Sophie's Christmas Wish* won Best Historical Romance of the Year in 2011 from *RT* Reviewers' Choice Awards, and *The Bridegroom Wore Plaid*, the first in her trilogy of Scotland-set Victorian romances, was a *Publishers Weekly* Best Book of 2012. Her Regency romances have received extensive praise, including starred reviews from *Publishers Weekly* and *Booklist*.

Grace is a practicing family law attorney and lives in rural Maryland. She loves to hear from her readers and can be reached through her website at graceburrowes.com.